LUCKY BREAK

Also by Jaclyn Westlake

Dear Dotty

LUCKY BREAK

A Novel

Jaclyn Westlake

AVON

An Imprint of HarperCollins*Publishers*

LUCKY BREAK. Copyright © 2025 by Jaclyn Raggio-Westlake. All rights reserved. Printed in the United States of America. No part of this book may be used or reproduced in any manner whatsoever without written permission except in the case of brief quotations embodied in critical articles and reviews. For information, address HarperCollins Publishers, 195 Broadway, New York, NY 10007.

HarperCollins books may be purchased for educational, business, or sales promotional use. For information, please email the Special Markets Department at SPsales@harpercollins.com.

FIRST EDITION

Interior text design by Diahann Sturge-Campbell

Lake house illustration © Danussa/Stock.Adobe.com

Library of Congress Cataloging-in-Publication Data has been applied for.

ISBN 978-0-06-334076-3

25 26 27 28 29 LBC 5 4 3 2 1

For all the rescued animals and the people who love them. Adopt your next pet from a shelter if you can. They're the best ones! Especially my little Indy. I love you so much, Bubs.

LUCKY BREAK

Prologue

I don't care what my superstitious Italian mother says, there's no such thing as luck. I've been around long enough (thirty-two years) to know *that* for certain. Everything has a cause and effect. That's why it's so important to always have a plan.

I'm a Virgo, so I come by my love of planning and exceptional organization skills honestly. They were literally written in the stars. (I don't actually believe in horoscopes, but as a card-carrying California native, I'm comfortable using astrological signs as shorthand for personality traits.)

I've had my life mapped out since my junior year of high school. My dad says that I'm goal-oriented. My therapist, Nora, says I have control issues and suffer from perfectionism. I don't get too hung up on labels.

It's not that I'm totally inflexible—I don't have to color-code my sock drawer or wash all the dishes before I leave the house or anything like that. I do love using a label maker, though. But that's just practical.

I've come to see life as a series of hurdles to clear, each one building off the last. Kind of like compounding interest. It works like this: scoring a 1500 on my SATs led to getting accepted to UC Berkeley, which led to an internship at Google, and then a job at Swayy, one of the top marketing agencies in Silicon Valley. I'm now the youngest account manager at my company and I'm on track to be an executive by the time I'm forty-five. This is an oversimplification, but you get the idea.

I have goals for my personal life, too, of course. I planned on meeting my future husband by the time I was twenty-seven (I met Marco days before my twenty-seventh birthday), start living with said future husband by thirty (conveniently, Marco already had a rent-controlled apartment in North Beach—close to Muni and walking distance to my parents' bakery), get married by thirty-two (we got engaged last year), buy a house by thirty-four (I've nearly saved up enough for a down payment on a condo), and have my first baby by thirty-five.

I've always wanted to have two daughters, but there's only so much you can control. Even I know that.

Chapter One

June
San Francisco

M arco tops off my wineglass and I resent him for it. I resent him for just about everything these days—the subtle Italian accent he claims to have picked up from spending summers with his grandparents in Sicily, the way his dark curls fall just so over his forehead, the fact that he no longer wants to marry me.

It's been four weeks since our relationship imploded, three since we told our friends and family, and about eight days since our last real conversation. Instead of talking, we've thrown ourselves into perfecting the art of avoiding each other—no easy feat in a one-bedroom apartment.

Marco returns to the pot of marinara he's been simmering and gives it a gentle stir. My traitorous mouth waters as the aroma of savory garlic and sweet tomatoes wafts through the kitchen. Marco makes the best pasta sauce I've ever tasted—aside from my mom's.

I kind of resent him for that too.

I don't know why he insisted on cooking me dinner tonight, but I have some ideas. And if I'm right, as delicious as Marco's marinara smells, I know I won't be able to choke it down. I take a big gulp of wine instead, which does nothing to settle my nervous stomach.

"So, Lize," Marco begins. His back is still to me, but it's like he's reading my thoughts. I used to like it when he did that. "I think it's time to talk about what comes next."

I shift on my barstool. "You mean the apartment."

As I say this, the old radiator in the living room sputters to life, completely unaware that it's technically summer. San Francisco has always refused to follow seasonal weather norms. It's been gray and drizzly all week.

Our apartment used to be my favorite place in the whole world. It was so quintessentially Marco, with worn parquet floors, arched doorways, the clunky radiator that reliably warmed our poorly insulated walls, a green velvet couch broken in just the right amount. If I'd had it my way, the entire place would have been brighter, lighter, more floral. But I liked his way, too.

Marco turns to face me and I look at him, really look at him for the first time in more than a week. His style could best be described as Italian Harry Potter meets East Coast Sherlock Holmes. Dark academia, I think the kids call it. It's sexy, yet understated as if to say, *I know I'm hot but I also have a brain so eyes up here, folks.* I found it to be incredibly appealing when we first met. It also seems to work like a charm with Marco's clients. He's the perfect antithesis to the typical clean-cut finance bro. Those guys are a dime a dozen. And there's only one Marco.

He furrows his perfect eyebrows. "Don't you mean *my* apartment?"

"No. I mean the apartment *we've* shared for the last two years. The apartment I helped you decorate. The apartment where we put up our first Christmas tree together and celebrated our engagement and logged god knows how many hours on that couch." I gesture emphatically in the direction of the living room.

Marco crosses his arms over his chest and assumes an authoritative, fatherly stance. "I lived here before we met," he says evenly. "And I'm the only person on the lease."

The past year has made Marco feel like a stranger to me, but this moment cements it.

"You want to kick me out?"

"You weren't planning on staying indefinitely, were you?"

Actually, I was. That was the entire reason I was still here. Under better circumstances, I would have moved out the night we ended things. But instead, I'd stuck around, hoping that Marco would be the one to go. I probably should have known better.

I run my finger along the deep brown grout lines in our countertops. They used to be beige, probably. I can't help but think this is a metaphor for our relationship. The idea of marrying Marco had once filled me with a sparkly, effervescent joy, but when I reach for that feeling now, all I find is a dull, gray void.

Marco proposed last year—right on schedule—after a romantic dinner at our favorite waterfront restaurant, complete with oysters and champagne (his favorite). We were walking along the Embarcadero, the lights of the Bay Bridge twinkling in the distance, when he dropped to one knee and presented me with an art deco gold band dotted with tiny rectangular emeralds. It was both beautiful and practical—just like Marco. I was barely able to gasp out a yes before burying my face in the warmth of Marco's tweed peacoat, savoring his cedarwood cologne, his arms wrapped so tightly around my waist that I thought I might burst.

I would have been perfectly content to burst.

"Why do you even want to keep this place?" I ask. "All you ever talk about is how much you want to live in one of those fancy SoMa condos with a gym and a doorman." I don't need to add that I can walk to my job from here or that my family's bakery is just down the street or that our place is rent-controlled and therefore one of the few apartments I'd be able to afford on my own. Marco knows that.

"I don't want to stay here," he says, his voice drops as his gaze falls to the floor.

I lean forward. "Then why are you asking me to move out?"

He shifts his weight from one side to the other before lifting his big brown eyes to meet mine. The way he sighs makes me feel small and pitied, which I can't stand. Then he hits me with, "Because the new tenant moves in a month from today."

"The *what*?" I say with such force that I nearly fly backward off my stool.

"The new tenant," he repeats, as if I hadn't heard him the first time.

"You gave up the lease?"

He shakes his head. "Of course not. Only an idiot would give up a rent-controlled apartment. I'm subletting it to one of my clients who's been looking for a pied-à-terre in the city."

My fingers find their way to my temples and I can feel my pulse beating against my skin. "Why wouldn't you just sublet to me? You knew I wanted to stay here." I'd been explicitly clear about that.

"I just think it's better if we have a clean break, don't you?"

Typical Marco, thinking he knows better. He doesn't have to add that he's five years older than me or that he earns more than double my salary or that he goes to Mass every Sunday and I haven't been in . . . well, who's counting. It's implied. I'm not sure when all of this started to grate on me, but it doesn't really matter. All that matters is that his holier-than-thou attitude is insufferable.

It wasn't always like this. It was actually really, really good for a while.

The reasons our once seemingly perfect relationship fell apart are myriad—we're both too stubborn, too rigid. He's traditional and old-fashioned and a bit of a snob about money. I'm pragmatic and driven and deeply disinterested in becoming the type of woman Marco now expects me to be. It's like he flipped a switch the moment he slid that ring onto my finger, his priorities shape-shifting until I no longer recognized the person I'd agreed to spend my life with.

The nail in the coffin was when Marco and I realized we wouldn't be able to give the other what they wanted most. Things unraveled pretty quickly from there.

I unglue my fingertips from my temples and shoot Marco a stare so withering that he actually flinches. "You need to tell this guy that he can't live here." He balks. "Come on, Marco. It's the least you could do for me."

He tilts his head to the side, his eyes pooling with something akin to sadness. "It's too late. We've already finalized the agreement."

"You're unbelievable," I say. Rage gathers in my stomach, but there's no point in fighting. I'm so tired of fighting.

Marco has the audacity to rest his hand over mine. It feels hot and heavy in all the wrong ways. I slide my hand out from under his. He doesn't resist. "I'm just doing what I think is best for us, Lize," Marco says. I can tell by the way his eyes bore into mine that he believes his words are comforting.

"I'm going to my office," I say. That's code for *I need to be left alone.* Marco knows better than to push back.

THERE'S A FUNKY little alcove nestled to the left of our entryway. When Marco first looked at this apartment, the Realtor tried to pass it off as a second bedroom but the lack of closets, windows, and square footage begged to differ. When I moved in, we used it as a catchall for our jackets and ever-growing collection of re-usable grocery bags until I got promoted and started working from home two days a week. I spent the better part of that sum-mer transforming the nook into my own little sanctuary, com-plete with botanical wallpaper, an antique writing desk, floating shelves lined with paperbacks, and a slender lounge chair. It's now my favorite spot in the apartment.

It's also where I've spent every night for the past month since Marco blew everything up.

I push aside a pile of neatly folded laundry before settling un-der a blanket on the chaise. As I wait for my laptop to come to life, I find myself imagining how nice it would be to have a little dog curled up at my feet.

I wasn't scheduled to adopt a dog until I turned thirty-four; after I got married but before I had my first baby. The dog was meant to be practice—the dry run before kids came along. It hadn't occurred to me that it might have been nice to have a dog around for moral support in case my carefully arranged life col-lapsed into ruin. I guess that's what I get for thinking I'd thought of everything. I curse myself for not insisting that Marco add me to the lease when I moved in. I shouldn't have trusted him. I should have made a backup plan.

No time like the present, I guess.

I pull up my inbox and start deleting advertising emails—a consequence of the online shopping habit I developed to distract myself from my failing betrothal—between sips of wine. For a mo-ment, I wonder if I should feel lame for spending my Friday night this way, when only a couple years ago, I would have been singing my heart out to Spice Girls songs at nineties night with my friends at our favorite subterranean dive bar. But there's no sense in wish-ing for things you no longer have. I've learned that the hard way.

I take a deep, steadying breath and return to the task at hand. I find clearing out my inbox to be akin to meditation. I'll never understand the people who have hundreds of unopened texts and emails languishing on their phones. It's depraved.

I've just snoozed a promo email from Pottery Barn when I spot a message from my best friend, Farah. The subject is *Mandatory Happy Hour!* I hold my breath as I open it. I've taken to subconsciously steeling myself around my friends since my relationship with Marco started to unravel.

When we were still in our twenties and unencumbered with any real responsibilities, Farah, Brittany, Carmen, and I would meet for drinks every Thursday at Starfish, a cozy sake and wine bar that was roughly equidistant from each of our respective offices. We'd feast on dumplings and half-priced bottles until Ren, the owner, would start wiping the wood slab that passed for a bar with an old rag, a signal that she was ready to close.

Now that we're older, each of us burdened with some combination of partners, children, or mortgage payments, we're lucky to see each other once a month. With Farah and Brittany already settled into life in the suburbs, I know that we're teetering on the edge of a new era, one filled with barbecues and kids' parties and T-ball games, but a part of me wants to hold on to the present for just a little bit longer.

I take another pull of wine, hoping to wash away my anxiety about the future and turn my attention back to Farah's email.

Hey Ladies!

It's been far too long since we all got together so I'm going to insist that we make happy hour happen this week. No excuses! I need a break from my kids, Brittany needs to escape home renovation purgatory, Carmen has to enjoy every second of freedom she has before the baby comes, and most importantly, Eliza needs us.

See you Thursday!

Love,

F

Brittany and Carmen had both already chimed in with a string of heart and wine emojis.

I know Farah has only the best of intentions, but all of this makes me feel like I'm being slowly smothered by a big, fluffy pillow embroidered with the words TURN THOSE TEARS INTO COCKTAILS, QUEEN! I suddenly want to run far, far away.

There is nothing in the world that I loathe more than being pitied.

Well, that, and a chaotic junk drawer. The Container Store makes organizers for those—there's just no excuse.

I pull up an apartment listing website, an exercise in futility, I'm sure, but I need to get a handle on the market. I'd prefer to live on my own—I'm probably too set in my ways to start fresh with a new roommate at this point, but I am a woman on a budget; I've always stuck to that rule about only spending 30 percent of your income on housing. Despite the raise I got over the summer, I'm worried that might not be realistic anymore. Whatever happens, I can stay with my parents if I have to. That's probably what I should have done in the first place.

It's no surprise to find that not only are the listings in my neighborhood scant, but all the one-bedrooms start at $4,000 a month.

So, I'm probably screwed.

Defeated, my eyes wander to a series of suggested articles that hover to the right of the listings on my screen. They're all travel- and home decor–related with one intriguing exception.

Looking for a Fresh Start? These Small-Town Charmers
Will Pay You to Relocate

Apparently the universe has a sense of humor.

"Okay, I'll bite," I mutter as I click the link. I'm met with a series of promotional photos of adorable little towns around the country, from Alaska to New Mexico to Alabama, each more charming than the last.

As a lifelong city dweller, I have always fantasized about what it would be like to pack up and move to a small town for a simpler life. My childhood best friend, Hannah, and I even hatched a plan to run away to Stars Hollow the summer after eighth grade. We were devastated when her mom caught on to our scheme and told us that our dream town only existed in the fictional world of *Gilmore Girls*.

The last city on the list is a small town in Minnesota called Juneberry Lake. I'm instantly taken by the idyllic photos of shimmering turquoise water, soaring pine trees, rows of colorful canoes, waterfront cabins, a life-sized moose statue, and a main street decked in twinkling lights.

Come for the fireflies and Juneberry blooms, stay for the annual end-of-summer festival, friendly neighbors, and the best bear claws this side of Lake Superior! The Juneberry Lake Committee for Growth will gift new full-time residents up to $10,000 to use toward the purchase of a home within the city limits. With median house prices hovering below $300,000, moving to this

> picturesque lakeside community will be the easiest decision you ever make.

I nearly spit out my wine. I couldn't buy a studio in the worst part of town for less than $500,000. Imagine the kind of house I could get in a place like Juneberry Lake. I could have a garage. And a guest room.

I could have a home office with a door.

When I was eight, my parents booked a house in Lake Tahoe for the Fourth of July. We rented Jet Skis and swam in the ice-cold, crystal-clear water and roasted s'mores around a fire. To this day, I can't smell pine trees without flashing back to watching fireworks exploding over the water, my brother, Enzo and I nestled under a nubby blanket.

I click on the Join Juneberry Lake website. I work in marketing, so I know when I'm being sold to, but with every lake life photo that graces my corneas, I become a little more convinced that a fresh start will solve all of my problems.

It's worked for me before.

The application is simple enough. It asks for some basic information, an updated résumé, a handful of short form essay questions. Why Juneberry Lake? What do you believe you would contribute to our community? Who will you be moving with? Tell us about yourself and your family (if applicable).

I start typing.

Chapter Two

I begin to turn on San Francisco that week. The parking? Impossible! The fog? Bone-chilling! Public transportation? Broken beyond repair! On Monday, I huff in disapproval when the man in front of me at Equator Coffee orders an overly complicated latte (but give myself a pass for ordering a flat white with oat milk—no foam!—as soon as he steps aside). On Tuesday, Minh, my favorite sandwich maker forgets to include extra pickles on the side of my tofu banh mi—again. I bet stuff like this never happens in Juneberry Lake.

I know they probably don't even make tofu banh mi sandwiches in Juneberry Lake. But still.

My fixation on a picturesque lake town in a state I've never visited is as good a coping mechanism as any, so I let myself indulge in the escapism as I slog through another week of Marco's pitiful stares. Especially since it's Wednesday and on Wednesdays, I stop by my parents' bakery for lunch.

The Colletti family goes back four generations in this city. My great-great-grandparents passed through Ellis Island on their way to San Francisco, where they lived for more than seventy years. They never bothered to learn English, but still managed to open what's now one of the longest-running bakeries in the city. My dad took over the family business right out of high school and now my mom and brother work there, too.

Mom beams as I walk through the door. She's always been

great about that, making me feel important no matter what else is going on. Her curly hair is tied in a knot at the top of her head and there's a smudge of frosting above her eyebrow.

Colletti's makes an assortment of Italian cakes and cookies, but my family is famous for their focaccia bread—and not the kind of focaccia you get in a breadbasket at a restaurant or use to make a deli sandwich. Our recipe is special. And a fiercely guarded family secret.

The bakery hasn't been renovated since, well ever, which if you ask me, is part of the charm. A letterboard menu, bleached from black to slate thanks to years of sun exposure, hangs over the tiled countertop and adjacent display case. A sizable wood-fired oven is built into the corner and three tiny bistro sets sit along the wall. Every year, my parents swear that they're going to install booths for additional seating, but they never do. I look back up at the menu and smile when I see the focaccia of the day is tomato.

It's tomato every day.

My brother emerges from the back wearing a red apron covered in flour. Enzo is an even better baker than Mom. He might actually be better than Nonna was but no one would ever dare say that out loud. "Hey, sis," he says, flashing his signature jerky wave. It looks more like he's tossing an invisible pizza than saying hello and it melts my heart every time.

When we were kids, Enzo was diagnosed with autism spectrum disorder. At the time, my parents were devastated. I think they were worried about what it would mean for Enzo's future, but ASD is what gives my brother some of his greatest strengths. He's meticulous about baking, very hard to distract, and incredibly reliable.

He's also pretty good with customers. Sometimes he goes into way too much detail about how best to serve the focaccia (same day if possible, and don't you dare top it off with cheese—it's not pizza) or the allergens in our tiramisu, but people can tell he means well. I'm sure Enzo will be running the place in no time.

Mom lifts a sheet of tomato from the line and begins slicing it into long strips. I pull up a stool at the modest tiled countertop and watch as she places a stack on a cloth napkin. I reach out my hands and flex my fingers greedily as she passes it to me. I could live on the stuff if I had to. I kind of wish I had to.

I bite into the focaccia and savor its warm, pillowy, salty dough, the sweet tang of tomato sauce, the delicate crunch of green onions as Mom looks on. Once she's satisfied that her firstborn won't go hungry on her watch, she starts with the familial updates. The headlines are that Cousin Talia got accepted to every college she applied to, Cousin Paul and his husband are adopting a baby, and two of my aunts aren't speaking to each other. Again. "Oh," Mom says, her eyes brightening. "Zia Michelle called to say that your cousin Alexandra set a wedding date."

Of course she did. My brother's big brown eyes catch mine. He's the only person who knows all the nitty-gritty details about my broken engagement with Marco. I did my best to spare my parents the worst parts.

"That's great. Congrats to Alex," I say before shoving a massive piece of focaccia into my mouth.

"Alexandra's fiancé proposed the month after Marco proposed to you."

"That's a fun fact."

"How are things going with Marco?" she asks, undeterred.

"The same," I say between chews.

"You really don't think you can work things out with him? He loves you."

Loved. Past tense. I don't correct her. "He asked me to move out and rented our apartment to some stranger without even consulting me, so no, Mom. I don't think we're going to work it out."

She throws her hands up and lifts her face toward the ceiling. "At this rate I'll never be a grandmother. Maybe I'm cursed."

"There's no such thing as curses, Mom."

She looks at me as if I've just told her the sky is green.

"Give Eliza a break, Mom," Enzo interjects. "She has a lot going on."

Mom looks from Enzo to me then back to Enzo. "You don't think I had a lot going on when I met your father?" she says indignantly. "I lived in a different country! I didn't speak English!" Mom grew up in Italy. She met my dad on a train in the Tuscan countryside and moved here when she was just twenty-two. I know it kills her that her daughter is an entire decade older than she was when she got married. Sometimes I think Mom longs for the simple way of life she left behind. I don't think she realizes that millennials are putting off marriage and babies in Italy, too.

The bell above the door jingles and I turn to see Dad, struggling with a box of fresh tomatoes. Colletti's bakery makes all of its sauces from scratch. Dad always says the only canned item allowed within these walls is San Pellegrino. And even then, he prefers the bottles. I jump up to help him.

"I've got it, Elisabetta," Dad protests. I pretend not to notice the relief on his face when I lift the box from his arms.

"Uh-huh," I say as I plop the surprisingly heavy mass of tomatoes onto the countertop.

"It's as though I'll never age," Dad says, flexing his tanned arms. Then he runs his fingers through his thick mane. "I'm sixty years old and almost no gray."

The fact that Dad has been dying his hair for years is an open secret, but I let him have it. "You're a modern marvel, Dad."

He beams in response. I pluck a tomato from the box and breathe in its sweet, sunny scent. Enzo does the same, squeezing his tomato to assess its firmness. He juts out his bottom lip in approval.

"So," Dad says, cocking his head to the side. "How are you feeling?"

"I'm fine, Dad."

He rubs my shoulder. "You don't have to pretend around us."

This sets my teeth on edge. I know Dad means well, but all I want is to get through one visit without my parents grilling me about Marco.

"I think you and Marco could still work this out," Dad continues. "Maybe we can have him over for dinner this weekend. What do you think, Elisabetta?"

I've only blown up on my family three times in my life. The first was when Dad donated my favorite toy, a stuffed owl named Mrs. Blinky to charity, the second was when Mom snuck chicken into her Christmas lasagna and told me it was vegetarian (she doesn't consider birds to be animals—it's a long story), and the third was during my junior year of high school when my parents decided to host our entire extended family for dinner the night before I took the SATs. I can feel blowup number four on the horizon, a distant rolling thunderstorm. I want to scream and bang my fists and beg them to stop treating me like I'm a helpless, injured little bird. But then my eyes find Enzo's. He's holding a vine full of ripe tomatoes above the floor.

He winks.

Then he lets them drop.

My mouth falls open as the tomatoes splatter all over the penny-tiled floor in spectacular fashion. Mom gasps, Dad tugs at his unnaturally dark hair, Enzo mouths "you're welcome." My brother loathes messes—especially sticky ones—and he hates wasting food. But this is so Enzo. He avoids hugs and will rarely say *I love you*, but he finds all kinds of ways to show how much he cares. I couldn't have asked for a better brother. I mouth "thank you" back to him as my boiling rage cools to a manageable simmer.

A knot twists in the pit of my stomach as I watch my parents scramble to clean up Enzo's mess, Dad scooping goopy seeds into his hands, Mom mopping up juice with a towel.

I hate myself for this, but all I want to do is turn and run out that door.

Chapter Three

I'm putting the finishing touches on a marketing campaign for Fido, a buzzy start-up that claims to have developed a virtual assistant for dogs, when my phone rings. I glance at the time—nearly 1 p.m. I should be heading to lunch soon. On Thursdays, I get an arugula and walnut salad with raspberry vinaigrette (the best I've ever had) from the Swayy cafeteria. Unless it's raining. Then I'll get pumpkin soup.

I don't know why I answer. I never pick up my phone. And don't even get me started on voicemails.

"Hello?" I say.

"Hey there," comes the reply. It's a human woman, not a robot, and she sounds friendly. "I'm looking for Eliza Colletti." The way she says my last name makes me think she's never met an Italian person before.

"You found her," I say cautiously. I'm almost positive this is some kind of sales call. Or a scam.

A good-natured chuckle floats out of the speaker. "Great. Well, this is Trish Miller. I run the Join Juneberry Lake program."

"Oh," I say, perking up in my chair. "Hi."

"Is this a good time?"

I look at my monitor. A scruffy mutt in a lime-green hoodie rests his little paw on an iPad. A word bubble hovers near his mouth. The text inside it says, "Hey, Fido, fetch me some treats." My boss, Jordan, had squealed with delight when I sent them the mock-up.

"Now's fine," I say.

"Excellent. Well, I want to start by thanking you for your interest in our program. The team here thought your application was outstanding. You're just the type of person we're looking to attract to Juneberry Lake—a young techie professional with a great job and a genuine interest in being part of our little community. The committee especially loved what you had to say about giving yourself a fresh start and getting to know your neighbors."

My chest bangs with excitement. "Oh," I say. "That's so . . . great?"

The dog stares back at me. His friendly expression has morphed into one of judgment. It was one thing to indulge in the fantasy of moving to a picture-perfect lake town, but this—whatever I'm doing right now—is another thing entirely. And this dog knows it.

Trish Miller launches into a detailed overview of the Join Juneberry Lake program. She explains that the city has been trying to attract higher income remote workers to give the economy, which currently relies almost entirely on tourism, a much-needed boost. Last year, thirty new people relocated from around the country and all of them still live in town. They're hoping to attract the same number this year and have already met more than half their goal. If I were to buy a house within the city limits and commit to living there full time for at least a year, I'd be gifted with a $10,000 stipend to put toward my new home. The details come back to me as Trish elaborates. Then my wheels start turning. If I could get Jordan to agree to let me work remotely, this could be a win-win. Worst case, if I absolutely hate it there, I can rent the house out or sell it after a year, no questions asked.

Even better, I could get out of my depressing rut. A change of scenery could do me good.

I grip the phone more tightly. "How long do I have to decide?" I ask, hoping that Trish doesn't notice the desperation in my voice.

"We can hold your spot for two weeks," she says, before sighing. "For legal reasons that I won't bore you with. Plus, we have a decent-sized waiting list. But don't let the quick turnaround intimidate you—you don't have to move right away. We'll help to get you set up with housing and all that good stuff first."

Two weeks? That's way too fast. My mind goes blank; I don't know what to say.

"Have I scared you off?"

"It's just so sudden."

"Well you don't have to decide right this minute," her voice is warm and reassuring. Almost familiar, in a way. "But I do have something that might sweeten the deal. This great little cabin just came on the market—the former owner moved rather abruptly, so, lucky for you, no one's had a chance to jump on it yet. It's lakeside and it comes with its own dock."

Trish says this as if I had a use for a dock. I know nothing about boats. I don't even own a car let alone a water-bound vessel. Nevertheless, the idea of having my own dock is appealing.

"I'll shoot the listing over to you. It's a real charmer."

"Okay," I say, at a loss for anything more.

Trish assures me that I can call her if I have any additional questions and promises to check in with me later this week. Within seconds of hanging up, my inbox pings, alerting me to a new message. My pulse quickens when I see Trish's name. I skip over the content of the email, eager to see the cabin she'd mentioned.

Newly Renovated 2 Bed / 1.5 Bath Lakeside Cottage

Live the lakefront dream in this sweet two-story charmer. Situated on a large lot in a friendly cul-de-sac, this freshly renovated home boasts an open-concept kitchen/living room/dining nook with breathtaking lake views, a finished basement, and a dedicated dock.* Enjoy a morning cup of joe by the stone fireplace or an alfresco dinner on the screened back porch. Sold furnished. Just bring your toothbrush!

* Dock is designated for homeowner use but may also be used by the owner of a neighboring house. Sharing is caring! Inquire for details.

The house looks like something out of a storybook, with brown shingles and dark green trim, colonial-style windows, a sweet little front porch, and a stubby, stacked stone chimney that rises from the second floor. The calm blue waters of Juneberry Lake glisten in the background.

I'm instantly smitten.

If mapping out your life were an Olympic sport, I'd be a favorite to win gold. But my old game plan has been ripped to shreds. Metaphorically speaking, I've suffered a career-threatening injury. I need to change tack.

A new plan begins forming in my mind—I swear I can actually see the pieces falling into place. I could leave all of this behind, at least for a little while. Sort of a time-out from my current situation.

A much-needed break.

There are thousands of reasons why I should nip this in the bud, delete Trish's email, and chalk this all up to a misadventure in magical thinking or temporary grief-induced insanity.

But the thing is, I really want to say yes.

Chapter Four

"T his kitchen renovation is taking twice as long and costing us twice as much as the contractors promised," Brittany groans, her face pinching. "It's going to be the death of me."

My friends and I are squished into our usual booth at Starfish, an array of dumplings, samusas, spring rolls, and a platter of firecracker cauliflower scattered between us. As has been customary for our last three happy hours, Brittany kicked things off with her latest complaint about the trials and tribulations of living through a home renovation.

"I bet your contractors feel the same way," Carmen says. She has a famously low tolerance for first-world problems.

Brittany juts her chin out in indignation. "You'll understand when you buy a house someday," she says, somehow managing to sound both superior and defeated.

"Have you settled on a backsplash yet?" Farah asks, ever the peacekeeper. We've been a foursome since college, but Farah is the glue that holds our group together. She's the one who introduced us. We're just little planets orbiting her sun—we'd all probably have gone our separate ways a long time ago if it weren't for her.

Carmen swallows her dumpling and swivels in the booth, facing away from Brittany and toward me. "So, Eliza, how are you doing?" Her tone is gratingly, uncharacteristically gentle.

Farah perks up at Carmen's query. Brittany pouts, unhappy about ceding the floor. That makes two of us.

I decide to rip off the Band-Aid and bring my friends up to speed on the latest developments with Marco and our apartment as I watch their expressions transform into uncanny impressions of that sad, watery-eyed emoji people usually use when they see a picture of a puppy.

"What are you going to do?" Brittany asks, her voice barely above a whisper. She's acting like I just lost all of my earthly possessions in a fire.

I look down at my bare finger. The tan line that my absent engagement ring left behind has begun to fade. "I'm thinking of moving, actually." My unexpected candor makes me suddenly aware of how desperately I want their approval and how terrified I am that I won't get it.

That's probably because I can tell they haven't approved of any of my decisions lately, no matter how many different ways I've tried to explain myself.

Brittany squeals. "Are you finally coming to the East Bay? There's a house for sale down the street from Brad and me that would be perfect."

Brittany and Farah have been trying to get Carmen and me to move to the suburbs with them for years, but Marco and I had agreed that we wanted to start our lives in San Francisco. And Carmen had made it clear that she would die before she left the city, insisting that she felt her soul wither a little every time she came within a mile of a tract home.

I'd been chewing on Trish's offer for the past week, growing increasingly drawn to the idea with each passing day. But saying it out loud to my friends will make it real.

Here goes nothing. "I'm thinking about moving to Minnesota."

Brittany gasps. Carmen chokes on her water.

"Minnesota?" Farah fixes me in her mom stare. She and her

husband, Gabe, have three-year-old twins, which enabled her to perfect *the look* in half the time it takes most women. "Eliza," she says in the same warning tone she uses with her boys when they're holding a marker dangerously close to a wall. "Rearranging your entire life is probably the last thing you need right now. Do you think you might be having a midlife crisis?"

"What if rearranging my life is exactly what I need right now?" I shoot back. "And who are you calling middle-aged?"

"Yeah I take offense to that part, too," Brittany says.

Farah huffs in exasperation. "That's beside the point!" She reaches for the wine bottle and tops off her glass. Back in the day, we used to go through at least three bottles in one sitting, but tonight Farah and I are the only ones drinking. Brittany is "not *not*" trying to get pregnant and Carmen is abstaining in solidarity with her pregnant wife.

I take the opportunity to wrest back control of the conversation. "The point is, this is something that I might want to do and I would really appreciate your support while I figure it out."

"What's there to figure out?" Farah asks. "Running away isn't going to solve anything. And what about all of your plans? You've worked so hard to get where you are. You can't just throw it all away because you've had a run of bad luck."

There's no such thing as luck—good or bad. Farah knows that. I shoot her a look.

Farah changes tack. "You can't leave your family. Or us." She looks around the table. "We're your support system."

I swallow an uncharitable scoff. The truth is, these past few months, my "support system" has either been fleeing city life for babies and backyards or peppering me with unsolicited advice. They're either (understandably) distracted or (less understandably) meddling and neither feels particularly supportive.

Besides, I never hang out one-on-one with Brittany or Carmen. Only Farah. It's always been the four of us all together or one of us and Farah. What she's really saying is, you can't leave *me*.

"It was bound to happen eventually," Carmen says. "The chances of all of us living within twenty miles of each other for the rest of our lives were pretty low."

"But why does it have to be Minnesota? It's so far away. And they have *seasons*." Farah crinkles her nose. "I bet it snows there."

"Maybe I'll like the snow."

"What if you don't have anything in common with your neighbors? What if a pipe explodes and you don't know who to call?" Farah says this as though I've proposed a solo mission to Mars.

"I don't have anything in common with my neighbors now and I'll Google whatever else I need. I'd be moving to another state, not traveling back in time."

"What about Marco?" Brittany asks.

I roll my eyes. "It's not really any of his business anymore, is it?"

They all stare at me, unblinking.

"You're really serious about this, aren't you?" Farah asks.

I hold Farah's gaze. "I am."

"But what if you miss my baby shower?" Brittany says through an indignant pout.

"You're not even pregnant yet," Carmen says, exasperated.

Brittany gasps. "Carmen!" Her eyes find mine. "That's such a mean thing to say."

Carmen chugs the rest of the water in her glass and then fills it with wine. "You all are driving me to drink tonight." Then she adds, "Don't tell Daisy."

MY THERAPIST'S REACTION surprises me the most. "I think it's a great idea," Nora says in her matter-of-fact way. Nora and I have been meeting every week for the last year—ever since things started going south with Marco—and I still can't get a read on her. No matter how hard I search her neutral facial expression for clues, she continues to be inscrutable.

"Are you serious?"

"I am." She nods to further affirm her support. "This is the first time I've seen you show any willingness to deviate from your goals. I think this is a healthy new development."

I twirl the tassel of one of the decorative pillows that adorn Nora's couch between my fingers. Her office is otherwise unremarkable, with cream-colored walls, a plain wooden desk, and a clear glass coffee table that sits between identical brown pleather couches. I think the pillows are her attempt to signal to her clients that sure, this is therapy, but that doesn't mean we can't have a little fun, too! "Where's the 'but'?"

Nora considers me. I think I detect a hint of amusement in her eyes. "Well, are you familiar with the expression, *wherever you go, there you are?*"

"Are you trying to tell me that running away won't fix all of my problems?"

She pulls her lips into a thin smile. "Yes."

"Do you think that's what I'm doing?"

"Do you?"

"Nora."

"Fine." She sits back in her chair, a signal that she's going to level with me. I love it when I can get her to level with me. "Yes and no. I think you feel like you're stuck and maybe a little trapped, so wanting to escape the situation is a natural reflex. That said, sometimes, life-altering events can be the catalyst for real, necessary change."

Intellectually, I understand what Nora is saying. The only

problem is, I'm not sure if my motivations are driven by the former or the latter.

"What are you hoping to get out of an experience like this? What's a best-case scenario for you?" Nora prompts.

I've been turning that question over in my mind on a loop for the past week and a half, but I'm still not sure. "There is definitely a part of me that wants to get away—not forever—I don't want to disappear or anything like that. I just want some space to breathe and to think. To regroup, I guess."

Nora tilts her head to the side but doesn't say anything. I know that means she wants me to keep talking.

"I have this feeling," I say, pressing a fist against my diaphragm, "that if I dismantle my old life, I'll be able to build a new one. Is that weird?"

Nora's face softens, then shakes her head no.

"My friends think I'm having a pre-midlife crisis."

Nora runs her hands along the tops of her creaseless pants. I don't think I've ever seen her clothes wrinkled. I've long suspected that she's a control freak like me. It's probably why we work so well together. "So what if you are?"

"I don't want to have a crisis."

"Well no one *wants* to have a crisis. But we don't really have any control over that. What we do have control over is how we respond. Whether we allow ourselves to grow."

I bury my face in my hands, as if hiding from this conversation, this decision, this reality will change anything. "This is not at all how I'd planned on my life going."

"Plans don't always keep you safe, Eliza."

I scoff. Nora was right about a lot of things, but not that.

Definitely not that.

"Sometimes bad things happen for no good reason at all," she adds gently.

My hands tighten into fists without my permission. It happens every time Nora tries to steer the conversation in this direction. "I don't want to talk about Hannah."

"Who said anything about Hannah?"

"It was implied."

"Have you been thinking about her lately?"

There isn't a day that goes by that I don't think about my childhood best friend. Hannah and I met the first day of sixth grade and were instantly inseparable. *ElizaandHannah*. A package deal. Until she died the summer before our junior year, before either of us even turned sixteen.

I don't like talking about it.

Hannah's death had taught me two things: first, that it's best to stick to a plan if you want to avoid disaster. "It's just so unimaginably unfortunate," I'd overheard one of our friend's moms say at the funeral. As if Hannah's life had ended simply because she was unlucky. I'd mentally retraced every single one of her movements that day, pinpointed the decisions, the changes in plan that got us here—luck had nothing to do with it.

The second thing Hannah's death taught me was that a fresh start can do wonders for a person. Hannah's death hung over me like a rain cloud for the rest of high school. It wasn't until I went away to college that I found the sunshine again.

Everything that has happened with Marco and me over the past year kind of reminds me of that feeling. I can't seem to shake the cloud.

Hannah's freckled face, her tangled, copper-colored hair, her unabashedly loud belly laugh, all flash through my head. To this day, there are moments when I can picture her so vividly that I feel like I could reach out and touch her. "I haven't been thinking about her any more than usual."

"What do you think she'd tell you to do about all of this?"

The thought makes me smile because I know exactly what Hannah would want me to do. "She'd tell me to go."

Nora tilts her head to the side. "How does that make you feel?"

Conflicted. The truth is, Hannah was reckless. Since she died, the guiding principle of my life has been doing the opposite of whatever Hannah would have done. I threw myself into schoolwork, I didn't go to parties or drink alcohol (until college, of course), I started a savings account.

And I most certainly didn't ride around in trucks with cute football players in the middle of the night.

But maybe this was the first thing Hannah and I had agreed on in a long, long time. Fifteen years, eight months, and twenty-one days to be exact. Not that I'm counting.

I take a long, deep breath. Then I say, "It makes me feel like I have a very big decision to make."

I DECIDE TO go straight home after therapy. I want to enjoy as much time alone in my little office nook as I can before Marco steals it away from me. Plus, I have a lot to think about.

But, when I push open the front door, I'm not alone.

Marco is standing in the kitchen with some dude in a fleece vest, the kind all the tech bros think make them look cool. My former fiancé's handsome face twists with confusion when he sees me standing in the doorway. "Lize, what are you doing here?"

"I live here."

"I didn't think you'd be home until later."

I cross my arms over my chest, keys still dangling from my right hand.

Marco arranges his lips into a tight smile. "This is Kwame," he says, gesturing toward the vest guy. "My client that I told you about?" The way his voice ticks up carries a subtle plea. He doesn't want me to make this awkward.

I turn to Kwame. "Nice to meet you," I say, regretting my compulsion to be unfailingly polite no matter the circumstances.

Kwame shoves his hands into his pockets. "It's a great place you have here."

I look back at Marco. "Not for long."

Marco lets out a nervous laugh. "I was just telling Kwame that you'll probably be taking the furniture in your office and a lot of the . . ." He sweeps his hand around the room, his eyes grazing over the art deco bar cart, bust of Cleopatra, and a framed photo of an aristocratic-looking pug. ". . . stuff you bought for decorations."

It wasn't *stuff*. Everything I'd bought for our apartment—with the exception of the things in my office—I'd chosen *for* Marco. To suit *his* tastes. He used to love it when I'd bring home my latest finds.

"Would you mind removing the wallpaper in the alcove, too?" Kwame ventures, his nose crinkling. I guess tech bros can't have whimsical design elements in their pieds-à-terre.

Something about the image of me peeling the pretty floral design I'd carefully selected from the wall piece by piece breaks my steely resolve, sending inconvenient tears to my eyes. I blink them away, hoping no one notices.

Kwame tilts his head to the side. "I'm sorry, I didn't mean to upset you. I know you're going through a lot."

And there it is again. That cloud. I didn't want Kwame's pity. I didn't need Kwame's pity.

He should be getting *my* pity. He's the one wearing an unflattering vest.

That's when I make up my mind. I uncross my arms, drop my keys on the entryway table, and start tugging off my jacket. "I'll be out of here before the fifteenth," I say, with all the casual breeze I can muster. I turn my attention to the brass coat rack I'd picked up at the Treasure Island Flea Market last year. "But I'm afraid I won't be able to take any of the furniture with me," I say as I drop the jacket over a hook.

Marco's eyes flash. I can tell he thinks I'm being irrational. Or worse, *hormonal*. "Why not?"

I take a breath so deep that it reaches all the way down to my stomach. Then I smile. "Because I'm moving to Minnesota."

Chapter Five

July
Juneberry Lake, Minnesota

Summer in the Midwest is not just a season. It's an experience. The moment I step off the plane, I'm smacked with a wall of moisture and heat so thick and syrupy that I have to force myself to move through it. By the time I get to my Lyft, my hair has frizzed up to twice its usual size and my clothes cling to my body, heavy and damp.

"Juneberry Lake, huh?" Doug, my driver, asks, flicking his eyes to the rearview mirror to meet mine. "Beautiful town. A little sleepy in the off months, but you'll like it."

I'd bought the lake house without ever stepping foot inside of it, which is so out of character that it gives me vertigo if I think about it too hard. But I did a virtual tour with the Realtor and the home inspector assured me that the house is in excellent condition. By that point, I was so in love with the idea of my new life by the lake that I didn't need much convincing. "That's the hope," I tell Doug.

"The lake shares a border with Wisconsin, you know," Doug continues, shaking his head. "Nice enough people but their football team . . ." He makes a *tsk*ing sound. "You're not a Packers fan, are you?"

"I don't really watch football," I say. Ever since I saw that Will

Smith movie about CTE I haven't been able to enjoy a game. Not that I'd ever been a die-hard fan or anything.

"The Vikings'll change that," Doug says, tapping the Minnesota Vikings air freshener that hangs from his mirror. He's wearing a purple and gold jersey and I can't help but respect his commitment. "Preseason is just around the corner. Do yourself a favor and head into town to watch a game at the Common Loon. They have every kind of beer you could want and their cheese curds are out of this world."

I'm charmed by the local flavor Doug is previewing for me. Cheese curds and a football game at a dive bar couldn't feel further away from my life in the city. Just like I wanted.

"I'll be sure to check it out," I say, meaning it. "Thanks."

"Anytime," he replies with a wave of his hand.

Doug proceeds to regale me with trivia about the state (Did I know that Minnesota is called the land of ten thousand lakes but there are actually more than eleven thousand? Or that Prince was born and raised in Minneapolis?) while I soak up the scenery as it whizzes by. It's beautiful and a bit foreign here but also comforting in a way that I can't quite put my finger on. The rows of corn and wide-open blue sky give way to simple houses situated on large, fenceless lots. I count fourteen above-ground pools and wonder if I should consider installing one at my new house. How else am I going to survive this humidity?

I suppose I could swim in the lake. Maybe I *should* get a boat.

I count six tractors too, but I know I won't need one of those.

"Here we are," Doug says, turning onto a cul-de-sac. He squints at the street sign and lets out a soft chuckle. "Loon Lane. Hopefully that's in reference to the birds and not the people."

The wide street is lined with mature trees. Five houses encircle the center, each distinctly different yet cohesive, somehow.

Besides my shingled cottage, there's a refurbished farmhouse with big picture windows and a wraparound porch, a small, simple cabin painted a dark shade of blue, a meticulously maintained Craftsman with a freshly mowed lawn, and finally, a cheerful yellow cottage with an array of flags gently flapping in the wind— I'm able to make out a pride flag, a Vikings flag, and one that appears to feature a dog's pawprint.

I'm pleasantly surprised by how much better my neighborhood looks in person. I guess the Google Street View images I'd scrutinized before I left haven't been updated recently. It's clear that my house isn't the only one that's been remodeled in the past couple of years.

"Home sweet home," Doug says as the car comes to a stop. My house—my very own home—sits in the center of the cul-de-sac, with two neighboring houses—the little cabin and the pristine Craftsman—on either side. I wonder what the people who live there will be like.

I open the car door, step back into the oppressive humidity and swing my duffel bag over my shoulder. Doug exits the driver's side and comes around in a bid to help me with my luggage. Or, as he quickly realizes, lack thereof. "That's all you brought?" he asks. I can't tell if he's impressed or distressed by my scant belongings.

Since my new house was sold fully furnished, I'd told Marco that he could do whatever he pleased with our old apartment and all of the "stuff" I left behind. He texted me to say that he'd signed a lease on a new condo along the Embarcadero with bay views and a private movie theater, so maybe he could take it all with him.

And I'm sure Kwame will be happy to help him dispose of my wallpaper.

All I had to do was pack up my clothes and toiletries and ship them across the country.

I squint toward the porch and can just make out the outline of a pile of cardboard boxes. "I shipped the rest," I say, pointing in the general direction of my stuff. That seems to appease Doug.

"Well, all right then," he pauses, as if gathering his thoughts. But all he says next is, "Welcome to Minnesota. You couldn't have picked a better state." Then he climbs back into his car and drives off. I watch as he disappears around the corner and feel a tinge of sadness. There was something reassuring about Doug's easy confidence about my future here.

I turn to face my new home and my body thrums with excitement as I take it all in for the first time. It's even better than the pictures.

I find the house key right where my Realtor said it would be (under a cheerful-looking statue of a beaver in a park ranger hat) and drag my boxes into the entryway, staging them haphazardly against a wall.

After texting my family to let them know I made it here in one piece, my first order of business is taking myself on a tour of the house. The layout is simple: there's a cozy living room (with a real-life, wood-burning fireplace!) to the left of the front door, a dining nook to the right, and a kitchen beyond. The living room and kitchen overlook the back porch, which has sweeping views of the tree-lined lake. It's downright idyllic. I find a small half bath off the kitchen and a pair of identically sized bedrooms upstairs with a full bathroom in between. Most of the furniture is covered with dustcloths, but the house itself has been cleaned recently. It smells faintly of bleach and artificial pine and I can't find a speck of dirt anywhere.

I open all the closet doors, pretending that I'm assessing the storage space when really I'm checking for murderers. Lucky for me, the coast is clear.

The basement is accessible through a small doorway under the stairs. I pull a chain overhead and am relieved by the sight of a tidy, well-lit stairwell.

I'm pleasantly surprised when I reach the bottom. The room is small and clean, with plaid carpeting and creamy white walls. It's several degrees cooler than the main level and smells of earth and cement. There are narrow windows toward the ceiling and I can just make out a couple of wildflowers sprouting from the grass.

I turn my attention to the rest of the basement. There's a laundry area, a love seat and coffee table in the center, an antique-looking wooden desk in the corner, and a row of metal storage racks along the far wall. The racks are largely empty, but three plastic bins line the bottom shelf. They appear to be full of papers. I lift the lid of one and pull out a stack of mail—some open and some still sealed—all dated last year and all addressed to Erica Donaldson, who I guess to be the previous owner. She probably just missed these in the frenzy of moving, but I make a mental note to mention it to one of the neighbors once I get to know them. Maybe they can help me return these to her or, better yet, confirm that I can toss them. I slide the envelopes back into the bin and close the lid with a satisfying *click*.

Back upstairs in the cheerful light of day, I take in the details of my new home with fresh eyes. There are folksy "lake life" touches everywhere—from the oars on the wall and the canoe-shaped lamp by the couch to the banister wrapped in rope. The decor choices would be corny back in San Francisco, but here, they're perfect. I don't want to change a thing.

Except maybe the coffee table, which isn't centered with the fireplace. That'll drive me nuts.

I yank the dustcover off the couch in the living room and the bench in the dining nook before snapping a few pictures to send to Farah, Carmen, and Brittany. *I've arrived!* I write. But I really mean: *See? It's perfect! I made the right choice!*

My friends had offered to throw me a going-away happy hour, which was sweet, but I told them not to worry about it. I know they mean well, but their attempts at being supportive don't do much to mask their pity and concern and I've already had enough of that to last a lifetime.

They promptly respond with a flurry of hearts on every photo and proclamations about coming to visit soon. I'm not sure if I buy their newfound enthusiasm, but I appreciate the effort.

Until a few minutes later, when I get an unwelcome text. From Marco.

> **Marco:** Sounds like you made it there safely. Call me if you need me.

I feel a pang of betrayal. It makes me wonder if Farah might be helping Marco keep tabs on me. She doesn't believe that this move is permanent, that my decisions are grounded in reality. She's just biding her time until I come back around.

I don't respond to Marco's text.

THE JUNEBERRY LAKE Committee for Growth left a welcome basket on the counter and I'm banking on it having enough wine and snacks to get me through the evening. Mom had sent me off with a batch of freshly baked focaccia, but I want to save it for when I really need it, for when I'm feeling really, truly homesick, and tonight isn't that night. I stick it in the freezer.

I'd been looking forward to exploring the town but feel suddenly exhausted by the idea of leaving the house. I remind myself that I took the whole week off work to get settled and that there will be plenty of time for new adventures as I grab the first drinking glass I can find (a Juneberry Lake Summer Festival mug) and the basket before heading to the back porch.

The sun is starting to dip behind the trees, and the humidity seems to have dropped along with it. The porch is screened, I'm assuming to keep the bugs out, but I can still see the property clearly from the forest-green Adirondack chair I plop down on. A wide lawn stretches toward the lake, connecting with a sturdy-looking wooden dock. A smallish white boat with blue writing on the back floats alongside. I can just make out its name: *The Tammy.*

I rummage around my welcome basket and produce a bottle of twist-top wine (either the committee is cheap or they were thinking ahead. I have no idea where the wine opener is or if the previous owner even left one behind for me), a bag of gourmet cheese popcorn, and a salted nut roll.

I sample both and find them to be equally delicious.

Something catches my eye just as I top off my mug of wine—a figure slinking away from the boat and up the dock. The person is a good fifty yards away, so while they're technically on my property, I don't feel threatened, exactly. More startled. I rise from my chair and walk to the edge of the porch.

My skin prickles ever so slightly as I remember Mom's parting words after my going-away dinner. She'd shoved the Tupperware container full of focaccia into my hands, pulled me into a crushing hug, and whispered, "Remember not to answer the door for strangers. And double-check all of your locks before you go to bed."

The man looks up in my direction, and I go still. Am I the

creep for standing out here watching him or is he the creep for trespassing in my yard? I remind myself of the terms of my sale: my next-door neighbor has shared use of my dock. That's probably him. My shoulders relax at the realization as I raise my hand in a friendly wave, all the while hoping he won't take it as an invitation to come to talk with me. I'm not quite ready to meet the neighbors yet.

The man just stares back. From what I can tell, he's not young, but not old, either. He's white, with brown hair and his eyes obscured by a pair of aviator sunglasses. Maybe he can't see me behind the screen.

An electric buzzing permeates the air, growing louder and more intense with each passing second. If I didn't know any better, I'd think I was in the path of a downed powerline. But, thanks to my brother and his extensive research, I know it's just June bugs.

I'm jolted out of my stare-off with Probably My Neighbor by my phone buzzing in my back pocket. I set my wine on the ledge of the deck and dig out my phone. I assume it's Mom or maybe even Marco, but instead, I see Trish's name lighting up the screen.

"Hello?" I answer, returning my focus to the man on the dock.

"Welcome to Minnesota! How are you settling in?" Trish asks, her Midwestern cheer dissipating the layer of unease that had settled over me.

"Good," I say, trying and failing not to sound distracted.

"How do you like the house?"

The man has started walking along the lakeshore, his head still turned in my direction.

"Eliza?"

I squeeze my eyes shut and shake my head in an attempt to concentrate on what Trish is saying. By the time I open them again—just mere seconds later—the man has disappeared.

"I'm here," I say. "Sorry, there was just . . . I think one of my neighbors was on my dock."

Trish lets out a good-natured *Huh.* As if to say that's odd but not terribly concerning. "What was he doing?"

"He was . . . walking? And looking at the house. I'm not sure if he could see me though."

I've never met Trish in person. I actually don't even know what she looks like—all her social media profile photos are the logo for Join Juneberry Lake—but I can picture her brow furrowing through the phone. "Probably just a lookie-loo," she says. "It's a small town and everyone knows your house went up for sale in a hurry—they're probably wondering why. We don't see a lot of turnover around here. I bet you'll get a few more of those over the next couple of weeks."

That sounds perfectly plausible. If Trish doesn't seem worried, I shouldn't be either. "You're probably right." I reach for my mug of wine and take a sip. "Thanks for the welcome basket by the way. That popcorn is incredible."

"Careful—that stuff's addictive. I've been known to polish off a supersized bag in one sitting." Trish laughs.

"I'll consider myself warned."

"Good. Anyway, I was calling to see if you wanted to meet for coffee tomorrow morning? I'd like you to see the town—you're going to love it. We can meet at Black Bear Brew on Main Street. Say ten a.m.?"

I spent most of the plane ride here making a *Juneberry Lake To-Do* list for myself. Exploring Main Street was toward the top, along with getting my boxes unpacked, my clothes put away, and making a new friend. I realize that I'm bouncing on my toes at the idea of checking an item off my list so soon.

I tell Trish that I'll see her tomorrow before settling back into my chair, and taking another bite of the salted nut roll. I scan the back lawn for any signs of movement, but my dockside visitor is nowhere to be found.

I pull out my phone to review my list in full. I'd been book-marking articles with advice about how to integrate yourself into a new city and as I browse all of the items on my list, I feel hope-ful that I'll be able to accomplish them well before this summer is over.

Week 1
- Start unpacking
- Explore downtown
- Find a coffee shop
- Go grocery shopping

Week 2
- Establish a routine
- Explore public transportation options or get a bike
- Meet my neighbors
- Finish unpacking

Month 1
- Get invited to a party
- Find a doctor & dentist
- Sample local cuisine
- Become a regular at a restaurant
- Swim in the lake
- Go to a Join Juneberry Lake mixer (ask Trish)

Month 2

- Host a housewarming party for new friends
- Attend the annual end-of-summer festival
- Celebrate my birthday
- Create new life plan and timeline

I remember Doug's recommendation and add *watch preseason football game at the local bar*. I set my phone down, feeling proud of myself for being so organized. I take another sip of wine as the June bugs start buzzing again.

I'm buzzing a little bit, too.

Chapter Six

Juneberry Lake is shaped like a kidney bean. Minnesota gets one half and Wisconsin claims the other, so you can technically cross over into a neighboring state by water. My new neighborhood is located on the south end of the lake, just a few miles from the Wisconsin side and the downtown is a little less than a mile to the north. I could technically walk there, which is a huge plus, but it was already soupy and humid by the time I woke up, so I decided to dust off the bicycle—an old beach cruiser—I found parked along the side of my house. I figure it's mine now—why would anyone leave a bike outside of a house that wasn't theirs? The bike is forest green with a tan leather seat and a metal basket attached to the front. There's some rust along the welding points, but it's in pretty good condition, all things considered.

It's been years since I rode a bike and I'd forgotten how liberating it feels. I relish the warm breeze blowing through my hair and the sunshine on my cheeks as I cruise out of the cul-de-sac and onto the main street. I pass a few other houses along the way before the road cuts in toward the lake. The view is a feast for my eyes: tall, mature spruce trees stand proudly along the shoreline and the water winks and sparkles in various shades of blue and green under the sunlight. In the distance, brightly colored kayaks dot the surface. I also spot some enviable mansions with sloping lawns and sprawling docks to the north. If I remember correctly, that's the Aspen Estates neighborhood. I read that it's full of rich people who only stay in their second homes during the summer months.

If I could afford a house like that, I'd never leave.

The ride to the edge of Main Street is quick—just a few minutes—and my eyes widen when it comes into full view. The vintage shop fronts and old-fashioned streetlamps make me feel like I've stepped into a Hallmark movie.

I park my bike outside of Black Bear Brew, a rustic, wood-paneled storefront with a doodle of a bear sipping coffee on the door. That's when I realize that I don't have a lock for my bike. I crane my neck in search of other bikes and spot a trio leaning up against the side of the pharmacy across the road. None of them are chained up. Back home, leaving a bike unlocked out in the open is a surefire way to ensure you never see it again. And while I know it would probably be fine here—Juneberry Lake is a far cry from the city—I can't bring myself to leave my defenseless cruiser out on the street.

I step into Black Bear Brew carrying my front bike tire. It's not a guarantee that the rest of it won't be stolen and used for parts, but I figure it's a decent deterrent.

The interior of the coffeehouse looks like a ski lodge from the eighties. The walls are painted a dark shade of green and covered in wooden snowshoes, plaid armchairs frame mismatched wooden tables, and the head of a friendly looking black bear looms over the espresso maker. It smells like coffee beans and cinnamon rolls.

Two women sit in the corner clutching steaming cups of coffee (why anyone would want to drink a hot beverage in this weather is beyond me), an older man in a newsboy cap flips through a magazine with a picture of a frog on the cover, and a thirtyish guy wearing cargo shorts, tennis shoes, and a JUNEBERRY LAKE

SUMMER FESTIVAL T-shirt sets a pair of cold brews on a table—without a coaster. He flashes me a smile as my eyes sweep over him. My first thought is that he looks like a tourist, but then I remember I'm not in San Francisco anymore. I suddenly feel wildly overdressed in my sundress and sandals.

"Eliza?" I turn to see a woman with locs and a nose ring, peering at me from behind the espresso machine.

I give her an unnecessary wave. "That's me."

The woman is grinning from ear to ear now. "Welcome to Juneberry Lake." She makes her way to me from behind the counter. "I'm Trish," she says, extending her hand. "It's so good to meet you."

"Likewise," I say, taking in her plaid apron and the telltale specks of flour that dust the edges of her hairline. "Do you run the Juneberry Lake program *and* work here, too?"

Trish flicks her wrist as if to say, *That's nothing*. "I don't just work here. I own the place."

I'm positively dazzled by Trish—her warmth, her energy, her charming-as-can-be coffee shop. "How do you have time to do all of that?"

Another flick. "This is nothing compared to my old job. I was the CFO at a big construction company in Minneapolis before I retired. Now I just work for fun." She does an adorable little shoulder wiggle.

"Have you met your neighbors yet?" Trish asks. I shake my head. She bites her lip. "All in good time," she says. "I'm sure they'll be happy to get to know you."

Trish almost seems nervous about whether I'm going to like my new neighborhood, but I can't imagine why. She probably just feels responsible for making sure every new resident receives a warm welcome.

As we chat, I can't help but notice the no-coaster guy stealing occasional glances at me. I assume it's because of my bike tire, but Trish doesn't mention anything.

"So, the committee hosts monthly get-togethers for all of our new residents and we have one coming up on Sunday at Cricket's—the restaurant just across the street. We're going to rent pedal boats and have a few drinks. You should come."

A thrill of satisfaction zips across my chest as I picture myself crossing another item off my list. "I'll be there."

"Fantastic," Trish says. "It'll be a great way for you to make some new friends in town. But, in the meantime, there's someone I'd like you to meet." She takes me by my free wrist and guides me farther into the café.

The guy in the cargo shorts stands as Trish and I approach. "Joel, I'd like to introduce you to Eliza."

He extends his arms in either direction. "Welcome to town," Joel says, radiating Midwestern warmth. "I'm Joel Jawowksi."

I take Joel in anew. He looks to be about my age, with short dark hair, deep brown eyes, and a small dimple in his chin. He bears a slight resemblance to Michael B. Jordan—if Michael B. Jordan dressed like a middle-aged dad and eased up on the workouts. I force myself to ignore the fact that he's handsome enough to star in a movie.

"Joel just moved to Juneberry Lake a few months ago," Trish explains. "And he's been kind enough to offer to show you around town today. I'd do it myself, but—" She turns to watch as a family of four gathers around the register. "I'm short-staffed this morning."

"My parents have a bakery back home," I say. "I totally get it."

"Where's home?" Joel asks.

"San Francisco."

"Nice. I've always wanted to visit."

"You should. It's the best. Where are you from?"

"Milwaukee, Wisconsin," Joel says. "Have *you* always wanted to visit?"

I laugh. "Should I?"

"Oh yeah," Joel says. I can't help but appreciate the way he stretches out the word "oh." "We've got it all—lakes, fish fries, corn, cows, Kaukauna cheese. There's nothing better."

"Except Juneberry Lake," Trish interjects, before looking back at the register again. "Well, it sounds like you two will have plenty to talk about. I'll leave you to it." She gives my arm a squeeze before returning to her post behind the espresso machine.

"Shall we?" Joel asks, gesturing to the table.

I lean my tire against the table and pull out a chair.

Joel takes his seat and passes one of the coffees to me. "I wasn't sure how you took your coffee, but it's hot out so I figured iced was the way to go." Then he jerks a thumb toward the bar. "I told them not to add anything, but you can dress it up however you want. They have every kind of milk you could think of, plus a bunch of syrups."

I follow his gaze to the bar where I spot a honey lavender syrup and a carafe of oat milk. I make a mental note to try a latte the next time I'm here. "I'm good with plain iced coffee for now, thank you."

Joel face brightens. "Nice, I guessed right." He raises his cup. "Cheers to your first full day in the best town there is."

It's so cheesy, but I can't resist humoring him. "Cheers," I say before taking my first sip of coffee. The caffeine hits almost instantly and I'm grateful for the boost. I slept better than expected last night, but I think it's going to be a few days before I'm used to the time difference.

"Okay," Joel begins, "I have to ask. What's up with the bike tire?"

I pat the rubber wheel. "Theft prevention."

He laughs. "You're *so* from San Francisco."

"And proud of it." I take another sip of coffee. "This is great by the way," I say, pointing to the cup.

Joel nods. "I know. We have some of the best restaurants in the state right here on Main Street." He sounds like he's recording a radio commercial, but his enthusiasm seems genuine.

"I'll have to try them all," I say.

"Are you hungry? They have a bunch of pastries—the bear claw is"—he mimes a chef's kiss—"perfection. Their breakfast burritos are pretty great, too."

"I don't think I can turn down a perfect bear claw at the Black Bear Brew House."

"You're right. You can't. I'll get us two." He's out of his seat before I can offer to get them myself. I watch as he steps behind the counter and pulls two pastries out of the display case. Trish doesn't seem to mind, flashing him a smile of approval.

When Joel returns with one bear claw for each of us, my mouth starts to water. It's drizzled with just the right amount of icing and smells of cinnamon and sugar and butter. Joel and I take simultaneous bites.

It tastes even better than it looks.

"Good thing Trish ditched that corporate job to make amazing pastries and brew perfect cups of coffee, right?"

"And she's so nice, too."

Joel makes a face as if to say, of course she's nice. Everyone in Juneberry Lake is nice.

"Is everybody around here that friendly?" I ask.

"For the most part, yeah," he says with a shrug. "People are happy here and happy people tend to be friendly. What are the people like in California?"

I bite into my bear claw and chew as I consider the question. "The people there are wonderful, actually," I say, thinking mostly of my favorite customers at Colletti's. "But we don't go out of our way to interact with each other. It's like everyone is distracted with their own stuff or assumes other people are too busy to stop and talk. But, if you were to go up to someone and say hi or ask for directions or something, they'd be happy to chat."

"Well, we're happy to have you here."

I know Joel can't speak for the entire population of Juneberry Lake, but the way he says it, I kind of believe him.

"So, AS YOU may already know, Juneberry Lake is named after the shrubs that grow along the lake, also known as Amelanchiers," Joel says, holding the door for me as we exit the coffee shop. "They usually bloom in June, hence the name. And when they're ripe, they're delicious—kind of like a pear or an apple meets a blueberry."

"I bet they're great in pies."

Joel wriggles his eyebrows. "They are. Aside from the fruit, Juneberry Lake is famous for three things: one, the annual end-of-summer festival, which everyone just calls 'Summer Festival'—it's best not to think too hard about it; two, the depth of the lake—it's three hundred and seventy-six feet, making it the fourth deepest lake in the state; and three, a couple of years ago, someone in the next town over won the super-mega lottery jackpot." He holds up a finger. "That last one doesn't really count, since it technically happened in New Hamburg, but things sound better in threes."

I nod, thinking there are surely more than a couple of fun

facts about this town. I've been here for less than a day and I'm already smitten.

"The official population is 4,882, but it goes up in the summertime because of all the tourists."

"Do you know everyone in town?"

"Juneberry Lake is small but it's not *that* small."

"Gotcha," I say, turning my attention back to Main Street. "So, where does the tour begin?"

Joel squints in the direction of town. "Let's start on the left side since it's still in the shade. Then we can grab some frozen custard for the walk back."

I've never heard of frozen custard before, but I think it's just what frozen yogurt is called out here. Kind of like how they call soda "pop." "Sounds like a plan," I say, before realizing that I'm still holding a bike tire. "Let me just reattach this first."

Once I'm satisfied that the wheel is secure, I turn the bike upright before stashing it behind a bush. Then I look back at Joel, who tries to hide an amused smirk behind his hand. I'm sure he thinks I'm a total weirdo.

I guess I kind of am.

"After you," Joel says, gesturing toward the row of shops.

I'm instantly taken with Main Street, enamored by the way it has everything a small town could need. There's the Elk General Store, a convenience-hardware-souvenir-clothing shop hybrid contained within an old-timey building made from dark-stained logs; the Main Street Market & Deli, a white brick facade with big, black framed windows; the Barn Owl Bookstore, complete with a hanging wood sign featuring a scarf and glasses–clad owl; and a shared dentist slash doctor's office in a beautifully maintained chalet-style house. Restaurants seem to have the run of the sun-drenched lakefront side of the street. I spot the Moose

Drool Custard & Candy Shoppe, another log cabin–style building; the Common Loon, the sports bar my Lyft driver had told me
about—as expected, a Minnesota Vikings banner hangs above
the front entrance—and Cricket's, a casual, farm-to-table dining
spot with a large dock and hourly kayak and pedal boat rentals.

Then there's the Starling Lounge.

My breath catches as I take in the wraparound porch, the crisscrossed twinkle lights, the stained-glass birds that dangle from
the covered patio, the outdoor stacked stone fireplace, and the expansive windows that boast a straight-through view of the lake. I
can only imagine what it looks like at nighttime, bathed in moonlight and framed by fireflies.

Joel, who's been greeting every single person we pass—by
name—follows my gaze to the lovely building across the street.
"The most romantic restaurant in the state," he says.

"It's beautiful."

"I know. You wouldn't believe how many engagements happen there every summer."

Joel has the air of someone untouched by the ravages of a bad
breakup. I assume he must be happily coupled, maybe even engaged himself. A tiny twinge of something—disappointment,
maybe?—dashes across my chest. I ignore it. Sure, Joel is cute, but
so are a lot of people. Besides, he's wearing cargo shorts. Joel gives
the lounge one final look before saying, "Anyway, are you ready for
some custard? I think they have the turtle special today."

Frozen custard is not the same as frozen yogurt. It's so much
better—thicker and tastier and an all-around gift to my taste
buds. I promptly devour the turtle special (a dreamy mix of caramel and chocolate and nuts) and wish that I'd gotten two. I intend
to go back for more tomorrow. "Is everything here this amazing
and delicious?" I ask Joel.

He grins. "Pretty much."

"So you're really happy here?" I ask, more for myself than for him. So far, I'm feeling great about my decision to move, but it would be nice to hear from someone who's been here longer.

Joel's eyes find mine as he considers my question. "I am. It's different, but good different."

"And it's not too far from home?"

"I'm not sure my mom would say that—she wasn't wild about me moving away. It's kind of a sore spot, actually. But yeah, I can visit my folks pretty easily. Plus, they have a house here on the lake. We used to come here every summer. My sisters and I would spend all day swimming or cruising around in our neighbor's boat or gorging ourselves on frozen custard and fried food. I've always loved this place, but I never thought I'd *live* here."

"What changed?"

A crease appears between his eyebrows. "I turned thirty. What would that be—a one-third-life crisis?" He laughs. "Not very catchy, but you get the idea."

"We'll workshop it," I tease.

He lets out a little laugh. "Thanks. I don't know, it's like I graduated from college and then next thing I knew all of my friends were married with kids and houses and ride-on lawnmowers and I wasn't. And it's not like I'm chasing that—I'm not. But, it just felt like I needed to do something different. Get to know myself in a new way. Plus, my company—I'm the program manager for a nonprofit that teaches underprivileged kids to code—decided to let everyone work from home, so I was free to go anywhere."

I'm not the least bit surprised to learn that Joel works for a charitable organization. He strikes me as the type of guy who earnestly ran for student body president in high school and volunteers at a soup kitchen every Thanksgiving. I bet he was a Boy Scout.

I also understand his crisis viscerally, but I'm not going to reveal all of that right now. Part of the appeal of a fresh start is that no one knows what I've been through.

"What about you?" Joel asks. "What brings you here?"

"A one-third-life crisis," I say.

Joel responds with a solemn nod. "I hear those are going around."

"So why did you pick this town?" I ask, keen to shift the focus back to him.

His face turns pensive. "I guess you could say that I followed someone here."

And there it is. I knew there was no way someone as cute and nice as Joel would be single. "That's sweet."

"I'd like to think so. Hopefully she agrees."

"You're not like . . . stalking her, are you?"

Joel chokes on a laugh and starts shaking his head emphatically. "Absolutely not. She's very happy to have me here. We're mutually happy about it."

"That's a relief," I say, summoning my supportive friend face. This is actually for the best. I don't need to be getting myself into any kind of romantic entanglements. I like the idea of having Joel as a totally platonic friend. That's what I need right now anyway.

Once we've finished our custard, I say goodbye to Joel, thanking him profusely for showing me around. When I catch myself smiling for no apparent reason on my bike ride home, I realize that while Joel and I were strolling Main Street, I forgot about all of my problems for the first time in months.

Chapter Seven

I get home from my tour of town, lean my bike against the porch, and head inside. I've never been more grateful for air-conditioning. My bike ride home left my hair stuck to the back of my neck and my dress feels heavy and damp. I tear open a wardrobe box and grab the first clean shirt I can find.

I've just slipped on a fresh T-shirt and cutoffs and pulled my hair into a bun when I hear the knock.

I open my new front door to find a woman standing on the porch. She's wearing a purple tank top emblazoned with Viking horns and clutching a foil-wrapped casserole. I'm pretty sure she was smiling before I even opened the door.

"Welcome to the neighborhood," the woman chirps. The way she's holding the dish reminds me of when Rafiki presents Simba to the animal kingdom at the beginning of *The Lion King*. "I'm Lynette Carr-Poole from two houses down," she adds, jerking her straw-colored ponytail to the right.

I nod. I know the house: a beautifully preserved white farmhouse with green shutters and a wraparound porch. "Nice to meet you," I say, flashing a smile. "I'm Eliza."

"What a pretty name," Lynette says.

"Your last name is Carpool?"

Lynette grins. "It's hyphenated. My maiden name is Carr and my husband's last name is Poole." She spells both out. "Neither

of us wanted to change our names when we got married, so we
compromised with Carr-Poole."

"It would have been a missed opportunity not to," I say.

Lynette bobs her head in agreement as she peers over my
shoulder. She reminds me of someone, but I can't put my finger on who. The cool, dry air inside my house mingles with the
sticky humidity outside. Goose bumps prickle at the back of my
legs as sweat beads on my forehead. Am I supposed to invite Lynette inside? Is that what people do here? Marco and I went years
without ever seeing the inside of our neighbors' apartments.

Lynette peels her gaze away from the cardboard boxes that line
my entryway. "So, what brings you to Juneberry Lake?"

It wasn't so much what brought me *to* Juneberry Lake as what
drove me *from* San Francisco. But she doesn't need to know that.
"I was accepted to the Join Juneberry Lake program," I say. "I just
got in from California."

Lynette brightens at the mention of my home state. "Isn't that
neat. What a great way to bring new faces into town. Kids these
days all want to live in the big city, don't they? Everyone wants to
be Carrie Bradshaw."

I look down at my ringer tee and distressed denim shorts. I'm
hardly a kid, but Lynette probably has about a decade on me. I was
in elementary school when *Sex and the City* premiered. Still, I get
the reference. "I guess so," I say. "It was just time for a change."

"Well this place will certainly be a change from California,"
she muses. "I've always wanted to visit. Is it like what you see on
TV? Does everyone surf and eat salads with no dressing?"

I'm charmed by the question. "Where I come from, it's more
about hiking and kombucha."

Lynette's face takes on a sunny expression, a delicate pair of
crow's-feet framing her grass-green eyes. "And is it just you? No

guy?" she asks, before quickly adding, "Or girl! We're a very welcoming bunch around here." She swats a hand at the biggest fly I've ever seen. "Have you met Marge and Gal? They're lesbians. *Married* lesbians."

The way Lynette elongates her vowels makes me feel like I could tell her anything. But I think better of it, instead pressing my lips together. "Not yet. And I'm newly single, actually. No guy." I do my best to sound breezy about my broken engagement, as if my life crumbling into a million little pieces was totally casual. No biggie!

Lynette tilts her head in sympathy. I'm so sick of people tilting their heads in sympathy that I could scream. But I don't. "I'm sorry to hear that," she says. "Do you know anyone in the area?"

"Not yet."

Lynette's cheerful expression falters, but she recovers quickly, one side of her mouth ticking up higher than the other. That's when it occurs to me that she bears an uncanny resemblance to Drew Barrymore. This puts me even more at ease. I adore Drew Barrymore. "Well, we're just going to have to change that."

Much to my relief, I think I like my new neighbor. When Lynette steals another glance over my shoulder, I push the screen door open and invite her inside.

I want to offer Lynette tea or a soda or something, but I haven't had a chance to go grocery shopping yet. All I have is whatever is left in my welcome basket. I should probably go to the market tonight. Subsisting on cheesy popcorn and savory nut loafs is fine every now and then, but two nights in a row would be a slippery slope.

"How are you settling in so far?" Lynette asks, as if reading my mind.

I let out an awkward half laugh, half smile. "I'm not, really. Not yet," I say, looking around at the array of boxes and half-covered furniture.

She nods sympathetically. "Say no more. We just remodeled our house a couple of years ago and basically had to camp out in the garage for months. I couldn't find a thing."

"Renovations can be tough." I say this as if I know, but my only point of reference is Brittany.

"Not as tough as moving across the country."

I rest my hip against the uncovered couch, its dustcover crumpled on the floor by my feet. "Yeah, I've got my work cut out for me."

"At least you don't have to redecorate."

My eyes sweep around the room, as if I'm taking it in all over again. The artful mash-up of plaid and wood with a nautical twist really is adorable. "True," I say. "Whoever owned this place before me had great taste."

A sad expression flits across Lynette's face, but she quickly replaces it with a smile. "She really did."

"Did you know her? The woman who lived here?"

Lynette frowns. "Of course," she says. I wonder if she's offended by my question. Juneberry Lake seems like a friendly place, maybe it's rude to imply that not all of the neighbors would know each other. "Erica was a coastal transplant, too. Like you," Lynette adds. There's a hesitant note to her tone.

"Do you mind if I ask why she left?"

Lynette shrugs. "Maybe she missed the excitement of the city—she'd moved from Manhattan. It's certainly a slower pace of life around here."

"Do you still keep in touch—"

"So when did you get in?" Lynette cuts me off before I can finish my question. If I didn't know any better, I'd think she didn't want me to ask, but there's no point in reading into it.

I wipe my hands against my shorts, brushing away imaginary dust. "Yesterday. I haven't even had a chance to run to the grocery store yet."

"Well then it's a good thing I brought you that hot dish. We can't have you going hungry."

I make a mental note to refer to casseroles as "hot dishes" moving forward and thank her again. "Have you lived here long?"

"Oh yeah, we all have. I take it you haven't met any of the other neighbors yet?"

I shake my head. "I think I saw one of them out on the dock last night. By the boat."

"The pontoon boat?" Lynette asks, as if I know what a pontoon is. I nod along like I do though. "That was probably Bob," she says, confirming my suspicions. "He's your next-door neighbor." She points out the window to the house with the perfect lawn.

"Bob is a widower," Lynette continues. "His wife, Tammy, passed away about eight years ago and he's become a bit of a curmudgeon since then."

The man I saw last night couldn't have been more than fifty. I can't imagine what it must have been like to lose a spouse so early in life. "His wife must have been young."

Lynette shakes her head. "She was sixty-eight. Not young, but not very old either."

"How old is Bob?"

"Eighty. I only know that because we threw him a little party to celebrate a few months ago. He hated it." She laughs.

So the stranger definitely wasn't Bob. Maybe it was his son or Lynette's husband or a mechanic. I decide not to ask Lynette about it because I don't want to seem paranoid.

"Bob's been teaching my kids to fish this summer and I couldn't be more grateful," Lynette continues, oblivious to my unease. "Entertaining two kids when they're out of school is basically impossible." She pauses. "I'm rambling aren't I?"

I shake my head. "Not at all." I like listening to Lynette talk. She's just so . . . open. Unpretentious. It's refreshing.

Lynette lets out a good-natured laugh. "You're sweet. I knew it wasn't true what they say about Californians." Before I have a chance to ask what "they" say about my home state, Lynette has moved on. "So, Bob keeps his boat on your dock—Erica let him use it. Actually, she let all of us use it. Yours is the only dock on the cul-de-sac with water deep enough for swimming or launching a boat." Lynette's tone—slightly tighter, less natural—gives me the feeling that there's more to the story. Maybe Erica was weird about everyone using her dock.

"Anyway, you've got Bob to the right and we're next to him," Lynette continues, her breezy tone restored. "My husband is Allan and our kids are Ruby and Ned. They're eight and five. You'll meet them soon, I'm sure—they sort of have the run of the neighborhood. But if they're ever bothering you, just say the word and I'll come wrangle them. I'm home full time, so I'm always just a shout away." She moves on before I have a chance to say that her kids could never bother me. "On the other side, you have Stuart—you may have heard of him. Stuart Sato? He wrote a bestseller called *Depth Charge*. Anyway, he can be a bit of a recluse but is a total doll when he's in the mood. And then you have Marge and Gal's place across the street. They foster animals with special needs out of their house, so they've got a rotating cast of cats, dogs, and the occasional bird coming through. It's a great way to get your pet fix without having to actually bring one home.

Ruby is desperate for a dog of her own and she insists she'll take care of it but you know how that goes."

I don't, but I can imagine. When I was eight, I begged my parents for a puppy. I swore up and down that I'd feed it and walk it every day. They finally relented and agreed to pick up a scruffy little mutt from the local shelter. I named him Spaghetti. It only took a week or two before Mom begrudgingly took over as his primary caregiver. She said he was more work than a human baby, but I also suspected that Mom liked Spaghetti more than her human babies (to be fair, Spaghetti was way cuter than Enzo or me), so I'd say it all worked out in the end.

All that said, I do love the idea of getting to hang out with the neighborhood dogs whenever I wanted.

"Well, I'll let you get back to it," Lynette says, her eyes doing a final sweep of the messy living room. "I'm sure you're eager to get unpacked."

I rise from my quasi-seat along the arm of the couch. "Thank you again for the hot dish," I say, giving myself an imaginary pat on the back for remembering not to call it a "casserole." "And the warm welcome."

"It's my pleasure. I'm excited to have another young gal on the block," she says with a wink. "I'll have to have you over for happy hour on our dock once you're settled."

This feels like the beginning of a promising new friendship, something I've found is rare to come by once you pass the age of twenty-two. I take Lynette's visit as further confirmation that moving here was the right choice. "I'd love that."

Lynette gives me a final wave before pushing through the screen door. It creaks shut before closing with a *click*. Alone again, I turn to survey my mess. I'm not even sure where to begin, but

I figure my closet is probably a safe bet, so I drag my duffel bag and the cardboard wardrobe box to the base of the stairs. The rest of my boxes are filled with the types of random things a person collects by the time they hit thirty: high school yearbooks, loose photos, picture frames, cheap, irreparably tangled jewelry, and the odd candlestick or novelty mug. The cluttered look of the living room is giving me anxiety, so I take the boxes of nonessentials down to the basement and shove them onto the storage rack for safekeeping.

It's only then that I realize I forgot to ask Lynette about Erica's abandoned bins.

Chapter Eight

The Join Juneberry Lake meetup that Trish invited me to was kind of a bust. I ended up chatting with Dora and Jerry, a khaki-clad fortysomething couple from Seattle who bought a place in Aspen Estates and Jade, a twenty-three-year-old influencer from Arkansas.

"We have so much space for the kids to run around now," Dora enthused.

"Three kiddos under five," Jerry added, with a laugh. "What were we thinking?" Jerry tried and failed to strike a self-deprecating tone. It was clear that he was quite proud of his and Dora's hyper-fertility.

"I love my hometown, but it was time to spread my wings, you know?" Jade, who stood off to the side, her sundress billowing just so in the afternoon breeze, had said. "I'll probably be married with kids in a couple of years, so I figured it was now or never."

My conversation with my fellow transplants only made me feel more alone. I'm not settled like Dora and Jerry, but I'm certainly not a fresh-faced ingenue like Jade. I'm not old, but I'm not young, either.

I'm just . . . here.

On the bright side, I was able to check *attend a Join Juneberry Lake mixer* off my list earlier than expected. And, by the time my second week in town rolled around, I'd mostly settled into my new house and gotten into a nice little routine (check and check). I get up just after the sun rises and ride my bike into town before it gets too hot and spend the morning catching up on emails and brainstorming campaign ideas from my favorite table at Black Bear Brew (*find a coffee shop* and *become a regular at a restaurant* have both been checked off as well). I figure this is a good way to familiarize myself with the locals. Plus, I like talking to Trish.

And I'm sure I'll bump into Joel there one of these days.

Marco has texted me a few times to "check in." His messages reek of guilt and obligation, so I've just been ignoring them.

I'm settling into a plaid overstuffed armchair in my upstairs guest room, the afternoon sun streaking across my legs, when my phone starts pinging in rapid succession. Without even looking, I know it's my group text thread.

Farah kicked things off with a picture of the twins covered in spaghetti, to which Brittany responded with photos of her nearly finished kitchen renovation, which prompted Carmen to share an anecdote about a conversation she overheard on Muni that morning. I perform the perfunctory hearting and thumbs-upping and ha-ha-ing at their many updates before switching my phone to do not disturb. I hate that I feel more like a stranger in my old group of friends with each passing day, but that doesn't change the fact that I do.

In high school, my identity had been irrevocably intertwined with Hannah's. First, as her best friend and then as the best friend of the girl who'd died. I never minded playing second fiddle to Hannah when she was alive—I was happy to bask in her glow. But after she died, I hated that I couldn't escape her shadow.

For the most part, kids at school were exceedingly nice to me. They treated me like I was a fragile piece of porcelain, like if they bumped me too hard, I'd crack. I'd feel people staring or hear whispers as I walked down the hall. *That's the girl whose friend died last summer.*

That is, until I got to college, where no one knew who I was. It took me a long time to tell Farah and the rest of the group about Hannah—I didn't want them to treat me any differently. To their credit, they didn't.

But ever since my relationship with Marco unraveled, I can't help but feel like I'm back in high school every time I hear from my friends. They've somehow managed to make me feel smothered and alienated all at once.

The thing is, I *am* lonely here, but I'm not homesick. I like Juneberry Lake. I just need to make some new friends.

I've slowly been making inroads with the neighbors. Lynette stops to say hello whenever she sees me ride past her house on my bike and everybody dropped off some variation of cookies, cakes, and casseroles—I mean *hot dishes*—within days of my arrival.

Well, everyone except Bob.

I haven't formally met him yet, but I did overhear him arguing with Lynette. And I think it was about me. The other night, I was having a glass of wine on the back porch and watching the sunset when Lynette popped over to Bob's with what appeared to be leftovers in a big Tupperware container. I couldn't make out the entire conversation—just the part where Bob raised his voice.

"Don't be naive," he'd practically hissed. "Keep your distance."

"But she's really sweet." Lynette's voice was elevated, but not as much as Bob's.

"Sweet won't protect any of us. I'm not taking any chances."

Protect them from what?

Lynette must have said something to appease Bob because he lowered his voice after that.

LYNETTE HAD MENTIONED that Bob was kind of a grump, so I can probably chalk his wariness up to that. Maybe he's not great with change. I wonder how he treated Erica when she moved here.

My little adventure in eavesdropping aside, my evenings are, admittedly quiet, so I find myself watching a lot of reality TV. I've started watching the neighborhood, too. I can see the entire block from the window in my upstairs guest room.

Two things have struck me so far: first, from this vantage point, it's even more apparent that my cul-de-sac is basically Pleasantville. My neighbors' houses are so meticulously maintained—with pristine landscaping, synchronized sprinkler systems, and freshly painted shutters. Even Stuart's house is in excellent condition, but that's probably because he appears to share a gardener with Lynette and Allan. The point is, this place is utterly idyllic. I've toured a good amount of Juneberry Lake on my bike since moving here, and outside of Aspen Estates, our street is easily the nicest one in town.

The second thing I've noticed is that my neighbors like to hang out with each other. Like, a lot.

Lynette hosts a neighborhood barbecue every Sunday afternoon. Marge and Gal always show up with a bag of fresh fruit and vegetables from the market and a rotating pack of mutts. Bob and Stuart usually bring some variation of chips and beer. I believe Stuart moderates a bimonthly book club (I've spotted Lynette, Marge, and Gal standing on his front porch with identical books tucked under their arms), and Bob has taken the neighbors out for at least three impromptu cruises on his boat.

I've witnessed more mundane interactions, too, like Gal walking a gaggle of dogs every afternoon, Bob teaching Lynette's kids, Ruby and Ned, to fish off the dock, Lynette leaving a freshly baked loaf of bread on Stuart's doorstep, Marge helping Bob load bags full of grass clippings into his truck, and Lynette receiving an inordinate number of packages (I think she has an online shopping habit—I've never seen her or the kids wear the same thing twice). It all feels so . . . wholesome.

But I'm not *in* with the neighbors. Not yet.

I've been expecting an invitation to Lynette's Sunday barbecue any day now, but two weekends have come and gone and this one isn't looking promising either.

I must be doing something wrong.

Chapter Nine

The more time I spend in my new house, the more curious I become about the woman who lived here before me. Normally, this isn't something that I would give much, if any, thought to—I never had the desire to know anything about the people who lived in my old apartment before Marco moved in. But, here, I'm surrounded by the minutia of this woman's life: her seersucker potholders and cast-iron skillet and chunky knit blankets; her carefully selected wall art and tufted couches and chipped LAKE LIFE coffee mugs. I find silver candlesticks tucked under a bench in the dining room and an old Nintendo console in the basement, *Mario Bros.* wedged into the gaming slot. It's almost as if one day she ran out for groceries and simply decided not to come back.

Of course, I know that's not what happened. She obviously took her clothes—the closets and dresser drawers were bare when I arrived. There wasn't a trace of makeup or lotion or nail polish remover in the bathroom vanity, no medications or ointments. And there isn't a single personal photo anywhere in the house.

I find myself wandering into the basement and popping the lid on the storage bins she left behind. I'm pretty sure it's a federal offense to open another person's mail, so I leave the sealed envelopes alone and instead I rifle through the letters that were already open. I haven't found anything scandalous or even vaguely interesting so far—it's mostly credit card offers, coupon booklets, home decor magazines, travel brochures, and a stack of old issues of the local newspaper, the *Juneberry Journal*.

I'm settled into a cross-legged seat on the floor flipping through the July 2021 issue when I come across an article about Erica and the Join Juneberry Lake program.

JUNEBERRY LAKE WELCOMES ITS FIRST
RELOCATION INCENTIVIZED RESIDENTS

There's a photo beneath the headline, a picture of a woman who looks to be in her thirties, with a friendly face, dark hair cascading in waves around her shoulders. She's holding a one-eyed poodle and standing beside a slick-looking man at least ten years her senior. My eyes dance to the caption: *Erica and Gary Donaldson with their dog, Phil.*

I scan the article, in search of what, I don't know.

Juneberry Lake is proud to welcome the inaugural members of the Join Juneberry Lake relocation incentive program! Hailing from New York City, Dr. Erica Donaldson, a veterinarian, and her husband, Gary Donaldson, an attorney, say they're excited to embrace the slower pace of life by the lake.

"It was time for a fresh start," Gary says. "We're thrilled to be here."

The couple purchased a modest lakefront home on the southwest side of the lake. "It's a bit of a fixer-upper," Erica says. "But we're excited to make it our own."

The Donaldsons are the first of five residents selected for the relocation pilot program, an initiative the city hopes will breathe new life into Juneberry Lake's modest economy. Trish Miller, the proprietor of Black Bear Brew, will manage the program.

When asked what they're most excited about, the Donaldsons said they're eager to get to know their neighbors. "They've all been so welcoming," Erica enthuses. "Within a day of moving in, everyone on our street had left a casserole on our front porch."

The Donaldsons say they wish they could return the favor. "We're New Yorkers, so cooking isn't our strong suit—we're takeout people," Gary explains. "But we appreciate the warm welcome."

This article raises more questions than it answers. Like, why hadn't Lynette mentioned Gary? And why did Erica, seemingly so excited about her new life in Juneberry Lake decide to leave only a couple years later? Perhaps most importantly, what happened to Phil the poodle?

I wonder if the Donaldsons were ever invited to the Sunday barbecue.

I reread the last line of the article, empathizing with the Donaldsons. I'm not much of a cook, either. Or a baker for that matter. Enzo got the lion's share of those genes.

And that's when it hits me. Maybe bringing each other food is some kind of Midwestern custom, a cultural norm that I've inadvertently violated.

If I'm going to show my neighbors that I'm serious about building a life here, I need to return the favor.

LACKLUSTER SKILLS ASIDE, I've decided to make a batch of Colletti's famous biscotti and personally deliver it to everyone's front door. I suppose I could bake cookies instead, but that feels too predictable. I want to present my neighbors with something that's a little more unique.

But I won't stop at biscotti. I'll ask Marge and Gal if I can give them a hand with all the dog walking they do, invite Lynette over for a happy hour, read Stuart's book so that I can talk to him about it, and pop over to Bob's to ask if I can pick anything up for him from the market the next time I go.

Hopefully that'll be neighborly enough to show them that I really want to be here, want to be part of their little clique.

I need them to know that I'm not just passing through like Erica.

"How MANY CUPS of sugar again?" I ask Enzo. He agreed to FaceTime with me while I attempt my first batch of biscotti. If I were still in San Francisco, I would have asked him to make it for me himself. Realizing how far away I am from my brother brings on the first bout of homesickness I've felt since I got here.

"Not cups," Enzo says, not bothering to mask his exasperation. "Only three-quarters of *one* cup. Biscotti isn't supposed to be sweet."

I bite my lip in concentration as I measure the sugar under Enzo's watchful eye. "Is this okay?" I say, holding the cup to the screen. I've propped my phone against the backsplash in the kitchen, which to my delight, was stocked with a gleaming array of bowls, measuring cups, baking pans, and wooden spoons. All from Sur La Table, no less. Mom would have a field day if she were here.

Enzo leans in to get a closer look at my work. "That's fine."

I dump the sugar into my mixing bowl before running my finger down to the next ingredient in Mom's recipe. She'd slipped some of her favorites (lasagna, cacio e pepe, and her famous marinara sauce) into my purse the night I'd said goodbye to my family. I didn't find them until I was on the plane. I spent the first hour of my flight tracing her loopy handwriting with my fingertips.

"You're making the vanilla bean recipe right?" Enzo asks, interrupting my reading. I nod. "Good. I don't think you're ready for the citrus one." I look up to meet his eye through the camera. He's smiling, amused by his brotherly jab.

"Funny," I say, as I drop one teaspoon after another of vanilla extract into the powdery mixture.

"Only let it sit for ten minutes after the first bake," Enzo reminds me.

"Yep."

"And remember to grease the pan."

"Will do." I grab a wooden spoon and start stirring. "How's life back home, Enzo?"

He narrows his eyes. "I'm being too intense about the recipe, aren't I?" I smile. "Sorry," he says.

"No need to be sorry. I just want to know how my little brother is doing. I miss you."

He leans back in his chair and stretches his arms. "Things are fine here. Mom keeps trying to book a flight to Minnesota and Dad and I keep stopping her. The bakery is busy as usual. I have a crush on one of our customers and Keith just got the newest version of *Dragon Blades*."

Keith has been Enzo's best friend since high school.

"That's awesome about *Dragon Blades*," I say. "But excuse me? You have a crush?"

"Don't make it weird."

"What's her name?"

"Allison."

"Do you want to tell me about her?"

"There's nothing to tell. She has nice hair and she likes focaccia. Sometimes we talk about movies."

"Do you think she likes you?"

Enzo pauses, his face pensive. "It's hard for me to tell."

"It's hard for everyone, I promise. It's not just you," I say, hoping to reassure Enzo. Sometimes he gets frustrated with himself for struggling to read social cues. I often have to remind him that there are plenty of social situations that almost all humans struggle with. Especially dating.

Enzo nods. "Okay. That's what I thought."

"Well, if you think that she might like you, you could ask if she wants to go to a movie," I suggest. "Doesn't Tom Cruise have something coming out soon?"

Enzo scoffs. "We wouldn't go to *that*."

I laugh. "Fine. Pick a movie you're excited about and ask her to go. If she says no, you can just go back to being friends who talk about movies when she comes in to pick up her focaccia."

Mom strolls through the kitchen holding a glass of red wine. Probably chianti. She's pretending that she isn't eavesdropping, but she's not fooling anyone.

"Hi, Mom," I call. She feigns momentary confusion, then surprise at the sound of my voice.

"Oh, hi, Eliza. I didn't even realize Enzo was talking to you."

"Yes, you did," Enzo says. He passes his phone to Mom and her face fills my screen, her big, curly hair falling over her shoulders. She always takes it down after the bakery closes. I love that I inherited my curls from her. It's one of the few ways in which we're similar. Mom is sweet and maternal and easygoing. I'm a bit more . . . rigid.

"What did you have for dinner?" she asks. What she really means is *I love you, I miss you, you'll always be my baby.*

"I haven't eaten yet."

Her face falls. She doesn't like it when I eat too late. "But I have a casserole in the freezer."

"Frozen casserole?" She practically spits the words out.

"From my neighbor."

"Is she Italian?"

"No."

Mom huffs.

I resume stirring. "How are you and Dad?"

She waves her hand dismissively. "We're fine. The bakery is good. When are you coming home for a visit?"

"I just got here."

Dad appears at Mom's side. "Remember what we talked about, Anna," he says gently. Mom frowns.

"We're happy for your new adventure, Elisabetta," Dad says. It sounds rehearsed, but I appreciate the effort.

"Thanks, Dad."

"And now I'll give you back to your brother." There's a brief struggle as the phone changes hands. When Enzo reappears, he's smiling in amusement.

"Did Enzo remind you to use a serrated knife when you cut the biscotti?" Mom yells over her shoulder as Dad escorts her down the hall.

"Of course, Ma," Enzo calls. He waits to make sure Mom is gone before returning his attention to me. "I forgot to ask why you're making biscotti."

I give my mixture a final stir. "It's for my new neighbors. I want to be their friend."

Enzo furrows his brow. "And you think biscotti is going to win them over?" He shakes his head. "You should have gone with éclairs."

ENZO HANGS UP with me once he's satisfied that I won't burn the house down with my biscotti.

I'm about ready to pull the first batch out of the oven when I realize that I don't have an oven mitt handy. As I rifle through the kitchen drawers, tossing whisks, spatulas, and a garlic press aside, my fingertips brush up against a thick piece of paper.

It's a business card for a financial adviser in Minneapolis. I'm about to throw it away when I notice something scribbled on the back. Someone—I'm assuming Erica—had written:

Trust Bob?

Despite the heat radiating off the oven, a small chill washes over me. Erica didn't think she could trust Bob. But, with what? And why?

The timer goes off and I set the card aside.

Chapter Ten

I place baskets filled with freshly baked biscotti, a personalized note, and serving suggestions (*these are great with coffee or a glass of port wine!*) for each of my neighbors in the front of my bike and pedal from house to house, leaving my special delivery on Lynette's, then Stuart's doorsteps. I'm pretty sure Lynette was dropping the kids off at summer camp and I don't think Stuart is awake yet, so I don't take offense when neither of them answers.

Then I go to Bob's house.

I'm a little nervous, given the note I found in Erica's kitchen and the fact that I overheard Bob arguing about me with Lynette. I've spotted him staring up at my house a few times, too, with a look that can only be described as disdainful. Hopefully a friendly visit will break the ice.

I park my cruiser at the base of Bob's driveway, next to a mailbox that reads THE HOLTS in big, practical black letters that make it feel like the mailbox is yelling at me. As I make my way up the well-maintained brick path, I'm careful not to brush up against the delicate, peachy-hued Juliet roses that line the walkway. Bob must have spent a fortune on them—I know because I'd looked into using Juliet roses in my wedding centerpieces. Marco had vetoed them when he saw how much they cost. Bob swings open his front door before I even make it to the porch. Looks like I'm not the only one who watches the world go by from my window.

"Can I help you?" he asks, his voice gruff. He's wearing a sensible white polo shirt and khaki shorts. His posture is impeccable.

I straighten my spine, then open my mouth to say hi, but the word doesn't have a chance to leave my throat before Bob interrupts me. "Whatever you're selling, I'm not interested." His hand, which never left the doorknob, begins to push the door shut.

"I'm not selling anything," I say urgently. "I'm Eliza. Your new neighbor?" I point toward my house.

Bob pauses the forward momentum of the door, but doesn't speak.

"I wanted to stop by to introduce myself, since we haven't formally met," I continue, my words running together. "I just moved here from California. Have you lived here long?"

Bob narrows his eyes into ice-blue slits. I guess I shouldn't be surprised by his chilly reception. I know he doesn't trust me, doesn't trust outsiders. It seems Erica didn't really trust him either. "Longer than you've been alive."

"Cool." I summon more artificial cheer and remind myself that we don't have to be best friends. I just want to be on good terms. "So you must like it here, then?"

"It beats California."

I look down at the basket in my hands. "I baked," I say, dumbly. I hold the basket out in front of me. "Have you had breakfast yet today? They're—"

He grunts. "Of course I've had breakfast," he says, his tone bordering on mocking. "Do you think I'm some kind of charity case?"

"What? No. Of course not."

"I manage just fine on my own."

"I—"

"You know, while I have you here, you need to remember to bring in your trash cans as soon as the truck comes by."

"Is that a rule?" I'm genuinely asking. Living in an apartment building with a trash chute at the end of the hallway has left me ignorant of trash day etiquette.

"It's common decency."

I nod. "Gotcha. Will do."

We stand in silence. It feels awkward to me, but he seems perfectly comfortable.

"Well," I say, shifting my weight from one foot to the other. "I guess I'll be going."

"You can leave your little"—he waves his hand dismissively—"crackers here. If you must."

"Okay," I say, taking a step forward and passing the basket to Bob. I start to turn on my heel. "It was . . . nice to meet you?" It comes out as a question because, actually, it was terrible to meet him but I'm a polite woman from a nice Italian American family so I would never say such a thing out loud.

Bob grunts but doesn't say anything so I turn and head toward my bike. I've swung my leg over the seat and disengaged the kickstand when Bob calls out to me. "Elizabeth?"

I don't bother correcting him. Whether or not this man knows my name is not my primary concern at the moment. "Yes?"

"Remember to turn your back porch lights off after nine o'clock," he says. "Some of us want to go to bed at a reasonable hour and can't sleep with a spotlight beaming through our bedroom windows."

My shoulders sag. "Will do. Sorry about that."

He raises his hand and holds it in the shape of a wave, elbow bent, fingers splayed, but doesn't complete the gesture. He just stands there like a statue as I pedal away. He never bothers to smile.

WHEN I RING Marge and Gal's doorbell, a chorus of barks erupts from inside. Gal answers holding a bug-eyed Chihuahua, its tongue dangling from the left side of its mouth.

Gal is wearing a bedazzled T-shirt, white capris, and tennis shoes. Her spiked pixie cut is dyed fire-engine red. Aside from her pink lipstick, she's not wearing a stitch of makeup.

"Well hello there," she says cheerfully, before turning back to shush the still-barking dogs. A pack of them—plus a one-eyed cat—has gathered behind a kiddie gate in the hallway, each jockeying for position. Gal's shushing has no effect.

"Hi, Gal. I just wanted to stop by to thank you for the delicious hot dish and to bring you these." I hold up the basket.

Gal lifts the cloth and peers inside. "How nice! Dog treats?"

"It's biscotti, actually. For humans."

"Ah."

"I could bake some dog treats for you though. My family owns a bakery back in San Francisco, we can pretty much make anything."

She takes the basket out of my hands. "Oh, that won't be necessary, hun. These dogs are plenty spoiled as it is. Isn't that right, Darla?" She gently jostles the little Chihuahua for effect. Darla peers up at her, eyes narrowed, as if miffed by the notion that there was such a thing as being spoiled enough.

"Well, I should probably take this batch out for their midday walk," Gal says. The barking has subsided and she's now backed by a chorus of persistent whines punctuated by shrill yelps.

"Would you like some help?"

Gal hesitates, as if she's weighing the pros and cons of letting the newbie tag along. Darla swivels her tennis ball head to look at me and her little tail begins to thump against Gal's side. Gal looks down at Darla and smiles. "You know what? A little help would be great."

MARGE AND GAL's house is surprisingly tidy. Gal leads me through the kitchen and living room and into an oversized mudroom with big accordion glass doors that open to the massive fenced yard. I catch a glimpse of a patio roofed with crisscrossing bistro lights, a new-looking cedar fence, a greenhouse garden, and a freshly mowed putting green. Given the number of animals they have (fourteen at the moment), I expected the house to be in a state of disarray. Instead, I see stacks of neatly labeled bins, a row of tidy kennels, and not a speck of dust. I spot a robotic vacuum cleaner in the corner. They must have to run that thing constantly to keep up with all the fur.

My eyes land on a postcard pinned to the refrigerator with a magnet. It's a picture of a white sand beach with water so blue it looks fake. When Gal notices me staring, she swipes it from its spot on the fridge and drops it in a trash can under the sink. "Been meaning to toss that," she says. "Marge doesn't like it when the refrigerator looks cluttered."

I want to ask where the postcard came from, but think better of it. "Where is Marge?"

"In a meeting," Gal says. She turns her attention to a row of leashes mounted on hooks along the wall and grabs one leash after another. They're ordered by color, like a rainbow. She deftly attaches one to each of the dogs who swarm around her knees and I notice they're each wearing a collar that matches their respective leashes. The planner in me can't help but admire Marge and Gal's color-coded system.

"I thought you were both retired?" I ask. I'd stopped to chat with Marge last week on my way home from the coffee shop. She was walking an adorable pair of elderly beagles. "Benny is fourteen and Tulip is twelve," she'd explained. "They're bonded."

If I hadn't known that Marge and Gal were a couple, I never would have guessed. Marge's style is prim and tailored—she's tall and lanky, wears her thick gray hair in a practical chignon, and favors linen that somehow doesn't wrinkle, while Gal is shorter, rounder, and dripping in rhinestones. I found Marge to be rather reserved, not quick to open up. But, she'd been friendly enough.

"It's not a work meeting," is all Gal says.

With the panting mob of wagging tails leashed up, Gal loads Darla into a carrier pack on her chest. "She's too little and too old to keep up," she explains. Darla peers out from the cocoon of her carrier like a queen surveying her subjects.

"I'll take the unruly mob," Gal says over the din of excited, clicking nails. "And I'll have you walk our newest addition. I don't think she's quite ready for the chaos of a group walk."

Gal unlatches a crate in the corner and a little dog emerges. She looks like a cross between a Chihuahua and a dachshund, with a sturdy little body, perky ears, and a very active tail. Her fur is golden brown, but her paws are white, almost as if they were dipped in paint. She has a white oval-shaped patch on her chest.

She also happens to be missing one of her front legs.

The little mutt does an indulgent stretch before shaking her entire body, as if drying off after a bath. The force of her shake leaves one of her ears upturned, but she doesn't seem to mind.

I can't explain it, but the moment I see this dog, I fall head over heels. I've never felt this way about anyone before. Not even

Marco. "Who is this?" I say, dropping to my knees and extending
a hand.

"We call her Potato," Gal says. "No reason."

Potato makes her way toward me with surprising ease. She
gives my fingertips a gentle sniff and then looks up at me expectantly. I flip her upturned ear back into its natural position.
She leans her head into my hand. "Hi, Potato," I say. "I'm Eliza."
Potato slowly closes, then opens her big brown eyes.

"She likes you."

"What happened to her leg?"

"Hit by a car. Poor thing. By the time someone brought her in,
the vet had to amputate. Her owner was nowhere to be found, so
as soon as she was strong enough, we paid off her medical bills
and Marge brought her home."

"Does that happen a lot? Owners don't come forward to claim
their lost dogs?"

Gal considers the question, subtly bobbing her head back and
forth. "Yes and no. It happens more often than you'd think, but
lots of our fosters are owner surrenders. Someone moves away,
someone has a baby, someone dies. Stuff like that."

If my dog ever went missing, I think I'd go to the ends of the
earth to find her. "I couldn't imagine ever voluntarily parting
with a pet."

Gal shrugs. "It's not always so simple. Sometimes letting go is
the best a person can do."

If I didn't know better, I'd think Gal was using pet surrender
as a metaphor for my breakup with Marco. But of course that's
not what she's doing.

"Don't get me wrong, some people are just garbage," she adds,
as she attaches Potato's yellow leash to her collar. She passes it to
me and smiles. "Shall we?"

GAL IS AN open book.

I asked her how long she's lived by the lake (thirty-two years this fall) and haven't had to ask another question for a solid ten minutes. There's something about her that I find transfixing. I don't know if it's her candy-apple red hair, or her blinged-out sunglasses, or the way her acrylic nails (gold glitter) sparkle in the sun as she gestures with her free hand. Her unabashed Gal-ness is disarming. I can't imagine anyone not liking this woman.

Gal grew up in northern Minnesota on a reservation called Leech Lake. Her mom worked at a casino run by the Chippewa and her dad was a fisherman. "I can clean and gut a fish better than just about anyone, but I haven't done it in years," she tells me. "It's a way of life for a lot of people, but I can't bring myself to eat animals, let alone kill them." She taught math at Juneberry Lake High School for thirty years and just retired two summers ago. "I don't know why people are so hard on teenagers. Sure, they can be jerks sometimes, but how is that different from any other age?" She's only left the state twice: first for Marge's sister's funeral and again last year when Marge convinced her to go on a Caribbean cruise. "I never saw the point in leaving Minnesota until I saw the water in the Bahamas," she says. "Aqua. Blue." She flashes her hands to punctuate each word. Gal also has an older brother who she hasn't spoken to in decades. "When my mom died, he pocketed her favorite ring. I could never prove it, but I know." She shakes her head. "Plus he's a homophobe."

"That must be hard, not having a relationship with your only sibling," I say. The mere thought of not speaking to Enzo tears at my heart.

Gal smiles. There's a smudge of bright pink lipstick on her teeth. "People always say that. It *would* be devastating if he were a decent person. I played nice for my parents' sake, but after they'd both passed, I was free. Not all siblings are created equal, unfortunately."

"I won the lottery with my brother."

Something funny flits across Gal's face, but I can't quite make it out behind her rhinestone sunglasses. Amusement, maybe? She strikes me as the type that doesn't believe in luck, either. She's a mathematician after all. "The lottery, huh?" she says. "Lucky you."

We follow the path by the lake in easy silence, Gal's pack of dogs happily trotting along, their leashes a tangled rainbow. Potato is surprisingly fast. There's a slight wobble to her gait, but she hasn't had a problem keeping pace.

"How does your mega jackpot of a brother feel about you moving across the country?" Gal asks. A follow-up question lurks behind this one. *Why are you here? What are you running from?*

Potato stops to sniff a patch of grass. "He's been really supportive. And he was especially excited about it being firefly season here."

"Lightning bugs," she says, wriggling her eyebrows. "They're pretty neat."

"The neatest."

"And I hear you're single?"

Hearing it stated so plainly, without even a tinge of pity, is refreshing. "It's kind of complicated, but yeah."

"Been there," Gal says wryly. "Everything about love is complicated until you meet the right person. Then it's—I don't want to say easy, because nothing worth having is easy—but when it's right it just . . . is."

"How long have you and Marge been together?"

She mimes long addition with her finger, muttering "carry the one" under her breath. I bet she was a fun math teacher. "We've been together for thirty years, married for twelve years next month. We went down to the courthouse the day it became legal."

"That's so romantic."

Gal shrugs. "It's just paper." She holds up a finger. "Important paper. Paper that everyone should be able to obtain if they want it, but being married didn't fundamentally change anything." She drops her finger and laughs. "Who am I kidding? It was romantic as hell."

"Do you have any kids?"

"We decided against it. I got my fill at school and Marge wasn't interested, so I didn't push. Plus, she's Jewish so we celebrate Hanukkah *and* Christmas." She shakes her head and laughs. "The month of December would have bankrupted us. All those presents."

The holidays are my favorite time of year. It must be so fun to celebrate Thanksgiving, Hanukkah, and Christmas so close together. Plus, I love latkes.

"What if she'd wanted them?" I realize this question might be too bold only after I ask it. But Gal doesn't seem to mind.

"Then we'd have had them. Truthfully, all I cared about was being with Marge. The rest would have just been a bonus. It's best not to get greedy with your blessings."

"Don't get greedy with your blessings," I muse. "I like that."

Gal nudges me with an elbow. "It's all yours, hun. So how are you liking that new house?"

"It's beautiful. Was Erica a designer on the side? Or a property flipper or something?"

"A house flipper? Like on HGTV?"

"Sure."

Gal shakes her head. "No, nothing like that. Erica just really loved that house."

"So why did she leave?"

Gal blows out a long breath, pink lips sputtering as she considers my question. "I think that's a question for Erica herself," she says, almost cautiously. It's the first time all morning that I've suspected that Gal might be holding out on me. But I get it. She doesn't know me. "Maybe she left Juneberry Lake for the same reasons you came."

The idea feels weighty, almost unwieldy. If I believed in tarot cards or magical coincidences, I might have gotten goose bumps. But I don't.

"Were you close with Erica or her husband?" I ask as we round the corner back onto Loon Lane. I haven't had a chance to ask Lynette or anyone else about Gary yet.

Gal shakes her head, but before she can answer, Bob bursts from his house, slams the front door, and marches purposefully toward his truck. Keys dangle from one hand and he holds a towel to his mouth with the other.

"Hey, Bob," Gal calls from across the street. "Everything okay?"

Bob pauses at the driver's side of his truck. "I mripped my mrooth," he shouts back.

"What's that?" Gal replies, cupping her free hand to her ear.

"I mripped my mrooth!"

Gal turns to me to see if I understand Bob. I give her an unhelpful shrug.

Finally Bob drops the towel and shoots me a withering look. "I chipped my damn tooth on those damned Bisquick crackers."

Gal's confusion lingers, but I understand perfectly.

Bob chipped his tooth on my biscotti.

Chapter Eleven

I toss a bag of cheesy popcorn into my cart and set off in search of the frozen foods aisle. (I'm pretty sure that the market sells Moose Drool Custard by the carton. A dream!) My cart is already loaded with wine, a basket of tomatoes, a couple heads of garlic, one fat onion, and a heap of basil. I'm in the mood for some home cooking and Mom's pasta sauce is my go-to comfort food.

It's also one of the only things I can cook.

After Bob got back from the dentist, I watched from my upstairs window as he zigzagged back and forth across the street, knocking on each of my neighbor's doors, gesturing emphatically toward my house as he told them about the biscotti incident. At least, I'm assuming that's what he was talking about. It could have been about the trash can thing.

Whatever he said, it must have worked, because another Sunday came and went without an invite to Lynette and Allan's. I really thought my family's biscotti would do the trick. Especially since Gal had been so receptive.

I snatch a box of spaghetti from a shelf as I roll by, visions of chopping, sautéing, and guzzling wine edging out the memory of my failed attempt to win Bob over. Enzo was right—I should have gone with éclairs.

Back to the drawing board.

"Eliza?" The sound of my name barely registers. Maybe because

I'm not expecting to run into anyone. I don't know anyone here. Not really.

It takes a few seconds for me to react. When I finally look up, there's Joel.

He's wearing cargo shorts, flip-flops, and a University of Chicago T-shirt, his hand is raised in a tentative wave. "Hey there. You okay?"

I realize I've been clutching the cart handle in a death grip. Then I remember that my ponytail has frizzed to twice its usual size and that I've almost certainly been scowling. Nonna used to call it my *"facia brutta,"* which is old-school Italian for "resting bitch face."

My mouth stretches into a forced smile. "Hi. Sorry, I'm distracted. How are you?"

He's holding a carton of frozen custard. "Why are you distracted?"

"Just a weird day, I guess."

He tosses the carton into the air, it does a little flip before landing back in his hands. "I like weird."

Something about Joel—probably his innate Midwestern friendliness—disarms me. Here goes nothing. "I tried to win my neighbors over with baked goods, but they were mistaken for dog treats. Then they chipped an elderly widower's tooth and now he's badmouthing me to the entire neighborhood."

Joel starts to laugh, but catches himself, slamming a hand over his mouth. "That's terrible," he says, still laughing.

I tilt my head toward the ceiling, hoping to spot an escape hatch. No luck. I look back at Joel who is continuing to lose his battle against the giggles. "It *is* terrible," I say emphatically. "I think he's gotten me blackballed from the neighborhood barbecue. They're all grilling—whatever it is they grill—without me as we speak. So, now all I want to do is go home and eat pasta and watch TV. Alone."

Farah had texted me to ask if I'd have time to catch up tonight, but I couldn't imagine explaining all of this to her. It was too ridiculous. I'd be better off wallowing in my solitude.

Joel shakes his head. "No. No way. You can't have a sad night all alone while the rest of your neighbors party without you."

"But I'm making pasta."

He winces. "I'm afraid the pasta loophole only applies if someone died. I'm taking you to the Common Loon." He flags down an employee in a Main Street Market apron. "Hey Pete? Would you mind bagging this nice woman's cart and keeping her groceries in the walk-in refrigerator? She'll be back to pick them up in a few hours."

Pete, who can't be more than nineteen years old, grins at Joel. "Of course, man. No problem."

Joel pats Pete on the shoulder as he heads off with my cart. Then he gestures toward the door. "Shall we?"

The Common Loon Saloon is a textbook dive bar. It smells vaguely of stale alcohol, limes, and disinfectant, but in that comforting, familiar way you expect all dive bars to smell. The simple, unstained pine walls are choked with pictures of smiling patrons and Vikings memorabilia—flags, jerseys, news articles, even a novelty bra—and a flock of taxidermied loons hangs overhead, their wings outstretched. A vintage jukebox plays Creedence Clearwater Revival on a loop from the corner.

Joel orders us a couple of lagers from the bar and we settle in at a high-top table by the dartboard. He absentmindedly spins a purple-and-yellow striped dart between his fingers as I detail my failed foray into neighborly baking.

"This Bob guy sounds like a clown," Joel says. "His teeth are probably made of glass or something."

I sigh. "I know. He's miserable. But the rest of the neighbors are friends with him. I just want them all to want to hang out with me. I know that sounds dumb."

"Are you kidding me? Getting invited to the neighborhood barbecue is peak Juneberry Lake. The stakes could not be higher." Joel positions the dart between his thumb and index finger and takes aim at the target. He throws and misses the board entirely.

"You're not great with the darts."

"It's not about that."

I arch my eyebrow.

"Throwing sharp objects is a stress reliever. Being good has nothing to do with it." Joel hands me a dart. "Give it a try."

I square my shoulders, line up my shot, and let the dart fly. It hits the bull's-eye. Joel lets out a long, impressed whistle. "Well, well, well," he says. "We have a shark in our midst."

"Throwing sharp objects at a wall has been one of my go-to stress relievers for years. I figured I might as well become a decent shot while I was at it." The truth is, I hate being bad at things. Even the trivial stuff. I've been known to dedicate entire afternoons to memorizing lyrics to my favorite songs, perfecting my nail-painting technique, or mastering a board game (I'm undefeated at Monopoly).

"Overachiever," he mutters, before taking a sip of beer.

If only he knew. "Want me to give you some pointers?"

Joel shakes his head vigorously. "Absolutely not. I refuse to care about being good at bar games. It'll take all the fun out of it."

"That's a refreshing perspective."

He winks. "Stick around, Frisco. I'm full of them."

I nearly choke on a sip of beer. "Oh my god," I say through a cough. "Please never call me Frisco again."

"Why not? It's where you're from."

"But no one from Frisco calls it Frisco."

"You literally just called it Frisco."

"I was using it ironically."

"Whatever you say, Frisco." He takes another shot with a dart. This time he at least makes it on the board.

"Fine. I'm going to call you . . ." I trail off. "What's a ridiculous nickname for Juneberry Lake?"

Amusement dances across Joel's face. "Sometimes locals call themselves Jujus, but I'm not from Juneberry Lake, remember?"

"That's right, you moved here with your girlfriend."

He shoots me a quizzical look. "I don't have a girlfriend."

"You said you followed a woman here."

Realization dawns across his face. Then he breaks into a laugh. "Oh, right," he says, shaking his head. "I told you that I came here to be close to someone, but no, she's definitely not my girlfriend."

"So . . . you broke up?"

He laughs again. "Not exactly."

I flash him a knowing look. "It's complicated?"

Dimples crease his cheeks. "You could say that."

"I get that. I came here to get away from something complicated. It's kind of an *Eat Pray Love* situation."

"I kind of figured." He takes another shot at the dartboard and misses again. "Love that movie by the way."

"The book was better."

He smirks. "Well obviously. It always is."

I take another sip of my beer, eyeing him with suspicion. Something about the crooked tilt of his mouth gives him away. "You haven't seen the movie or read the book, have you?"

Joel twists his face, feigning offense. "Are you calling me a liar?"

"Are you a liar?"

He holds my gaze a moment too long before breaking into a laugh. "Fine, you caught me." He shakes his head. "I was just trying to be supportive." Something about the way he says "supportive" makes me think he actually means "flirty." I bat the thought away.

"Just as I suspected." I take another sip of beer. "Anyway, now that you're here, you seem to like it. Do you think you'll stay for a while?"

Joel considers me with his deep brown eyes. "It's hard to say. I kind of take life as it comes. It keeps things exciting."

"I can't even begin to describe how much anxiety that would give me. I plan *everything*," I say gesturing with my hands for emphasis. Our server dodges my arm as I sweep it around the room. It looks like she's doing an impression of Keanu Reeves in *The Matrix*.

"Careful there, new girl," she says, righting herself. She holds a platter of cheese curds encircled by a variety of sauces—ranch, barbecue, ketchup, honey mustard. Remarkably, she didn't spill a drop.

"I'm so sorry," I say, dragging my hands down my face. "Today is not my day."

She swats her hand in the air, waving me off. "Don't sweat it. A flying arm is nothing. You should have seen this place when the Vikings made the playoffs."

"I heard it was like a war zone," Joel adds gravely. "Gertie has seen some things."

Gertie's eyes crinkle at the corners. "Hazards of the profession." She's wearing a tank top with a loon on the chest and her hair is pulled back into a French braid. She looks so cool and casual and summery that it makes me want to run home and see if my French braiding skills are still intact. It's been years since

I attempted one. "Well, enjoy your curds. I'll be behind the bar if you need me. See you later, *J Wow*."

Joel's face goes slack as Gertie walks away.

"J Wow?"

Joel shakes his head. "I never should have told Gertie that story."

"What story?"

"It's so embarrassing."

"I think the embarrassing part already happened. The J Wow thing is out in the world now. No turning back." I stare at Joel expectantly.

He sighs. "So, my last name is Jawowski and when I was in high school, I thought I was going to be a DJ."

"I'm already embarrassed for you. What kind of music did you play?"

"I was really into throwbacks, so mostly nineties hip-hop. And more than a little Will Smith."

I suppress a grin. "Very fly," I tease. "And I take it J Wow was your DJ name?"

He nods. "I made everyone call me that—my friends, my family, my teachers . . . and then *Jersey Shore* premiered. Do you remember that show?"

Of course. My parents had been horrified at the portrayal of Italian American youths. "A disgrace!" Mom had scoffed. But Enzo and I were fascinated. We'd watched every episode.

"Of course."

"So you may recall that there was suddenly a more famous JWoww on the scene—and she spelled it with more Ws than I did, which for some reason made her much cooler. My sisters haven't stopped teasing me since."

I can't help but laugh at the idea of a teenaged Joel being

upstaged by a reality show. I put my hand over my mouth to try to lessen the blow.

"So you plan everything, huh?" Joel says, in a feeble attempt to change the subject.

"Yes, J Wow. Everything."

He ignores my use of his nickname. "But don't you think that maybe, the unplanned moments are where life happens?" He pops a cheese curd into his mouth and chews. I watch the muscles in his jawline flex. "Like you almost smacking poor Gertie." He grins. "You can't manufacture that stuff."

I shake my head and pick up a cheese curd and examine it. "You swear these are good?"

He finishes chewing another and swallows. "Have I led you wrong yet?"

I don't answer, instead dipping it in ketchup and taking a bite. I was expecting something akin to a mozzarella stick, but this is entirely different—tart and gooey and salty and sour all at once. My mouth twists and my eyes start to water. "I do not like this."

Joel laughs. "Really? Because I couldn't tell from your face."

I chase the offending bite with the dregs of my beer.

"It's kind of an acquired taste," Joel agrees. "But look on the bright side. It got your mind off being bummed about your neighbors."

I scrape my tongue against the roof of my mouth. "I'm not convinced it was worth it."

Joel makes a show of looking over his shoulder before leaning toward me. "Just a word of advice—if you want to make friends around here, I'd keep your distaste to yourself. Minnesotans take cheese curds and football very seriously."

"Right, I'm supposed to become a Vikings fan."

Amusement plays across his face. "You catch on quick."

"I'm assuming you love the Vikings too?"

Joel pauses mid-sip. He sets his bottle on the table and considers me. "Can you keep a secret?"

"I'm a vault," I say, thinking back to the shoebox that Hannah and I stored under her bed. We'd written PRIVATE in big block letters and filled it with notes detailing our most sacred truths. Hannah's mom gave it to me after she died. I remember digging through the scraps of paper, tracing Hannah's bubbly writing with my fingertip.

I stole my sister's sweater.

My mom said she doesn't like my grandma.

I found ten dollars on the street and kept it.

As an adult, they all seem inconsequential, but still, I've never shared them.

"Okay what I'm about to tell you needs to remain confidential for all of time. If you ever breathe a word of this to anyone, I'll deny ever having met you."

"Are you about to tell me that you murdered someone?"

Joel scoffs. "God no." He leans in closer. "I wish."

I lean in a bit, too. "Well now I'm intrigued."

Joel's eyes latch onto mine again. I avert my gaze, dropping my eyes to his mouth, which leads to the realization that we're close enough to kiss. Not that we're going to. I don't know why that idea even entered my brain. "I'm a Green Bay Packers fan," Joel says, mercifully oblivious to my thoughts about his lips.

I lean back, snapping the invisible string that seemed intent on pulling me closer to him. I gasp dramatically. "That's really bad."

"Tell me about it."

"I won't say a word," I promise solemnly.

"I know," he says, flashing me a mischievous grin. "Because of mutually assured destruction. If you tell anyone about the Packers, I'll tell everyone about the cheese curds."

JOEL AND I ordered one more round of beers and a plate of french fries under the guise of cleansing the offensive curds flavor from my palate when really, I think we both just wanted a reason to hang out a little longer.

The air is still warm and sticky as we start the walk back to the market, the sky is a shade of orangish pink. "The sunsets here are unreal," I say, swiveling my head to take in as much of the vibrant sky as possible.

"They're something else for sure," Joel agrees. "You seem to be feeling better."

It's probably the beer-and-french-fry dinner, but I do feel better. The company doesn't hurt either. "Much better," I say. "Thanks for saving me from a lonely night of pasta and rotting my brain with bad reality TV."

"You were going to watch bad reality TV?" Joel asks. "Man, now I wish I would have joined you. I love shows that make my brain feel like mush."

I laugh. "Next time."

"Here's hoping." He crosses the fingers on both hands. "But until then, do you have any plans next weekend?"

I shoot him a look. "You know the answer to that."

He laughs. "Right. Your neighbors won't hang out with you. Well, I was thinking about renting a pedal boat from Cricket's and taking a cruise around the lake. You interested?"

I am interested. Very interested. I really want to be friends with Joel, but the way he's asking, coupled with his complicated relationship status, feels like he might be interested in more than just a friendly boat ride and I'm so not in that place. The mere thought of going on a date with another person makes my stomach lurch. "I'd love to," I say. "It's just that—I don't mean to make this awkward, but I feel like I need to tell you that I'm not ready to date again. Like, at all."

Joel's eyebrows tick up in amusement. "It's just a boat ride, Frisco. Not a marriage proposal."

My shoulders relax. "Okay," I say. "Then we're on. Just promise me something?"

"Name it."

I cross my arms. "That you'll never call me Frisco again."

Joel purses his lips as he bobs his head from one side to the other. "I will try my best."

"Don't just try. *Do*."

He nudges me with his elbow. "I'll see you next Saturday, *pal*."

I'm thankful that the sun has already set, that the sky is glowing pink. Because it hides the decidedly more-than-friendly way my cheeks flush when Joel touches me.

Chapter Twelve

Before

Romance of the love and marriage persuasion was not something I paid much attention to until I turned twenty-six. To be clear, I didn't want to get married at twenty-six—I wanted to be at least thirty before I made such a major commitment—but I knew that if I wanted to stick to my schedule, it was time for me to start looking.

I'd dated some in college. I'd even had a handful of (fun!) one-night stands. I wasn't a prude.

But trying to find a life partner—especially in a city like San Francisco where tech bros with terminal cases of Peter Pan syndrome ran amok—was going to be a challenge. I needed to take this seriously.

So I made a list.

I know some people get hung up on what they want their future spouse to look like, which to a certain extent, is understandable. You want to be attracted to your partner, of course. But compatibility goes well beyond physical appearance.

I wanted to find someone who was driven, who had a career and goals for the future.

Someone who was financially responsible.

We needed to be ideologically aligned, which given that I lived in California wouldn't be too hard.

He had to want kids, but not until we were older. I figured we'd want to enjoy each other and dedicate more time to building our careers first. Plus, I'd read that your late thirties were actually the perfect time to become a parent because you were more patient and more established.

I wasn't looking for a party boy. I wanted an adult. Sure, an adult who could have fun would be nice, but I didn't want to do mushrooms and go bungee jumping every weekend. Or ever, for that matter.

Most importantly, he needed to love my family. Especially my brother. Italian families tend to be quite close—sometimes closer than was comfortable for people who didn't grow up in a similar environment. And I knew I'd never be able to love anyone who didn't love Enzo.

Last but not least, he needed to like carbs. I couldn't possibly go through life with a carb-conscious eater telling me that bread would give me cancer. Bread was an integral part of my life—one of my few true passions—and I wanted to share that with whoever I ended up marrying. I reasoned that I could make an exception for a gluten allergy if I really loved the guy. But given that everyone in my family was invariably covered in flour, a concession of that magnitude wouldn't be without its challenges.

I shared my criteria with Farah, Carmen, and Brittany and asked for their feedback. They agreed that it was a largely reasonable list, and each added a few nice-to-haves on top.

"He should make enough money to support both of you if you decide you want to stay home with your kids for a couple of years," Brittany suggested.

"I think you should look for an Italian guy," Carmen said. "Maybe he could convince you to finally learn the language. And your kids could be bilingual." Carmen, whose parents were from

El Salvador, had been horrified to discover that my parents hadn't taught Enzo and me Italian when we were young. I could get by with some basic Italian if I had to, but my skills were gravely lacking.

"I think he needs to be from the Bay Area," Farah added. "You don't want to marry someone who's going to want to move to the East Coast when you have kids."

"Or worse—a flyover state," Brittany cracked. Carmen did a mock shudder.

I tried the apps with mixed results and my friends took turns setting me up with guys from work or friends of friends. Eventually, Farah even tried to get me to date her brother, Amir, who took that as a sign that it was time to come out to his family. Like any good Persian family, the Behzadis used Amir's news as an opportunity to throw him a massive party.

And that's where I met Marco.

I noticed his mop of curly hair first. Then his pants—freshly pressed and cropped at the ankle, hovering above a pair of Italian loafers; the same ones all of my cousins always wore to weddings.

We locked eyes and while it wasn't love at first sight—he was a bit too . . . polished—there was a familiarity that I couldn't deny. Like recognizing like.

"Great party, huh?" he'd said when he approached, casually resting an elbow on the bar.

I looked around the Behzadis' massive living room. There were upward of two hundred people in attendance, milling around tables piled high with food, crystal champagne flutes pinched between their fingers. A massive banner that read HOORAY, AMIR IS GAY! hung above the dance floor, where Farah's aunts and uncles danced to a vaguely familiar Persian pop song. "It reminds me of something my family would do," I said. "Except we'd use less crystal."

"And no bartender?"

"Not unless you count my dad's cousin Sal."

Marco laughed. "Our families sound similar."

"Are you Italian too?"

He grinned and held out his hand. "Marco Fanelli."

Check.

I took his hand and gave it a firm shake, the same one my friends and I used to practice before our business club networking events in college. "Eliza Colletti."

"*Parli italiano?*" he asked. His accent was flawless.

"*Non bene,*" I replied, the words stiff in my mouth, like a shoe that I hadn't broken in yet.

He laughed. "Maybe someday I can teach you."

Another check.

"If you're lucky," I said. It came out flirtier than I'd intended, but Marco seemed to like it.

"So," he said, his eyes not-so-subtly staring at my lower lip. "How do you know the man of the hour?"

"I'm his sister's best friend."

"Ah."

"And you?"

"I'm Amir's boss."

So Marco was older than us. I could see it now that I knew—he had an air of experience about him. "You work in finance."

"I do." He leaned forward conspiratorially. "This might sound kind of lame, but I love financial planning. Helping people plan for the future is kind of my passion."

A fellow nerd. My heart did the tiniest of flips. "Doesn't planning make everything better?"

He smiled. "Yes, Eliza Colletti. It really does."

MARCO AND I went on our first official date one week later.

He took me to the North Beach Restaurant, an institution within the San Francisco Italian community. It's the kind of place where you were just as likely to bump into a mayor (I did as a starstruck sixteen-year-old) or your aunt and uncle. My family had celebrated many a birthday there, both in the main section of the restaurant—a long, rectangular space with white tablecloths, arched ceilings, wood-paneled wainscoting, and flickering candles—and in the wine cellar downstairs, a cool, cave-like basement with stone floors where hunks of drying prosciutto hung from the ceiling.

"My dad worked here when he was a kid," Marco said, after we'd been seated at a little two-person table by the window. "I guess he broke like a hundred plates one summer. Our family isn't suited for the service industry."

When I told him about my family, that we're *those* Collettis, he stared at me, dumbstruck. "I think you might be my dream girl. I could live on Colletti's focaccia."

Another green flag, I thought.

We spent most of dinner—caprese salad, bucatini puttanesca, an incredible gorgonzola gnocchi, and naturally, a bottle of Tuscan red wine—talking about our families, our jobs, our goals for the future.

"How many kids do you want?" he asked as I speared fluffy gnocchi with my fork.

"Two."

"Boy and a girl?"

"Girl and a girl."

He nodded, his curls falling perfectly over his forehead. "That would be cool."

"Will your kids speak Italian?"

He gestured to his nose. "If they inherit my features, they're going to have to."

I gestured to my own nose. A Roman nose, Dad called it. "Same."

"Your nose is perfect," Marco said. "And I'm just kidding about all that. I mean, I'd love for them to know the language but not for the sake of vanity."

The idea of our future little olive-skinned, Roman-nosed children running around speaking Italian delighted me. I could picture it so clearly. "When do you think you'd want to have your first kid?"

He dabbed at his mouth with the cloth napkin. "Well I'm already well into my thirties, so sooner rather than later."

"I was thinking thirty-five."

His eyebrows ticked up, ever so slightly. I think he was intrigued. "That long?"

"I have things I want to accomplish first."

He chewed a rigatoni noodle, considering my stance. "Makes sense, actually. The maternity leave in this country is embarrassingly bad. Plus, you might want to stay home with the kids, so I can see why you'd want to enjoy your career before all of that."

We went back and forth like that all night, bouncing hopes and ideas and goals off each other. I felt comfortable with Marco. We were so similar.

That's not to say that we were a perfect match across the board. Marco was a little older, a little more traditional. He was a practicing Catholic and, much to my mother's dismay, I was very much not. But he didn't seem to mind.

I knew my parents were going to love him.

Our friendship was instant, but the chemistry would prove to be something of a slower burn. This didn't concern me in the least. I wanted to build a lasting partnership. The thrill of a new relationship was fleeting. When that inevitably faded away, I wanted to be sure that there was a strong bond to fall back on.

I wanted a relationship like my parents. Like my grandparents.

When Marco kissed me that night, his technique a pleasant blend of firm and tender, his lips tasting of salted caramel, it felt like a puzzle piece clicking into place.

With Marco, it wasn't so much that I fell in love with him as that I decided to love him.

I didn't think the distinction mattered.

Chapter Thirteen

ere's your usual," Trish says as she sets my avocado toast on the table. My mouth waters at the sight of a perfectly ripened avocado mash drizzled with olive oil and seasoned to perfection. I guess you can take the girl out of California, but you can't take the California out of the girl. Then Trish slides another smaller plate beside it. "And a bear claw on the house."

"You're the best," I say. I've been having a tough time focusing on work since the move and I need all the fuel I can get.

Trish wipes her hands on her checkered apron. "I know it." Trish swears she's sixty-six, but she looks way younger, with smooth brown skin, locs that she wears in a ponytail on top of her head, and a penchant for eighties hair band T-shirts. She's jarringly nice, but also has a cool, big city vibe that I find comforting. She'd be right at home in San Francisco. And between her bear claws and perfectly brewed coffee, she'd make a killing.

I cast a glance around the coffee shop, which I've yet to see busy on a weekday. "How is it that you have the best breakfast I've ever tasted and this place isn't packed with people?"

Trish shrugs. "It's chaos on the weekends, but we're creeping up on shoulder season. Tourism peaks here around the Fourth of July and slowly tapers off after that."

"What about the summer party thing?" It's impossible to walk more than five steps on Main Street without seeing a poster advertising the annual end-of-summer tradition.

"Summer Festival?" Trish asks, amused by my lack of knowledge. "Yeah, that's kind of our last hurrah. It gets pretty quiet in the fall. That's why we host the festival at the very end of the season—after the State Fair. We want to squeeze what we can out of that last summer weekend."

I look around the café. It's the perfect mix of rustic and modern, with kitschy decor and a handwritten chalkboard menu above the bar. I know it would photograph beautifully. "Are you on Instagram?"

Trish shoots me a look that says, *Do I look like the type of person who has time for that social media bullshit?* And honestly, I get it. If you think about it too hard, it *is* bullshit. But necessary bullshit.

I've built a career on it.

Trish twists the corners of her gingham apron between her hands, silently mulling something over. She pulls out a chair and plops down across from me. "I've been watching you this morning," she says carefully. "Is everything okay? Do you like your new house?"

"I love it," I assure her. "It's perfect, actually." Trish's shoulders drop an inch. It's sweet that she's so concerned about how I'm settling in. "I was wondering about something though," I venture.

"What's that?"

"Erica Donaldson. The woman who lived in the house before me?" Trish nods. "Do you know why she left?"

Trish blows out a breath and shakes her head. "No idea. It was all kind of abrupt."

"Did she have trouble making friends?"

"I don't think so. She used to spend quite a bit of time with her neighbors—your neighbors—if I'm remembering correctly."

That's not how Lynette or Gal made it sound, but Trish has met a lot of transplants over the years, so maybe she's not remembering clearly. "Did you know her husband?"

"Not really. He was . . . standoffish. They split up a year or two before she left."

"Do you know why?"

Trish opens her hands, fingers splayed and gives me a look that says, *Your guess is as good as mine.* "Your neighbors might know more than me."

"They said they weren't close."

A look of befuddlement dashes across Trish's face, but it disappears just as quickly. "Why the sudden interest?"

I'm afraid that if I tell Trish that I'm hoping to avoid whatever mistakes Erica made, I might seem neurotic or insensitive. I know it's not really any of my business. "Just curious, I guess."

Trish makes a *mmm* sound. "Sounds like you're looking for a distraction from whatever it is that's actually bothering you."

I crinkle my nose. "Is it that obvious?" She gives me a look that says *duh*. I sigh. Marco had texted me again this morning, begging me to at least confirm that I was getting his texts. I don't know why he cares. I wish it didn't bother me as much as it did. But I don't want to talk about Marco with Trish. So instead, I say, "Work." It's not a lie.

Trish laughs. "What an extremely specific answer."

I lower my laptop screen, bringing Trish's full face into view. Her expression is equal parts amusement and sympathy. "There's this campaign I'm working on for a new client and I can't figure out how to approach it," I explain. "I've been feeling a little off my game lately."

Trish drops her chin onto her fist. "Well you did just move to a strange new town where you don't know anyone. Do you think that might have something to do with it?"

That would be a logical conclusion, but no. I launched the Dyno-Soar drone rebrand in the midst of my relationship with Marco disintegrating. I crushed my pre-SATs a few weeks after Hannah died. As dark as it is, I'm able to compartmentalize my grief. I thrive under duress. My feelings toward my job these past few weeks are more akin to ambivalence. I've never felt that way about work before. It makes me nervous.

"Maybe," I say.

"Well, what's the company? Maybe I can help." The way she says it reminds me of how Dad used to sit with me at the kitchen table while I struggled with math homework. *We'll work this out together, Elisabetta,* he'd say. And we usually did.

"I'll figure it out."

"Just because I'm an older gal doesn't mean I'm out of good ideas," she says. She's joking, but surely there's some truth behind it. That must suck, being discounted because of your age. "I'll have you know I graduated top of my class at business school."

I don't doubt Trish's business acumen for a second, but when I open my mouth to explain what this company does, something stops me. The thing is, the product is ridiculous. The client, a self-improvement company called BetterMe, is rolling out a new behavior modification product—the MeMeter—a wearable device that's supposed to help users stick to their goals or break bad habits. When a user engages in an undesirable behavior, like sitting for too long, drinking alcohol, or biting their nails, for example, the MeMeter will deliver a tiny electric shock. Sort of like a Fitbit meets snapping a rubber band on your wrist.

I've worked on countless campaigns for all types of oddball products—Silicon Valley has cooked up some real doozies over the years—but for the first time in my career, I'm a little bit embarrassed about what I do for a living. Something about discussing this with Trish—normal, stable, salt-of-the-earth Trish—has brought this to the surface.

"Try me," Trish insists. Maybe talking to a normal person about the MeMeter will be helpful. Like an everywoman test case. I take another long drink of coffee and give it a go. Trish nods along as I talk, her brow furrowed. When I'm done, she starts asking questions.

"What about people with heart conditions?"

"There's also a vibrate mode or an auditory component."

"Auditory component?"

"The device will make a very loud, very annoying sound."

"I see. And who is the target demographic?"

"The company is big into the self-improvement space—diet, exercise, mindfulness—that kind of thing. So, it'll probably be sold as a companion piece to their existing suite of products."

The space between Trish's eyebrows has grown as deep as the Grand Canyon. She considers me for several moments, and then says, "I'm not going to lie to you, Eliza. This meter thing sounds dumb as hell."

"That's what I was afraid of," I groan.

She holds up a hand. "I'm not done. It sounds dumb, but if the company already has a loyal fanbase of people who are into all that life optimization stuff"—she waves her hand dismissively to make it clear that she's not one of those people—"they'll probably be eager to try it."

She's right. It's Marketing 101. Cater to your audience. "I know you're right. I'm just feeling a little blocked is all."

The way Trish looks at me, really looks at me, reminds me a bit of Nora. I bet Trish would make a great therapist. "I'm not one of those follow your passion, find a job you love and you'll never work a day in your life kind of people. Work is work. It's not always going to be fun or exciting—it's right there in the name. But the minute you start feeling uneasy about how you're spending those working hours is the minute you should start thinking about moving on."

I appreciate Trish's sentiment, but I usually love my job. Jordan is great—they let me go fully remote to move here and didn't touch my salary, which is something of a miracle. Plus, I get to be strategic and creative at the same time. I like using both sides of my brain. And seeing my work out in the world still sends a thrilling little zip up my spine.

When I was a kid, I loved to draw. I'd lock myself away in my room for hours on end, sketching portraits of my family members, our dog, the bakery, my favorite tree. Hannah used to ask me to draw her pictures of things that had happened at school. I'd spend the better part of my lunch hour working on funny little doodles to slip in her locker. I loved the way she'd howl with laughter at my depiction of our vice principal's stop-drop-and-roll demonstration at the annual safety assembly or the time our school's unofficial mascot, Sally the Seagull, finally succeeded in stealing Freddy Rodriguez's tuna sandwich.

I stopped drawing after she died.

I think the current issue is that my new environment seems to be shining a different light on the type of projects I work on and it's not exactly flattering. I can't really picture anyone I've met here using any of the products I represent. The thought of Marge and Gal unleashing Fido AI on their pack of dogs is downright laughable. And I can't imagine Lynette flying a drone.

There is a chance that Bob would like the MeMeter, though. He has kind of a masochistic vibe.

I return Trish's stare. "Thanks. I think I'm just a little distracted."

She pulls her lips into a knowing smile. "I heard you were at the Common Loon with Joel last night."

My lips sputter involuntarily as my mind fumbles around for an appropriate response.

Trish's grin widens. "Welcome to life in a small town."

I encircle my iced latte with my hands. Despite the air-conditioning, beads of condensation are already rolling down the sides of the glass. "We bumped into each other at the grocery store," I say, before adding, "and that's not what has me distracted."

Trish pats my hand. "Well you're welcome to be distracted by *work* here anytime you like." She gives me an exaggerated wink. "That is until winter rolls around. Then only on the weekends."

"What do you mean?"

Trish has already risen from her chair. She pushes it closer to the table and then stands with her hands resting on her back. "At a certain point, we lose more money with the doors open than closed."

Selfishly, the prospect of losing my pseudo-office is disappointing, but as someone who was raised in a bakery, I know how much of a hardship reduced hours can cause. There's a rhythm to places like this, value in the daily routine—inventorying measuring cups, plates, bags of flour; wiping tables littered with sugar and sticky with honey; lining freshly baked muffins or cookies or cakes on doily-clad baking sheets; grinding beans and brewing coffee. With enough time and care, these become almost automatic, sufficiently humming along on their own. But when hours get wonky or experienced employees leave, things get gummed up. I wonder how many of Trish's baristas come back after the winter. Longevity and seasonal work don't exactly go together. This has to be more of a hardship on Trish than she's letting on.

But I don't say any of this. Instead, I eloquently say, "Well that sucks."

Trish shrugs. "It's the cost of doing business in a small town."

"Does all of Main Street shut down in the winter?"

Trish's forehead creases. "More or less." When my face falls, she adds, "But only during the week. You'll still have plenty to do here on the weekends."

I suppose I shouldn't be surprised. The Join Juneberry Lake program—the very thing that brought me here—was created to help with this exact problem. I want to ask Trish what the impact has been, but I don't want to offend her, either. I make a mental note to ask Joel, instead.

Trish taps the back of the chair. "Anyway, no need to worry about all of that now. We have to get through the Summer Festival rush first." Trish's hand comes to rest on the chair again, her sensible gold wedding band glinting under the overhead lights. "And you need to get back to work. Those torture devices aren't going to sell themselves."

I can't help but laugh. "I'm not sure that they can sell at all. But I'll do my best."

"That's the spirit." She gives me a parting wave before disappearing behind the counter.

I lift my laptop screen and see a new Slack message from Jordan. Do you have the bandwidth to take on the CanScan pitch?

If I remember correctly, CanScan is an app that provides recipe suggestions based on the contents of a users' pantry. I'd be lying if I said I wasn't curious about what the app might recommend for someone whose pantry contains a truly random assortment of items—say, a bag of beans, canned peaches, and a bottle of soy sauce. There had to be some limitations.

I fire off a reply to say *sure! I'd be happy to!* and *I'll get to it as soon as I can.* Then I spend the rest of the day building a marketing strategy for Trish instead.

Chapter Fourteen

"Walk me through it one more time," Farah says distractedly over the sound of running water. I hear the scrape of a sponge against dishes and if I listen closely I can just make out the sound of her boys playing with Gabe in the background.

My neighbors' collective weirdness around Erica's departure, coupled with the note I found on that business card in the kitchen have been gnawing at the back of my mind. I can't make any sense of it, so I decided to get Farah's take.

When she and I first met, we bonded over a shared love of mysteries. We even—embarrassingly—joined the campus Mystery of the Month club where we'd spend the last Sunday afternoon of every month wandering the campus in search of clues our adviser had planted. Our solve rate was the highest in the group. There was something reassuring about looking at a seemingly impossible outcome and working backward to piece together the series of events that led up to it. I think it reinforced my sense of order in the world. Everything—especially the bad stuff—had a cause and effect.

I recount it all again. "Weird, right?"

"I don't know," Farah says through a sigh. "It's not a lot to go on. It sounds like this Erica person just broke up with her husband and went back to New York."

"But why would she have written down Bob's name?"

"Maybe she needed him to watch her dog."

"You're probably right," I say, defeated.

But something tells me that Farah is wrong. Maybe Erica witnessed a crime and was whisked away into the witness protection program (I picture her holed up in a convent like Whoopi Goldberg in *Sister Act*), or after years of close calls, she'd finally made it as an actor and was cast as the lead in some off-Broadway play, or perhaps she'd decided to travel the world, touching down on every continent.

Maybe she's in Antarctica right now, watching penguins waddle by.

I know the reality is likely much less glamorous. Erica probably grew tired of this little town and wanted to move on. Her old furniture and belongings would be too specific to work in her new house—wherever that was—and moving all of it would have been too big a hassle. There's a part of me that hopes it was more complicated than that, though. It makes Erica feel like a kindred spirit.

Farah and I haven't connected on much lately, but I thought maybe if I told her about the Erica stuff, it might be a first step toward rekindling our friendship. Instead, this conversation has left me feeling like a frivolous kid talking to a busy mom with more important things to worry about.

"How are you settling in otherwise?" Farah asks, the faux cheer in her voice betraying her. She still doesn't think this move was rooted in logic.

"Fine," I say, absentmindedly flipping through another issue of the *Juneberry Journal* from September 2022. It's mostly just pictures from the town's annual end-of-summer festival. I don't want to have to explain my decision again, so I decide to change the subject. "How are the kids?"

Farah launches into a long-winded story about preschool enrollment as I continue to skim the photos—in search of what?

I'm not sure. I see pictures of the watermelon-eating contest, the corn maze, and the Ferris wheel, and even spot Trish holding a giant stuffed bear triumphantly over her head.

I'm about to turn the page when I recognize Lynette, beaming at me from the lower righthand corner of the paper. She's sandwiched between Bob and a woman holding a little one-eyed dog, her wavy hair tied up in a ponytail.

It's Erica.

My eyes scramble over the page in search of the caption. It reads: *Bob Holt, Lynette Carr-Poole, and Erica Donaldson, members of the "Loon Lane Gang" enjoying the festivities.*

They're all wearing matching T-shirts.

I'm about to cut Farah off to tell her what I've found when I hear a knock at the door. "Shit," I mutter as I start frantically tossing the mail and newspapers back into their bin.

"Tell me about it," Farah says. She thinks I'm empathizing with her preschool story.

"Hey Fare—someone's at the door. I have to go."

"Oh—okay. No problem. I have to start dinner anyway."

I FIND LYNETTE standing on my doorstep. "Hey there," she says brightly. She's more dressed up than usual, today she's wearing a white dress dotted with yellow daisies that hugs her ample figure. Her hair appears to have been freshly highlighted. She looks beautiful. "What are you up to?"

I figure it's best not to say, *Rifling through your old neighbor's mail,* so instead I say, "Just getting organized."

Lynette makes a face as if to say, *Moving, amiright?* I appreciate her solidarity.

"Well, I've been meaning to thank you for the biscotti. Allan, the kids, and I devoured them."

A rush of smug satisfaction washes over me. The biscotti actually worked! I allow myself the subtlest of fist pumps.

"I'm so glad," I say. "Bob wasn't exactly a fan."

Lynette waves her hand dismissively. "That old grouch isn't a fan of much these days. Don't worry about him."

Lynette is the type of person Mom would call "a doll." I can almost hear her saying, *That Lynette is such a doll, Elisabetta. That's the kind of friend you want.* "You're very nice, thank you."

Another wave of the hand. "Anyway, I stopped by because Allan's taking the kids to his parents for the night and I have the house to myself." She raises her eyebrows suggestively. "How does happy hour at my place sound?"

"Sounds great. What time should I come over?"

Lynette's grassy eyes light up with amusement. "I was thinking now?"

"Like right now?"

"Yep."

It's been ages since I engaged in an impromptu hangout. After college, every aspect of my life—including my social life—had to be scheduled and, for the past few years, logged into the calendar I shared with Marco. This grown-up equivalent of a friend knocking on my door and asking if I can come over to play stirs something in me that I thought was long gone. It's more than a little thrilling. "I'll get my shoes," I say. My tone reminds me of the way I used to say, *I'll check with my mom!* when Hannah would call to ask if I could sleep over.

When I emerge from my house, donning a gauzy sundress and a pair of flip-flops, my mass of hair swept into a ponytail, I see Lynette standing at the base of my driveway with Stuart. It startles me for a moment, as I've come to think of him as a bit of a recluse. From what I can tell, he generally keeps to himself. The few times I've spotted him around the neighborhood, his face is always drawn, his mouth downturned. But today, he's smiling, laughing even. Lynette seems to have that effect on people.

"Eliza," Lynette says as I approach. "Have you met Stuart yet?"

"Not officially," I say. "Hi."

Stuart dips his sharp chin in acknowledgment. Up close, he's much handsomer than I'd imagined. His thick hair is turning salt-and-pepper gray and his dark eyes look almost sultry behind his horn-rimmed glasses. "You're the one who left the biscotti on my doorstep," he says. His voice is deeper than his slight frame would suggest.

"And you dropped shortbread cookies on mine."

"Nice to put a face to a baked good," he says. Lynette laughs.

I've been listening to the audio version of Stuart's novel, *Depth Charge*, about an underwater welder who discovers a secret network of enemy submarines off the coast of California. It strikes me as aggressively masculine, the sort of book my friends' dads read exclusively when we were kids. But, the writing is good, and the main character's partner is a woman, whose entire identity doesn't hinge on having gravity-defying boobs, which is more than most of the other novels of its kind can say for themselves.

"I'm a big fan of your work," I tell Stuart, hoping I sound genuine.

For a moment, he looks almost stunned by the compliment, mouth ajar, eyes wide. But then he recovers. "You mean *Depth Charge*?"

I nod. "I love Rita's character. She's a spitfire."

"Thank you, that's very kind." His tone signals that this will be the end of the conversation.

So much for that. I was hoping flattery would get me somewhere, but clearly I was wrong. On the bright side, I can stop listening. The story was giving me the heebie-jeebies anyway.

Living alone in an empty house makes scary stuff—no matter how ridiculous—seem more plausible.

I'm grappling for something else to say when an old Crown Vic turns down our cul-de-sac. Its faded gold paint job stands out in stark contrast to our picture-perfect neighborhood. Lynette and Stuart stiffen at the car's appearance. Loon Lane is a dead end, so there's virtually no traffic. My neighbors don't seem to have a lot of visitors—aside from each other—either.

The driver cruises by without stopping and hangs a U-turn in front of Stuart's house. He looks in our direction as he passes and I catch a glimpse of aviator sunglasses, brown hair, and a pale, unremarkable face. He almost looks familiar, but I don't think I've ever seen him before.

"Do you know that guy?" Lynette asks me.

I shake my head. Stuart and Lynette exchange a look.

"He's probably just lost," Stuart says.

Lynette mutters something under her breath. We stand in eerie silence for a moment too long.

"Anyway," Lynette says brightly, deftly changing the subject. "We're going to have a girls' night at the house." She turns to look at Stuart. "But I'll bring your leaf blower by later." I get the sense that Lynette is the one holding this neighborhood together, kind of like she's everyone's big sister.

Stuart's lips tighten into a straight line that could almost be a smile. "Sounds good," he says, taking one, then two steps backward. His hands are shoved in his pockets. "Have fun, you two." He gives us a wave and heads back toward his cabin. Before he goes inside, he turns to scan our street. I can't help but think he's looking for that Crown Vic.

Chapter Fifteen

The Carr-Poole family's house sits on a large corner lot at the entrance to our cul-de-sac. It's painted white with a brown shingled roof and a porch that encircles the entire home. Their expansive green lawn is only slightly overgrown and I notice a couple of children's toys lying discarded on the grass as we approach.

Allan is loading bags into the van—a new-looking Toyota minivan hybrid which is exactly the type of vehicle a family named the Carr-Pooles *would* have—when Lynette and I arrive at the base of their gravel driveway. Their oldest, an eight-year-old girl, her curly hair knotted into a pair of space buns on top of her head, waves at us from her sparkly purple wheelchair.

"Mom," she calls, "did you remember to pack my swimming suit for Grandma and Grandpa's?"

"Yes. Did you remember your manners?" Lynette jerks her head in my direction.

The girl places her little hand over her mouth. "Sorry," she says to Lynette. Then she turns to me. "Hi, I'm Ruby." She smiles broadly, revealing a gaping hole where one of her front teeth should be.

A little boy in a lizard T-shirt appears from the other side of the car. He has an Afro and is wearing a pair of orange swim goggles on his head. "I'm Ned!" he shrieks. Ruby giggles, then makes a show of covering her ears.

"It's nice to meet you both," I say, marveling at their cuteness.

"We're going to our grandparents' house," Ned announces.

"On our dad's side. Mom's parents live in Illinois, which is two states over," Ruby adds, as if Ned has left out an essential piece of information.

"That sounds fun."

Ruby bobs her head emphatically. "They have a pool."

"And a water slide," Ned says, pulling his goggles down onto his eyes.

"It's so cool," Ruby says, her enthusiasm palpable.

"Do you like to swim?" Ned asks, his big brown eyes have taken on a bug-like quality through the goggles.

"Of course," I assure them. "But I was never lucky enough to have grandparents with their very own pool."

Ned lets out a whoop, apparently thrilled to learn that he's among the fortunate ones. Ruby tilts her head to the side, her face sympathetic. "I bet they're still good grandparents who did their best."

Allan extracts himself from the SUV and takes a step back, examining his work. "I think that's everything," he says to no one in particular. But he can't seem to tear his eyes away from the Tetris-style stack of bags.

"Honey?" Lynette says, in the strained but loving tone of a longtime partner who is accustomed to tolerating the other half's idiosyncrasies. "I want to introduce you to Eliza. Our new neighbor."

Allan nods absentmindedly before giving his handiwork one final look. Then he turns to introduce himself. He's handsome, in a middle-aged dad at a barbecue kind of way, with deep brown skin and a bald head. He's wearing a red T-shirt with a cartoon badger and a big W on it.

"Lynette and I met in college," Allan says, when he notices me staring at his shirt. "University of Wisconsin–Madison."

"We met in statistics class," Lynette adds.

"She was failing, so I offered to tutor her," Allan jokes. Lynette swats his arm. The way they look at each other makes me miss Marco. Or at least the idea of him.

Allan turns to Lynette. "We should hit the road." He gives her a quick kiss on the cheek. "Nice to meet you, Eliza."

"You too," I say, as Allan whisks Ned into his seat. I step off the driveway and onto the grass as Lynette helps load Ruby into the van. She tells both kids to behave before kissing them each on the head. It's the kind of sweet scene that I've seen play out between parents and their children a billion times, but it hits me differently today. I force myself to look away, toward the lake.

I tell myself it's just the breeze that's making my eyes water.

LYNETTE POURS A sunny concoction from a glass pitcher into two heavy-looking red goblets. They remind me of the kind of glasses my parents had in the nineties. I find the hit of nostalgia comforting. Lynette seems to have that effect.

Lynette has arranged a little spread on the patio off her back porch, complete with a cheese wheel, fat purple grapes, a semicircle of Ritz crackers, a tray of assorted nuts and—I kid you not—a ramekin of sour cream and a tin of caviar nestled atop a bowl of ice.

"I know it's a splurge," Lynette says, when she sees me eyeing the golden tin. "I just like to treat myself every once in a while. I had to talk the owner of the market into special-ordering this for me—they don't usually carry caviar." I watch as she drops a dab of sour cream onto a cracker and tops it off with a scoop of tiny green pearls. She holds it out to me. "Want to try?"

I've never had caviar before, but after my less-than-stellar experience with cheese curds, I'm going to hold off. I know it's wildly expensive, and I don't want to insult Lynette if I make a face. I'm terrible at hiding it when I don't like the taste of something. "I'm good, but thank you."

Lynette flashes her crooked grin. "More for me then." She pops the cracker into her mouth and closes her eyes as she chews.

The lake winks in the distance, the sun casting tree-shaped shadows along the shoreline. Lynette's backyard is a kid's dream—there's an in-ground trampoline, a cedarwood swing set—complete with an accessible swing for Ruby, and a level, rambling lawn. I take a sip of my drink and my shoulders do an involuntary wiggle as the refreshing taste of lemon dances across my tongue. "What's in this?"

Lynette swallows another bite before answering. "It's gin and lemons and muddled mint. We call them Bootlegs." She'd garnished each goblet with a mint leaf and a lemon wedge. "It's sort of the unofficial cocktail of the season here. At least in the summertime. In the fall and winter, I drink Loon Juice—it's cinnamon and apple cider—delicious," she says, flashing me a crooked smile. "It'll put you right in the holiday spirit."

"Sounds nice."

Lynette sighs longingly. "It tastes like autumn, which is my favorite time of year. I love it when the leaves change and the air gets crisp. And Halloween is so much fun with the kids. I make their costumes myself."

"What are they going to be this year?"

She considers my question. "Well, Ned wants to be a lizard. He's obsessed with them—he catches skinks around the rocks near the lake and drops them into old jam jars. Allan has to make sure he lets them go every night. I don't know how Ned would react if he woke up to a jar full of dead lizards."

"And Ruby?"

Lynette's face softens at the mention of her daughter. It's the look of a parent who wants to protect her kid from the worlds' cruelty. I still catch Mom making the same face every once in a while, when she thinks Enzo doesn't know she's watching him. "She wants to be an astronaut. I'm going to try to make her chair into a rocket ship. Hopefully I can pull it off."

"An aspiring woman in STEM. That's awesome," I say this with genuine admiration. The only thing I aspired to be when I was Ruby's age was a professional ice cream eater.

"Ruby's wanted to be an astronaut since she was six," Lynette says, staring out at the lake. "She wants to live in zero gravity so she can move around without any help. It's why she loves swimming so much."

"Can I ask why she uses a wheelchair?"

"Of course. She was born with spina bifida."

Lynette says this plainly, clearly uninterested in any kind of sympathy, and yet my knee-jerk reaction is to say, "I'm so sorry." I regret the words as soon as they've left my mouth. It's not the same, but I've always hated it when people acted like Enzo's autism was some kind of tragic diagnosis when really it was just a confirmation of who he was: unique, yes, but certainly not in need of pity.

"No need to be sorry," Lynette says. "We've had our challenges, but Ruby is perfect just the way she is."

I think back to the evenings I spent watching the neighborhood from my upstairs window, when I first spotted Ruby playing with Ned on the front lawn as Lynette and Allan looked on, Ruby in her bright purple wheelchair and a matching purple dress, Ned wearing swim trunks and lime-green goggles. Ruby was blowing bubbles at her little brother and giggling as he tried in vain to pop them. They'd reminded me of Enzo and me when we were young.

"She seems like such a cool kid," I say. "Both of them do."

She beams with pride. "Yeah, we'll keep 'em."

A jingle of collars and a flurry of tiny footsteps passes by on the street behind us. Lynette and I turn in unison to see Marge walking a pack of dogs. She waves but doesn't stop, which I've come to expect from Marge. She's friendly in passing but reserved. Nothing like Gal.

I strain my neck to get a better look at who Marge is with. Bubbles, a paraplegic French bulldog in a little cart leads the pack with Tulip and Benny, the bonded beagles; Titan, a bouncy dalmatian who Gal told me was diagnosed with cancer three years ago—"It doesn't seem to bother him," she'd said with a shrug—and Carl, an absolutely ancient wire-haired Jack Russell terrier in tow.

Much to my disappointment, I don't spot Potato.

"I'm glad Ruby isn't here right now," Lynette says with a shake of her head. "She's still asking for a dog. I don't know how much longer I can hold out. Allan is already caving. He always makes me play bad cop."

"It's so cute that you two have been together since college."

"We like to think so," she says. "But don't let the sweet story fool you—marriage is not all daffodils and sunshine. Especially when one of you is a workaholic and the other aspires to be a lady of leisure." She sighs. "We have our problems."

Ah. Allan's commitment to work explains Lynette's ability to afford to enjoy a tin of caviar on a weeknight. Not to mention the steady stream of packages that show up on her doorstep every day.

"Every relationship has its challenges," I say. Lynette concedes with a smile and I sense an opening. "Speaking of relationship issues, I didn't know Erica was married."

Lynette blinks hard. "Where'd you hear that?"

"From Trish. Small towns, right?" I say with a conspiratorial shrug.

That seems to ease Lynette's discomfort. She looks back out at the lake. "Erica didn't really share any details about her personal life. And I never got to know Gary."

"Did they have a hard time fitting in? Being from New York?"

She blinks again, apparently surprised by how much I've gleaned about her former neighbor, but she doesn't push back. "Gary definitely stood out," she says. "He wasn't very friendly."

"What did Bob think of them?"

Lynette arranges her face into a sympathetic expression. I think she thinks I'm asking for myself, which I suppose I am. "Bob was Bob."

Enough said. "So you all never hung out?"

Lynette pushes out her bottom lip and shakes her head. "Not really."

But I know that's not entirely true. I want to know more, I want to ask why, but I don't want to offend Lynette in my quest to figure out whether or not Erica did something to offend her. I decide to leave it alone for now.

The temperature seems to drop a few degrees the instant the sun sinks fully below the tree line. I feel myself relax a bit more into the patio chair. Lynette does too. "Finally," she says, fanning herself. "How have you been adjusting to the muggy Midwest?"

I pop a cheese-laden Ritz into my mouth, relishing the combination of tangy cheese and salty, flaky cracker. I consider Lynette's question as I chew. "I don't really mind it," I say, before gesturing to my hair. "Aside from the aesthetic challenges."

Lynette runs a hand through her blown-out hair, which has fallen limp. "That's why I usually don't bother doing anything with mine. It always ends up like this."

I'm flattered that Lynette got all dressed up to invite me over.

"It's been a nice change of pace, actually," I say. "We don't have a true summer back home. At least not like this. I'm a summer girl—the sunshine, the warm nights, the *barbecues*," I say, un-artfully attempting to hint around for an invitation to Lynette's weekly party. "They're so . . . all-American." I can't say I've ever used that term before. I know I'm being super awkward, but Ly-nette pretends not to notice. She's a total girls' girl, I can tell.

But she doesn't say anything about the Sunday barbecues. In-stead, she asks, "Did you and your friends get together for cook-outs or potlucks back home?"

I think back to the year that my friends and I snuck a twelve-pack of beer, a party-sized bag of salt-and-vinegar chips, and a George Foreman grill onto the rooftop of Carmen's building. Farah brought a pack of veggie dogs and a ziplock bag full of ketchup packets she'd had in her car since college. We settled in next to the neighbors' definitely-not-legal marijuana garden and tried in vain to catch a glimpse of the Pier 39 fireworks show. The best we got was a dim glow against the fog. "Not really. Just for Fourth of July," I say.

"That's it?"

"Well, we did have an annual Friendsgiving tradition for a while. But none of us really liked Thanksgiving food, so instead, we'd just make whatever we wanted." I brought Mom's lasagna, Farah would make *tahdig*, this delicious crispy Persian rice, Brit-tany brought tacos, Carmen and her wife baked cookies. I liked that we'd made it our own, now that I thought about it. I probably didn't appreciate it enough at the time. "We haven't done it for years, though. Mostly because half of my friends moved out of the city."

Lynette smiles in understanding. "Well, maybe you can bring it back when you go home for the holidays this year."

"Maybe."

"Do you miss home?"

It feels like an allusion not to San Francisco, but to my former life, to the before. The truth is, my life feels like it's been cleaved into three distinct eras: before Hannah died, before I broke up with Marco, and now. Missing home feels pointless. The old version of home doesn't exist anymore.

"I miss my family," I say. That'll have to be enough for Lynette for now.

She doesn't push.

LYNETTE STRAPS STUART's leaf blower to her back and walks me home, the moon lighting our way. Our cul-de-sac doesn't have any streetlights, so it can get pretty dark, which is probably why Lynette said she'd walk with me. But tonight, the nearly full moon casts the street in a lovely blue glow. "This was really nice," she says, pulling me into a hug. "Thanks for keeping me company."

"Thank *you*," I say. "It's nice to have a friend to hang out with."

"Come by anytime."

"Are you sure you don't want me to wait for you to walk back home?"

She shakes her head. "Nah, I could navigate every inch of Loon Lane with a blindfold on." With that, she sets off toward Stuart's house, the leaf blower's hose dangling by her side like an extra arm.

When I reach my front porch, I find a stack of books, all titles I've never heard of, on my doorstep. There's a note from Stuart scribbled on a torn sheet of yellow legal paper. *These are much better than* Depth Charge. *Trust me.* He also included a little doodle of a smiley face with spikey hair. A word bubble hovers next to its mouth. *Enjoy*, it reads.

I decide that Stuart isn't so bad.

Chapter Sixteen

August

In spite of the evening I spent on Lynette's patio and the inroads I'd made with Stuart and Gal, last week's Sunday barbecue came and went without an invitation. And things weren't looking promising for this weekend, either.

"I just don't understand why they haven't invited me yet. I've been here for a month now," I say to Joel before digging my spoon into my frozen custard. He'd arrived at Cricket's with a cup of the turtle special in each hand. We now sat on a splintered wooden bench along the dock, waiting for Jimbo, the owner, to give us an orientation on how to use a pedal boat.

Joel gives me a sympathetic look. "I get why it's bugging you," he says. His kindness makes my heart skip. He barely knows me and is already patiently entertaining my neurotic fixations, which is more than I could say for Enzo.

"What is it that you're hoping to get out of going to this party?" my brother asked during our last FaceTime call. Even from two thousand miles away it still felt like my brother could see right through me.

I'd shrugged like it was obvious. "Friendship. Acceptance. Community?"

"And this barbecue is the only way to do that?"

"It's a cultural thing. Getting invited would mean that I'm in, that I've made it."

Enzo stared at me through the screen. He didn't need to remind me that I'd only been here a month, that I needed to be patient. "Do you think it might be time to delete that to-do list you made when you moved?"

"Of course not," I say, offended. "I just don't like being left out."

I could tell Enzo didn't agree, but what was he going to do about it from across the country?

A bead of sweat rolls down the back of my neck. I'd wisely swept my hair into a ponytail and slathered my body in sunscreen before I left the house this morning. Hopefully I don't sweat it all off before lunch. I swallow another bite of custard in an effort to regulate my body temperature. "Do you think they're hiding something?" I ask Joel.

He smirks with amusement. "Like what?"

"I don't know. A cult? A secret society? A pack of werewolves?" Joel scrunches his face. "You're right. I'm spiraling. Living alone is making me weird."

"It is weird, isn't it?" he asks. I nod, relieved that he doesn't think I've completely lost it. Joel looks around the empty dock before leaning in closer. "This is kind of embarrassing, but sometimes, I can't go to bed without checking all of my closets for serial killers."

"I do the same thing!"

"Really?"

"Well, it's not specific to serial killers. I'm worried about one-off murderers, too."

Joel shakes his head. "Not me. I figure I could take a first-timer. But a skilled expert?" He gulps. "I wouldn't stand a chance."

I raise my eyebrows. "You've really thought about this, haven't you?"

Joel nudges my arm with his elbow. "Oh, like you can talk. You're the one who thinks your neighbors are hiding a secret werewolf cult."

He's got me there.

Jimbo, a gregarious, ruddy-faced man who I guess to be in his midsixties emerges from the restaurant and waves us over to the row of pedal boats along the dock. "You kids ready?" he asks.

I offer to throw away our empty custard cups while Joel grabs us a pair of life jackets from the hooks along the railing.

"Do I have to wear this?" I ask, as he hands me one.

Joel narrows his eyes in suspicion. "Can you swim?"

"Of course I can swim."

"But can you swim *well*?"

"I wasn't on the swim team or anything, but I'm not going to drown if the boat tips over."

"Well I wasn't a lifeguard, so I won't be able to save you if something goes wrong out there." Joel sighs dramatically. "But, I'll take your word for it. Just don't make me regret this."

You MIGHT THINK that after what happened to Hannah, I would be more risk averse, but I actually like a little adventure—within reason. Sometimes I feel guilty when I catch myself enjoying life too much or doing anything that borders on risky. Even after all these years, I'll think, *Hannah would have loved this.* Nora is always reminding me that trauma and grief manifest differently for everyone.

The pedal boat is a cheery shade of red with a retractable striped awning. We settle side by side as Jimbo unties a rope and tosses it into the back. "One hour!" he calls as we slowly float away.

It takes us a couple of tries before we fall into a steady rhythm, our legs churning in unison. "You're a natural," Joel says. He takes control of the steering console between our seats, guiding the boat toward the south end of the lake.

A merciful breeze tickles my cheeks, blowing the loose curls around my face. I breathe in the refreshingly cooler air. It smells of sun and trees and minerals. Like summer.

"I hear you've been spending a lot of time at the coffee shop," Joel says, interrupting my moment of zen. I must look confused because he adds, "Trish mentioned."

"I hope I haven't been imposing. I just like it there."

Joel flashes me a dimpled smile. "I think the feeling is mutual."

"She told me that most of Main Street closes down in the off-season."

Joel sighs. "She prefers 'limited hours,' but yeah, 'closes down' is accurate."

"Has the Join Juneberry Lake program helped?"

Joel tugs the steering handle to the right and the boat turns ever so slightly toward shore. "I think it'll be at least another year or two before the town sees a real impact. And who knows if we'll even get the chance."

"What do you mean?"

"Well, not everyone in town is thrilled with the program."

"Why?"

"For starters? It could drive up house prices—which is a double-edged sword. Property values going up is good for the homeowners but it makes it harder for locals to break in. Not everyone in town can afford these lakefront places, either, so the more expensive things get around here, the harder it is on the long-term residents. And then there are the people who are worried about too much changing all at once."

"Doesn't the town need more people?" Trish had told me that Juneberry Lake used to have a big paper factory just outside of town, but that it closed down about ten years ago after some big embezzlement scandal. The old building is now a Walmart.

"The dissenters are definitely the minority, but they're also the loudest. You know your neighbor with brittle teeth? Bob?"

"Unfortunately."

"I thought he sounded familiar, so I asked Trish and she confirmed it. He's leading the charge."

I groan. "Is this because of the biscotti thing?"

Joel starts laughing. "I'm sure it didn't help. But no, he was salty about it long before you got here. I've been going to town hall meetings with Trish as kind of an ambassador for the program and he's always there griping about something."

My heart sinks for Trish, for the town. For myself. "Do you think they'll shut it down?"

Joel tilts his head from side to side. "The mayor has to approve a continuation next year and she tends to be conflict averse. She's done some great things for this town, but if Bob and his pals make enough noise that she starts to feel like her job is in jeopardy, I think she'll side with them."

I let Joel's words sink in as we pedal on in silence, save for the sounds of the water gently lapping against the boat and the chirping birds in the distance. Finally, I say, "I don't want to overstep, but I sketched out a marketing strategy for Black Bear Brew. I think if Trish invested in some targeted advertising, she might be able to bring more customers in year-round."

"I think the problem is people in nearby cities have plenty of options within a few minutes of their own houses. Why would they drive a half hour out of their way?"

"For the space. For peace and quiet. For the best bear claw in the state," I say, the words tumbling out in a jumble of excitement. "There's tons of parking in town and the café is usually pretty empty. I know my friends back home had a hard time working from coffee shops. They get so overcrowded. There's nothing more annoying than trying to edit a complicated spreadsheet while the guy next to you is on a Zoom call about sales forecasting."

"Sounds like a city problem."

"Exactly. Minneapolis is a city and there are tons of dense suburbs within a half an hour. Besides, it wouldn't hurt to try, right?"

Joel gives me a nod of concession. "People aren't going to drive thirty minutes through a snowstorm for a cup of coffee."

"Well then maybe Trish can do deliveries or sell baking kits or do virtual cooking classes when the weather gets too rough. There are tons of ways to get creative."

Joel's face turns pensive. "You should talk to her. What brought this on anyway? You've been here for like five minutes." I think I detect a hint of admiration in his voice.

"I have a soft spot for small businesses."

"You really love your family."

His observation catches me off guard. That wasn't the point I was trying to make. "Of course."

"The Collettis," he muses, drawing out the *coh*.

"A nice Italian family," I say. "What about the Jawowskis?"

"The Jawowskis are a nice Polish family. A half-Black, half-white Polish family," Joel says proudly. "They're great."

"Have they come to visit you since you moved?"

Joel's face tenses. "I haven't invited them out yet." I can sense that there's more to the story there. Maybe his parents don't approve of the woman Joel followed here? Or maybe they were the cause of his one-third-life crisis (I still haven't been able to think of a better term for it). But before I can inquire further, Joel changes the subject. "What about your family? Was it hard to move away?"

My mouth twists. "Yes and no."

Joel steers the boat closer to shore. "You're kind of mysterious, you know."

I could say the same thing about Joel. "I'm not trying to be. I guess I'm just trying to figure out what to do with myself next."

"Any luck with that?"

"Aside from scheming ways to get invited to a neighborhood barbecue?" I shake my head. "Not yet."

"I'm sure it'll come to you."

"I hope you're right."

He grins. "I'm right like fifty-two percent of the time, so you're in good hands."

I've been so engrossed in our conversation that I hadn't been paying attention to where we were going. I suddenly realize that I'm looking at my back porch. From the water, it looks smaller than I'd imagined. The whole cul-de-sac does. I point out my house to Joel.

"Looks like a great place," he says, his tone approving. "So tell me about these neighbors. Who lives where?"

I wonder if Joel knows any of them, but as I list each person's name, he doesn't react. I guess he doesn't spend much time south of Main Street.

I go house by house, assigning an overly simplified descriptor to each neighbor. Stuart is the reclusive writer; Lynette and Allan are the college sweethearts with two kids; Bob is the grumpy widower. Joel points to Marge and Gal's house, visible between Bob and Lynette's. "And what about them?"

"They foster special needs dogs," I say. "Gal taught math at the high school for like thirty years. Marge helped run a dance studio. They're both retired now."

Joel's face falls for a second, but he recovers quickly. If I didn't know any better, I'd say that something about Gal and Marge's life made him sad. But I couldn't imagine why. Maybe he misses his family dog or something.

"So, where do *you* live?" I venture. For a second, I worry that I'm overstepping, but then I remember that we're currently staring at my neighborhood from the lake.

Joel rubs the back of his neck with his palm. He winces. "My parents' house is in Aspen Estates."

That explains why he doesn't know anyone who lives on my street. "Riiiiiiich," I tease.

"Well, it's not right on the water or anything. And they bought it like thirty years ago."

I shift on the plastic seat to face him. "You don't need to be modest about it. I'm not judging you."

His hand is still cupped around his neck. "I don't know. It's bad enough that I'm living in my parents' vacation home. The fact that it's in a fancy neighborhood makes it sound like I'm a spoiled rich kid or something."

"I know spoiled rich kids and you're not one of them," I assure him. I mean it, too. Joel helps underprivileged kids for a living and has clearly gone out of his way to learn about Juneberry Lake and the people who live here. "Besides, what are you supposed to do? Not use the house? That wouldn't help anyone. You don't need to go out of your way to make your life more difficult to make up for what you have."

Joel turns to meet my eye. He shrugs. "You're probably right."

"I'm right like ninety-nine percent of the time, so you can trust me."

Joel gives my arm a playful push. Then he makes a show of wiping his hand on his swim trunks. "You're all sweaty!"

"It's like four hundred degrees out here!"

"Don't be dramatic. It can't be more than two hundred and fifty." He tilts his face up toward the sky. The sun blares down on us from directly overhead. "Should we go for a swim?"

I'd worn a bathing suit under my dress on the off chance that I fell in or something, but I hadn't planned on voluntarily stripping down. Especially in front of Joel.

Joel doesn't wait for an answer. He stands up, sending the little boat rocking and pulls his shirt over his head and tosses it to the side.

I know I just got out of a long-term engagement and that Joel is in some kind of mysterious situation-ship, but I can't help but watch. And let's just say *wow*. He's been hiding a lot under those frumpy Juneberry Lake T-shirts.

I'm relieved when Joel jumps into the water before I can stare for too long.

Now I feel even hotter and stickier than I did a minute ago.

"The water is perfect today!" he calls. I can hear him splashing around off the side of the boat. "You coming in or what, *Frisco*?"

I shudder at the awful nickname. That does it. Without a second thought, I shimmy out of my sundress and execute a flawless cannonball into the water.

I let myself sink several feet toward the rocky bottom, relishing the sensation of the cool water enveloping my body. Now that I think about it, I can't remember the last time I went swimming. I almost forgot how refreshing it is, how alive it makes me feel.

"Nice splash," Joel says when I break through the surface. He's treading water just a foot away. "I nearly drowned."

I shoot him a smirk. "That was for calling me Frisco."

"Well, if calling you Frisco means I get to see you in a yellow bikini, I'm going to do it again."

I tell him he's an idiot. Then I dive under the water.

I don't want him to see me blush.

Chapter Seventeen

Before

You might think that the first thing Marco and I did after getting engaged was jump straight into planning our wedding. But you would be wrong.

The first thing we did was make an appointment at a fertility clinic.

It took me years to get Marco on board with this plan, which he insisted was completely unnecessary. "You're still young, Lize," he'd say. "I don't think this is something we're going to have to worry about. Besides, I'm not really comfortable with the whole idea of IVF. It kind of feels like we're playing God or something."

I couldn't have felt more differently. Swayy offered fertility benefits so we'd only have to pay a fraction of the typically astronomical costs. And why wouldn't we take advantage of all that science had to offer?

"But what if God is the one who created IVF?" I'd asked.

Marco didn't have a counter to that.

Eventually, given my commitment to holding off on kids until we were a bit older, Marco agreed it would be wise to freeze a few embryos, as long as I agreed that we'd try to have a baby unassisted first. This was just an insurance policy.

A baby savings account.

"This is the time to do it," Dr. Ramirez, a gray-haired woman with a kind, broad face enthused, nodding with approval. "I only wish more young people were as thoughtful about planning for their futures as the two of you are."

Marco and I beamed at each other. We thought we were so damn smart.

Marco sat diligently by my side as Dr. Ramirez walked me through all of the hormones I'd be injecting my body with, holding up empty sample boxes and dummy syringes as she went. "These two will stimulate follicle growth. The idea is to get your ovaries to mature multiple eggs at once, as opposed to the single egg they typically release during a normal cycle." She held up another package. "This one will prevent you from ovulating too early. We want to grow as many follicles as possible before the ovaries release them."

I turned to look at Marco, whose eyes had glazed over. I was barely following along myself and I'd been ovulating for almost twenty years.

"And this one will be your trigger shot. You don't have to worry about this one until the end. This is what will tell your body it's time to release all those eggs you grew." She set the box down. "Then we'll do the retrieval, fertilize the mature eggs with Marco's sperm, and go from there. Easy peasy."

I remember nodding along with smug certainty. Two weeks of discomfort in exchange for years of peace of mind? Easy peasy indeed.

After we completed all of the pre-cycle testing (everything looked normal, normal, normal!), Marco bravely attempted to help me with my injections. But the way his hands shook when he picked up the needle made me nervous, so I made a game-time decision to do it myself.

Holding a needle to my abdomen stirred something primal from deep within me, a long dormant survival instinct. It's almost as if us humans are wired to *not* poke ourselves with sharp objects. My hands froze, my body stiffened, and I could have sworn that an invisible forcefield appeared between the needle I held in one hand and the piece of fat pinched between my fingers.

It took me six tries to psych myself up enough to plunge that first needle into my flesh. When I finally did, I was pleasantly surprised to find that it didn't really hurt at all. I was stronger and braver than I'd given myself credit for. "I did it!" I called out to Marco, who'd gone to the couch to lie down. He let out a supportive groan. I think all the needlework had made him nauseous. With the seal broken, I completed my next injection.

No looking back now.

On day five, I went in for my first ultrasound to see how my follicles were progressing. I told Marco he didn't need to come with me since it's not like I was pregnant or anything. I scrolled through work emails on my phone as the technician wordlessly maneuvered a wand around my cervix.

"Dr. Ramirez will call you later today with the results," she said, tugging off her gloves. "You can go home once you're dressed."

It occurred to me that I was fortunate to be going through this process now, as a preventive measure. If this was a last resort, I think the transactional nature of harvesting eggs would have felt immeasurably cold.

I was still at work when Dr. Ramirez called. She wasted no time in cutting right to the chase. "So, at this point, we typically expect to see at least a handful of follicles developing in each ovary," she said. "Unfortunately, your body doesn't seem to be responding to these particular hormones."

"What does that mean?" My hand was resting on top of my wireless mouse when I asked this. For some reason, I'll aways remember that.

"Well, in your case, it looks like you've only got one follicle starting to form. When we do a retrieval, we do our best to get as many eggs as we can—ideally at least ten—so that we can minimize the number of times a patient has to go through the procedure. With that in mind, at this point, I'd like to cancel this cycle. We can try again next month, with some new meds. How does that sound?"

OVER THE NEXT year, we attempted three additional cycles after our failed first attempt.

The second round produced six eggs (low for my age), only one of which was mature enough to be fertilized. That one fertilized egg failed to progress beyond two cells.

The third round (this one included steroids to improve my egg quality, which worked wonders on my mood, and more tests for Marco, all of which came back pristine) produced five mature eggs, three of which fertilized, and one of which made it to genetic testing. The results were chromosomally abnormal.

The fourth round went exactly the same as the third round.

Each of these cycles were punctuated by additional testing, bloodwork, and physical exams. My body came to resemble a pincushion. My abdomen became tender, swollen, and bruised. Eventually, I was diagnosed with ovarian dysfunction. Which is basically a vague way of saying, something's wrong but we don't know what or why or how to fix it.

"We can keep trying," Dr. Ramirez said at our last meeting. "But it's very unlikely that you'll ever be able to conceive a biological child of your own."

I remember Marco reaching over to take my hand. "We're not going to give up," he answered for us.

I pulled my hand away and placed it in my lap.

Chapter Eighteen

I'm sitting on my back porch enjoying the chilled pasta salad I'd picked up at the market this morning while I weigh whether or not to delete Marco's string of unanswered messages. It's clearly bothering him that I'm no longer at his beck and call, that I'm moving on. But this is what he wanted.

Now all I want is for him to let me go.

I'm shoveling a forkful of fusilli into my mouth when I spot Ned wandering around my yard. He has a glass jar tucked under his arm. He must be looking for lizards.

"Hey, Ned," I call. He turns toward the sound of my voice, a lizard dangling from his fingertips. "Catch anything good?"

As if on cue, the lizard Ned is holding drops to the ground and disappears under a rock. Ned's left holding the stubby tip of its tail. I remember Enzo telling me that skinks can detach their tails when they feel threatened. "It grows back," he'd reassured me. Ned must be aware of the skink's regenerative abilities, because he appears completely unfazed.

"Will you help me find a salamander for my sister?" he calls.

I set my pasta salad aside and walk toward the edge of my porch. "Does Ruby *want* a salamander?"

Ned shrugs. "Lizards always make me feel better when I'm sad."

My heart twists at the thought of Ruby feeling sad, and then twists again at Ned's thoughtfulness. Even if it is a bit misplaced.

Ruby is more of a dog kid than a lizard kid, but it's the thought that counts.

I make my way down the lawn toward Ned and his little jar. He's wearing his water shoes, swim trunks, and a T-shirt with a picture of a dinosaur on it. His swim goggles rest on the top of his forehead. "Why is Ruby sad?"

"Her friends wouldn't let her play basketball with them. They said if she couldn't dribble the ball, it was trawbling and that was cheating."

I take trawbling to mean traveling. "That's terrible," is all I can think to say. I'd have much sharper words for the kids who excluded her. And even sharper ones for their parents.

Ned does an exaggerated shrug of his shoulders. He's still holding the stub of the skink's discarded tail. "Ruby is really good at basketball. She beats me all the time."

"They should have let her play," I agree.

Ned sighs. "I know."

"It's very sweet that you want to do something nice for your sister."

"All I can find are skinks though."

"Hmm," I say, tapping my index finger to my chin. I scan the rocks near the lake, as if a salamander will magically appear. But the rocks are lizard free and the water on the lake is smooth as glass. The only sign of wildlife is the sound of June bugs in the distance and fireflies sparking to life, little embers floating along the grass. "What if we catch her some fireflies instead?" I suggest. "Ruby can keep the jar in her room for the night."

Ned jumps up and down. "Like a night-light!"

"Exactly," I say. With that, Ned tosses the disembodied lizard tail into the water.

We drop a damp paper towel and a handful of grass into the

bottom of the jar ("For their hawbitat," Ned explains) and start collecting bugs. Up close, fireflies look like a smaller, lankier version of a beetle. If it weren't for their little flashing bottoms, I wouldn't have thought much of them. There's a metaphor for not judging a book by its cover somewhere in there. I mention this to Ned.

"It's what they have inside that makes them special," he agrees, then his face falls. "My friend's dad pulls the light off and puts it on his shirt," Ned says, his voice somber. "It keeps flashing even without the bug, but I feel bad for the bug."

"Yeah, that doesn't sound very nice."

"It's not." Ned holds his forearm up horizontally in front of his face as a firefly crawls along his wrist. "But we won't do that to you, okay?" he says to the bug before nudging it into the jar.

It's nearly dark out by the time Ned declares that we've collected enough bugs. He wanted exactly thirteen because that's Ruby's favorite number. "She can't wait to be a teenager," he says. "I don't know why. Teenagers are so old."

If Ned thinks teenagers are old, he must think I'm ancient. I decide it's best not to mention that I'm old enough to be the parent of a teenager.

Lynette is scrubbing dishes in her farmhouse sink when Ned bursts through the back door. He's dragging me behind him with one hand and clutching the fireflies with the other. "Ruby, I made you a night-light," he declares, holding the jar above his head like a trophy. Ruby sits at the kitchen table, reading a book. She squints at the jar.

"He wanted to find Ruby a salamander," I say to Lynette. "But we decided on fireflies instead."

The creases in Lynette's forehead smooth with relief. "Thank you," she mouths.

Ned flips the overhead kitchen lights off and pads over to Ruby. He sets the jar in front of her on the counter as Ruby leans forward to peer into the glass. Her eyes widen with excitement. "I love them," she says. Her little voice is so sweet.

"Eliza helped," Ned says.

Ruby's cute little face makes me feel like I'm going to melt. "Can I come next time?"

"Of course," I say. "I'll help you two collect fireflies anytime."

"And maybe another time we can swim in the lake?"

"Don't get greedy, missy," Lynette says. "Eliza has a life, you know."

Lynette is being generous—I don't have a lot going on these days. I give her a reassuring look before telling Ruby that I'd love to go for a swim. She looks at Lynette, triumphant. "See, Mom?"

"Do you want to stay for a drink? I have a bottle of Rombauer open." Lynette gestures to the island in the center of the kitchen where a bottle of chardonnay sweats on the countertop. My eyes sweep around the room—it's the first time I've been inside the Carr-Poole home. The two times I've been over, we hung out on the patio and their dock, respectively. The kitchen appears to be freshly renovated, with tall, open beam ceilings, creamy marble countertops, and dark-stained wood cabinets. It's accessorized with copper rooster statues and red dish towels with fat hens on them.

Lynette's style is well-worn in a good way. Like returning to a childhood home.

My stomach growls, a low, gurgling rumble. As much as I'd like to stay, to soak up the warmth of this house and this family, my empty stomach won't allow it. My pasta salad is probably warm by now, but I'm still hungry. I was going to have the rest for lunch tomorrow, but after all that firefly hunting, I might polish it off tonight. "Maybe another night," I say. "I've got dinner waiting back home."

"Well if you change your mind, I'm around."

"Thanks for letting me help you with the night-light," I tell Ned. "And Ruby? You're welcome to come over anytime."

I'm halfway out the door when Lynette says, "By the way, if you aren't doing anything this weekend, Allan and I are having everyone over on Sunday. We're grilling brats. You should stop by."

I don't know what brats are (or is it braaht? Lynette's Midwestern dialect is rather strong) and I don't care because I finally did it. I'm *in*. All it took was one quasi-successful batch of biscotti, four walks with Gal, one brief conversation with Stuart about the books he left on my doorstep (I said, "You were right, *Torchlight* was great." Then Stuart nodded and said, "Okay, good. See you around"), two pitchers of Bootlegs with Lynette (not in one sitting), and an offer to bring Bob's trash cans in with mine (he'd refused, looking offended).

My hand leaves the screen door and flutters over my chest. "I'd love to." Then with as much casual energy as I can muster, I add, "I'll bring dessert. Something softer than biscotti."

Lynette smiles. Her hands are still submerged in the sink. "Great. We'll see you then."

When I get home, I have a missed call from Farah and a text from Marco.

> **Marco:** Do you think breaking up might have been a mistake? I really miss you, E.

I don't respond to either of them.

Chapter Nineteen

I check to see that my platter of Italian cookies is still intact be-fore heading over to Lynette's. I spent the better part of an hour arranging the soft, chocolate-dipped duettos (Enzo's recommendation) just so.

When, I knock on the Carr-Pooles' big wooden front door, no one answers. I knock again. Nothing. I check my phone to confirm that it's 3:17 p.m., which I felt would be just the right amount of late—polite without being too eager. I'm about to knock for a third time when I hear what almost sounds like yelling coming from the back of the house.

As I round the porch I see a barbecue in full swing: Stuart and Gal sit on a pair of folding lawn chairs, each cradling a koozie-clad beer, Lynette works the grill as Allan dumps chips into a bowl at a folding table that's been draped in a red-checkered cloth. And finally, I see Marge and Bob standing off to the side. Arguing.

Lynette lifts a spatula and waves it in my direction when she spots me on the porch. "Eliza, you made it," she calls loudly, her eyes darting toward Marge and Bob. "Look everyone," she continues in an exaggerated tone, "Eliza is here."

"That's the problem," Bob shoots back.

The note I found in Erica's junk drawer flashes through my mind. *Trust Bob?*

I certainly didn't. Marge flicks Bob's shoulder and whispers something that sounds like "don't make this worse" before turning toward me. "Don't pay this old curmudgeon any mind. We're happy to have you."

Now everyone is staring at me in silence, waiting to see how I'll react. It's obvious that Bob doesn't want me here, but I'm certainly not going to give him the satisfaction of getting under my skin. I decide to go with easy breezy, flashing a wide smile and wiggling my fingers in a wave. Lynette drops the spatula onto a plate and rushes toward me, wiping her hands on her apron as she goes. She pulls me into a hug (I'm thrilled that we're on hugging terms) and says, "Let's get you a drink."

Lynette leads me over to a vintage metal cooler next to the barbecue and offers to take my plate of cookies. "These look delicious," she says, eyeing the hand-dipped chocolate topping. "I'm going to go pop these in the fridge so they don't melt. Help yourself." She jerks her ponytail in the direction of the cooler before heading toward the back door. I fish out a spiked seltzer and pop the lid before realizing that I may have made the wrong choice; everyone else is drinking beer. Except maybe Marge. It's hard to tell under her LAKE LIFE koozie. I think back to that one anthropology class I took in college and vaguely recall something about blending in and adopting local customs, but it's too late now.

Allan tosses a Wisconsin Badgers koozie in my direction. "Good to see you again, Eliza."

"You too," I say. I tug the sleeve onto my drink, grateful for the disguise.

"Where are the kids?" I ask.

Allan scans the massive lawn. "They're around here somewhere," he mutters before turning back to me. "Did Lynette tell you she finally agreed to let them get a dog?"

I'd figured it was only a matter of time. I wouldn't be able to tell Ruby no if she asked me for anything. "That's great," I say. "One of Marge and Gal's?"

"Oh yeah. The one in the dog wheelchair." Allan smiles. "It was love at first sight for her and Ruby."

As if on cue, Ned and Ruby come tearing around the corner with Bubbles hot on their heels. The kids squeal with laughter as Bubbles bounds across the lawn, the wheels of her little cart spinning.

The trio comes to a stop a few feet from where Allan and I stand. Ned and Ruby are rosy-cheeked, Bubbles is panting.

"Eliza we got a dog!" Ruby says.

"Her name is Bubbles!" Ned yells.

"I see that," I say, bending down to pat Bubbles on the head. Bubbles pants in appreciation for the attention.

"She's in a wheelchair like me," Ruby says proudly.

"And she's five like me," Ned adds.

"The three of you belong together."

Ruby flashes her gap-toothed grin as she hikes up her shoulders. Ned nods emphatically. Bubbles licks her chops. They're all in agreement.

With that, Ned throws a tennis ball toward the lake and Bubbles runs off in pursuit. Ruby, then Ned bring up the rear.

I MAKE MY way over to Gal and Stuart, who are talking animatedly, Darla the Chihuahua and Carl the terrier on their respective laps. Potato is lying on the grass between their chairs, but springs to her feet when she sees me approaching. Before I know it, she's crawled into my lap, placed her front paw on my shoulder and started covering my face with licks. Potato is making such a scene, that Gal turns away from Stuart to comment. "Someone missed her best friend."

She could be talking about either me or Potato. I scratch behind her ears as we stare meaningfully into each other's eyes.

Lynette approaches, a fresh, ice-cold beer in each hand. She
passes one to Stuart and one to Gal. "How's it going over here?"

"I was just asking our famous neighbor when we can read his
next book," Gal says, lifting her chin in Stuart's direction. "He's
very secretive these days."

Stuart flinches at the mention of his work.

"He doesn't like to brag," Lynette says.

"He *pretends* he doesn't like to brag," Gal corrects her. She
jerks her thumb toward Stuart. "This one acts like he's too good
for literary snobbery, but he rejects every book I choose for our
book club."

"You only read romance novels," Stuart mutters.

"People like romance novels," Gal says.

"What's wrong with romance novels?" I ask.

"They make people happy," Gal answers for Stuart.

"I am happy," Stuart says, sounding anything but.

"What do you like to read, hun?" Gal asks me.

I used to read a ton as a kid. But I hadn't had much time for reading. Until recently, that is. "I've always been big into mysteries—
especially the cozy ones. I think they make me feel like the world
isn't quite so chaotic. Like, if you look hard enough there's an explanation for everything." I'm rambling, but the group is nodding
along politely. "But I like romances too," I assure them.

"I don't care about the genre as long as there are some hot
lovemaking scenes," Lynette says with a giggle. Stuart blushes.

"Guess who got us into those new spicy romance books?" Gal
says dryly.

"No, that was Er . . ." Lynette lets her voice trail off. Stuart
clears his throat. Gal shifts in her lawn chair.

Lynette waves her hand in front of her face. "It doesn't matter whose idea it was. I'd never read anything like it before and I've really expanded my palette since then. Gal got us started on this new series, Coffee Cove, and whew." She fans herself. "That's some hot stuff."

"Coffee Cove is garbage," Stuart huffs.

"It's smut," Gal corrects him. "And we love smut."

I never, not once, in all of my days pictured myself standing around at a neighborhood barbecue discussing sexy books with a couple of Midwestern gal pals, but here I am.

I like it.

"Can I come to the next book club?" I ask.

It's immediately apparent from the sudden, tense silence that I've overstepped. Gal starts hemming and hawing, as if she's about to haggle at a garage sale. "Maybe to the next one?" she offers, her voice ticking up into a question at the end.

Lynette agrees a little too enthusiastically. "That might work." She turns to me, her face apologetic. "It's just that we've already read the book for this one."

"And assigned all the discussion questions," Gal says.

"Not to mention the snacks," Stuart adds.

"Yes," Lynette says, sounding like a person who's just been tossed a life preserver. "The snacks are already set."

Maybe there's some type of book club etiquette that I don't know about. Are you supposed to wait to be invited? I assume they want to see how I do in a group setting first, which is fair. This is the first time we're all hanging out together.

"Of course," I say, trying to sound casual and reassuring. "I totally get it. Maybe next time."

They all breathe what appears to be a collective sigh of relief.

Lynette turns back to look at the grill, which Allan has taken over in her absence. "It looks like the food is just about ready. Let's go grab some plates. We'll sit on the dock."

LYNETTE AND ALLAN's dock is so much more than a dock. While mine is simple and utilitarian—a long, narrow row of planks that extend into the deeper portion of the lake—theirs is an expansive platform, probably a twenty-foot square, that hovers above the shallow, marshy water. They've erected a gazebo at the center, which provides ample, merciful shade for the picnic table. A small table for Ruby, Ned, and Bubbles sits off to the side. Ned and Ruby have already dug into their respective plates, their little dog looking on hopefully.

We all settle in around the table (Potato curls up by my feet under the bench), which has been set with cheery red plastic plates and gingham napkins encircled by wicker napkin rings. The food has been arranged at the center, all in matching red bowls. I'd been stressing about the whole bratwurst situation, but Gal brought a couple of tofu dogs to share and Lynette and Allan grilled veggie kebabs, too. I've piled my plate high with zucchini and bell peppers, pasta salad, and potato chips. I try not to make a big show out of being a vegetarian. I've found that people can get pretty weird about it, as if my choices are an indictment of theirs (which they aren't, obviously).

Not all people react badly, of course, just some. Like Bob.

"No brats for you, Golden State?" Bob asks, eyeing my plate. I suppose this is Bob's idea of a conversation starter, but it's impossible to miss the hostility in his tone. "What are you, some kind of *vaygan?*" He attempts a smile, but it looks more like he's gnashing his teeth together. I can't tell which one my biscotti chipped.

I slide my hands under my legs. "Something like that."

"Ignore him," Marge says, patting my shoulder. "Bob survives exclusively on meat and potatoes, so it's hard for him to wrap his mind around the fact that some of us prefer different food groups."

Gal raises her veggie dog in solidarity.

"Cheers everyone," Lynette says, raising her beer. "To another beautiful day in the neighborhood."

The neighbors clink their respective cans before digging into dinner. As everyone falls into what appears to be a companionable routine—passing condiments and complimenting the chef and exchanging inside jokes that I assume harken back to barbecues past—I'm struck by a sudden bout of homesickness. The way these people interact feels much more intimate than any group of neighbors I've ever known. They act more like a family.

I can feel Bob eyeing me as I stab at the remains of my macaroni salad. "So, California," he says between chews. "What part of the state are you from?"

"San Francisco."

Bob huffs. "Figures. Let me guess—you're fleeing the rampant crime and homelessness."

Bob's out-of-touch opinion of my hometown aside, I kind of wish it were that simple. But I hadn't fallen out of love with San Francisco, and I certainly wasn't running from the city itself.

Lynette leans forward. "Leave her alone, Bob. She's going through a breakup." Everyone but Bob nods along gravely, as if that explains everything. Which I guess it kind of does.

"There's plenty of fish in the sea," Gal says reassuringly.

Marge elbows Gal in the ribs. "Don't rush her. She might not be ready."

"Yeah I think that's a ways off," I agree.

I swear I can see Bob's eyes narrowing behind his sunglasses.

"Well you're not going to meet anyone in a small town like this," he says. "I bet you don't last through the winter."

"I don't know about that, Bob," Stuart interjects. "I think Eliza's tougher than you're giving her credit for. Something tells me you'll be shoveling snow out of her driveway for many winters to come." I flash him a grateful smile.

"Not a chance," Bob grumbles.

"You did it for Erica and you'll do it for Eliza too," Allan says, before taking a swig of beer. I could swear Lynette pinched his leg under the table. He winces ever so slightly.

I don't even mind that Bob's being a jerk because he's given me the opening I've been waiting for. I decide to seize on the opportunity. "Oh," I say, holding up a finger. "Speaking of Erica—did she leave a forwarding address?"

The way my neighbors fidget at my question makes me realize that for a second time today I've inadvertently overstepped.

"Why do you ask, hun?" Gal asks. Her tone can only be described as cautious.

"She left some bins in the basement. I was just hoping to return them to her."

"What's in the bins?" Marge leans forward, her tall frame stretching over the table.

I shrug. "Just some mail. And a handful of newspapers."

Stuart raises his eyebrows. "Newspapers?"

"They're a couple of years old." I'd skimmed the articles and most of them were typical small-town fare—an elementary school dance performance, a Fourth of July parade schedule, information about local elections—but there were a few that were a bit more titillating. A city councilmember was fired for misconduct, a well-known TV show about rich people behaving terribly filmed a few scenes across the lake in Aspen Estates, a winning lottery ticket was sold in the next town over, a lawyer in that same town was disbarred for misappropriating client funds. Erica had folded the pages down on a couple of real estate listings, but as far as I knew, she hadn't stayed nearby. Maybe she was looking for the right person to sell her house.

Allan clears his throat. Marge and Gal exchange a look.

I look around the table. "What am I missing?"

Lynette rests her hand on my wrist. "It's just that, when Erica left, she didn't . . . tell us where she was going."

"Can you just text her to ask where we should send her old mail?"

Lynette shakes her head sadly. "It's been a year since any of us have heard from her. She changed her number after she left."

"Did you have some kind of falling out?"

Lynette forces a laugh. "No, no. Nothing like that."

"So why hasn't she been in contact? Did she say why she was leaving? Or leave any hints about where she was going?"

Bob laughs and somehow manages to make it sound condescending. "Easy there, California. I'm the interrogator around here."

Gal told me that Bob used to work for the FBI. The thought of him being a professionally trained interrogator makes me uneasy.

"Sorry," I say. "I don't mean to overstep. I'm just curious is all."

"You're fine, hun," Gal says. "Go ahead and toss whatever's in those bins. Erica doesn't need it."

Marge nods her agreement.

Lynette clears her throat. "Well, I think that's enough with the past." Her tone is light, but firm. She wants me to drop it.

And maybe I should. If my neighbors say there's nothing fishy going on here, I should believe them. They haven't given me any reason not to.

I've gotten what I wanted, haven't I? I'm at the barbecue. I'm in.

It might be time to stop looking backward. That's why I moved here in the first place, isn't it?

"Who's up for a game of bocce ball?" Allan suggests.

I BID MY new neighbors goodbye and walk home just as the sun has started to drop, casting spiky shadows along the pavement. The evenings are rapidly becoming my favorite time of day—it stays light well past eight o'clock and the air is warm but not too humid. Plus, this is when the fireflies come out.

We'd spent the better part of the afternoon playing bocce ball on Lynette and Allan's expansive lawn. Bob and Gal had been designated captains and—no surprise here—Bob had made a point of not picking me, which was his mistake because I'm amazing at bocce ball. Marco and I were in a league together back home. It took me a few tosses to get a feel for the grass (I usually played on gravel), but once I got the hang of it, I was unstoppable. Gal's team won all three rounds.

The day ended with Bob kicking the pallino so hard it almost landed in the lake. With that, everyone decided to call it a night, each of them muttering something about Sunday chores and it being a "school night."

All in all, I'd say today was a success.

Stuart even said, "See you next week" as I was leaving.

My phone buzzes as I walk through my front door, and when I see that it's my brother calling, I do a little happy dance.

I take a cup of tea out onto the back porch while I catch up with Enzo. He runs me through the usual updates: Mom still hopes I'll come home any day now, Dad thinks he's finally perfected his minestrone recipe (he's been tinkering with it since before either of us were born and I swear every iteration tastes exactly the same), and Enzo went to the movies with his crush, Allison, but doesn't offer any details beyond that. I tell him about the town, my new favorite coffee shop, and meeting Joel. I'm just about to get into my day with the neighbors when I notice lights flipping on at the edge of my dock. Then Bob's boat engine whirs to life.

"Eliza? Are you still there?"

I shake my head, trying to pull myself back to the conversation with Enzo. "Yes." My voice drops to a whisper. "Sorry."

"Why are you whispering?"

"My neighbors are outside."

He doesn't reply, which means his wheels are turning as he tries to parse the social nuance. "You don't want them to overhear you talking about them?"

"Something like that . . . It's just that they all acted like they had to get home, like they were all going to leave right after me. But now it seems like they just wanted me to leave so they could hang out without me." Or worse, talk about how weird I am.

"Maybe they didn't want to hurt your feelings."

I peer over the railing to watch Stuart helping Lynette onto the boat. Marge and Gal settle in under a striped blanket. I don't see Allan, so I guess he stayed home with the kids. At least one person was telling the truth. "Yeah," I say with a sigh. "You're probably right."

After I hang up with my brother, I go about my nightly bedtime routine. I never got very into the whole skin-care thing—not like some of my friends. Brittany has so many products that she keeps a tiny refrigerator on her bathroom counter—but I can't get into bed without washing my face and dabbing mom's favorite night cream under my eyes. She'd given me a jar on my

thirtieth birthday. "You don't look too old yet and you should try
to keep it that way. At least until after you're married."

Little did she know how far off that would be.

I change into my pajamas and plug my phone in on the night-
stand, but before I turn off the lights in my room I can't resist
peeking out the window one last time.

Bob's boat is back. My neighbors are nowhere in sight, probably all tucked away in their own beds.

Chapter Twenty

On Monday morning, I'm removing my bike from its new parking spot on my front porch when I hear footsteps approaching. I turn around expecting to see Lynette or Gal, but instead, it's a man I don't recognize. He's parked a dingy-looking Crown Vic in front of my driveway.

"Hi there," he says, smiling broadly. "Hope I didn't startle you."

He hadn't startled me, but something about this man's sudden appearance does unnerve me. "Can I help you?"

The stranger removes his aviator sunglasses, which I realize were the most remarkable thing about him. He's average in every way—he's probably in his fifties and just under six feet tall, with brown hair, brown eyes and ruddy cheeks. He wears a green polo shirt and khaki shorts that neatly camouflage the slight pouch of his belly. He looks like millions of other American dudes, but for some reason, the way he's standing, peering up at me from the lawn triggers a disconcerting sense of déjà vu.

"I'm Van Fischer," he says, as if that explains everything. "I was in the neighborhood, so I just thought I'd stop by."

Without even thinking, I've positioned the bike between me and this Van character. "Why?"

He squints up at the house, and that's when I recognize him. This is the man I'd spotted walking along my dock on my first night in Juneberry Lake. I steal another glance at his car—it's the same car that had crept down our street when I was outside talking with Lynette and Stuart. I don't like this. "I was wondering if Erica was around?"

I take a small step toward my front door. "Erica doesn't live here anymore."

"Oh yeah, I know. It's just that, well, I thought she might have been by to pick up some of her things now that her house sold."

I shake my head. "I haven't seen her. I've actually never even met her."

"Huh." Van shifts his weight from one leg to the other. His thumbs are hooked in his beltloops. "Did she leave a forwarding address?"

"No," I say, "not that anyone knows of."

Van shakes his head. "That's a real shame."

"Why do you need to get in touch with her so badly?"

Van makes a face that I think is intended to look sympathetic, but in reality, he just looks constipated. "I'm not the one who wants to get in touch. It's her husband. He hasn't heard from her in more than a year." He makes a *tsk*ing sound. "Poor guy. He's worried sick."

I drum my fingers against the handlebars of my bike, a subtle signal that I'm in a hurry and don't have time for whatever this is. Van doesn't take the hint.

"Have your neighbors told you much about Erica?"

I arrange my face into a thoughtful expression. "No," I say, my tone vague, disinterested. "Just that she'd moved away and no one talks to her anymore." I also recently learned that she worked as a part-time veterinarian at the local clinic and she was definitely chummier with at least some of my neighbors than they're letting on, but I'm not going to volunteer any information because while I may not know what's going on here, I do know that I don't trust Van Fischer.

Van smirks. "That's convenient." He pulls a wallet out of his back pocket and extracts a white business card. "Well, if you do hear anything, give me a shout."

I reluctantly take the card. "Will do," I say, my voice monotone.

Van hesitates, considering me. Then he sighs. "I really hope you mean that. I'd hate for this to get complicated."

My stomach dips. Was that a threat?

Van smirks. "Anyway, thanks for your help, Eliza." He turns on his heel and saunters back toward the old Crown Victoria.

He unlocks the door and turns around. "Hope you're enjoying the new place. That Join Juneberry Lake program sure is something." Then he winks, gets in his car, and drives away.

Despite the stubborn humidity, an unsettling chill runs the length of my entire body. I know I didn't introduce myself and I'm certain that I never mentioned the Juneberry Lake program. When I look down at the card, I realize that my hands are shaking.

"A PRIVATE INVESTIGATOR?" Joel asks. I nod. "That's strange."

Trish sets a plate of bear claws in the center of the table before sliding into the chair beside me. I'd planned to talk with her about my marketing ideas before work today, but Van's morning visit derailed that. Instead, she'd put on a fresh pot of coffee and texted Joel. He'd arrived within a few minutes, looking like he'd just rolled out of bed. I don't think Joel is a morning person. He's been working at the cafe almost every day lately, but he doesn't usually get here until well after ten.

"Eat up," Trish says. "I read somewhere that cinnamon is good for rattled nerves." I'm dubious of the science behind Trish's claim, but as a lifelong consumer of baked goods, I anecdotally agree. Joel and I each grab a claw. Trish smiles with satisfaction.

I take a sip of my coffee. It's decaf—Trish insisted. "He did give me the creeps," I say. "But he's clearly only interested in finding Erica. I think talking to me was kind of a shot in the dark."

Trish makes a face. "I don't like it. A strange man sniffing around for information about a woman who clearly doesn't want to be found? It's not right."

"So what do you know about this Erica person?" Joel asks. He's already polished off his bear claw.

I recount everything I know, which really isn't much. When I finish, Joel sighs. "It is a little weird that she left without a trace," he concedes.

"But I talk to people who want to leave their current lives behind for one reason or another almost every day," Trish says. "Just like you, Eliza."

"My friends and family at least know where I am," I say glumly.

She pats my hand. "I'm just teasing."

"Did you know Erica? Did she ever come in here?" I ask.

Trish's eyes go to the ceiling as if recalling a memory. "Oh sure. She was lovely—smart, vibrant, pretty. And very outgoing. She always had that little dog with her, but I never saw her with her husband."

"Did she ever talk about wanting to move?"

"No, we never talked about anything that serious. Mostly just the weather or the festival. She always seemed to be in a good mood. Although . . ."

I perk up at that, scooting forward on my seat.

"Although?" Joel says, mirroring my posture.

"Well, there was this one time. She came into the coffee shop with this other woman—the one with bright red hair?—and she seemed pretty rattled."

"Gal," I confirm. "Do you know what she was talking about?"

"She kept saying 'He's going to find out. He's going to take everything.'" Trish scrunches her nose. "I figured it had something to do with the divorce. Gary had already moved to Minneapolis by then."

I sigh. Just last night, I'd resolved to let the Erica thing go. But there's no way I can do that now. "This might sound dumb, but I feel connected to her. I mean, I'm living in her house surrounded by a bunch of her stuff, hanging out with her old neighbors, drinking out of her wineglasses. And now there's this private investigator . . . I have to know where she went. And why."

"It might not be any of your business," Trish says gently.

"But what if she's running from something? Or needs help? What if her husband is a monster and someone needs to warn her that he's looking for her?"

Joel clears his throat. "This is dark but, is it possible that she could be, you know . . . dead?"

I shake my head. "No. She took all of her clothes and personal belongings. She definitely left on purpose."

"Right. Good," Joel says. "We don't need a murder in Juneberry Lake."

"That sounds like a *Dateline* episode," I say.

"Exactly," Joel says gravely. Trish lets out a throaty laugh.

I take another sip of coffee and I swear I can taste the absence of caffeine. I might have to sneak over to Cricket's for a coke or something after this.

"What about the Realtor?" Trish suggests. "She used Donna Chu—maybe she'll know something."

"Donna's my neighbor. I'll give her a call," Joel offers, standing.

"You don't have to do it right now."

"It'll just take a minute." Joel smirks. "Besides, you've piqued my curiosity."

Trish shimmies her shoulders. "This is kind of fun. I like having you in town."

I rub my temples in exasperation. "I don't want to make any trouble," I groan.

Trish rests her hand on my shoulder. "You're not. I think it's sweet that you care. I don't think most folks would expect someone like you to give a hoot about the people of this town."

I look up at her. "Why?"

She shrugs. "People just have ideas about what it means to be from different parts of the country."

I start to say that's not fair, but she's absolutely right. I moved to Juneberry Lake expecting everyone who lived here to be exceedingly friendly and uncomplicated. They are friendly, but life here certainly isn't without complications. Nothing is.

Joel rushes back into the bakery, his brown eyes twinkling with excitement. "I talked to Donna," he says, slightly out of breath. "She couldn't disclose much, but she was able to tell me that Erica's house was sold through a trust. A blind one."

"What does that mean?"

"It means she never met with Erica—they only spoke on the phone twice. The executor of the trust managed everything on her behalf."

"Who's the executor?"

Joel shakes his head. "She couldn't say. But she did tell me the name of the trust." He looks down at his phone. "TRH Holdings." Joel looks at me. "Does that sound familiar?"

I tap my pursed lips, thinking. "I don't think so. At least not off the top of my head."

"I bet it'll come to you," Trish assures me.

Joel bobs his head in agreement. "Definitely. And in the meantime, Trish and I are dying to hear about your ideas for taking Black Bear Brew international."

My temples were just starting to throb, so I welcome the change of subject. But I definitely need to manage Joel's expectations. I'm good at my job, but not *that* good. "Let's not get ahead of ourselves."

"National?"

I bring my hands together, signaling something even smaller. "I was thinking regional."

Joel grins. "I like that. Think global, act local."

I grin back. "Something like that."

We must hold each other's gaze a bit too long because Trish starts waving her hand between us. "Jeez, get a room you two," she teases. I know she's just joking, but my cheeks warm ever so slightly. Joel doesn't seem to notice.

The three of us spend the rest of the morning discussing my laundry list of ideas, including, but not limited to a social media campaign, newsletter, holiday catering, a delivery and to-go service, winter baking classes, and a remote worker loyalty program. Trish's eyes only cross a few times and she promises to think everything over before our next meeting. I should feel good about the whole endeavor, but in the end, my thoughts keep drifting back to Erica.

Chapter Twenty-One

The next morning, I decide to forgo my usual trip into town to work at the coffee shop so that I can talk to Lynette while the kids are still at camp. This Erica thing is spiraling out of control. What started as a bid to avoid whatever missteps my predecessor made has turned into something much bigger. People are looking for Erica and my neighbors are hiding something.

I find Lynette sipping coffee on her back patio with Stuart. They're sitting under a big striped umbrella, facing out toward the lake.

"Eliza?" Lynette says, rising from her chair. "Is everything okay?"

"Can we talk?"

She looks at Stuart and then turns back to me. "Of course," she says, gesturing for me to join them at the patio table.

Stuart takes a hurried gulp of his coffee as I approach and then stands abruptly. "I was actually just leaving," he says. "Thanks for the lattes, Lynette."

Lynette gives Stuart an absent-minded wave before he disappears around the front of her house. "He comes over for coffee when he gets writer's block," she explains. "Which seems to be about every day lately."

I'd never allowed myself the luxury of having writer's block—not that writing marketing copy was the same as writing a wildly popular novel—but still. The idea of being creatively stagnant seemed like an indulgence.

"So what's going on?" Lynette asks as she settles back into her chair. Her hair is swept up into a claw clip and she's wearing a matching rust-colored terry cloth tank top and short set. If I didn't have more pressing matters to discuss, I'd ask her where she got her outfit.

Lynette's cheeks, reddened by the summer heat drain of color as I begin to detail my run-in with Van Fischer. By the time I tell her about his parting words, she's sunken back into her chair, her face drawn.

"I don't like to gossip," she says. It feels like the beginning of something, so I don't respond. She looks up at me, her green eyes pleading. "Erica and I were friends, but her life got . . . complicated. It's not my story to share."

I nod in understanding. Maybe all of Lynette's caginess around Erica was out of loyalty to her friend. "Gary moved out years ago," she says more to herself than to me. "I can't imagine why he'd be trying to contact Erica now."

"Did you know him well?"

She shakes her head. "He's in-house counsel for some big corporation in Minneapolis, so he wasn't home much. I was under the impression that he and Erica lived separate lives."

"Do they have any kids?"

"No, just her dog, Phil. They tried when they first got together, but it didn't happen for them. I think Erica felt that it all worked out for the best, given what a huge ass he was."

I absorb the information like a blow, my heart sinking for Erica. "So they've been divorced for years?"

Lynette tilts her hand back and forth. "Erica held off on making things final because Gary is such a high-powered attorney. He'd gotten all of his buddies to tell Erica they couldn't represent her. She was worried she wouldn't get anything in the divorce. She was trapped in this limbo, separated but still married."

This was why I'd insisted that Marco and I sign a prenup. Not that we ended up needing it. "What changed?"

Lynette shrugs. "I don't know," she says. She sounds tired. "Gary got engaged to someone new—I'm pretty sure she's an executive assistant at his firm. She's a good ten years younger than Erica."

"Typical."

Lynette rolls her eyes. "I know. Anyway, Erica was tired of fighting and Gary was suddenly motivated to play ball. I don't know the details, but it worked out that Erica got the house and Gary got to waive spousal support."

"Do you think he's mad that she sold the house?"

"Your guess is as good as mine." She rubs the bridge of her nose. "Maybe? But I can't imagine why it would matter to him."

I bite my lip. "Should we try to warn her?"

"I can try her old number," Lynette says. "But let's not get our hopes up. In the meantime, if that investigator comes back, don't tell him a thing."

"I won't," I assure her.

"Good," she says, biting her thumbnail. "That's good."

WORD ABOUT VAN's visit got around the neighborhood faster than I could say "scummy private investigator." Stuart brought me a bottle of chokecherry liqueur, Lynette dropped off a hot dish, Marge tucked her cell phone number on a scrap of paper inside my mailbox with a note telling me that I could call her anytime.

Bob went out of his way to let me know that he owns a gun, which, given his temperament, made me feel even less safe.

On the bright side, my neighbors were suddenly much more forthcoming with information about their relationship with Erica. It's not that they didn't like her, it's that they hated Gary.

And I think they might also be hurt by the way Erica left. I believe them when they say they don't know where she went. The whole thing just feels like a sore spot, a bruise I've been poking at.

I feel partially responsible for dredging up the past, like my arrival to town and my curiosity about Erica summoned Van Fischer.

"Erica's ex was a real piece of work," Gal says, during one of our now daily afternoon walks. Marge never joins, always flitting off to one of her mysterious meetings. "I never liked him."

While I genuinely appreciated my neighbors' shows of support, their reactions also made me a bit nervous. "He's not like, dangerous is he?"

"Gary?" Gal laughs at the thought, Darla the Chihuahua bouncing along in the bedazzled carrier Gal has strapped to her chest. "No, not in the least. He's a sleaze, but he wouldn't hurt a fly."

I swipe my arm along my forehead in an attempt to stave off a flood of sweat. The sun has positioned itself directly overhead and there's not a cloud in the sky. "What about the PI?"

Gal moves Benny's leash from one hand to the other in an effort to untangle the pack. "You've been reading too many of those books Stuart loaned you. That guy was just rattling your cage to see if you know anything, which you don't. I bet you won't see him again."

With a shiver, I think back to Van staring up at my porch the day I arrived. I hope she's right.

We continue along the lake path and Potato quickly finds a shady spot to take care of her business. I pull a baggie out of my back pocket to pick up said business as she supervises. I've only known this little dog for a few weeks, but she's already the boss of me.

"But that reminds me," Gal says. "There's something I wanted to ask you about."

I tie a knot in the top of the bag and toss it into a designated pet waste bin along the trail. Potato leans against my leg, whining softly. That's her signal that she's done walking for the day. I pick her up and she gives my chin a single lick as if to say, *thank you.* "Okay."

Gal pushes her sparkly sunglasses to the top of her head. "Marge and I have been talking and we figured that since you probably get a little lonely in that house of yours, you might want some company." Her eyes float from me to Potato and then back to me. "Would you be interested in adopting Potato?"

My hand is pressed against Potato's little chest and I can feel her heart beating against her sternum. It's as if she knew Gal was going to ask me this question and is now nervously anticipating my answer.

My brain automatically kicks into analytic mode. Weighing pros and cons is a reflex for me at this point, like breathing. On one hand, I wasn't supposed to get a dog for a couple more years. I was of course going to adopt from a shelter because I didn't want to disappoint Sarah McLachlan. But that plan—along with the rest of my life—has gone to pieces. I'm probably not in the best position to embrace any more change.

On the other hand, it would be nice to have a companion, especially if Van shows his face again. Not that Potato is much of a guard dog, but that's beside the point. I *did* come to Juneberry Lake for a fresh start, so I should be open to unexpected opportunities like this.

I look down at Potato and take in her big brown eyes, her soft ears, her wet little nose. I think about the way she cocks her head when she's confused and the wrinkle that forms between her eyebrows when she's worried and the way her entire body wiggles with excitement when I come over to walk her.

I swear I hear Sarah singing "in the arms of the angel" in my head. Maybe this is one of those decisions that can't be made with logic. I've fallen in love with this dog and I want her to be mine. So I say yes.

Gal does an excited little jump. "I was hoping you'd say that. You were meant to be her mama."

I don't know if it's Gal's enthusiasm, or Potato's warm little body, or the idea of me being this sweet dog's adoptive mom or that damn Sarah McLachlan song, but I'm suddenly flooded with tears. I sink to the grass with Potato still in my arms and she swivels around to lick the salty streams rolling down my cheeks.

Gal digs a tissue out from her fanny pack and dangles it in front of me. "I hope those are good tears."

I'm honestly not sure, but I nod all the same before accepting the crinkled Kleenex. It's a good two minutes before I can talk again, but when I do, I feel so much lighter. Like I've finally let something go.

"I'm sorry," I say, dabbing at my eyes. "I don't know what came over me."

Potato hops out of my lap and starts sniffing at Titan's backside, apparently satisfied that I'm going to be okay.

"No need to apologize for having feelings, hun. Feelings are good. They remind us that we're alive."

"Thanks, Gal." I climb to my feet.

She gives my arm a reassuring pat. "Why don't we swing by the house and load you up with dog supplies? No need to waste a trip to the pet store when we have everything you'll need at home."

Gal's kindness makes me feel like I could start bawling all over again. But I force myself to hold off on any further displays of emotion until Potato and I get home.

Chapter Twenty-Two

Before

Marco was a miracle baby. His mother had been told by multiple doctors that she wouldn't be able to carry a child to term, but after years of trying and far too many losses, along came Marco.

"We prayed him into existence," Marco's mom would say whenever she told the story. "Our little miracle."

Marco and I didn't mention our struggles with fertility to our parents because we were all but certain they wouldn't understand. First, the idea that we would resort to medical intervention *before* we'd ever tried to have a baby the old-fashioned way would have been incredibly confusing to them. Second, the fact that we were doing this before we were even married would have set off a chorus of Hail Marys. And finally, the news that biological children might not be in the cards for us might have sent at least one of our parents to an early grave.

My mom, bless her, was an old-school Italian in just about every way. The woman still believed that pregnancy was contagious.

I did confide in Enzo, who couldn't have been more supportive about the whole thing. "I researched your condition," he told me. "I know it's disappointing, but there are a lot of women who go on to have children in other ways. You could get a donor egg or you could adopt. There are also plenty of women who don't have children but live very fulfilling lives." He sounded like he was reading from a Wikipedia page, which he probably was. Research was one of his love languages.

I don't remember the exact phrasing I used when I shared the news with my friends at our monthly happy hour, but I do remember their collective expressions of horror, pity, and grief.

"You should just start trying to get pregnant unassisted now," Brittany said. "You never know what could happen and you don't want to waste any time. This same thing happened to my friend from high school. She was told she couldn't have kids but now she's pregnant with her second."

"Definitely get a second opinion," Carmen added. "It might just take a few more rounds, but it'll be so worth it in the end." That was easy for Carmen to say. Her wife, Daisy, had been the one to endure "just" a few rounds. They'd banked six healthy embryos and if I'm being honest were kind of smug about it.

"You and Marco have to have kids," Farah said. "You'll make the best parents ever and you'll look so cute pregnant."

None of it was what I wanted to hear. What I wanted to hear was that this didn't change the way they looked at me, that I didn't have to have kids to make myself whole, that no matter what happened, things would be okay. Toxic positivity belonged on Instagram—not in my uterus.

Finding out that I was infertile in such a roundabout way was disorienting, and eventually I realized that I needed to talk to a therapist.

That's how I found Nora.

We met every Thursday afternoon for months. I couldn't see it at the time, but I was slowly making my way through the stages of grief: denial (*Those first two rounds were just flukes! This is go-*

ing to work out fine), anger (*If Dr. Ramirez was good at her job, she would have known to start me on these steroids sooner!*), bargaining (*Maybe this is my fault for wanting to wait until I was older. If only I hadn't drank so much Red Bull in college. Maybe I can make up for it now by tripling my folic acid intake?*), depression (just a lot of sobbing), and eventually, acceptance.

"I'm not going to be able to have a biological baby," I finally said. I remember looking out the window of Nora's office and noticing that it was sunny.

"How does that make you feel?"

When I first started seeing Nora, the answer would have been crushed. Devastated. Inconsolable. The possibility of never holding my newborn baby in my arms, of never watching her take her first steps or hanging her artwork on the refrigerator or making her pose for way too many photos in her prom dress elicited a grief like I'd never known. I'm not saying that feeling was gone now—Nora had helped me to see that it would always be a part of me—but it no longer held the same power.

"I feel . . . relieved."

Nora leaned forward, resting her forearms on the tops of her thighs. A pair of glasses dangled from her left hand. "Interesting. In what way?"

I knew by then that when Nora said something was interesting we were getting close to a breakthrough.

"I wish I could have a baby of my own, but I can't keep putting myself or my body through these treatments. I'm relieved because I know I tried and now I know it's time to move on."

"What do you think moving on looks like?"

"It looks like telling Marco that I'm not going to do another round. Ever."

"How do you think he's going to take it?"

I looked down at my clasped hands, fingers intertwined. I did that sometimes to comfort myself. "I'm worried that he's going to be disappointed."

"That's valid. And Marco is an adult who can handle being disappointed."

I knew Nora was right but it would take me months to tell Marco the truth. As far as he was concerned, we were just taking a break so that we could focus on the wedding. I don't think he ever moved past denial. And he refused to go to therapy.

Not even as a couple.

Eventually, Nora and I started to talk about what my life after infertility could look like. Maybe Marco and I would carve out a different path to parenthood, one that would feel even more meaningful and miraculous in the wake of everything we'd been through.

But a new vision started to emerge too, one I'd never considered.

I didn't *have* to have a baby.

I thought about my aunt Paula and my dad's cousin Rex, one divorced and one never married, both living full, happy, successful child-free lives. I made a list of public figures I admired who never had children—Oprah, Helen Mirren, Sandra Oh, Louisa May Alcott.

The idea that I could be happy whatever my future held—kids or not—filled me with a newfound sense of hope. I could continue to work toward my goals, and live a full life, and love my family, and hang out with my friends. Infertility wouldn't define me.

I was ready to shed the scarlet I.

More than anything, I was excited about deciding on a path forward together. With Marco.

This wasn't some self-protective defense mechanism. It was a realization that I'd worked toward, slowly and ploddingly, a concept that emerged alongside my grief. It wasn't a conclusion I'd reached lightly.

But in the end, none of that seemed to matter to anyone but me. It was like Marco and my friends were stuck on some kind of programming loop.

But you can't give up. You're still grieving. You're meant to be a mom. This is your mountain to climb, your Everest to conquer. It'll all be so worth it in the end.

It was like they couldn't wrap their minds around my new reality. I desperately wanted them to understand that I wasn't giving up. I wasn't quitting. I was making a conscious choice to move forward with my life, to be okay. The fact they refused to believe me hurt more than a lifetime of needle jabs and swollen ovaries ever could.

I never would have imagined that the hard-won epiphany that brought me so much peace would be the very thing that would threaten to throw my closest relationships into turmoil.

I found myself missing Hannah more viscerally than I had in years. She would have understood. She would have known just what to say.

For some reason, the thought also made me angry, too. Because she should have been here.

Chapter Twenty-Three

I can't believe that I've lived my entire adult life without a dog.
Aside from a couple of miscommunications about potty breaks
and Potato's penchant for stealing my sandals and making me
chase her around the house, she's settled in remarkably well. At
first I was a little worried about how she'd navigate the stairs, but
she flies up and down them like a champ. She loves sitting in my
lap on the porch in the evenings while I watch the fireflies and
we sleep snuggled side by side every night. In the mornings, she
wakes me with a gentle lick on the tip of my nose.

It's only been a few days and I'm already having a tough time
remembering what life was like before Potato. It feels like she's
always been mine and I've always been hers.

My parents have taken to FaceTiming me first thing in the
morning for their daily Potato fix. Dad marvels at her resilience,
declaring, "And she does it all with just three legs," at least once
during every call. Mom peppers me with suggestions for treats that
I can give to Potato. "Spaghetti used to love carrots and apples," she
reminds me, before gravely adding, "But he hated blueberries."

The way my parents manage to dote on Potato through a
screen makes my heart ache. They would make such wonderful
grandparents.

"When can we come visit?" Mom asks. She's clutching a
steaming cup of coffee. It's only 5 a.m. their time but honestly,

she doesn't need the caffeine. Mom has more natural energy than anyone I know.

"We can't leave Enzo alone at the bakery," Dad reminds her. His voice sounds heavy and a bit sluggish. He's never been much of a morning person.

"So we'll close the bakery," Mom says. "We'll come for your birthday."

"How about you all come the week of Christmas," I suggest. Mom makes a face like she's just swallowed a spoonful of vinegar. "It'll be here before you know it and you've already planned to close for the holiday."

It hadn't occurred to me when I agreed to adopt Potato that my ability to travel would be hindered. I have no idea how she'd do on an airplane and I certainly don't want to leave her behind if I make a trip home. Gal said that Potato was welcome at their house anytime, but I'm worried that she might misinterpret that as me returning her to them. So, I'm staying put in Juneberry Lake for the time being. At least until Potato has lived with me for enough time to trust that I'll always come back for her.

Dad bobs his head in agreement. "That's a great idea, Elisabetta. Maybe Enzo and his new girlfriend can come too."

Enzo and Allison had been on two dates (a movie and dinner—not on the same night), so I was pretty sure they weren't an official couple yet. But I appreciate Dad's optimism.

"It's settled then," Dad says. "We'll come for the week of Christmas."

"I'm going to book our flights when we hang up," Mom agrees. She looks like she's about to bounce through the screen.

"Great. You can all stay with Potato and me."

"Where else would we stay?" Mom huffs.

"If you have any emergencies before then, we'll fly out to you right away," Dad reiterates. "And if it's very urgent, your nonno had a cousin—Jerry—in New Jersey. I'll get you his number."

"The flight from New Jersey is just as long as the flight from San Francisco."

"Just in case," Dad says.

"Didn't Nonno's cousin Jerry go to prison for stealing a bunch of money from a charity?"

"So?" Dad asks. "He's family."

I suspect Dad would use the "it's family" card to excuse just about anything. *Didn't she invade a sovereign country under false pretenses? Yes, but she's* family.

I hang up with my parents and give Potato a scratch behind the ear as I marvel at how she's managed to make me feel closer to them than I have in a very long time.

I STARTED TO feel guilty about ignoring my friends back home, so I texted them some pictures of Potato. One is of her lounging in an Adirondack chair on my back porch, another is an action shot of her running around the yard, and the final is a selfie of the two of us. We're both smiling.

Brittany: ???

Farah: OMG

Carmen: What is happening

Farah: She's so cute!

Brittany: Is it missing a leg

Carmen: So you're really not coming back are you?

Farah: She can still come back!

Brittany: The leg though?

It was probably my fault for texting them out of the blue without any context, but I couldn't pretend I wasn't hurt by their mixed responses. Especially Brittany's. I'm starting to wonder whether we're even friends anymore. I can't remember the last time she said something that made me feel supported or understood or even vaguely amused.

I give them a quick backstory and tell them how much I adore Potato. Carmen says that's great, Brittany hearts my message, and Farah texts me on the side.

Farah: I'm really happy for you and Potato! She's the cutest dog in the world. I miss you! Can we maybe schedule a phone date soon? Maybe a FaceTime so I can meet Little Miss P?

Me: I'd love that

Me: BTW have you talked to Marco?

Farah: Of course not! Team Eliza all the way

Farah and I have always been the closest of our group. If she were the one helping Marco to keep tabs on me, I'd be devastated. I want to believe her.

I'm about to tell her I'm free next week when I get a text from Marco.

> **Marco:** I hear you got a dog? Send pics.

> **Marco:** Maybe we can FaceTime soon?

I DECIDED TO work exclusively from home for the duration of Potato's first week with me, but today is the day that she makes her debut at Black Bear Brew. I couldn't be more excited and by the way her whole body wiggles as we walk out the door, I think she's excited, too.

I load Potato into the basket on the front of my bike, where I've added a pillow in the bottom and lined the sides with a soft blanket to make sure she's comfy. Her ears fly back as I take off down the lane and I wonder if I should pick up a pair of doggles for her.

When we pull up in front of Black Bear Brew, I'm pleasantly surprised to see Joel standing outside. A small part of me hopes he's been waiting for me, but I know that's ridiculous. He just likes working at the coffee shop.

"Who's this?" he practically coos as Potato and I pull up. My stomach does a heady little thump when I see the way Joel looks at my dog.

I engage my kickstand before taking Potato out of the basket and setting her on the sidewalk. She immediately runs to Joel. He bends to greet her like she's an old friend.

"You got a guard dog," he says, without taking his eyes off Potato. Her little tail wags back and forth so quickly it's a blur.

"Something like that," I reply. "This is Potato."

When Joel looks at me, his smile is wider than I've ever seen it. "I *love* that name."

"Me too. It suits her."

Potato finishes her introduction to Joel and trots back to me. I give her a reassuring pat on the side.

"Is that where you've been all week? There's no way you're getting any work done with this cutie around."

I pick Potato up. "She's actually an excellent coworker," I say, thinking of all the hours she's already logged by my side as I concoct marketing strategies for an array of increasingly ridiculous products. "I mean, she doesn't help at all, but she's happy to nap next to me while I work."

"What a life."

"Tell me about it." I kiss the feathery soft fur behind her ear.

He sighs dramatically. "Now I want one."

"You should meet my neighbors," I say. Joel's face tightens ever so slightly. "They have a rotating pack of foster dogs that they'd love to find homes for. My other neighbor just adopted one, too. Her name is Bubbles."

At that, Joel's shoulders drop. "Bubbles," he says, placing his hands over his heart. "Adorable."

"She is. But not quite as adorable as Potato."

"Obviously."

Potato gives my cheek an appreciative lick.

"Well, I'm glad you're here. I was hoping to run into you. Are you busy this afternoon?" Joel asks.

"No more than usual," I tell him. "Why?"

"I was thinking we could go to city hall."

"Why would we do that?"

He flashes me a conspiratorial smile. "To figure out who's behind the TRH Holdings trust."

Between adopting Potato and trying to keep up with all the work my boss had piled on, I haven't had a chance to fine-tune my strategy for figuring out where Erica went. But I would love to get to the bottom of it. In addition to being plain old curious, I'm also concerned. Erica doesn't want to be found for a reason and it must have something to do with her husband. If I can figure out where she went and put her in touch with Lynette, someone she seems to have trusted, maybe we can warn her before Van has a chance to track her down.

I know all too well how difficult it can be to leave everything you know behind. If I can help someone else hold on to their fresh start, I'm going to do it.

Joel taking the initiative to help me means more than I would have ever expected. I'm momentarily stunned. "Really?" is all I can think to say.

"Oh yeah. I can't resist a good mystery. I'm invested now." He shrugs. "Plus, Pat, the receptionist owes me a favor that I've been dying to call in."

I realize I'm practically beaming. "That would be great," I say. I make a mental note to text Gal to let her know that I won't be able to make our afternoon walk today.

Joel returns my almost-beam. "I'm glad you think so."

AROUND LUNCHTIME, TRISH plops a platter of tomato and hummus sandwiches—seasoned with dill and lemon zest—and a carafe of iced coffee down on the center of the table before setting a glass in front of me and then Joel, who doesn't look up from his laptop. "Is now a good time to talk about your presentation from the other day?" she asks.

I take a sip of Trish's coffee, my second cup of the day. My caffeine tolerance is going to be sky high before this summer is over. I'd been planning to work through lunch so that Joel and I would have enough time at city hall today, but I'm too excited to hear what Trish has to say to turn her down. I gesture for her to join me at the table.

"Well," she says, as she eases down into the chair beside me, "I've had some time to digest everything we talked about and I have to say, I've never seen such a thorough, thoughtful presentation before in my life." It sounds like a compliment and a critique.

I take it in stride because it's not the first time I've heard that. I'm nothing if not thorough in all aspects of my life. "I know my ideas can be a little overwhelming."

"Like drinking from a firehose," Trish says.

"Or Niagara Falls," Joel jokes. He closes his laptop. I guess he's invested in this now, too.

"In a good way," Trish adds.

"Wow, you two are hilarious," I say sarcastically, before turning my full attention to Trish. "So what're you thinking?"

She picks up a sandwich from the plate at the center of the table and examines it thoughtfully. Potato leans forward in my lap, her little nose twitching. "I know you said that we should focus on a few key ideas, so I'm thinking the baking classes, the loyalty program, and the holiday catering." She sticks out a finger as she lists each one.

I scrunch my shoulders with excitement. "Those were the ones I was hoping you'd pick."

Trish's face lights up. I love the way her cheeks crease when she smiles. "Great minds think alike." She takes a bite out of her sandwich.

"No delivery business?" Joel asks. "Isn't that what worked for your parents' bakery?"

"Her parents' bakery doesn't get snowed in."

"Fair point," Joel says. "So, what's next?"

I rub my hands together. "Now the fun begins."

By the end of my meeting with Trish I feel more energized about work than I have in years. And I'm not even getting paid! I like the challenge of working with limited resources and a discerning customer base. I think designing campaigns that center on delicious baked goods might be my calling.

After lunch, Joel steps out to call ahead to his friend at city hall as I help Trish bus our table. Potato follows at my heels. "He sure has been spending a lot of time here," Trish says, jerking her head toward the window.

My phone pings and I ignore it. I'm almost positive that it's Jordan checking my progress on the MeMeter pitch. I promised I'd get it to them a week ago, but I had to ask to push my deadline back. And I haven't even started on CanScan yet. I'm just not as fast or efficient here. Maybe the slower pace of life has started to affect my work.

"What do you mean?" I ask.

Trish shoots me a look. "Come on, Eliza. You're a smart woman."

My neck feels suddenly hot. "He probably just gets bored working at home all the time," I say, sounding more defensive than I mean to. I cross my arms. "Besides, he's in like—a situation-ship—or something."

Trish balks. "First of all, that's not a real word and second of all, I haven't seen him hanging around with anyone but you," she says, stepping behind the counter.

With that, Joel walks back into the café. He's wearing almost the exact same outfit as the day we met—a T-shirt from a local brewery, cargo shorts, and sandals—but I don't see a dorky tourist anymore. I see Joel. Sweet, smart, do-gooder Joel.

I just wish he wasn't so cute.

Chapter Twenty-Four

City hall isn't a hall at all. It's a well-preserved Victorian mansion, with a steep pitched roof, an expansive front porch, and ornate cast-iron railings. Sunlight reflects off the stained-glass windows, winking yellow, red, and green. I feel like I'm stepping back in time as I climb the front steps. I wonder who lived here back when it was a home. Whoever they were, I hope they didn't have to wear those awful corsets.

A woman behind an imposing wood desk who must be Pat jumps up at the sight of Joel in a way that's not dissimilar from how Potato reacts when I tell her it's time for dinner. She's wearing a white blouse and a floral skirt; her hair is pulled back into a smart gray bun. "There's my Joel," she says, her raspy voice drips with affection.

"Hey there, Pat." Joel leans over the desk to give her a hug. She unironically pinches his cheeks. They catch up briefly as Potato and I hang off to the side. Joel asks about Pat's daughter and she asks about his parents. They're both looking forward to the Summer Festival at the end of the month.

Joel gestures to me and Potato. "So, my friends and I were hoping to take a little peek at the records room."

When Pat looks in my direction, she makes a half-hearted attempt at curving her lips upward. I'm not offended in the least—Joel is much more charming than I am. "You got it," she says, as she starts digging around in a drawer. She produces a

ring of keys and passes them to Joel. "You're technically supposed to make an appointment and fill out a form for this sort
of thing, but I'll let you slide."

"What did you do to get that woman to love you so much?" I
mutter under my breath as we make our way down the hall.

Joel twirls the key ring on his index finger. "A gentleman
never tells."

"Shut up." I laugh, giving him a playful shove.

Joel returns my grin. "Her house flooded a few months back
on the weekend of her daughter's wedding. I offered to put her
whole family—six people, two kids, and three cats—up at my
place. I guess I kind of saved the day."

The fact that Joel would open his home up to a family in need
doesn't surprise me. The fact that he has room for that many
people (and cats) does. "How big is your house?"

Joel stops in the middle of the hallway, feigning annoyance.
"Haven't we been over this? A gentleman never tells."

"It's huge then?"

Joel flashes me a suggestive smirk that sends my stomach into
a backflip. "That's for me to know and you to find out." It feels
like maybe we aren't talking about his house anymore.

The mood instantly shifts when we step inside the records
room. It's dimly lit and not particularly large—maybe about the
size of my basement—and smells like an old library. The door
creaks closed behind us. "Pat said that each of these cabinets are
labeled by category," Joel says. "We're looking for marriage and
divorce records, estates and trusts, and home sales." He points
to the right. "You want to go that way and I'll go this way?" he
gestures with his head toward the left.

I run my finger along the old filing cabinets, squinting at the
peeling labels as I go. I pass municipal ordinances, meeting

minutes, census data, election records, and personnel files before I find a cabinet labeled divorce decrees. The fact that it's a smaller cabinet than the adjacent one that contains marriage licenses gives me a little zip of satisfaction. Leave it to Juneberry Lake to best the national average. Even if they've yet to digitize their files.

Erica's last name is Donaldson, so I figure her file will be toward the top. I slide the first drawer open and look for the Ds and quickly find a manila folder with Erica's name on it. I skim the pages in search of pertinent information—although I'm not even sure what would be considered pertinent. I've never seen a divorce record before. Erica and Gary finalized their divorce on August 8, 2023. The reason for the dissolution of the marriage was irreconcilable differences. Gary wouldn't pay Erica any alimony and Erica would retain ownership of the house. Gary kept his sizable 401(k) but they divided their savings and bonds up evenly—each walking away with the equivalent of about half a million dollars.

Erica would get custody of Phil the one-eyed poodle, thank god.

I read through the remainder of the document, but nothing of interest jumps out at me. No one was changing their name, there were no children to argue about custody over, no restraining orders. From what I could tell, this looked like a pretty straightforward divorce. Just like Lynette had said.

I make my way over to Joel with the file in one hand and Potato in the other. When I find him, he's standing over an open drawer, flipping through the contents of a red folder. "Find anything?"

Joel furrows his brow. "I struck out with TRH Holdings. There's no record of it here in Juneberry Lake. Maybe it was opened in another city or with the county."

"I think the divorce record is a bit of a dead end too," I say, passing him the file. "Everything looks pretty straightforward."

Joel skims it and nods. He passes the file back to me.

"I can't believe we're striking out."

"Don't lose hope yet," Joel says, returning his attention to the file he was reading before. "I'm looking over the property records for your house now. Maybe there will be some mention of the trust."

"Maybe," I mutter before returning the divorce file to its proper cabinet. I circle back to where I left Joel, but this time, instead of finding him poring over pages of real estate jargon, he's holding up a piece of paper as if it were a prize catch.

"Did you find something?" I ask, my voice rising involuntarily.

He passes me the paper. It's a petition to add a party to the deed.

"Erica requested that Bob Holt be added," Joel blurts before I can finish reading.

"As in the old curmudgeon who lives next door to me?"

"One in the same."

I look at the paper again, needing to see his name in black and white. It's there. Right next to Erica's.

"Do you think he might have anything to do with TRH Holdings?" Joel asks.

Realization dawns slowly at first and then all at once. Bob's wife's name was Tammy and Bob is, of course, short for Robert. Their last name is Holt. TRH.

Trust Bob. The note I'd found scrawled on the business card at the bottom of Erica's junk drawer wasn't a question of whether or not she could trust Bob. It was about Bob's trust.

"Bob is behind TRH Holdings."

"Are you sure?"

For a moment, I curse myself for not putting it together before. But why would I have? From what I know of Bob, there's no earthly reason why Erica would want him on the deed to her house. It doesn't make any sense.

"Positive," I say. "But I have no idea what to make of it."

"We'll figure it out," Joel says reassuringly. Then he snaps a photo of the petition before tucking the file back into its place. I watch as he eases the cabinet closed.

Even though we got what we came for—or at least some of it—I find myself wishing we could stay here in this quiet, dimly lit room just a little bit longer.

Chapter Twenty-Five

I've just sat down to put the finishing touches on the MeMeter presentation I owe Jordan by the end of the day (I'm cutting it closer than ever) when Joel texts me.

> **Joel:** Any luck with the deed?

> **Me:** I haven't mentioned it to my neighbors yet. Don't want them to think I'm digging into their lives.

> **Joel:** Fair enough. Any other ideas?

That's when I remember Erica's mail. As far as I know, Lynette hasn't been able to get in touch with her, so it doesn't look like I'm going to have any way to return it. Maybe it's time to dig into those unopened envelopes.

> **Me:** Maybe. Are you free tonight?

> **Joel:** I'm all yours.

I'M A LITTLE nervous to have Joel over to my house, but I know I shouldn't be. We're friends.

Still, I rush through my presentation and send it off to Jordan without taking my usual third, fourth, and fifth review passes so that I can spend the rest of the day tidying up and assembling an Instagram-worthy charcuterie board before slipping into my favorite sundress. I even chill the wine.

Joel shows up at the back door, as if he's been over a million times before. "Too embarrassed to be seen with me?" I ask as I open the screen.

He's wearing a short-sleeved button-down shirt and shorts without superfluous pockets. It's the most dressed up I've ever seen him. "I thought it'd be nice to walk around the lake path," he says, turning back to look at where he'd come from. "It's more scenic."

Potato wriggles at my feet, eager for Joel to join us. I step aside and gesture for him to come in.

"Great place," he says, taking in Erica's decor.

"I can't take any credit—it's all Erica. Do you want anything to drink? Wine? Lemonade? Sparkling water?"

Joel nudges me with his elbow. "Someone's been to the market."

"Just wait until you see my charcuterie board."

He raises his eyebrows. "Sounds like we're in for quite a night."

This is weird. Are we flirting? There are a million and one reasons why I shouldn't—can't—flirt with Joel. I clear my throat. "Drinks?"

He crinkles his nose. "Will you think less of me if I ask for a glass of rosé?"

"Are you kidding? I hail from the land of rosé all day. I've never felt better about our friendship." If Joel is put off by the way I emphasize the word "friendship," he doesn't show it.

I pour us each a glass of cool, crisp pink wine—the type of wine Marco refused to drink with me. Not that I'm comparing. Joel scoops Potato into his arms and holds her like a baby. He accepts the glass with a free hand. "Cheers," he says. "To . . . becoming amateur detectives?"

I clink my glass against his. "And to breaking federal laws."

He nearly drops his wine. "I'm sorry what did I just agree to?"

"It's probably best if you have a whole glass under your belt before we get into the specifics."

He shakes his head. "You're something else, Frisco." He takes another long drink.

"THIS IS AWESOME," Joel says, his head swiveling as he looks around the basement. I'm not sure why I expected Joel to be as uneasy about my subterranean lair as I was the first time I saw it. He's a born-and-bred Midwesterner. This is normal to him.

I plonk the bottle of rosé down on the coffee table in the center of the room. "I guess it's not so bad down here."

"Are you kidding? In this part of the world, a finished basement is goals. You've made it."

"Where I'm from, a finished basement is affordable rent," I say, thinking back to Brittany's first apartment, a below-ground one-bedroom with a converted living room/bedroom setup. It was under a restaurant and natural light was nearly impossible to come by, but it was the only way she could afford to live in the trendy Marina neighborhood. Sure, she had a minor rat issue, but we could walk to all of our favorite bars from her place.

The things you tolerate in your early twenties.

"So why did you lure me down here? Should I be nervous?"

I gesture toward the storage bins full of Erica's mail. "We're going to sort through someone else's mail." I go on to explain my earlier discovery and my reasons for wanting to open the letters I hadn't looked at yet.

When I finish, Joel twists his mouth, a signal that he's

considering his options. "Okay, I'm in." My shoulders sag with relief. "On one condition."

My shoulders creep back up again. "What's that?"

"That you'll let me play that vintage Nintendo when we're done."

I've been meaning to see if that thing still worked. It's been years—decades actually—since I played old-school Nintendo. I like these terms. "You're on. But I hope you don't mind losing because I'm basically an expert at video games."

"Well prepare to be wowed because I'm an incredibly gracious loser."

"Don't you mean prepare to be J Wowed?"

Joel raises his chin in mock indignance. "I'm going to pretend you didn't just say that."

I pull the bins off the shelves and we settle cross-legged on the floor. Potato curls up in my lap and falls asleep almost instantly. We start by setting aside the mail I've already looked through, along with the newspapers, which leaves us with about one bin's worth of envelopes.

Joel picks up a pink envelope and places his finger along the lip. He tears it open unceremoniously, pulls out the paper and scans it before tossing it aside. "Junk," is all he says. And so it begins.

As we work our way through the never-ending pile of mail, pausing to examine, then discard the contents—me neatly and Joel haphazardly, which I try not to hold against him—we start talking. About work, about our families, about life.

"I'm sort of the oddball of my family," Joel muses. "My parents and my sisters are super organized. They do all the right things in the exact right order. Graduate college, get a job, fall in love by twenty-five, buy a house with a white picket fence, have two children, own a golden retriever."

I know the type all too well. "It sounds like we'd get along swimmingly."

"You're not like that. Last year, I bet you'd never even heard of Juneberry Lake. And now you live here. My family would never."

"But you did."

He shrugs. "Like I said. I'm the oddball."

"Why do you think that is?"

"I have my theories, but ultimately I'm just not wired like they are. I wouldn't say I have wanderlust, necessarily, but I am allergic to feeling like I don't have options. I hate the idea of my whole life being planned out from the moment I was born. What's the point of living if you already know what's going to happen?"

"I think it makes some people feel safe."

"But they aren't really, are they? Life is unpredictable. I just think it's better to roll with the punches and adapt as you go."

"That's one way of looking at it."

"Right? Look at me broadening your perspective. Aren't you glad you met me?"

I toss an empty envelope in his direction. "You're all right."

He crumples a piece of paper and throws it at me. It bounces off my shoulder and lands near Potato's head. She doesn't wake up. "I'm a delight and you know it."

"A delight?"

"Yes. A delight. Why? What word would you use?"

I pause to give it some thought. How would I describe Joel? A lovable goofball? A charming do-gooder? A guy who looks unreasonably hot in the shirt that's currently straining against his biceps?

"We can go with delight."

He puffs up his chest. "I told you."

I roll my eyes.

"So, how's the whole *Eat Pray Love* thing working out for you?"

I look around the room and sigh. "Well, I'm waist-deep in a pile of someone else's mail, so clearly it's all coming together."

Joel gives me a sympathetic smile, revealing a pair of dimples. "You're doing better than you give yourself credit for."

I mumble a half-hearted thank-you to Joel, but my focus is no longer on him. Because I'm holding a payment reminder for Erica's student loans. She owes more than a thousand dollars a month and that mostly just covers the interest. She's more than $200,000 in debt.

"Did you find something?"

"Maybe." I hold up the bill. "Erica had massive student loan debt."

Joel takes the paper and his eyes widen as he looks at the amount. "Almost a quarter of a million dollars? Damn. Was she a doctor or something?"

I nod. "A vet."

He passes the paper back to me. "Put that in the keep pile."

The bills pile up in quick succession after that. Maxed out credit cards, past-due notices from contractors, a massive home equity line of credit. It looks like Erica had a serious amount of debt, mostly incurred from house projects, clothing purchases, supersized grocery bills, and a company called Dynamo Inc. All pretty reasonable, for the most part. But interesting, nonetheless. I suppose this explains her myriad credit card offers. Those companies can smell blood in the water from miles away.

"What's Dynamo?" Joel asks. "I keep seeing a bunch of charges, all for about twenty bucks."

I take out my phone and type the name into Google. An online gaming company pops up. "I think it's a digital casino."

"Gambling addiction. I knew it."

I shoot him my most sarcastic smirk. "You don't know anything."

We return to the task at hand, ripping open envelopes with renewed vigor.

"Ouch," Joel hisses. He sticks his index finger in his mouth.

I wince. "Paper cut?" He nods. "Want me to find you a Band-Aid?"

He takes his finger out of his mouth and examines it. "No, I'll be fine. It just stings a little."

I set another bill on the growing pile as Joel rises from his spot on the floor. He stretches his arms and arches his back. "I'm going to see if I can find a letter opener. I can't afford another injury." He starts toward the desk on the other side of the room.

"It's empty," I warn, but Joel's already opening drawers and feeling around the back.

He pulls out a few crumpled lotto scratchers and u-pick tickets. He holds them up like evidence. "It's safe to say this lady liked to gamble." He sets them on the top of the desk and resumes his search. "There's something stuck behind this drawer."

When he finally extracts his arm, he's holding a crumpled envelope. He smirks with satisfaction as he passes it to me. "Not so empty after all."

I open the letter and extract a heavy piece of paper. At the top, there's a logo of a cow encircled by writing. It's a little wrinkled, but I'm able to make out Happy Hooves Animal Sanctuary.

"I know this place," I say. "There was a big write-up about them in the *San Francisco Chronicle*. They rescue and rehome farm animals, and the ones who can't go to a new home get to live at the sanctuary." I run my finger over the seal, lost in a memory. I'd always wanted to go to one of their volunteer days with Marco. It seemed like it would be a fun little date.

I'd actually made a list of all the dates I wanted to go on with

Marco—the pumpkin patch, a mixology class, an arcade night at Dave & Buster's. That seems so dumb now.

Joel sinks down beside me. "What does it say?"

My eyes fly over the page. "It's a note for Erica, thanking her for a donation."

I sense Joel deflating. "Oh, so it's nothing then. Man, I thought I'd made an important discovery."

"I'm not finished," I say, my hands trembling with excitement. "It was a donation of one million dollars."

"So, WE KNOW that Erica owed a ton of money but that she also gave a roughly equal amount away," I muse, my hand absent-mindedly stroking Potato's back. She and I settled in on the couch after Joel and I finished sorting through all of Erica's mail.

"And it all happened around the same time," Joel says from his seat on the floor. "Around two years ago."

I nod.

"It all has to be connected somehow, doesn't it?" I ask. "She was getting a divorce and her ex-husband was marrying a much younger woman, so she went on a spending spree. Maybe she did it to stick it to him? Spend all their money, declare bankruptcy, and disappear."

"That actually kind of makes sense."

"Or it could be some kind of tax loophole."

My knowledge of taxes and loopholes is limited to the handful of times I've submitted my own returns on TurboTax. And for the past couple of years, Marco had handled all of that stuff for me. "How would that even work?"

Joel shrugs. "No clue. My parents might own a big lake house but they aren't tax-evasion rich."

"Same."

My stomach growls so loudly that it startles Potato from her nap. "I don't think we're going to get anywhere else tonight. Let's eat a bunch of cheese and olives."

"You don't have to ask me twice."

Joel and I proceeded to devour my charcuterie board (he graciously made a point of telling me how impressed he was with my ability to arrange the contents in such a visually appealing way) before suggesting that we fire up the Nintendo.

The only game cartridge that I can find is the original *Mario Bros.*, which is fine by me because that one was always my favorite. I blow on the cartridge for old times' sake before turning the TV and the console on. I'm relieved to see that they both work. I don't know what else Joel and I would do together if it didn't and I wasn't quite ready for him to go home.

We sit on the couch with Potato nestled between us. There's something about being in the dimly lit basement, alone with a guy and basking in the glow of an old, boxy TV, delightfully full and heading toward pleasantly drunk that reminds me of college, when everything felt new and possible. I like it.

"I don't think it's fair for you to play *Mario Bros.* against me," Joel says as the robotic *boo doo doo doo do do do do* of the *Mario Bros.* theme song begins to play.

"Why?"

"Because you're Italian," he says. "Mario and Luigi are your people."

"My people?"

"You can understand their accents."

I laugh. "That's not how real Italian people sound."

"It's how you sound."

I give him a playful shove. "I don't even have an accent."

"Oh yes you do!"

"Ohh yes yooh dooh," I mimic his elongated vowels.

"Oh my god, like, how dare you."

"I don't sound like that!"

"Okay, Miss California."

We return our attention to the game, both smiling. "So if Mario and Luigi are my people, who are yours?"

"Well there's no Black people in this game," he gives me a playfully pointed look. "But if I had to pick, I'd say I'm a Yoshi guy, through and through."

I hit the A button and Mario leaps to collect a row of floating coins. A satisfying tinkling sound floats from the speakers. "Well first, on behalf of my people, I apologize for the shameful lack of inclusion."

"That means so much, thank you," Joel cracks. "I've been waiting for you to say something."

I give a solemn nod of acknowledgment before shifting into my next point. "That said, I can kind of see you being a Yoshi guy except that Yoshi doesn't talk."

Joel pauses the game before setting the controller on the coffee table. He picks up the wine bottle, freshens my glass, and passes it to me. "Yoshi lets his actions speak for themselves."

My fingertips brush his as I take the wine and my whole body feels like it's covered in miniature sparks, like I've been struck by a million tiny lightning bolts. I wonder if he feels it too. The way he's holding my gaze makes me think he does. I turn my attention back to the TV and restart the game before either of us has a chance to make a mistake that might ruin everything.

Chapter Twenty-Six

Before

The more I opened my mind to the possibility of pursuing a different route to parenthood or maybe even forgoing parenthood altogether, the more Marco dug in.

We went back and forth about what to do for months, which would invariably end with one of us in tears. Usually me.

Eventually, inevitably, we reached our breaking point.

That night, I was sitting on my usual barstool and Marco was standing across from me, the kitchen counter separating us.

"I'm my parents' only child," Marco said. "And Enzo isn't sure if he wants kids. We're their only shot at grandchildren."

"Our kids would have your last name—regardless of whether they have your genes."

Marco sighed. "I've just always looked forward to catching glimpses of my grandparents and my parents, and yes, even myself in my kid. Maybe she'd look like my nonno or have my dad's eyes . . ." He looked at me. "And I'd imagine your family wants the same."

I totally understood where Marco was coming from. Even though it's never been about that for me, I know that's something that a lot of parents look forward to. The decisions people make about having children are rarely rooted in logic. It's usually tied to something much deeper.

Marco rubbed his jaw. "I think that maybe we went about this all wrong. We should have tried on our own first. Let's do that. That's what my parents did and it all worked out."

"Miracle babies are the exception, not the rule," I said gently.

"We have to try."

"We've done four rounds of IVF."

He shook his head. "No. I think we should get married first and then start trying for a baby. The traditional way."

I flexed my fingers in frustration. "And when that doesn't work? Would you be willing to adopt?"

"I'd rather try IVF again."

"I don't want to try IVF again. Ever." I wished that I could make him understand the roller coaster of inflicting physical trauma on my body only to be rewarded with an inevitable emotional letdown. It wasn't just that the side effects often rendered me virtually unable to work for days on end, but that every failed attempt broke my spirit a little bit more. It had affected every aspect of my life—our relationship, my friendships, my job. I was finally feeling like myself again and I couldn't go back.

But when I said all of this to Marco, his only response was, "Is your job really more important to you than a family?"

I groaned with exhaustion. I'd had a long week and was feeling particularly impatient. "You did not just say that to me."

"Maybe you should start coming to Mass with me," Marco pressed. "Not every week, but just sometimes."

"That's not what we'd agreed." I was fully supportive of Marco's beliefs, and he'd always assured me that it didn't bother him that I felt differently, so long as I'd let him take our future kids to church. Enzo and I had gone to Mass with my parents until we were teenagers, so I didn't have a problem with it. Besides, Marco wasn't extreme by any means—he was pro-choice and very supportive of the LGBTQ+ community—if he weren't that would have been an instant deal-breaker for me. His connection to the church always felt more cultural, ritualistic. But the science of creating life—his potential future children's lives—made him deeply uncomfortable.

"Is any of this what we'd agreed to?"

I blinked, stricken. "What's that supposed to mean?"

Marco braced himself against the counter. "Look, Eliza. I love you and I love your family and I love what we've built together, but . . ." His voice was just above a whisper, like he was afraid of what would happen if he admitted his true feelings too loudly. He met my gaze, his eyes glossy. "I didn't sign up for a life without children."

And there it was.

I alone would not be enough for Marco.

Maybe he wasn't enough for me, either.

I know that I could have kept trying. But I wasn't willing to subject myself to all of that for him, for his dreams. The reality was, I always expected that I'd have children. I'd counted on it, in the same way I counted on having air to breathe. But not once did I stop to ask myself how *badly* I wanted children—or what I was willing to do to have them.

There are women who would sell their souls to the devil himself if it meant they could have a baby, and my heart broke for them. But I couldn't count myself among their ranks. I'd already taken things as far as I was willing to go. I'd had the supersized ovaries and bruised abdomen to prove it. But it turns out, a baby, at least a biological one, was not something I was willing to pursue at all costs.

"Well, if you aren't willing to consider an egg donor or adoption, a life without kids is a real possibility. So, where does that leave us?" I asked.

Marco fixed me with the same pitying stare I'd been on the receiving end of for months. "I don't think we need to jump to any dramatic conclusions here, Lize. We should probably focus on the wedding anyway. Or at least pick a date."

"How can we talk about spending our lives together when we can't even talk about this?"

"I don't know what else to do at this point," Marco said, his fingertips curling on the tile countertop. "If I had known that you didn't want children, I never would have proposed."

In an instant, I was on my feet. "I *never* said I didn't want children!" I'm not sure if I was screaming or whispering. It felt like both. Tears streamed down my face and I banged my hands on the counter. "Do you understand what I've been through? Do you understand how hard I've worked to make peace with all of this?"

"I didn't mean that," he said, taking a tentative step toward me. "I'm so sorry."

He wrapped his arms around me and I sobbed into his chest. But we both knew that his mask had slipped, that the truth had finally come out.

We both knew the damage was done.

Chapter Twenty-Seven

On Friday afternoon, a knock at my back porch sends Potato into a fit of barks. As she tears toward the door with me hot on her heels, I feel a pang of gratitude. I haven't heard a peep from Van Fischer, but the idea of having Potato by my side if he were to come back is comforting. She may be small, she may be missing a limb, but she is mighty.

I find Lynette and Ruby at my back door, both donning bright pink plastic sunglasses and matching swimsuits. They smell like the kind of sunscreen Mom used to put on Enzo and me when we were kids. Potato runs to greet Ruby, tail whirring.

"It's a boat day!" Ruby proclaims. Potato yips in response.

"Bob's taking the neighbors out for a cruise on *The Tammy*," Lynette explains. "We were hoping you could join us."

After I finished the MeMeter pitch, I dove straight into Can-Scan. I'm nearly finished with the slide deck, but the idea of finally getting to take a spin around the lake on Bob's boat is too tempting. I've been waiting for this invitation all summer.

Plus, maybe I can get some more information about Bob's relationship with Erica out of the other neighbors. And that would give me an excuse to hang out with Joel outside of the coffee shop again—platonically, of course. He's just as curious as I am.

In light of all the digging I've done into Erica's business over the past couple of days, my suspicions that Bob knows way more than he's letting on have only grown.

I'm starting to wonder if he's blackmailing her. What other reason would she have had to give him the deed to her home?

Maybe he's in cahoots with Erica's ex. Sort of an old boys' club kind of thing. That would be on-brand for Bob.

I promise myself that I'll finish my presentation before I go to sleep tonight. I flash Lynette a smile. "I'll get my suit."

I STAND ON the dock with all of my neighbors, watching Bob's boat rock gently from side to side. The air is thick with humidity, but a cool breeze drifts off the water. "She's coming too?" Bob asks Gal, not bothering to drop the volume of his voice for my benefit.

"Yes, she's coming," Gal shoots back. "And her name isn't *she*. It's Eliza."

Bob grunts.

If Gal wasn't wearing her bejeweled sunglasses, I suspect that I might see laser beams shooting out of her eyes. "This young woman has been nothing but nice to you. Show her some respect, you old grump."

"I'm not much older than you."

"Exactly. I'm old too."

Bob doesn't respond. Instead, he returns his attention to one of the ropes that's attached to the dock. He unties it, holding the loose end in one hand, and gestures for us to step aboard. I hang back and let everyone else on before me, watching as the boat bobs up and down with each new passenger.

Bob narrows his eyes as I pass. "Watch your step," he mutters. It's the nicest thing he's ever said to me.

Despite our mutual distaste for each other, I'm internally thrilled to finally be aboard *The Tammy*. I've watched my neighbors cruise out to the center of the lake without me so many times; finally being included feels like unlocking a new level in a video game.

The layout of the boat is remarkably simple: It's essentially a floating rectangle with a waist-high aluminum railing around the perimeter, bench seating in the back, a steering wheel in the front, and a retractable awning. I can't imagine it goes faster than a few miles per hour.

Simplicity aside, it's in immaculate condition, which given the state of Bob's lawn comes as no surprise.

"Over here, Eliza," Lynette calls from a bench in the back corner. She pats the top of a cooler to her right.

I lay a towel over the cooler and settle in next to her while she and Allan strap Ruby and Ned into their respective life jackets. I wonder if I should consider getting a life jacket for Potato, although I doubt Bob would let me bring her on the boat. I felt bad leaving her at home, but Marge and Gal had taught me that Potato was fine staying home alone as long as I made her a cozy little bed on the couch and put *CSI: Miami* on the TV.

"Does she like all of the *CSI*s?" I'd asked.

Gal responded with a solemn shake of her head. "Only *Miami*."

I felt weird letting my sweet little dog watch a show about murder, so I tried introducing her to the Food Network, but that backfired when one of the hosts started shucking corn. Potato leaped from the couch and started running in circles, barking her head off the whole time. Apparently she found corn offensive, but gratuitous violence? Not so much.

Bob fires up the engine and a puff of gray smoke floats up behind me and for a moment, I find myself relishing the nostalgic smell of airborne pollutants. It reminds me of the city. Specifically, waiting for the bus. Music starts playing from a speaker attached to a pole overhead. It's some country artist that I've never heard of.

Marge and Gal sit on the bench opposite Lynette and the kids while Stuart and Allan join Bob at the helm. "Did you do much boating back home? Out on the bay?" Gal asks.

When Hannah and I were in high school, we were obsessed with the Rocket Boat, a tourist attraction that took off from Pier 39. For a while there, we went every other week. We'd scream our heads off as that thing ripped around the bay. By the end of every ride, we'd be wind-blown and soaking wet. We'd take bets on whether or not any of the tourists would throw up by the end. It was usually a fifty-fifty shot.

But aside from that, no. "Not really."

"Well you're in for a treat."

Stuart steps off the boat to untie the last rope that was holding us to the dock. He tosses it on the small swim deck before hopping back onboard. Lynette flashes him a thumbs-up.

I watch my house shrink as the boat steadily churns toward the center of the lake. The sun is just starting to disappear behind the tree line, but the temperature remains stubbornly in the eighties. Perfect for a late-afternoon boat ride.

The neighbors all pass around some variety of beers and strawberry lemonades.

"How long has Bob had this boat?" I ask.

Lynette ponders my question. "I don't know, a couple of years?" she guesses, looking to Marge and Gal for confirmation.

Gal nods.

That's about the time that Erica filed the paperwork to change the deed on her house. Right after her divorce was finalized. "Were Bob and Erica close?" I ask, hoping it's a softball.

"They certainly got along," Lynette says. If I didn't know better, I'd say she was choosing her words carefully.

"What about Bob and Gary?" I press. "Were they close?"

"No one liked Gary," Marge says firmly.

"Speaking of exes . . ." Lynette says, not so subtly steering the conversation away from Erica. "You're going to have to tell us what happened with yours eventually."

"We have a pool going, you know," Gal says, amusement dancing across her face. "Lynette thinks the bastard left you for your best friend, Marge thinks you got cold feet. Stuart and I agree that you might have murdered him."

Strawberry lemonade threatens to shoot out my nose. "Murdered?" I sputter.

Gal laughs. "Not really."

Lynette leans toward me. "But we are curious."

"And if you did murder him. You can tell us. We won't snitch," Gal adds, holding up three fingers as a signal of Scout's honor.

I'd thought about opening up to Lynette about Marco and me a couple of times and nearly told Gal everything on our most recent walk, but I'd held back, afraid they'd react the way my friends back home had. But, if I wanted my neighbors to let me in, I had to let them in, too.

I RUB MY hands against my bare legs, staving off nonexistent goose bumps. "Well, let me assure you that no one got . . ." I look over at Ned and Ruby who are taking turns honking the boat horn. I lower my voice. " . . . murdered. No one cheated either."

"Cold feet then?" Marge asks.

"Infertility," I say, before letting out a long, cathartic exhale.

Lynette puts her hand on top of mine. Gal lifts her sunglasses. Her eyes look watery. Marge pats my shoulder. I tell them everything.

"I'm going to kill him," Gal says, matter-of-factly.

"You dodged a bullet," Marge says.

It's a long time before Lynette speaks. The way she's looking at me makes me feel like she understands what I've been through on a visceral level. I wonder if she struggled to get pregnant with Ruby and Ned.

Lynette squeezes my hand. "Eliza," she says firmly. "You did absolutely nothing wrong. This isn't your fault and you are no less valuable as a person because one of your organs doesn't work the way it's meant to."

I know that but hearing it from someone who isn't my therapist or my brother means more than I ever could have anticipated. My lip quivers and the tears quickly follow. But they aren't sad tears.

My neighbors encircle me in a group hug. I can't believe I've only known them for a couple of months.

"I really am going to kill him," Gal says.

AFTER WE ALL gather ourselves, Marge excuses herself to chat with Ned and Ruby and Lynette turns her attention to the front of the boat. "Hey, Eliza, do you mind grabbing me a couple of waters from the cooler?" she asks. I fish a pair of bottles from my makeshift seat and pass them to her. "Thanks. I'll be right back."

I wipe my icy hands on my shorts and watch as Lynette makes her way over to Allan, who's engrossed in a conversation with Bob. I can't imagine what about. Bob has the personality of an angry lobster.

Actually, that's not fair to lobsters.

Lynette gently rubs Allan's back to get his attention, but he barely looks away. She slides the water into his hand before settling in next to Stuart, who sits alone in the middle of the boat. Stuart is alone a lot. I wonder if that's a writer thing.

"She looks after him," Gal says, following my line of vision. "We all do, in our own way."

I've fallen into a friendly rapport with Stuart, but we've never really chatted one-on-one. I hardly know anything about him.

The boat rocks from side to side as the wake from a distant Jet Ski laps against the hull. No one seems to notice. They probably all have their sea legs by now. Or is it lake legs?

"That little cabin was his family's summer house way back when," Gal continues. "Stuart moved in after his folks passed away about a decade ago. He doesn't have any siblings, so we're kind of it for him."

"What about friends?"

"Stuart's quite the introvert, in case you haven't noticed. I think he has a few close friends from childhood, but they're all back in Wisconsin. He goes to visit them every spring for a week or so. They're all married with kids, so I think he gets his family fix there."

"Has he written anything new since *Depth Charge*?"

Gal shakes her head. "He's always writing, every day. But it seems like whatever he's working on has him stuck. It's been years."

That explains his decision to live in his family's old cabin. It's almost certainly paid off, so Stuart can live like a starving artist without actually starving. Maybe that's why Lynette is always bringing him food.

"Do you think he's depressed?"

Gal strokes her chin, considering my question. I wonder if she's ever thought about whether Stuart was happy or not. "I think he's quite content, actually. In a lot of ways that's even better than being happy. Happiness is fickle. Contentment is steady."

Gal and I cruise along in easy silence for several minutes as Ned and Ruby laugh at Marge's jokes, Bob blabs Allan's ear off about diesel versus gasoline engines, and Lynette and Stuart talk in hushed tones between sips of water. I'm happy to take in the scenery: the flock of loons floating a few yards away, a fish leaping out of the water in the distance, kayakers paddling by.

And my god, the sunset. The sky has turned a brilliant shade of pink, accented with strokes of purple and orange.

Eventually, Marge makes her way back to us and Lynette finishes her conversation with Stuart, who rejoins Bob and Allan at the helm.

"So, Eliza," Lynette says, as she settles back into her seat. Her tone is playful, like she's a cat dangling a mouse between her claws. "A little birdie told me that you had a gentleman caller last night."

In hindsight, it's laughable that I thought I could get away with having Joel over. I swear the trees in our neighborhood have eyes. I feign confusion, trying to buy myself time. "Gentleman caller?"

"Mm-hmm," Lynette says through a smug smile. "I hear he was there pretty late."

"Oh, you mean Joel?" I laugh, maybe a bit too forcefully. Marge leans forward. Crap. I've drawn more attention to myself. "He's just a friend."

"Sure he is."

"Really," I say emphatically. "He's new to town too. Trish introduced us."

"You said his name was Joel?" Marge has tilted even farther forward, her body nearly folded in half.

I nod. "Joel Jawowski. Do you know him?"

For the briefest of moments, Marge looks momentarily stunned. I almost expect her to tell me that Joel is a notorious serial killer or something, but she then juts out her lower lip and shakes her head. "Doesn't ring a bell."

Lynette places her fist under her chin and leans forward. "So what's he like?"

I sigh. I want to tell them that there's nothing to label, but I know it's futile. "Joel is a really nice guy that I like hanging out with—as friends. We're about the same age and he's easy to talk to and we have a lot of similar interests. That's all."

"He sounds pretty perfect," Marge says, the rays of the setting sun illuminating her face. Lynette and Gal are wearing identical grins. The three of them are even worse than my mom.

It's twilight by the time we make it back to the dock and the lake is still. The water is smooth and glassy. I can't detect even a hint of a breeze. Bob docks the boat with Stuart and Marge's help, the three of them moving in concert, like they've done this thousands of times.

Lynette and Allan insist that we all go ahead since gathering the kids will take them a while. Stuart offers to stay behind to help Bob with seat covers. I say thank you and good night before starting up my lawn with Gal and Marge on either side of me.

"Oh shoot," Gal says. She stops in the middle of the lawn, her hands feeling around the top of her head. "I forgot my sunglasses." She looks to Marge and says, "You go on ahead. I'll meet you at home." She gives me a quick wave and starts jogging back toward the boat.

"She loves those hideous sunglasses," Marge says, her voice dancing with amusement.

"They suit her."

"They're very Gal," Marge agrees. I can hear the affection in her voice.

We walk on in silence, the grass squishing quietly under our footsteps, infinite stars twinkling overhead, crickets chirping in the distance. I'm not sure what to talk to Marge about, but I've pegged her to be more of a strong, silent type. So I let the quiet linger.

Then Marge surprises me. "Are you a football fan by any chance?"

"I'm familiar with the concept."

Marge laughs. It's an elegant sound, much different from Gal's barking chuckles. "What a tactful answer." She tugs at the beach towel on her shoulders. She'd wrapped herself in it when the sun finally set and the temperature dipped into the seventies. "Well I'm meeting some friends in town tomorrow night to watch the Vikings preseason game. They're playing your 49ers, so I thought you might want to join."

They're hardly *my* 49ers—they don't even technically play in San Francisco anymore—but I feel a pang of longing for home all the same. Marge has always been harder to read than Gal. Maybe because she's not around as often. It's helped her to preserve an air of mystery, even if it's unintentional.

"Sure," I say. "Is Gal coming?"

"She prefers to watch at home. She says it's too hard to concentrate on the game when there's a crowd of people around."

"But it's just a preseason game."

"Don't let Gal hear you say that."

I laugh. "Noted."

Marge reaches out to touch my shoulder. The gesture feels surprisingly maternal. "I'll see you at the Common Loon at seven tomorrow night. And whatever you do, don't wear anything that'll make you look like you're from California."

I wonder why Marge is suddenly interested in hanging out with me. Maybe it's because I finally opened up to her about things with Marco. Or maybe she feels bad for me. Whatever the reason, I like the way that I can still feel the lingering imprint of her hand long after she's disappeared across the street.

Chapter Twenty-Eight

I don't own anything purple. I slip on a canary-yellow tank top and a pair of denim shorts and hope that'll be good enough for Marge and her friends.

"You don't have any Vikings stuff?" Marge asks when I find her in the back corner of the Common Loon. She's next to the dartboard where Joel and I sat the first time we hung out.

"I haven't even been here for two months," I say.

She blinks. "That's plenty of time."

My mouth opens, then closes. Marge and I have yet to spend more than a few minutes at a time alone together and to be honest, she intimidates me a little.

"I'm just playing," she says. Then she claps her hands together. "These are my friends." She introduces me to a man named George and a woman named Seema, both of whom appear to be in their late forties or early fifties.

"Great to meet you both," I say.

"You're not from Minnesota," George says.

Marge holds her hand up to the side of her mouth. "She's from California," she says in a stage whisper. "But we're trying to keep it on the down-low tonight."

George makes a sympathetic face, as if I've just revealed that I have an incurable disease. "Probably best if she doesn't talk too loudly then."

Marge swats at George.

"How do you all know each other?" I ask.

Seema arches an eyebrow as she looks at Marge. "You didn't tell her?"

"It hasn't come up," Marge says.

Seema turns back to me. "We're in AA together." She gestures to George. "He leads our group and Marge became my sponsor a couple years ago when she started coming to meetings again."

George claps Marge on the back.

I return my attention to Marge. I'd noticed she wasn't a drinker, but I hadn't ever asked why. "I'm twenty-nine years sober," she says by way of explanation.

Suddenly it clicks. The meetings Marge is always running off to must be for Alcoholics Anonymous. I don't know how I hadn't put it together before. I clutch my hands to my chest. "Marge, that's incredible. Congratulations."

She waves me off like it's nothing, but I know it's not.

"Do you think it's weird for a bunch of former drunks to be hanging out in a bar?" Seema asks.

"It's a little unconventional," Marge says before I can formulate a response. "But it's the best place to watch the game."

"We've swapped an addiction to alcohol for an addiction to Vikings football," Seema says. "Much healthier."

George gives her a high five.

Gertie comes around with a tray full of cheese curds, onion rings, and bottles of Vernors ginger ale. I politely decline when Seema offers to scoop a pile of curds onto my plate. But I'm already planning to go back for seconds on the onion rings and ginger ale.

"I got sober shortly after I met Gal," Marge explains. "I had my first drink at thirteen and my last one at twenty-eight."

"Fifteen years," George says. "A solid run."

Marge dismisses his comment with a good-natured flick of her hand. She turns back to face me. "Gal told you that I used to live in Manhattan?" I nod. Her face softens. "I loved it there. I got cast in a few off-Broadway productions, I auditioned for the Rockettes twice. I was called back both times. I even had drinks with Bernadette Peters once."

Marge's eyes sparkle, like she's enjoying sharing this with me. "But I also did a lot of things I wasn't proud of," she adds, before popping a cheese curd into her mouth. I do my best not to make a face. "I used to get blackout drunk and sleep with anyone who'd have me. Which is all fun and games until someone leaves you with a souvenir. I was lucky I didn't end up with AIDS. Some of my friends weren't so fortunate."

An ache builds in my throat as I process everything that Marge has been through. I swallow hard. "Marge, I'm so sorry."

"Like I said, I'm lucky." She sighs. "There were other consequences though, like a handful of broken bones and multiple prescriptions for antibiotics. You really want to avoid chlamydia if you can."

My face softens. "You've been through a lot."

"It's just part of my story. It made me who I am. I did the best I could at the time and now I do even better."

"What changed?"

She folds her hands in front of her on the table. "I hit what I thought was my rock bottom, so I moved home to live with my folks. I even stopped drinking for a few months. Once I was feeling better, I took a job teaching summer dance and drama at the high school, which is where I met Gal."

"I didn't know you met at work. That's so cute."

"Quite the meet-cute," she agrees. "It was love at first sight. Gal came by the theater to chat with one of her students about an extra-credit assignment and I was onstage running the kids through some choreography. As soon as we locked eyes, I knew I was done for." Her gaze grows distant and I imagine that in her mind, Marge is back in that high school auditorium. "We went to the Summer Festival for our first date and the sparks flew. Gal won me this purple stuffed dog that I still have to this day. We ate sno-cones and cotton candy. Our first kiss was at the top of the Ferris wheel."

Marge's life could be a movie.

She smiles and for a moment, I catch a glimpse of the young woman she was then. "The only problem was that I'd started drinking again." She unclasps her hands, splaying her fingers. "I'd naively thought that since I was able to take a break, I had it under control. Which of course wasn't the case. Within a few months, I'd gotten fired from work, embarrassed myself in front of Gal's friends, and been kicked out of my parents' house. Then Gal gave me an ultimatum. She told me that she wanted us to be together forever and that she'd do everything she could to support me, but she would not spend her life cleaning up after a drunk. The thought of losing Gal terrified me. That was my true rock bottom."

She slaps her hands on her knees. "So I went to rehab and got sober for real, which was not easy. I worked all of the twelve steps." She holds up a finger. "Also not easy. It took months and months, and then a few weeks after I hit a full year of sobriety, I moved in with Gal."

"And the rest is history?"

A shrug. "Yes and no. I had a lot of guilt and shame about my addiction. I became convinced that Gal was compromising to be with me. I felt like I had this defect, this disease inside of me and it was hard for me to believe that Gal wasn't harboring a secret resentment that we couldn't drink wine together while we made dinner or go out to happy hour like normal couples."

What Marge is describing strikes a chord somewhere deep within my gut. I know infertility and alcoholism are apples and oranges, but I feel a kinship with Marge nonetheless. She was scared that Gal couldn't accept her, warts and all, that Gal might wake up one day and realize that she'd prefer to be with someone who didn't have any defects. I know this feeling intimately and acutely.

But when I hear all of this coming from Marge, as an outsider, I can see how flawed her logic is. When it's right, truly right, the person you choose to spend your life with will want you just as you are.

I'm not sure why Marge decided to open up to me tonight—perhaps it's the contagious feeling of camaraderie among the Vikings fans in the bar or the intoxicating tang of ginger ale—but whatever the reason, I'm glad that she did. Because something about hearing her story helped me to understand my own.

A man in a hat shaped like a wedge of cheese enters the saloon and is instantly greeted with a chorus of boos. He appears to relish it, gesturing for the crowd to keep it coming. "Packers fans," Seema mutters. "They aren't even playing tonight."

"Maybe he just wants to see what it's like to watch a superior team," George says. Seema high-fives him again. Now I understand why Marge told me not to wear any Niners gear.

Marge holds up her ginger ale. "Anyway, enough of the serious stuff, let's have some fun."

I clink her glass in agreement as the opening promo song starts to blare over the speakers. I look around the Common Loon, which seems to have tripled in population since I arrived. Every seat has long been taken and fans in bright, grape-colored jerseys mill around the bar. I spot Jimbo, the owner of Cricket's and Doug, the Lyft driver who dropped me off at my new house for the first time in the crowd. It feels full circle somehow.

The song ends and the footage cuts to the field where players line up for kickoff. I watch as the rosy-cheeked bartender climbs onto the counter. He's wearing a horned helmet. The crowd quiets as he raises his arms. Then the bartender claps his hands together over his head and yells, "Skol!"

Everyone else in the bar with the exception of me and the Packers fan clap in unison. "Skol!" they yell, so loudly it rattles my innards.

"This is the Skol chant," Marge says gleefully into my ear. "A long-held Viking tradition. We stole it from Finland!"

The bartender proceeds to lead the crowd in the chant as it increases in pace and intensity. Finally, he yanks a horn off his helmet and blows into it like a conch. The crowd goes wild. And then the 49ers kick things off.

It's been years since I've watched a football game and although I wince at a few of the rougher tackles and am a little conflicted about wanting to root for my home team, I'm wholly invested by the end of the first quarter. I hug a jumping Marge when the Vikings run a punt back for a touchdown, I join in a Skol clap after the Vikings score a field goal, I pull at my hair when the referee misses an obvious call.

It's pure, uninhibited fun.

At halftime, Marge turns to me. "So you and this Joel guy."

"Marge," I say, tilting my head back in exasperation. "There's no me and Joel."

She almost looks offended. "Why not? Are you not attracted to him?"

"What? No. I mean—it's not about that."

"He sounds like a nice young man. And you're a nice young woman."

"Well, he came here for someone else. I think it's complicated. We haven't really talked about it."

"He came here for someone else," she repeats to herself. I nod. "But he's spending his free nights at your house?"

My thumb instinctively rubs the spot where my engagement ring used to be. "I think it's too soon," I say, my voice tight.

Marge furrows her eyebrows. "For who? You're not still hung up on your ex-fiancé, are you?"

There were moments when thinking about Marco made my chest feel all tight and knotted, but that's not the same as missing him. "No." I sigh. "I just don't want to get hurt again."

Marge tilts her head in sympathy. "Well that's not entirely in your control, my dear. But you never know what'll happen. Sometimes you just get lucky."

Enzo had called me the other day to tell me that after six official dates and a successful introduction to his best friend, Keith, he and Allison had decided to define their relationship. He delivered the news in his usual matter-of-fact way, but I know he was excited. He wouldn't have called to tell me otherwise.

Talking to Enzo about Allison reminded me how thrilling the early days of a new relationship can be. When you first meet someone new, it feels like anything is possible, like you might be at the beginning of your happy ending. I've been around long enough to know that those feelings fade with time, and that there is no such thing as a fairy tale, but in spite of all this, I've found myself longing for that feeling all the same.

I'd be lying if I said I hadn't let myself flirt ever so briefly with the idea of what it might be like to kiss Joel.

"That's not what I moved here for," I tell Marge. It's wholly true. I'd never figured someone like Joel into my new plans.

Marge leans forward. "One of life's greatest joys is when something unexpectedly wonderful falls into our lap." She pats my hand. "Trust me on that one."

I suppose she has a point.

Much to my relief, another Skol chant breaks out before I have the chance to respond.

Chapter Twenty-Nine

September

M y workweek kicks off with a panic-inducing email from Jordan. First of all, it's terrifying that they're sending emails at this time of day—it's 4:00 a.m. in San Francisco. But second and more importantly, they're angry with me. That's never happened before.

Let's talk.

That's all they said in response to the presentation I sent over the weekend. *Let's talk.* What does that even mean? It's so terse. So unfeeling.

This is very un-Jordan. They're the best, most understanding boss I've ever had.

I'll admit that I've been a little distracted since the move. Between getting unpacked, digging into Erica's life, and working with Trish on her winter marketing strategy, I've been stretched rather thin. But I don't think that's affected the quality of my work. I would never let that happen.

If I'm being brutally honest, I suppose that I've started to feel like my job is a little ridiculous. More specifically, that our clients are ridiculous. The start-up and tech companies that Swayy tends to attract seem to operate in an alternative reality, a place where everyone is laser focused on "optimizing" their lives and "driving efficiency" and finding ways to "work smarter." It's a world where cars drive themselves and wearable devices remind us when to eat and when to pee. It's sort of a quasi-*Jetsons* bubble, which I used to think was cool, but now that I don't exist in that world every day, it all feels kind of silly.

That aside, I know I nailed that CanScan presentation. I scroll to the bottom of Jordan's email to find the attachment I'd shared over the weekend. Reviewing my top-notch work product should help to ease my anxiety. But, when the attachment opens, my sleepy brain takes its sweet time processing why the deck I'd created for Trish fills my phone screen. I close out and try again only to be greeted by Trish's presentation once more.

Oh my god.

I didn't send the CanScan deck to Jordan. I sent the Black Bear Brew marketing pitch.

I leap out of bed, startling Potato from her slumber and rush to my laptop. I quickly—but carefully—forward Jordan the right presentation, along with an emoji-laden apology. Thirty minutes later, my phone rings once again startling Potato, who had just fallen back asleep.

It's Jordan.

Somehow they sound more awake than I do. "Thanks for sending this over," they begin. "It looks great. No surprise there."

"I'm glad you're happy with it," I breathe. "I'm sorry again."

"It happens." I picture Jordan shrugging on the other end of the line. They're probably wearing pajamas that are cooler than any of my normal clothes. "It's just that it doesn't usually happen to *you*."

That sends my esophagus into a freefall. I start to sputter an incoherent response, but Jordan saves me from myself. "It's totally fine if you're taking on freelance work on the side. I really don't care—you can spend your time however you want."

My esophagus creeps back into its proper position. "Really?"

"Of course. But if you ever don't want to be here anymore, I need you to tell me."

I tighten my grip on the phone and do my best to keep my voice steady. "Jordan, that's not it at all."

A pause. And then, "I'll take you at your word. But if that changes, just give me a heads-up. No hard feelings."

I swear up and down I'm fully committed to my job and even laugh when Jordan cracks a joke about how I should probably make time for some fun extracurriculars outside of work rather than just taking on more marketing projects. "You're young," they say. "Go live."

The thing about Jordan is, I know they mean it. They're married with two kids, they sit on the board of a shelter for queer and transgender kids, and they're deeply committed to pickleball.

Even with the would-be crisis averted, I'm rattled by Jordan's line of questioning. Why on earth would I ever want to leave a job that I'd spent my entire career working toward? I'm probably only a year or two out from my next promotion. Soon enough, I'll be managing an entire division. There's no way I'd bail now.

And yet, sometimes I daydream about doing just that.

THE NEXT MORNING, I catch myself staring at Joel in between emails. I take in his full bottom lip, his long, dark eyelashes, the way his hands grip his coffee mug.

When he pushes back from his laptop and heads over to the bar for a refill, I involuntarily inhale his scent: pine trees and soap and a dash of mint.

When Trish stops by to tell me she reserved a booth at Summer Festival, I tune her out, Marge's words echoing in my mind.

Maybe I should just go for it with Joel. I'm probably overthinking everything.

I wonder if he's a good kisser.

"You okay over there?" Trish asks, her eyebrows raised. She has her hair tied up with a checkered ribbon today. I swear she's been cheerier these past couple of weeks. I think she's genuinely excited about our vision for Black Bear Brew.

"Yeah, I'm great," I say, shaking my head. "I guess I'm just still recovering from my weekend."

Joel's head jerks up at that and my heart does a panicked flutter. I don't want him to think that I was hanging out with some random guy. "I had a lot of work to do," I add quickly. "And I watched the game with my neighbor. Her wife doesn't like to watch at the bar so she invited me."

With that, Joel's shoulders drop ever so slightly.

BY THE TIME we wrap up with Trish, the humidity outside must be close to 100 percent. Leaving the air-conditioned coffee shop feels like walking into a thick, hot, mushy wall. I'm not sure I'll ever get used to that.

"Hot enough for you?" Joel says. He holds the door open for Potato, who refuses to leave the comfortable indoor climate behind, her disdain for the ungodly temperatures written all over her little face. She grunts with relief when I end up bending down to take her into my arms.

"Maybe too hot," I say back, but I'm not sure if I'm talking about the weather. I never should have opened up to Marge about Joel. Now it's all I can think about and I can't look Joel in the eye without breaking into a nervous sweat.

Joel squints up toward the sun and I start to worry he's going to melt. "Yeah, sometimes we get these last-gasp heat waves before fall comes through. It'll probably start to feel a little less like hell soon."

The thought of summer coming to an end makes me a little sad. Sure, I'd love to be able to sit outside in the middle of the day without evaporating, but I worry about what'll happen to my routine once the weather turns. I haven't even thought to ask whether my neighbors get together for Sunday barbecues all year-round snow or shine. And I hate the thought of not getting to see Trish most days.

Or Joel.

"So, I'm going to be working from home for the next couple of days," Joel tells me. "My company is doing a virtual all-hands conference and I'm going to be presenting."

I don't love the idea of not seeing Joel at the coffee shop for the rest of the week, but I play it cool. "Okay." I shrug. "Trish and I will miss you."

I turn my attention to settling Potato into her little basket. I'd left my bike in its usual shady spot under a big sycamore tree where the temperature feels mercifully bearable. It's been a long time since I worried about someone stealing it.

When I look back at Joel, his hands are dug into his pockets. He almost looks nervous. "Yeah I'll miss you and *Trish* too," he says with a grin. "Maybe we could make up for it though? Are you free on Friday night?"

Most of my neighbors are meeting for book club at Stuart's on Friday, so I'm definitely free. "I think so, why?"

He smiles, flashing those dimples. "Good." He takes a breath, his face suddenly serious. "So, I know you said at the beginning of summer that you weren't ready to date, but it's almost fall and . . . I'd really like to take you to dinner."

My jaw falls open ever so slightly, but before I can formulate a response, Joel adds, "And I'm not hung up on anyone else. I know I kind of let you think that I was, but I'm not. I'm single. Very single."

This sends my heart into chaotic flutters, but I do my best not to show it. I let out a long slow breath. "You're single."

"Yep."

"And you want us to go to dinner together."

He tries and fails to keep his face neutral. "It's good to know you're following."

For the briefest of moments, thoughts of Marco and our would-be wedding and the house we won't buy and the children we won't have flash through my mind. But they dissipate as quickly as they come. It's just one dinner. I straighten my spine. "Yes," I say.

"Yes, you're following?"

"Yes, and I'd love to go to dinner with you."

The way Joel's face lights up—like he's just learned he won a free car or something—makes my stomach feel all gooey. "I'll pick you up at seven," he says. "And let's not overthink anything—it's just dinner. If you don't have a good time, we'll go back to being friends."

"It sounds like you're the one who's overthinking."

He laughs. "Oh, I'm definitely overthinking."

I do an embarrassing spirit fingers gesture with my hands. "Welcome to the club."

Joel mimics my jazz hand thingy. "Glad to know I'm in good company." Then he shoves his hands back into his pockets and tells me he'll see me on Friday. I have to wait for him to disappear back into the coffee shop before I can mount my bike because my legs feel like they're made of Jell-O.

I don't know how I'm going to make it all the way to Friday.

Chapter Thirty

When I hear Joel knock on the door, it's the back door. I don't know why he doesn't bother with the front, but I suppose I'm glad he's comfortable enough with me to be so informal. I open the door with Potato cradled in my arms. Her tail thumps against my hip at the sight of him.

"Wow," he breathes. "You look amazing."

Lynette had stopped by earlier today to wish me luck on my date and to lend me her favorite necklace (a ruby pendant on a delicate gold chain) and matching ring. I'm not a jewelry expert, but the ring would be better described as a bauble. It has to be a least a few carats and probably costs more than Bob's boat. I had to will myself not to cry at her sweet gesture.

"This is a big night," she'd said, as she fastened the pendant around my neck.

"It's just dinner," I'd said.

Then she took one look at my outfit—a fitted burnt orange jumpsuit that didn't *not* emphasize my boobs and strappy sandals—and replied, "Sure it is. And a firefly is just a bug."

I promised her I'd come over for coffee in the morning for a full debrief.

I feel my cheeks flush. "Thanks," I say to Joel. "You're not so bad yourself." He's wearing a linen button-down shirt and a pair of shorts with only one set of pockets. I think he has a fresh haircut too.

"We're being weird," he says with a laugh.

"I know. Let's stop. It's just dinner, right?"

"Exactly."

"Where are we going by the way?"

He clears his throat. "The Starling Lounge?"

As in the most romantic restaurant in the tri-county area and the epicenter of summertime proposals. That feels decidedly not casual. "Cool," I say, trying and epically failing to sound relaxed. "Let me get Potato settled and we'll head out."

I set Potato on her blanket and kiss the top of her head, leaving a smudge of lipstick smack in the center. "Wish me luck," I whisper. She thumps her tail three times before turning her attention to Horatio Caine and his sunglasses.

THE HOST AT the Starling Lounge, a fiftyish woman named Dina with a round, kind face and an asymmetrical haircut, gives Joel a wink when we check in. "Joel, you've finally brought a lady friend along with you," she says through an approving smile. "I've been waiting for this day." Then she looks at me and says, "He usually eats alone at the bar."

I knew Joel loved this place so I'd assumed that he would have brought his mysterious ex-girlfriend here at least once before. The thought of him dining alone in such a romantic setting is charming and sweet and sad all at once.

Also, I'm kind of flattered.

Dina escorts us to a table on the back patio overlooking the lake. We're seated under a wood pergola draped in market lights. A handful of stained-glass birds dangle overhead. "Best seats in the house," she says as she hands each of us a menu. "Bon appétit."

Joel looks at me over his menu. "Is that a new necklace?"

I touch the pendant with my fingertips. "My neighbor insisted on letting me borrow it."

"It looks pretty on you."

Our server arrives with glasses of ice water in hand. She lights a candle at the center of the table and asks us if we're ready to order drinks. We decide to split a bottle of sauvignon blanc, which arrives in its own freestanding ice bucket.

"Cheers," Joel says, holding up his glass. The wine sparkles in the golden light of the setting sun.

I hold mine up too. The stem is cool between my fingers. "To our first date?" I venture, instantly blushing at my boldness. I don't know why, but calling this a date makes it feel more delicate. More real.

Joel tilts his head to the side. "I thought this was like our third or fourth date." My face must give away my confusion because he starts ticking off all the things we've done together. "Darts at the bar, the pedal boats, video games and criminal activity at your place?"

"Those weren't dates," I say through a laugh.

"They were to me."

I suddenly feel like I'm filled with tiny, effervescent bubbles. I clink his glass. We sip our wine in unison.

"I'm really glad you decided to move to this random little lake town," Joel says.

"I think I am, too." It certainly hasn't been perfect—Joel knows that better than anybody. But I can't deny that this change of scenery, this new pace of life has been good for me.

I pick up my menu. "So what's good here?"

Joel's eyes light up. "Everything."

I scan the menu and decide on a cavatelli pasta with roasted summer corn and fresh basil before returning my attention to

Joel. He's looking at me over the top of his menu. "That necklace really does look pretty on you."

The server returns to take our order (Joel's having a beet salad that I plan to make him share with me and the catch of the day). She leaves us with a basket of bread and a little bowl of olive oil before taking our menus. It takes a minute, but soon we relax back into our usual cadence. The wine probably helps.

We talk about almost everything—our childhoods (largely idyllic), our siblings (I tell him all about Enzo and he tells me about his two older sisters, both married with kids, both living within a few blocks of their family home), and our parents (still married and actually like each other). He tells me about the time he said "pro boner" when he meant to say "pro bono" during a high school speech (he was class president, just as I'd suspected) and I tell him about the time I broke my toe playing kickball in gym glass. We both agree high school was the worst.

I don't tell him about Hannah.

Our food comes and goes. Joel gamely shares his beets with me and my pasta is one of the best dinners I've ever had, but given how well the night is going, I think I would have been just as happy with a peanut butter and jelly sandwich.

Eventually, the sun disappears over the lake and the fireflies spark to life. As the band plays "Harvest Moon," the restaurant falls away and we are all that's left.

"You're a little hard to read, you know," Joel says. He's not being accusatory in the way that Marco used to say it, just observant, curious. "What's something that I don't know about you? You can't be this perfectly put together all the time."

I laugh. "You mean neurotic?"

"You must have like—I don't know, some kind of deep dark secret or weird flaw or something." He leans back in his chair, appraising me. "Do you save every bottle cap from every pop you've ever drank?"

I shake my head.

"Did you escape a sunflower-worshipping cult?"

I laugh. "No."

"You eat frogs?" I make a face. "You hate frogs?"

"I don't think I'm going to be able to have children—at least not biologically," I say, without even thinking. Opening up to Joel feels like a reflex more than a conscious decision. Maybe it's the beautiful, open water of the lake, or twinkling lights, the break from reality. Or maybe it's because I know that whatever this is between us is probably temporary, a rebound. The stakes would feel much higher if I thought he might be "the one." Navigating the fertility conversation with someone who could reject me again, the same way Marco did, would be terrifying.

Whatever the reason, I tell Joel everything.

He listens intently, his brow furrowed in sympathy. "That's brutal." He sighs. "I'm so sorry."

One of the things I've come to appreciate about Joel is that he doesn't pity people. I don't feel like he's looking at me any differently. His "I'm so sorry" feels more like a straightforward acknowledgment that I've been through something shitty and that sucks, but that I'm not damaged or fragile because of it.

"It's okay," I say. He gives me a look. "Really," I assure him. "It's sad. But I think the way I found out made it easier to digest, somehow. I wasn't ready to have a baby yet anyway, so it all felt more abstract. I didn't feel like anything tangible had been taken from me."

"What about your fiancé?"

"He was in denial, I think. His mom had trouble getting pregnant, so I think he was hoping we'd be as lucky as she was."

"Yeah, it doesn't always work that way."

"I kept telling him that, but he couldn't let go of the vision he had for his future family. It made me feel like I wasn't good enough anymore. Like part of the reason he was with me was for my reproductive organs and when it turned out they were defective, my value dropped."

"That's awful." Joel leans forward, his eyes not leaving mine. "No one should ever make you feel that way. You are enough just as you are." He bites his lip. "More than enough, actually. You're amazing."

I look away, needing to gather myself. This is exactly what I'd longed for Marco to say, for my friends to tell me. But they never did.

"Can I ask if you ever considered surrogacy? People do that all the time, right?" Joel scrunches his face. "You don't have to answer if that's too personal."

"I don't mind." It actually feels good to talk about all of this with someone who isn't acting like I've just revealed that I only have hours to live. "Surrogates are wildly expensive, but more than that, Marco just wasn't on board. He's pretty traditional— and Catholic—so he wasn't very comfortable with IVF in the first place. I think using another woman's eggs would have pushed him too far."

Joel nods. "I wouldn't feel that way, but I'm not going to judge him for it."

"Same," I agreed. "And the other issue was that I started coming around on the idea that maybe a life without kids wouldn't be so bad. We could travel, spoil our friends' kids, adopt a bunch of dogs, eat out whenever we like, not have to endure sleepless nights or tantrums or getting peed on."

Joel leans forward. "I've definitely thought about that before.

It's kind of surprising more people don't forgo the whole kid thing altogether."

"That's what I said. But there's such a stigma around it. Everyone made me feel like I'd never be complete if I didn't have a kid, like I'd be doomed to a selfish half-life devoid of real love."

"You know that's bullshit, right?"

"I do now. And so, I guess I landed in this strange place where I could see myself being happy either way."

"Schrodinger's cat."

"In a way, yeah. I'm in this weird limbo where my life can go one way or another and I need to figure out what I want, because either way, I'll need to plan ahead."

"So I take it adoption was out of the question, then." There's an edge to the way Joel says this, something that wasn't there before.

I swallow my last remaining sip of wine and shake my head. "For my ex it was, but I would have been open to it. I actually think that adopting could be really amazing."

Joel considers my answer. I get the impression he's debating something. Then he rolls his shoulders, takes a breath, and says, "I'm adopted. Actually, in my family we call it being *chosen*." He grins. "But yeah, adopted. We all are—me and my sisters. My parents said they always knew they wanted to build their family that way."

This catches me off guard, although I'm not sure why. I guess I never thought about it one way or another.

"That's the reason I moved here," he continues before I can react. "I was looking for my birth mom."

I blink, stunned. "*That's* the woman you followed here?"

Now he meets my eye. "It is."

"Why did you let me think it was for a girlfriend?"

Joel rubs his face. "Mostly because I wasn't ready to talk about the whole looking for my birth mom thing. But there was a part of me that was kind of relieved when you assumed I'd come here for a girl I was dating. I figured that since you were going through a breakup, it might be better to let you think I was only interested in friendship. I was fine with being just friends too, of course. But I was sort of hoping that I might grow on you." He winces. "Are you weirded out?"

I shake my head. "No, I get it." And I think I do. When I first moved to Juneberry Lake, going on a date with someone new was completely out of the question. If I'd known Joel was single, I probably wouldn't have let myself get too close to him. Thinking he was hung up on someone else made him feel safe.

He sighs, relieved. I reach across the table and touch his hand for the first time. Our eyes meet and there's that spark again. It's small, but undeniable. I think Joel feels it too. I withdraw my hand and return my attention to the lake because I'm scared of what would happen if I hold his gaze for too long. Joel follows suit.

"So, did you find her?" I ask, my eyes still on the dusky water. "My birth mom?"

I look back at him and nod.

He smiles, looking a little wistful. "I did. We've been getting to know each other, meeting up for coffee, taking walks around the lake. We like to get sandwiches from the market and eat them on this one picnic bench over by Aspen Estates. It's been nice."

"Do you have a lot in common?"

He weighs his words before responding. "I think we have similar outlooks on life. We're both practical but also hopeless romantics with a mild case of youthful wanderlust. And we both care a lot about this town. We get along really well."

"Did she tell you why she gave you up?"

"She did and I totally get it. There are no hard feelings there. Given her situation, she was being the best mother she could be. Plus, I have the greatest parents ever. They're my mom and dad in every sense—I wouldn't trade that for anything."

I think about what Gal said about the people who surrender their pets. She'd said something similar—sometimes admitting that you can't care for someone in the way they deserve and letting them go is the most loving thing you can do. "I hope I can meet her someday."

He looks surprised by this. Maybe I'm jumping the gun on the whole meeting the parents thing, but I don't mean it that way. "I'd like that too. We haven't introduced our respective families to each other yet—all in good time." Then he flashes me a crooked half smile that makes my stomach do a thrilling little flip. "And maybe you've already met her and you don't even know it. Juneberry Lake is pretty small."

I like to think that I'd recognize Joel's birth mother if I ever saw her. For a moment it crosses my mind that it could be Trish, but I've spent tons of time with both of them this summer and I've never gotten the sense that they're overly close. Besides, they don't look alike. I want to ask if his birth mom is married or if she had any other children, but I don't want to be too nosy. I decide to leave it for now. "What about your birth father?"

"He might be harder to find since she's not in touch with him. But, I'm going to try to do one of those DNA tests to see if I can track down some relatives."

"Can I ask how your parents feel about all of this?"

"They're supportive in theory," he hedges. "They've always said that if any of us wanted to look for our birth parents, they'd be behind us, but I'm a little worried that they might feel differently when it actually happens; when she's real. My sisters don't have any interest in finding theirs and I don't want my parents to feel like they weren't enough or like I'm trying to replace them. That would never happen."

My hand finds his across the table again. This time, I'm not scared of what might come next.

It's close to midnight by the time Joel walks me home. We might have stayed at the restaurant all night if Dina hadn't chased us out.

Our pace slows as we approach my porch, I don't think either of us want the night to end. But we have nowhere to go, June-berry Lake isn't exactly an up-all-night sort of town. I reluctantly climb the steps before turning to face Joel, my back to the front door. I forgot to flip the porchlight on before I left, so the only light we have comes from the moon and stars.

He takes a step toward me. "I had a great time tonight."

I twist Lynette's ring around on my finger, suddenly feeling like I've landed in a nineties rom-com. "I did too."

"I kind of want to kiss you."

I bite my lip as my eyes fall to his mouth. He really does have the nicest lips. He tilts my chin upward ever so gently with the tip of his finger and our eyes meet, brown on brown, and then I'm stepping toward him and his hands are framing my face and my hands find his back. The anticipation only lasts for a second, but it contains an entire universe. I'm about to cross a threshold. I don't so much step across as leap headlong.

When Joel kisses me, it's a full-body sensation. I melt into him, into his soft lips, his strong arms, his intoxicating scent.

"I've been wanting to do that since the first time you walked into the coffee shop," he murmurs, his mouth still tantalizingly close to mine.

"Even though I was holding a bike tire?"

He exhales a laugh. "*Especially* because you were holding a bike tire."

Then he kisses me again. It's firm but gentle and slow but urgent. Kissing Joel is impossible and inevitable and I want to savor this moment for as long as I can. Then I want to do it again and again and again.

WHEN JOEL AND I finally manage to pry ourselves apart, I float into my house on a euphoric cloud and sink down onto the couch beside Potato, who stares up at me expectantly, like she's waiting for details. "We kissed," I tell her. She misinterprets this as a request for a kiss and promptly licks my chin.

"Let's go potty and then snuggle in bed," I say. Potato reluctantly rises from her blanket nest and stretches. She hops off the couch and ambles dutifully to the back door. I stand on the steps of my back porch while Potato sniffs around on the lawn. The night feels fresh and warm and new. I close my eyes and take a deep breath. I feel content.

I feel at home.

Stuart's porch light is off and the lights in his cabin are dimmed and flickering. I wonder if the reason I never see him before noon is that he stays up into the wee hours of the morning writing by candlelight. The notion is kind of romantic, if not a little brooding.

I don't know what makes me shrink against the side of my house when his door swings open—instinct, I suppose. My breath quickens as he steps out onto the porch because he isn't alone. Lynette is there too. And before I know, I know. The way they linger in front of his doorway, illuminated by moonlight, heads dipped together, mouths moving in gentle whispers says it all. I don't gasp when Stuart takes Lynette's chin into his hand and brings his lips to hers. I can't help but watch as she runs her fingers through his salt-and-pepper hair and presses her body into his. It's an eternity before they draw apart.

Potato comes trotting up the lawn and I pray that they don't see her. I press my finger to my lips in a sign to be quiet. She seems to understand, slowing her pace and gently creeping toward me.

We slip back into the house unnoticed.

Chapter Thirty-One

When I wake up the next morning, my first thought is of Joel. Of our night. And that kiss.

But then I remember another kiss, a much more complicated one. I briefly let myself imagine that I might have dreamed the whole thing, but the memory snaps back into focus, sharp and vivid, and I know it's true. Lynette and Stuart are having an affair.

And now I have to meet Lynette for coffee at her house.

Lynette was the first person to welcome me to the neighborhood and she's been nothing but a good friend to me ever since. My loyalty lies with her, not Allan. But I can't go on like everything is normal. I can't pretend that I don't know about Stuart. I can't lie to her face. Even if she's been lying to everyone else's.

I find Lynette sitting at a table under an umbrella on her back patio. A carafe of iced coffee and a pair of blue drinking glasses rest in front of her. She practically explodes from her chair when she hears me approaching.

"How was your date?" she asks, her voice bubbling with excitement. "Tell me everything."

I sit on the chair beside Lynette. Despite the shade of the umbrella, it's sweltering. It's not even 10:00 a.m. yet. Potato flattens herself against the pavement under the table in an effort to stay cool. I force myself not to join her.

"We kissed," I say, eyeing Lynette more pointedly than I mean to. She squeals with excitement. "How was it?"

I smile, but there's a sadness lurking beneath. If only I hadn't taken Potato out at that exact moment. If only Lynette had stayed inside a little longer. In an alternate universe, she and I are bonding over the excitement of my budding relationship with Joel, speculating about how he might be feeling, wondering when he'll call, dreaming up our next date. But I live in this universe. This is my unfortunate reality.

I set a small package on the table—I'd carefully wrapped Lynette's necklace and ring in craft paper before I left the house this morning. I didn't want to lose them.

"Thanks for the jewelry," I say. "Joel really liked the necklace. He complimented it more than once."

Lynette beams and I realize that all I'm doing is stalling.

I rest my hands on my thighs and draw a steadying breath. "I have to tell you something," I say.

Lynette, sensing the graveness of my tone, returns her glass to the table. The way she's looking at me, eyes full of trust and concern stings. I remind myself that I haven't done anything wrong. I just want to be honest.

"I saw you with Stuart last night."

Her mouth flops open, then closed, then open again. Shakes it off. "Oh that?" She flicks her hand. "I was just returning a book I'd borrowed from him. After the kids went to bed."

"I saw you *kissing* Stuart," I say gently.

Lynette wilts like a flower in the scorching hot Minnesota sun. "Oh," she says quietly.

"I'm not judging you," I tell her. And I mean it. I know all too well that relationships can be complicated. I also know that cheating is something a lot of couples can overcome, if they want to. "I just couldn't pretend—"

She bobs her head. "I understand. You have every right to be angry with me."

I reach out to her, my hand landing on her knee. All I want to do is comfort her. I'm not trying to be confrontational. "I'm not angry. I'm confused and worried. But I'm definitely not angry."

She heaves a breath. "Allan doesn't have to work as much as he does," she says quietly, as if this explains it all. She looks back at the house. "It's Saturday and he's upstairs working while I'm out here enjoying this beautiful view alone. I'm glad he has a career that he loves, he deserves that, but all the time away from me and the kids . . . it's a conscious decision."

I think about how often Lynette is on her own, how often I've seen Allan's car pulling up long after the sun has gone down. The number of times he's taken the kids to his parents' for the weekend when Lynette didn't join. Maybe she hadn't been invited.

"That must be so tough. I can't imagine."

She dips her chin. "I don't know how it happened. After the kids came, we started to grow apart, bit by bit until it felt like we were just roommates. All we talk about is the kids. We're never alone together. We haven't had sex since our anniversary last year—" Her eyes widen at her own revelation. "Sorry, that's way more information than you needed."

"It's fine," I assure her.

"We're a good team when it comes to parenting. Allan is a wonderful dad."

"Of course he is. You're both great parents."

She sniffles. "But it's been years since we felt like a real couple. And then when Erica—" She stops abruptly then waves her hand as if she's swatting away a fly. "When Erica moved away, I was more alone than ever. Gal and Marge have their own lives and Bob is, well, Bob. Stuart and I started meeting up for coffee and I guess one thing led to another. As cliché as that sounds."

So this isn't new. If things started around the time Erica left, it's been well over a year. "Do you . . . want to be with Stuart?"

She shakes her head emphatically. "We don't want to be together, no. It's not like that. Besides, Allan and I splitting up would be . . . complicated."

"Because of the kids?"

"Among other things."

I get the sense that she doesn't want me to dig any deeper. At least, not any deeper than I already have. So I leave it.

"Please don't tell anyone," she pleads. My hand is still on her knee. She picks it up and squeezes it. "I know I need to sort all of this out, but I just need a little time."

I totally understand. She wasn't expecting to have this conversation today. Or ever. "I won't," I promise. "All that I ask is that you don't ask me to cover for you. I don't want to have to lie to Allan. Or anyone else for that matter."

"I would never do that."

I pat her hand. "Do you need a hug?"

"You have no idea," she says. I wrap her in my arms and she starts to cry.

I try to tell myself that telling Lynette was the right thing to do, but now I'm not so sure.

VAN FISCHER IS sitting on my doorstep when I get back from Lynette's, which is exactly the opposite of what I need. I'm already feeling icky enough. Telling your friend you know about their affair doesn't exactly elicit the warm fuzzies.

I think we were able to end on an okay note. I probably wouldn't have made the same choices Lynette has, but I also haven't been married for twenty years. I don't have two kids.

"Good to see you again," Van says as I approach.

"Nothing has changed since the last time you were here," I say tiredly. "Please leave."

Van examines his nails. "Nothing, huh? That's not what I hear."

I stop short of my front steps and tighten my grip on Potato's leash. She doesn't like him, I can tell. The bristly fur along her back is standing at attention.

Van rises from his seat and takes one step toward me. "I hear you've been doing some digging."

I arrange my face into an expression that I hope conveys that I think Van is a complete idiot.

"Find anything interesting?"

"I don't know what you're talking about."

"Sure you do."

"I can assure you I don't." I cross my arms. "Now please leave me alone. If you come back again, I'm going to call the police."

He holds up his hands. "Easy there, tiger. I'm just trying to help."

I point toward the street. "I mean it, Van. I don't want you coming back here. You're not welcome at my house."

"Have it your way," he says, as smarmy as ever. He starts toward his car, jingling his keys. He's steps away from the old Crown Vic and turns on his heel. "Before I go, I'll just leave you with this." Van jerks his head toward Bob's house. "I'd watch out for old Bob here. He knows more than he's letting on."

I'd already suspected that, given what Joel and I found. Of course Van would have uncovered the same things we did. He's probably already figured out that Bob was behind the blind trust and that Erica was drowning under a tsunami of self-imposed debt. But he doesn't know that I know and I have no intention of letting on.

I roll my eyes. "I meant what I said about calling the cops."

I turn away from him and lead Potato up the stairs. When I hear his car door slam, I don't bother to look back.

Chapter Thirty-Two

For decades, Juneberry Lake has hosted a festival to celebrate the end of summer on the weekend of the autumnal equinox. Every year, the recreational area along the lake is transformed into an elaborate carnival: a Ferris wheel is erected, a concert stage is constructed, jump houses are inflated, food booths line the entrance. I'm told the corn maze is not to be missed. It's clearly a point of pride for the town, the evidence is everywhere—people wear T-shirts from years past, shops hang posters in the windows, it comes up in almost every conversation.

The Juneberry Lake Summer Festival draws quite a crowd to our little town—the local hotel is fully booked, vacation rentals are maxed out, and signs directing out-of-towners to a makeshift parking lot a few blocks away have appeared along Main Street. That's why I volunteered to help Trish set up a food booth for Black Bear Brew. Given the number of people who will be passing through the festival, we agreed that this would be the perfect opportunity to spread the word about the café. We'll be passing out bear claw samples and catering order coupons and loyalty reward cards all weekend. My hope is that our ground game coupled with the localized social media campaign I designed will help to expand Trish's customer base through the fall and winter months.

Getting ready for the festival has been a welcome distraction. In the two weeks since I discovered Lynette's affair and endured yet another ominous visit from Van Fischer, throwing myself into work has felt like coming home. Never mind that I've continued to neglect my actual job, which I'm sure Jordan is less than thrilled about. It's not that I've missed a deadline or delivered a subpar work product—I would never allow myself to do that. But, I haven't been my typical overperforming self. I've been doing the required minimum. I simply haven't had the bandwidth for anything more.

"This looks so good." I look up from the display I've been fussing with to see Joel. He's wearing his signature cargo shorts and last year's Summer Festival T-shirt. My mouth quirks up at the corners at the sight of him.

"Hi," I say.

He steps into the booth. "Hi." Now we're both smiling like idiots.

"Hi."

He takes another step closer. "You already said that." Then he dips his head to kiss me. It starts out as a sweet peck, nothing more than lips brushing lips. But soon I've wrapped my arms around his neck and his hands find my hips. We're melting into each other.

Joel and I have kissed exactly six times since our first date, not that I'm counting. I still get the same heady, dizzying thrill every time. I know it's only a matter of time before we do more. Much, much more.

"Ahem," Trish clears her throat. We untangle ourselves from each other, grinning like a couple of sheepish teenagers who just got caught making out in the back seat.

"Oh, hey, Trish," I say, casually smoothing the Black Bear Brew Crew T-shirt she'd gifted me with the day before.

Trish is wearing a smirk that says *I called this from a mile away*.

Joel loops his arm over my shoulder. "The booth looks great, doesn't it?"

Trish sweeps her eyes over my handiwork, taking in the buffalo plaid curtains I draped at the entrance, the wooden bear statue to the left of sample display, the cozy seating area I arranged in the corner in an attempt to mimic the charm of the café. "Our girl has quite the touch," she says.

"She sure does," Joel agrees.

"I'm proud of you kids," Trish says. "Now can one of you go get me one of those sno-cone things? It's hotter than Hades out here."

Despite the temperature inching toward ninety degrees before lunchtime, I can *feel* summer coming to an end. The heat and humidity remain, the days are still bathed in sunshine, but the evenings are getting cooler and the air carries a refreshing breeze. Fall is edging its way in.

Change is coming. I can feel it.

My BIRTHDAY IS on September twenty-first, which happens to fall smack in the middle of the festival. When I told this to Joel, he insisted on taking me to celebrate on Saturday night. I also promised the neighbors that I'd meet up with them on Sunday. Having plans for my birthday *and* a group of friends to go to the festival with feels like a massive accomplishment given that I didn't know a soul when I got here at the start of the summer. I'm excited to visit the Ferris wheel with Marge and Gal to pay homage to the site of their first kiss, to play carnival games with Ned and Ruby, to drink frozen Bootlegs with Lynette.

As far as I know, she hasn't told Allan about her affair and I have no idea if she's ended things with Stuart, but I trust her to make things right in her own time. I'm certainly in no position to judge how a person navigates a complicated relationship.

Now that I know what I know, hanging out with everyone all together is a bit tricky, but I'm hoping the merriment will provide plenty of distraction. Who has time to feel awkward when there's a corn maze to navigate?

But that will all be tomorrow's problem.

Although I spent Friday night holding down the fort at the Black Bear Brew booth, I resisted the temptation to explore the festival grounds. I wanted to see them for the first time with Joel.

Now, as we walk under the crisscrossed twinkle lights that hang over the main path, I'm so glad I waited.

Rows of carnival games—ring toss, squirt gun races, a dunk tank are to my left, a beer garden and picnic area is to the right. I see the entrance to the famous corn maze beyond. The Ferris wheel is straight ahead. It's painted a rusty red, the same as the Golden Gate Bridge. Ambient music drifts from the distant stage.

Joel entwines his fingers with mine. "Okay, birthday girl, where to first?"

I peer around, trying to soak up the scene in its entirety. My eyes land on a balloon dart game. As if on cue, a balloon pops. I flash Joel a mischievous grin. "There."

He follows my line of sight and groans when he realizes what I've chosen. "You would," he says, giving me a playful nudge. "You better win me something."

I win Joel a giant snake that he insists on draping over his shoulders. He names it Kaa after the snake in *The Jungle Book*. Joel didn't hit a single balloon (I hit all ten, but who's counting) but he plucks along, undeterred. I wonder if his consistently sunny demeanor is a result of his Midwestern upbringing. Or perhaps it's genetic. For all I know, his birth mom is the same way.

Joel holds the snake's head at my eye level. "We're going to the duck pond next," he says, attempting a hypnotic tone.

I play along. "Duck pond," I say in a faux trance.

"It actually worked," Joel whispers to himself. He examines the snake's face.

We hit the duck pond where Joel nets a duck worth twenty game tickets. A fortune! This leads us to the milk can toss (we're both terrible), Skee-Ball (we're both surprisingly decent), and the high striker, which no surprise, Joel beats me at. He hits the little platform with the mallet so hard the bell dings.

"My hero," I cry as I throw myself into his arms. He lifts me off my feet, spins me around, and then kisses me. No one in the crowd bats an eye, but I feel like I've landed smack-dab in the middle of one of Gal's romance novels. It's been so long—years and years—since I've let loose like this. I'm honestly not sure if I ever really have.

Next, we head to the beer garden for a drink (we both opt for rosé) and a funnel cake. Joel uncoils the snake from his neck and sets it on the bench. "I'm going to keep this little guy forever and ever," he says, patting it on the head. "No one's ever won me a carnival prize before."

"Stick with me, kid. There's more where that came from."

"Kid? Are we in an old-timey Hollywood movie?"

"Is saying 'kid' an old Hollywood movie thing?"

Joel fights off a smile. "I'm honestly not sure."

"You're cute."

He cups his cheeks in his hands. "I've been waiting for you to notice."

I take the opportunity to steal the last bite of funnel cake. Joel doesn't seem to mind.

"So, how are . . . things?" he says instead.

I've, of course, brought Joel up to speed on Van's ominous warning about Bob and my unfortunate Lynette and Stuart spotting. I figured it wouldn't be betraying Lynette's confidence if I told someone who'd never met her. Besides, I needed someone to talk to about all of it.

"Things are the same. Nothing new to report."

"So have you given up on finding Erica?" He makes an exaggerated face, like he's just had a massive epiphany. "Wait . . . was the Erica stuff all just a ruse to get close to me? You can tell me. I won't be mad. It's kind of flattering, actually."

I toss a crumpled napkin in his direction. "Don't flatter yourself."

"Too late."

I drop my fork onto the now-empty plate. "I guess I'm just out of ideas. None of my other neighbors seem to have any clue where Erica went or how to contact her. Van said Bob knows more than he's letting on, which is probably true, but Bob and I don't exactly have a warm relationship."

"Yeah, Trish said he just filed another complaint with the city. Something about nosy newcomers snooping around . . ."

I smack Joel's arm. "No, he didn't."

"No. But he did make a stink at last week's town hall. He says we haven't seen any benefits."

"He sucks."

"Agreed."

By the time we finish our wine, the sun has set and the air borders on cool. The glow of the festival has taken on an essence reminiscent of a Disney movie. Specifically, *The Princess and the Frog*. One of my favorites.

Music starts playing from the stage overlooking the lake. It's twangy and unfamiliar but fits the night perfectly. Joel grabs my hand. "Come on."

A ceiling of market lights crisscrosses the dance floor and while I don't know any of the songs this band is playing, I don't care. They're surprisingly good.

The only time I've ever line danced was—inexplicably—in my fifth grade PE class. Unless the Cha-Cha Slide at my cousin's wedding counts. Joel says it doesn't. I've always found organized dancing to be kind of embarrassing, but now that I'm doing it, it's actually fun. It's not very hard either—it's basically just a series of grapevines and kicks and shuffles and turns. It kind of reminds me of the dumb little dances Hannah and I used to make up in middle school. I think Mom still has videos of a few of them, but I've never been able to bring myself to look.

Naturally, I can't help but appreciate how orderly it all is. Plus, dancing with Joel makes me feel all sparkly.

By the end of our third dance, I've just about gotten the hang of the Tush Push (you can't make these names up). "Want some water?" Joel says into my ear. My face feels warm and I'm getting thirsty, so I nod. He spins me one more time before leading me off the dance floor.

"NOT SO BAD for a small town, huh?" Joel says in between sips of water.

"Not bad at all," I agree. The warmth of the dance floor has faded and the air is just cool enough to make me shiver. I wrap Joel's snake around my shoulders.

"Looks like someone needs a Summer Festival sweatshirt," Joel says, gesturing toward a merch booth.

"An official Summer Festival sweatshirt? I guess I really am a local now."

Joel offers to buy it for me as a birthday present, but I insist on getting it for myself. I want my first Juneberry Lake novelty clothing item to come from me because, as silly as it sounds, this feels like a moment. I pick a green crewneck and tug it over my head. I think it's the first time I've worn a sweatshirt since I moved here.

"It's getting kind of late," Joel says.

I haven't thought about the time since we got here, but this brings me back to reality. "I should probably get home to Potato soon."

"Okay, but we can't go home without riding the Ferris wheel," he insists.

Jimbo yanks a giant lever and the churning wheel grinds to a stop. He lets a couple of high school kids off before gesturing for Joel and me to climb in. "Have fun up there, you two," he says with a wink as we glide away.

Joel drapes his arm over the back of the cart as we climb, and I relish the warmth of him beside me as the wind gently dances across my cheeks. My breath catches as the lake comes into view, glimmering under the stars and festival lights. If the sun were still out, I'd almost be able to see my house from here.

"You know, two of my neighbors had their first kiss right about . . ." I wait for the cart to climb to the very top. "Here."

"Oh yeah?"

The Ferris wheel lurches to a stop and the cart rocks gently forward and back. I wonder if Jimbo is doing us a solid. Joel brushes my cheek with his thumb, then tucks a curl behind my ear. The feeling of his fingers on my neck is electric. I don't know how long we're stuck up there, because soon we're kissing and time acts a bit funny when we do. I completely lose track.

Things are bordering on PG-13 when the ride jumps to a start again. We pull away from each other, both of us catching our breath.

It feels like we've started something new tonight. Something I'm not sure I can finish.

But I think I'd like to try.

Chapter Thirty-Three

It took everything in me not to invite Joel in last night. Like, everything.

We kissed on my back porch for what felt like hours until I heard Potato scratching at the door, which distracted me just long enough to break the spell.

In the light of day, I'm glad that I waited. Not because I have any hang-ups around sleeping with someone too soon or anything. It's just that, the way I feel about Joel scares me a little. I really, really like him.

Marco left me a voicemail to wish me happy birthday yesterday and then texted me again last night, insisting that he had something he needed to tell me. I can't imagine what there is to talk about, but I'm *this close* to blocking his number, so maybe I owe him a conversation first. I told him we can talk later next week, after the festival is over. He hasn't written back yet, which is unlike him, but maybe it's a good sign. Maybe he's finally getting over whatever weird sense of guilt or nostalgia or pity has compelled him to keep reaching out.

I hope so. This needs to end for good.

Potato's little tail twirls with excitement when she sees all the neighbors milling around the entrance to the festival. It's almost like she knew what she'd missed out on yesterday. Bubbles is the first to greet Potato and the two promptly begin exchanging butt sniffs.

"Happy birthday, Eliza!" Ruby calls. "Mom said I can ride the big slide and the Ferris wheel!"

Lynette told me that she'd tried to steer Ruby away from the rides in years past, but that Ruby's doctor had finally convinced her that it was perfectly safe. "That's so exciting," I tell Ruby. "Who are you going to ride with first?"

"Me!" Ned says.

Allan rests his hand on Ned's little shoulder. "We'll see about that, mister wiggly."

Ned responds with an over-the-top full-body wiggle. Ruby laughs so hard she has to cover her face.

"So, Eliza here's the deal," Marge starts. She tosses me a yellow T-shirt with LOON LANE GANG written in big block letters across the chest. The rest of the neighbors are already wearing theirs and I promptly pull mine on over my tank top. Even though it's hardly fashionable, I've never felt cooler. "There are a few key things we have to do today—it's a neighborhood tradition." She holds up her fingers and begins counting. "They include the watermelon-eating contest, the giant slide, the frozen Bootleg booth in the beer garden, and the fireworks show." She looks around at the rest of the group. "Did I forget anything?"

"The corn maze," Bob says.

"That was really more Erica's thing," Gal says, before quickly adding, "What about the concert?"

"That's right before the fireworks," Lynette says.

"And don't forget about lunch at the brat stand," Stuart adds. Everyone bobs their heads in agreement.

The conversation quickly devolves into a swirling mass of logistics and scheduling. Marge and Gal take the lead, ensuring everyone gets a chance to do all of their favorite activities, while also reminding the group that we need to stick together as much as possible so that no one misses out. I pour water into a pop-up dog bowl for Potato. She and Bubbles lap it up gratefully.

Eventually, a consensus is reached. Our first stop will be the giant slide.

Allan carries Ruby up the steps of the huge, gleaming slide and sets her on my lap. Ruby declared that she wanted to ride with me on the walk over and honestly, I couldn't think of a greater honor.

Ruby and I shimmy into a potato sack next to Ned and Allan. The teenager supervising this whole operation wastes no time in giving us a nice big push to kick off our descent and I'm a little surprised by how quickly we pick up speed. Do they grease this thing up with butter? Ruby shrieks with delight and I can hear Ned howling with laughter behind me. We fly over a dip and land harder than I expected. For a moment, I worry about Ruby, but when I look down at her little face, all I see is pure happiness.

"We *have* to do that again!" Ruby cries after we crash into a pile of foam blocks. Her voice is filled with so much joy that I'm suddenly relieved to be wearing sunglasses. I don't need Ruby to see me crying.

I hug her little body. "We'll go as many times as you want."

After Ned and Ruby finally got bored with the slide (I lost count after our tenth trip down), we take in the watermelon-eating contest. Stuart surprises everyone by entering and then landing himself in the finals.

"I don't know where he put all that watermelon," Gal marvels. "He's a string bean."

"He's pretty amazing," Lynette says. I don't care for her doe-eyed expression or the way she wraps him in what I now know is a more than neighborly hug when he steps down from the podium, a third-place medal draped around his neck and his lips stained red.

Lynette had promised me she was going to sort all of this out, but now I'm wondering if she likes things this way. She can have her watermelon and eat it too.

"You're going to be pissing all day," Bob says.

"Is a watermelon going to grow in your stomach now?" Ned asks.

"Why would you say that?" Allan responds. He's holding Ned's hand.

"Because he ate *a lot* of seeds." Ned holds his hands as far apart as he can. "One of them has to grow."

By the time we've worked our way through most of the group's itinerary, dusk has settled over the festival, but the temperature remains well into the eighties. It's warmer tonight than last night. I probably didn't need to bring my sweatshirt.

We nestle in at a large, picnic bench across from the corn maze as everyone finishes their brats and Bootlegs. Ned and Ruby got frozen custard. I'm a little jealous. I alternate between staring resentfully at my Bootleg and eyeing Lynette and Stuart, who sit arm to arm on the bench across from me. Allan is fully engrossed in his bratwurst and doesn't seem to notice.

Bob stands abruptly, staring at his phone. He looks around at everyone at the table until his eyes eventually land on me. He seems to be weighing his options, but for what I have absolutely no idea.

"I'll be right back," Bob eventually says to the group. He walks off, toward the entrance to the corn maze clutching his phone before disappearing behind a crowd of teenagers, all donning some variation of crop tops and frayed jean shorts, which I'm sure Bob hates. The idea brings me more than a little joy.

A man dressed as a giant ear of corn strolls by, waving to the crowd. "There's the festival mascot," Stuart announces. Potato, who'd been napping on a patch of grass under the bench springs to life, barking and lunging at the corn.

She pulls so hard on her leash that it nearly yanks me off the bench. "She hates corn," I say helplessly.

"You never know what it's going to be with these dogs," Gal says, shaking her head in amusement. "We've seen it all. Shoes, plates, garbage cans, palm trees, the word 'pickle'—"

"Actual pickles," Marge adds.

I do my best to settle Potato down, but for some reason the corn is driving her wild. I don't think she wants to hurt the giant corn man, but she certainly has some unresolved issues with the starchy vegetable. When she finally plops her little butt down into the dirt, still whining, I take the opportunity to readjust her leash, which has been digging into my palm.

That's when Potato takes off.

I cry out, half yelling, half wailing her name as the leash slips from my hands. Without thinking, I'm on my feet and setting off in pursuit of my dog, who is in pursuit of giant corn. I can sense Marge, Gal, and Allan behind me, but I don't look back, my eyes are locked on Potato. That is until I run into that crowd of teenagers, none of whom are in any hurry to get out of the way.

"I lost her," I say when Gal catches up to me, panting.

"I think I saw her go into the maze," Allan says.

"Let's split up, the four of us," Marge says, gesturing to the rest of the neighbors. "We'll get her back."

I nod and take off toward the towering rows of corn.

EVERY POSSIBLE SCENARIO races through my head as I search for Potato with increased desperation.

Is this what being responsible for another living being is? Lynette must feel this way all the time about Ned and Ruby.

It's terrible.

The corn maze is more disorienting than I expected. The stalks are quite high and packed together so densely that you can't see to the other side. I consider sticking my head through the wall to find a shortcut, but then I remember that M. Night Shyamalan movie with the aliens in the cornfield that Hannah made me watch and I think better of it.

After what feels like hours and more twists and turns than I'll ever remember, I spot the corn man leaning up against a pole in the middle of the maze. I run toward him at full speed. As I get closer, it becomes evident that he's cradling something in his arms.

Potato.

I flail to a stop a couple of feet from my dog and her new best friend, dust kicking up in my wake. When I approach, Potato looks up at me casually, as if to say, *Oh hey, Mom. Fancy meeting you here.*

"I take it she belongs to you?" the man asks. He never stops scratching under Potato's chin. I nod, too out of breath to form a proper sentence. He smiles and I realize that I know him—he's the bartender at the Common Loon. I almost didn't recognize him without his Viking horns. "She came running at me like she'd been shot out of a cannon and leaped into my arms. Does she have a thing for corn?"

"Apparently," I say, shaking my head. "I thought she hated it but . . ." I glance down at Potato who is staring at the corn man with what can only be described as cultlike devotion. "I guess she's a fan. I'm so sorry."

"Are you kidding? This made my day."

After I text the neighbors to let them know that I've found my runaway, it takes me several minutes to pry Potato away from her pal. She finally bids him a reluctant farewell and I promise that I'll bring her to the Common Loon so that they can visit again soon.

"I'll even wear the corn suit!" the bartender says. I'm not sure that's a great idea, but it's not worth saying anything right now.

I start back in the direction that I came, but soon realize that I'm not sure which direction that is. I turn back to Potato's new friend. "How do I get out of here?"

He shrugs. "Beats me."

You'd think a man made of corn would know his way around a corn maze, but I guess that's what I get for making assumptions.

It's fine. I'm just a little turned around, but I know I'll find my way out eventually. I scoop Potato into my arms and take a right.

Then I take a left.

And another right.

It's a dead end.

I take a moment to gather my bearings, hoping that someone who knows the way out will come along. And that's when I hear Bob.

It sounds like he's just on the other side of the corn wall. And he's talking to a woman. I can make out snippets of their conversation from where I stand.

"Wish you were here."

". . . not the same without you."

"Can you see okay?"

It sounds like he might be on a FaceTime call.

I shouldn't be eavesdropping, but I can't help myself. I've never heard Bob speak this kindly or gently to anyone before. If I didn't know any better, I'd guess that he was talking to his son, but the voice on the other end of the call is clearly a woman's. She asks a question and Bob's tone shifts. "Yeah, he's been poking around, asking the new girl a bunch of questions, but I've got it handled."

Am I the new girl?

"No, no," he says. "You'll stay put if you know what's best for you. You know what'll happen if you ever come back."

I can't tell if he's threatening this woman or warning her. I'm about to peek around the corner to see if I can get a look at who he's FaceTiming with when I hear him say, "All right, Erica. We'll talk again soon."

Chapter Thirty-Four

I've checked almost everything off my Juneberry Lake to-do list with one major exception: hosting a housewarming party.

Despite some recent complications (namely Lynette and Stuart's affair and discovering that Bob is in contact with Erica), things with my neighbors have been even better than I'd hoped. And I want to thank them in the best way that I know how.

Italian-style lunches are a time-honored tradition in my family. Ever since I can remember—and surely since way before I was born—the extended Colletti universe has gathered around a long table piled high with carbs and meats and cheeses for a marathon lunch. Everyone is usually seated by noon and we don't typically head home until well after the sun has gone down. No one's seat at the table is permanent—it's an ongoing game of musical chairs as cousins and siblings and aunts and uncles rotate from one conversation to the next in an attempt to squeeze in a visit with everyone.

I've seen it all at these lunches—family secrets revealed, sibling rivalries come to a head, arguments over who makes better ravioli, tears of joy (helped along by carafes of wine), and even an engagement. In my family, these lunches are where bonds are strengthened. I'm hoping that my Midwestern version of an Italian lunch will serve a similar purpose.

Lynette agreed to lend me a set of folding tables, chairs, and a surprisingly comfortable bench that she sets up at Thanksgiving when all her relatives come to visit, and Erica had stocked her house with just about everything else I need. I've pushed Lynette's tables together under a big shady tree and draped them in a red and white tablecloth. Luckily, the weather today is perfect—midseventies with a light breeze. If this lunch had been a day later, I would have been screwed. There are thunderstorms in the forecast tomorrow. Erica's plates (a charming mishmash of forest green and white that must have been collected from antique shops and rummage sales over the years), burlap napkins, and her big glass goblets are the perfect addition. As I garnish the table with sprigs of rosemary, I take a moment to admire my work. It's quite the tablescape if I do say so myself.

I spent all last night preparing my platters. I pulled out all the stops—chopped salad with homemade vinaigrette; spaghetti with Mom's marinara sauce; a cheese platter complete with Fontina, Provolone, and Taleggio; a small plate of cold cuts; ciabatta rolls; breadsticks; caprese; and of course, prosciutto with melon. I've also prepared a vegetarian option sans prosciutto. Cantaloupe is just as delicious with a dash of sea salt sprinkled on top.

I was pleasantly surprised by the selection at the market. My expectations were low given that I grew up in San Francisco where Italian delis are abundant. But this spread should do just fine.

The pièce de résistance is my family's focaccia. I've shown remarkable self-restraint since the move and have only defrosted one sheet so far. That left me with three to share. It's a big sacrifice, but I think it'll be worth it. Focaccia isn't nearly as good after it's been defrosted, but I figure since my guests haven't ever had it fresh from the oven, they'll still be pretty blown away.

I'm adding a couple bottles of chianti and a sparkling Italian soda for Marge to the center of the table as my neighbors begin to descend on my backyard. Lynette and Allan arrive first, without Ned and Ruby, who are with their grandparents for the weekend. They look odd together without the kids, incomplete somehow. I wonder if they've been using the time alone to reconnect. Not that it's any of my business.

Gal and Marge, with Darla the Chihuahua in tow arrive next, carrying a bouquet of flowers that Marge picked from her garden. Then Stuart, who smiles tightly as he greets Allan, never bothering to remove his sunglasses.

Bob shows up last, which is no surprise. Honestly, the only real surprise here is that he actually came. I'm still not sure what to make of the phone call I'd overheard, but I know I have to say something soon.

Everyone settles into their seats as I start passing platters, explaining each dish, and recommending my favorite pairings. Soon enough, everyone's plates are full. Bob is the only one who complains that he's not a fan of cold cuts.

The afternoon unfurls at an easy pace. We talk about the Summer Festival fireworks show (Gal insists it was the best one yet; Stuart disagrees); Lynette promises to invite us all over for mulled cider when the leaves start to change (Marge is certain it'll be any day now); we all laugh when Darla tries prosciutto for the first time and her bulgy little eyes light up with joy. Something about a big Italian spread in the middle of the day seems to make everyone slow down. Just like back home. It works every time.

After everyone has gone back for seconds and in some cases, thirds. I run inside to get my tiramisu. With Enzo's guidance, I also baked some oatmeal walnut cookies for Marge, since I'm not sure how strict she is about alcohol consumption in baked goods. Tiramisu is soaked in rum.

I catch a glimpse at the clock on my way out and realize that I've completely lost track of time. Joel could be here any minute. I'd told him he could come over around six and it's well past that. I send him a quick text to say that lunch is running long.

When I reemerge from the house with Potato at my heels I realize that I'm too late. Lynette is chatting up Joel, who leans awkwardly against the trunk of the tree that shades our lunch table. My stomach constricts at the sight. Not because I don't want Joel to meet everyone, but because I didn't want him to meet them via ambush.

I make my way back to the group as quickly as possible, which isn't very quick at all given that I'm balancing a spongy tiramisu atop Erica's vintage cake stand.

"Hey, Joel," I say tightly, not sounding nearly as casual as I'd hoped to. I set the cake stand in the center of the table.

"We saw Joel trying to sneak away after he spotted all of us," Lynette says. "But I convinced him to stay."

My eyes meet Joel's as I attempt to arrange my face into an apologetic expression, but I probably just look like I've eaten too many olives.

Which I have.

"So this is the mystery man," Gal says, making a show of looking Joel up and down. "He's cute."

"Gal," Marge hisses.

Gal looks at her wife and shrugs. "Well he is."

Bob stares at Joel and I can tell he's trying to place him. "Hey," he says, realization dawning on his stern face, "you're the guy from the city hall meetings. You're one of those Join Juneberry Lake people." Bob says this as though he's just recognized Joel from an episode of *America's Most Wanted*.

Marge shoots Bob a withering look.

"Why don't you have a seat?" Stuart says patting a space next to him on the bench. Stuart seems to be taking some degree of lighthearted pleasure in watching us squirm. I swear to god, I'll start talking about Stuart's book in front of everyone if he keeps needling Joel.

I curse myself for not timing things better as Gal and Lynette pepper Joel with every question under the sun. Marco endured something similar at his first family lunch back home. It's something of a rite of passage, but I feel terrible for Joel. He hasn't been properly prepared.

I've never seen him look so uncomfortable. The man who knows—and actually *enjoys* talking with—almost everyone in town now sits stiffly beside me, his shoulders creeping toward his ears, eyes darting around the table. His gaze lands on Marge but she doesn't acknowledge him.

The tiramisu can't even diffuse the tension, which is usually a sure thing.

Bob resumes his interrogation through bites of cake, peppering Joel with questions about his job (as if he even knows what coding is), needling him about why he left Wisconsin, and once again, circling back to his Join Juneberry Lake discourse.

"Don't we have enough people here?" Bob asks the table before flicking his eyes back to Joel, who just shrugs helplessly. He's acting so strange. Sure, Bob is a lot, but it's not Joel's first encounter with him. I watch as he steals another glance at Marge, who has her fingertips pressed against her temples.

Whatever the reason for Joel's discomfort, I can't watch him squirm another second longer. I need to redirect everyone's attention. It's a split-second decision, one that I hope I won't regret. "So, Bob? Was that Erica I heard you talking to at the festival?"

I was planning to bring this up to Gal or Lynette in private, but I suppose now is as good a time as any.

I'm not exaggerating when I say that the whole table freezes. Even the crickets stop chirping. My neighbors look like statues, but their eyes are darting every which way. Gal appears to recover first. She clears her throat then says, "Bob's not in touch with Erica anymore."

Marge, who has been uncharacteristically silent says, "None of us are."

Bob directs his icy glare at me. "Were you spying on me?"

My eyes widen at the accusation. "Of course not. After I found Potato canoodling with the corn . . ." I pause because the ridiculousness of that sentence does not fit how serious this conversation is. "Potato and I got a little turned around. We hit a dead end in the maze and I heard you on the other side of the wall."

Bob's right eye twitches at the mention of the corn maze. "It was Erica that you were talking to on FaceTime, right?"

I never technically saw Bob's phone, but given his eye twitch, I'm pretty confident I've got him on the ropes.

Bob sputters, "You're lying."

That's rich, coming from the person who's been lying to everyone. I look around at my neighbors who have become my dear friends. My surrogate family, really. Their faces are all masks of stunned disbelief. Lynette has gone white as a ghost. Stuart is sweating profusely. They deserve better than this. I straighten my spine. "No, Bob. You're the one who's lying. You've been lying to all of them for more than a year." I turn to address the table. "Bob is not only in touch with Erica, but he told her not to come back if she knew what was good for her. I heard every word."

Gal takes a long drink of wine straight from the chianti bottle. Marge drapes a hand over her eyes. But no one says a thing. I figured they'd be upset to learn about Bob's duplicity, but the news seems to be hitting them harder than I expected.

"I'm really sorry you all had to find out this way," I say. Joel shifts uncomfortably beside me. Maybe I should have just let Bob keep grilling him. That might have been less awkward.

"Eliza," Lynette says gently.

"Don't," Bob warns.

"She already knows," Stuart grumbles, defeated.

Bob looks from Allan to Gal to Marge. They all appear to sigh in resignation, agreeing to something that I don't understand. Bob looks back at Lynette, defeated. "Go ahead," he sighs.

Lynette swallows. "Eliza, we know that Bob is still in touch with Erica."

Now it's my turn to be stunned. It takes me more time than I would like to gather my thoughts. "But you told me that she didn't leave a forwarding address, that she never answered your calls. You said there was no way to get in touch with her."

"I know that's what I said."

The realization that Lynette has been deceiving me lands as a painful thud in my chest. "You've been lying to me about this too?"

Lynette flinches at the word "too." Allan's eyebrows tick upward. "I didn't have a choice," Lynette says quietly. The way she's framing it, as though she's somehow the victim gnaws at me. Without realizing, I look from Lynette to Allan and then Stuart. Allan's head ping-pongs between his wife and his reclusive neighbor, a look of puzzlement on his face.

"She's telling the truth, hun," Gal says. "We all agreed not to tell you. It wasn't easy, but we felt it was for the best."

"And we tried our darndest not to get too close to you—to keep a friendly neighborly distance—but you won us over," Marge adds. None of this makes me feel any better.

Worse, I have absolutely no idea what is happening. I can't help but feel betrayed.

"Can someone just tell me what's going on here?" When no one responds, I add, "Or should I just call Van Fischer?"

That seems to get their attention. Joel's hand finds my thigh. I don't know if he's trying to be supportive or suggesting that I take it down a notch.

Lynette leans forward, her face grave. "Eliza, you haven't been in touch with Van Fischer, have you?"

I shrink, feeling like a kid who broke a window and lied about it. "No," I say a touch too defensively. "But I don't think he plans on leaving me alone until he finds Erica."

"That is a problem," Stuart says. His voice is quiet, but it's not unkind. More like resigned.

"Are we really doing this?" Lynette asks.

"Maybe Eliza's friend should go," Gal suggests.

Allan and Stuart nod along. Bob turns to Joel. "I think she's right, son." The way Bob says it sounds like he just told Joel to take a long walk off a short pier.

"Don't call him 'son,'" Marge says. She's barely said a word since this debacle began. I can see that her hands are shaking. I don't know if it's from fear or anger or anxiety, but whatever it is, she's not okay.

Bob looks genuinely confused.

Gal rubs Marge's back, which seems to settle her nerves. She crosses her arms over her chest as Gal looks on in concern. I don't know if any of us have ever seen Marge like this.

"I can go," Joel says into my ear. "I'll just wait for you in the house, okay?" He looks at Marge before rising from the table.

"No," I insist loudly. Maybe too loudly. I adjust my volume and turn to address my neighbors. "Joel should stay. He's been helping me try to find Erica and he's my—" I stop short. Joel's not my boyfriend but he's not just my friend either. I settle on, "My Joel."

He's my Joel? What does that even mean?

"It's fine," Joel says. "Really." He turns and addresses the table. "It was nice to . . . meet you all."

"You too, hun," Gal says with forced cheer. The rest of the table remains silent.

Joel gathers Potato from the bench and heads toward my house. When he gets to the porch, he looks back over his shoulder, but I'm not sure if he's looking at me.

Chapter Thirty-Five

We all sit in silence, save for Darla's little snores from her carrier on Gal's chest. She's slept straight through all of the drama.

Gal speaks first. "We were all very close with Erica—ever since she moved to town. We knew all about her philandering husband and their crappy marriage and she knew all of our stuff, too. She was one of our closest friends. She still is."

"Which is why we all agreed to protect her," Lynette says.

"From what?" I can't imagine what could possibly be so big and bad that they would need to cover for her so elaborately.

"As you may have figured out, Erica loved to gamble. And for as long as we knew her, she was convinced that she was going to win the lottery someday." Lynette laughs at the memory. "She had a methodical system—every week, she'd drive to the most rural gas station she could find, this rinky-dink mom-and-pop place one town over and buy exactly ten tickets."

"And she'd never pick her own numbers," Gal adds. "She read somewhere that it's statistically better to let the machine pick."

Lynette nods. "Anyway, she did this for years. She'd always show up to Friday night book club with Mega Millions tickets tucked into the pages of her book."

"That's why you haven't been invited to book club by the way," Stuart interjects. "Erica still calls in every month."

I still don't see where this story is going, but I do take some solace in knowing that I wasn't being excluded based on something I'd done.

"Let's cut to the chase," Bob butts in. "Erica picked up tickets for the whole neighborhood every week for years and then we won."

"You *won*?"

They all nod.

"What does that mean?"

Bob rolls his eyes. "It means we won. We won seven hundred million dollars."

"To be exact, it was 722.85 million dollars," Allan says. "Cut that in half for taxes."

"I don't understand. You're telling me you're all multimillionaires?"

"She's quick, this one," Bob cracks.

"But . . . how did you *all* win?" I ask. That's probably not what I should even be focusing on at the moment, but I'm suddenly desperate to wrap my mind around the logistics of this revelation.

"We all chipped in to Erica's lottery fund—a couple dollars a week," Stuart says. "The agreement was that if our numbers were ever drawn, we'd split the money equally amongst the five households."

"It was just a verbal agreement," Lynette adds. "We never thought we'd actually win. Besides, we all trusted each other."

"We aren't dummies either, though," Gal puts in. "We drew up a contract after we won, just to be safe."

"Mostly to protect our portion of the winnings from Gary," Marge says.

"So . . . why do you still live *here*?" I think every living adult has fantasized about what they'd do if they won the lottery someday. I'd pay off my parents' debts, buy myself a house, gift a chunk of my winnings to Enzo, set aside a little money for everyone in my extended family, buy a new wardrobe, make a massive charitable donation, quit my job, and travel the world. In no particular order. But from what I could tell, my neighbors—my uber-wealthy neighbors—had done no such thing.

"Ever heard of the curse of the lottery?" Gal says. "None of us ever expected our lives to change overnight like that."

"Except Erica," Bob says.

Gal concedes his point with a flick of her hand. "Anyway, we decided that we didn't want our lives to change in a dramatic way and we didn't want our friends and family to treat us any differently. So, we didn't tell a soul."

"How is that possible? You have to come forward when you win the lottery. They have to give you the big check."

Allan shakes his head. "Not in Minnesota. Winners can choose to remain anonymous here."

"Which was especially important for Erica," Lynette adds.

"On account of that son of a bitch she was married to," says Bob.

Gal picks up the rest of the story. "Luckily, the bastard had already changed his tune about getting a divorce. He'd convinced his assistant to marry him, poor thing. Erica was only weeks away from being free of him once and for all when we won. But if he'd found out . . ."

"He would have taken her for everything she had," I say, realization settling in.

Gal points a pink fingernail in my direction. "Bingo. So, we kept it quiet. The divorce was finalized and Erica's ex was none the wiser."

"But then she started renovating the house," Lynette says. "Among other things."

Gal cups her hands under her chest and mouths "boob job."

"It got back to Gary, somehow, which piqued his curiosity. He knew exactly how much money Erica had gotten in the divorce and the way she was spending, she would have blown through it in a matter of months. He was always too smart and too nosy for his own good," Lynette continues. "The law is a bit murky, but Gary might be able to make a claim to Erica's money since they weren't technically divorced when she won it. And given his connections, Erica decided that it would probably be for the best if she sold the house and got out of town. The hope was that it would look like she'd been renovating the house as an investment so that she could sell it and start fresh somewhere else."

My stomach roils. I can't believe that I've inadvertently kicked up such a massive hornet's nest. And I'm even more shocked that Bob was actually trying to do the right thing. "That's awful," I say. "Poor Erica."

Gal presses her pink lips together. "It's been rough on all of us. Maybe this is our version of the curse."

"Or she is," Bob says, jutting his chin out at me.

"Where is she now?" I ask.

Bob scoffs. "Like we'd ever tell you that."

I actually understand where he's coming from. "Of course," I say. "I'm sorry. I don't mean to pry."

That elicits a laugh from the table at my expense. I deserve it, but it hurts. "I won't pry any *further.*"

"I think the damage is done," Bob says. "What have you told Van Fischer?"

I shake my head. "Nothing."

"Maybe this could be useful," Stuart interjects. "We can find out everything he knows and fill Erica in."

"We might be able to throw him off the scent," Gal agrees.

"I'll do whatever you want me to do," I say. And I mean it. I'm desperate to fix this, to put the toothpaste back in the tube.

"Erica is like a daughter to me," Bob says. "If this goes sideways . . ." He lets his voice trail off. He doesn't need to finish the sentence. If this goes sideways, Bob will be the least of my worries. I think I'd lose my new friends for good.

NONE OF MY neighbors bid me a proper goodbye as they scatter to their respective houses. I can't blame them—I've just exposed their big secret and opened them up to all kinds of scrutiny.

I watch as Gal leads a shaken Marge up the lawn and across the street. Bob slams his door, which I don't think was an accident.

I hear Lynette whisper to Allan that she needs to tell him something and my whole body goes numb. Stuart catches my eye as he's leaving. I think he heard it too.

I drop my head into my hands, curling my fingers into claws, letting them tangle my hair. Joel must have been watching from the window, because he and Potato join me outside. He rubs my back. She licks my arm.

"Do you want to talk about it?" Joel asks.

"I wouldn't know where to begin," I say. Which is the truth, but also, I'm not sure if I should reveal my neighbors' secret. I shouldn't even know about it.

"You don't have to start at the beginning. I already know everything."

My head snaps up. "What? How?"

Joel shifts on the bench next to me. "Don't get mad," he starts. "But I overheard you."

I turn to look at Joel, who wears a charmingly sheepish expression. "How did you overhear everything?"

He winces. "Maybe 'overheard' is the wrong word. I eaves-dropped on everything. Potato and I sat on your back porch and, well, your voices carried."

"Joel Jawowski!" I say with mock offense. Honestly, I can't blame him. I probably would have done the same thing.

"I figured you wouldn't mind since I'm your . . . *Joel*." He taps his knee against mine under the table and if I weren't so dis-traught, I'd kiss him. I don't know how he manages to be ador-able and sexy all at once.

"Do you think I'm a monster for outing them?"

"You didn't know," Joel says. "You were trying to help."

I release my hair and turn my head to look at Joel. "But I didn't help, did I? I made things so much worse."

"You didn't know," he repeats.

"I wish they would have just told me. Why lie for so long?"

Joel draws a breath. "People lie for all kinds of reasons about all kinds of things."

This perks my antenna up. I'm probably just on edge because of everything that came out today, but I still have to ask. "Why do I feel like there's something you aren't telling me?" I ask, bracing for impact.

Joel looks up at the sky, maybe searching for the courage to confess something awful. But then he says, "You know how I came here looking for my birth mother?"

I nod, head swimming.

"It's Marge."

"Marge?" My voice trails off as the puzzle pieces start to click together in my mind. Marge's past in New York, her temporary sobriety when she returned home to the safety of her parents' house. She'd been pregnant. With Joel.

That's why Marge had fallen silent when Joel arrived and

taken such offense to Bob's rudeness. She was protecting the baby she'd put up for adoption.

My head spins as I remember that it was only after Lynette told everyone that Joel had been over to my house that Marge showed an interest in spending time with me one-on-one. In hindsight, she'd been instrumental in pushing me to give Joel a chance. A mother meddling in her son's love life.

"Was Marge the reason you decided to ask me out on a date?"

His expression turns sheepish. "She might have mentioned something."

"Does Gal know?"

His smile falters. "Yes and no. She knows about me, but we haven't met yet. Until today, that is."

"Is that why you never came to my front door?"

"I just didn't want to catch Marge off guard. And my instincts were right because look how she responded today. Marge doesn't have much of a poker face."

"I really blew everything up today."

"Eliza, you're too hard on yourself. Sometimes things just happen. I just happened to be adopted, and my birth mom just happened to live in Juneberry Lake, and you just happened to move here and your lunch just happened to run late today. None of this was planned. I couldn't have orchestrated any of this. That's not how life works."

"I know."

"I'm not so sure that you do."

I wipe a traitorous tear from my cheek, but another one follows. Joel catches it with his thumb.

I raise my eyes to meet his. I want to tell him I'm so happy he's here, that I'm so happy he found Marge, that I don't know what I'd do without him.

I want to tell him that I'm falling for him.

But then my screen door slams behind us.

"Eliza?" The sound of his voice triggers an involuntary wave of comfort and nostalgia and home. I look up to see the one person I never expected standing on my back porch. He looks entirely out of place in his checkered shirt and rolled sleeves and Italian leather loafers.

But he's real. And he's really here.

Marco.

Chapter Thirty-Six

Instinctively, as though I've been caught in the throes of an illicit affair, I push Joel's hand from my cheek. He recoils from me, wounded, and I hate myself for it.

Marco pretends not to notice. He digs his hands into his pockets as he makes his way down my back steps. It feels like it's all happening in slow motion. He looks around at the lake, letting out a low whistle. "Quite a place you've got here. It's even better than the pictures."

I step out from behind the table to intercept Marco. There's a part of me that wants to run to him, to hug him, to cry into his chest as I have so many times before. He's a piece of my home and as dysfunctional as our relationship had become, his familiarity is comforting.

"I take it that's your fiancé," Joel says from behind me.

I turn to look at Joel. He's set Potato on the grass and is standing now, too. "Ex-fiancé," I correct him.

He dips his head in a slow, sad nod. "I'll let you two talk."

"Joel, wait—"

"It's fine, Eliza. There are some things I need to take care of anyway. We'll talk soon."

He turns to leave before I have a chance to reply. I almost start after him, but then I sense Marco at my side.

"So," Marco says. I turn to look at him, my swirling conflict of emotions surely written all over my face.

Marco's expression softens. He jerks his chin toward Joel. "That's the guy you've been seeing?"

I can tell he's trying to be strong, but I've hurt him. We've hurt each other. It's something we've gotten quite good at these past few months. "Yes," I say as neutrally as I can. But then I realize that there's no way that Marco should know I've been seeing anyone. I made a point of not mentioning Joel to my friends.

The only person I've told was Enzo.

"Your mom told me," Marco says. And while I should—and do—feel betrayed, I'm mostly just relieved that Enzo hadn't been the one to go running to Marco. Mom is a meddler. And an eavesdropper. She also adored Marco, thought of him as another son. Plus, I haven't shared the gory details of our breakup with her. I suppose I shouldn't be surprised.

It hits me that I owe Farah an apology. And an explanation. But I can't deal with that right now.

One disaster at a time.

"Do you really think it was appropriate for you to be keeping tabs on me through my mom?" Now I'm annoyed again.

Marco looks offended. "She was going to be my mother-in-law. We were family."

I sigh. "What are you doing here, Marco?"

"You said we could talk."

"I meant over the phone."

"After all we've been through together, don't you think I deserve a chance to talk with you face-to-face?"

This is meant to make me feel guilty, and to a certain extent, it does. I never really said a proper goodbye when I left for Minnesota. To be fair, I didn't think we had anything left to say to each other.

Clearly Marco disagrees.

I sigh. "Okay, we can talk. But first, I need you to help me clean up this mess."

MARCO AND I have cleaned up after our fair share of family lunches together and we quickly fall into our old routine: me stacking plates, him scooping salvageable leftovers into Tupperware containers and scraping the rest into the garbage. I rinse dishes and he loads the dishwasher. I don't tell him anything about my neighbors or why I'd hosted them today and he doesn't ask.

Once the table has been packed away and the kitchen wiped clean, the hum of the dishwasher providing us with ambient noise, I pour each of us a small glass of wine. I'd barely touched my chianti at lunch, too busy enjoying my neighbors' company. But now, I'm desperate to take the edge off. "Let's talk on the back porch," I say.

Marco takes a sip of wine, before casting his gaze around my screened-in porch. Potato sits in my lap, staring at Marco with wary uncertainty. It's not that she doesn't like him, but I think she's picking up on my trepidation. It feels so strange to see this totem from my past sitting here in my present.

I have to remind myself that only a pair of months separate the two.

"So," he starts, tentatively. "I've missed you. The last couple months without you have been brutal."

I dip my chin in acknowledgment but don't say a word.

His eyebrows knit together. That's not the response he'd hoped for. Was he really expecting anything different? "How do you like it here?"

Marco has no idea how complicated that question is, and while I'm tempted to spill every last detail in a bid for comfort and support, I stop myself. Marco is not my person anymore.

"It's different."

"Good different?"

I stare into my wineglass, as if I'll find the answer there. I settle on, "Yes."

He shifts in his seat. He looks so out of place in an Adirondack chair. I realize that I'd never really seen Marco out of his element. "Is this really it then? You're staying here?"

After today, I'm honestly not sure. But Marco isn't just inquiring about which state I'm planning to reside in. He's asking about us.

I rest my hand on Potato's head. "I am."

Marco visually deflates, broad shoulders drooping. "I never should have kicked you out of the apartment. I'm so sorry."

"It worked out the way it was supposed to," I say. And I mean it. If he hadn't forced me out, I never would have come to June-berry Lake.

"I don't get how this all went so wrong," he says, his voice glum. "We were perfect together."

I used to think so too. It was one of my favorite things about us as a couple. We were completely in sync, our trains chug-ging along side by side on identical tracks. Until suddenly they weren't. "Were we though?" I wonder aloud. "Is there even such a thing as two people being perfect for each other?"

Marco opens his hands, fingers splayed. "I just . . . I under-stand that infertility is hard on couples. It's the worst-case sce-nario." He looks up from the floorboard he'd been keeping his eyes fixed on. Now they're fixed on me. "But you just gave up."

I sigh. "In what way did I give up?"

A puzzled look crosses his face. "You said you didn't want to try to have a baby on our own and you said no more IVF. It was like all of a sudden you were onto the next thing, talking about what if we adopt instead or maybe we just won't have kids at all. I watched you, your wheels turning as you formulated a new plan. *Oh, this won't be easy so I'll just scrap it and move onto the next.*" He's getting agitated, but he doesn't seem angry. He's sad.

And so am I. He still doesn't seem to grasp that.

Marco and I have been through this more times than I can count, but I will myself to give it one more go in the hopes that maybe this time he'll finally hear me.

"The doctors said it would be virtually impossible—" He starts to interrupt and I hold up my hand to stop him. "Please just listen. If you want to understand, you have to listen to me." He sinks back into his chair. I take a breath. "I couldn't marry you knowing that you had this unrealistic expectation that a baby would miraculously appear in my uterus. Where would that leave us if it didn't?"

"Where would it leave us if it *did*?"

Potato shifts in my lap and I wrap my hands more tightly around her. She makes me feel grounded, clear. I'll never be able to repay her for that. I return my attention to Marco, and my voice comes out strong and firm. "I couldn't stay in a relationship that was contingent on my body performing a miracle. Think about how much pressure that puts on me. Think about how much rejection I'd be setting myself up for. If we weren't able to have a baby, I would have wasted years of my life with someone who, no matter how great of a partner I was, would have looked at me as a disappointment."

Marco shrinks. He's taken on the posture of a partially inflated balloon. "I really made you feel that way?"

If *yes, you idiot* were a facial expression, that would be the look I give him.

"But we'd always talked about having kids together." His voice is weak.

"I never took that off the table. I just wanted us to move on to the next option. And I wanted to keep enjoying our lives while we figured out what that would be. But you made it perfectly clear that you weren't willing to compromise."

He's quiet for a long moment. Then he asks, "Did you ever even want them?"

"Of course I did. Why do you think I went to the trouble of trying to freeze embryos with you four times? For kicks?"

"But even that right there," he says. "You wanted to freeze embryos because you wanted to put off having kids for years."

"Wanting to wait and not wanting them at all are not the same thing."

"I think for you it might be."

Marco may be right. I don't know how I would have felt when the time came to start trying to get pregnant if everything had gone to plan. Maybe I would have hesitated or had some kind of epic meltdown. But it's just as possible that I would have been thrilled. There was no way to know. "I never lied to you, Marco."

He nods. "Okay." Then he seems to disappear into his own thoughts. I can tell because he's tugging on his bottom lip.

"I understand that this was hard for you," I continue. "But I need you to acknowledge that this was hard for me too." I shed more than my fair share of tears over my diagnosis and every subsequent failed round. The difference is that with each disappointment also came resignation. And ultimately, peace.

"I know it was," he says quietly. He looks at me again, and this time there are tears in his eyes. "I'm sorry for what I said, about how I would never have proposed to you if I knew you couldn't have kids. That was awful."

"That's probably the cruelest thing anyone has ever said to me." There's no venom in my words, just simple truth. "But I'm glad you said it, because I know you meant it. And if I'd known you'd react that way to my having a medical condition that's beyond my control, I wouldn't have said yes."

He drops his head. He looks defeated. Something has gotten through to him and he knows this is it for us. "I think I could come around on adoption, eventually. I just really wanted to have biological kids with my wife. I can't explain it, it like, defies logic." He presses a balled fist to his chest. "It's just in me. I have to try it this way. Is that a bad thing?" he asks, his tone pleading.

I shake my head. "No. But, it doesn't matter now."

"I wish it did."

"I did love you, Marco. We just weren't meant to be."

He doesn't say anything, but we both know it's true. We're no Marge and Gal. Without children, Marco and I aren't nearly as compatible as I once thought. The worst part is, if it weren't for a few twists of fate, I might never have known.

Regret or maybe sad resignation pools in Marco's deep brown eyes. "I'm going to miss you, Eliza."

"You'll find your person," I tell him. "But can I give you some advice for when you do?"

He gestures for me to go ahead.

"Make sure that you're really in it with her—no matter what. Life is unpredictable—people get sick, they have miscarriages, they lose their jobs, they change their minds. It's not fair to expect them to check off every box on an arbitrary list or to be the exact same person year after year."

"I hear you," he says, his eyes pooling with tears. "I really do."

I reach over to pat his left hand, the hand that'll never bear a ring from me. He places his free hand on top of mine.

There's nothing more to say.

Chapter Thirty-Seven

When Marco leaves the next morning, having spent the night in my guest room, I am finally, profoundly alone. We are done. It's the right thing and I'm relieved, but something about the finality of it reminds me of death.

I linger on my front porch, surveying the neighborhood. It's eerily quiet and there's the subtlest of chills in the air. I rub my bare arms for warmth, sparking a tiny shock of electricity when my fingers touch my skin.

There's a storm coming.

Potato follows me inside and watches as I pour myself a massive cup of coffee. I grab a blanket for us and we head out to the back porch. That seems to be the place where I do my best thinking.

I take a long drink of coffee, not caring when my tongue starts to burn. I hardly slept at all last night, but not because my ex-fiancé was in the next room. I couldn't stop worrying about my neighbors and their secret fortunes and Erica's whereabouts and Van Fischer.

And Joel.

After I'd gotten Marco settled, I'd dashed over to my room with Potato in tow to text Joel.

> **Me:** I'm sorry about Marco. We needed to have a conversation, but it's over.

> **Me:** I'd really like it if we
> could talk tomorrow.

My heart swelled as three little dots appeared on screen. But, Joel's response wasn't exactly what I'd hoped for.

> **Joel:** I understand. Glad
> you were able to talk.

> **Joel:** Catch up later this week?

Something tells me that doesn't bode well.

My stomach twists as I replay the events of yesterday and how horribly, horrendously wrong it all went. My actions may have jeopardized Erica's finances, her well-being, maybe even her safety and they'd certainly alienated all of my neighbors.

My obscenely rich neighbors.

How had I missed it? Was I really that oblivious? Farah always said that money talked but wealth whispered. That was an understatement. I thought it just meant that uber-rich people bought Gucci clothes without the logo.

With the exception of Allan, none of my neighbors work. This hadn't seemed out of the ordinary, given that Marge and Gal were in their sixties and Bob was probably approaching eighty. I'd just thought they'd all retired.

I knew Stuart's book had been quite successful, and given that his parents left him the cabin, it seemed plausible that he was able to live off royalties. Now I wonder if he's even bothered to write a single word since he hit the jackpot. Maybe he just spends all of his time sneaking around with Lynette.

Allan doesn't have to work so many hours, she'd told me when I confronted her about Stuart. Her words now carry much more weight. Allan technically doesn't have to work *at all*. I'd assumed that Allan was working himself to the bone as some sort of noble provider, determined to take care of his wife and their two kids (and to support Lynette's shopping hobby). But that wasn't the case.

Cheating was never a solution—obviously—but Allan played a bigger part in this mess than I'd realized.

There are more things that I missed, too. The fact that Marge and Gal run what must be an expensive animal fostering operation, what with vet bills and food and supplies. I'd never stopped to wonder how they funded it. Everyone's houses were recently remodeled, too. Everyone's cars were new. Nothing fancy, but new. Not to mention Bob's dumb boat.

Now that I think about it, almost every one of my neighbors had mentioned something shifting in their respective lives about two years ago—Gal retiring, Marge going back to AA meetings, Erica's divorce, Lynette's marital troubles. And I'd never stopped to wonder.

I'd been too involved in executing my stupid little plans. I had blinders on. I missed everything.

My phone vibrates, startling me from my rumination spiral. Potato pops her head up, irked that I interrupted her morning nap. I whisper an apology as I tap my phone screen, hoping to see a message from Joel.

It's from Mom, asking if I can talk.

I understand why Mom stayed in touch with Marco. Now that I think about it, I'm not even surprised. But I am angry with her for passing along information to him that I hadn't even shared with her directly and that I certainly didn't want shared with Marco.

In the end, maybe it was for the best, but I'm not in the mood to talk to her today.

I call Enzo instead, but he doesn't answer.

THERE WON'T BE a barbecue at Lynette and Allan's this Sunday— everyone had agreed to skip this week in lieu of yesterday's lunch. Surely we were all regretting that now. I know Marge and Gal had plans to make chili and watch *When Harry Met Sally* to celebrate the first rainfall of the season. I have no idea what Stuart or Bob are up to. But I do know that Lynette will be home. She said that she and Allan were going to have a quiet day to themselves. She'd been looking forward to it.

The walk down the street to Lynette's house feels slow and ominous. Every step is an effort. I feel as though I'm walking through quicksand.

The howling wind doesn't help.

When Lynette answers the door, her eyes are red-rimmed and her nose is sniffly. She's been crying, but she manages to muster a half-hearted smile.

"Hey, Eliza." My jaw relaxes at her warmer than expected greeting.

"I just wanted to apologize for yesterday—"

She waves me off. "You don't have anything to apologize for. It's not like you did it on purpose." Then she glances over her shoulder. "Allan knows," she whispers.

Her words send a boulder tumbling to the bottom of my stomach. "What? How?" I whisper back, although I already know the answer.

I think back to the look I'd given Lynette and Stuart when I called her out for lying to me. I know it had set Allan's Spidey senses tingling. Even if he'd already suspected, I felt terrible for playing a role in outing Lynette. "I'm so sorry. Does Stuart know that Allan knows?"

She nods. "Allan called Stuart late last night."

"Are you okay?"

She just shrugs.

"Can I do anything to help?"

"You're sweet to check in, but no. We have a lot to sort out before the kids get home."

"Do you want me to take them for a couple hours after Allan's parents drop them off?" I offer. It's a quasi-desperate attempt to make up for my role in blowing up Lynette's life. But it's genuine, too.

"No, we'll be okay. But thank you."

My eyes drop down to my feet. I hate not being able to help my friend. Is this how Farah felt when I told her about Marco and me? Utterly helpless? "Well if you need anything, I'll be home."

She gives me a tight smile before pushing the door closed.

I'm halfway down the steps when I hear it creak open again. When I turn around, I see Lynette and my spirits lift. Maybe I *can* do something to help her.

But all she says is, "Bob, Marge, and Gal don't know. Allan, Stuart, and I would appreciate if you didn't tell them. It would only make things worse."

I press my hands against my chest. "I won't tell a soul."

With that, she shuts the door.

Chapter Thirty-Eight

Stuart is waiting for me on my front porch when I get home.
"I'm not upset with you," he says, as I approach with obvious trepidation. "If I were in your shoes, I wouldn't have been able to resist digging around either. Curiosity is just part of being human."

"There's a reason they say it killed the cat though."

He smirks. "Yeah, I suppose so." He returns his attention to a stack of paperbacks that he'd placed on the railing. The spines are various shades of pastels—pink, purple, and yellow. Like a little bouquet of books. He picks up the pink one, considering it. "Stuart Sato hasn't released a book since *Depth Charge*," he says. He holds up the book. There's a charming drawing of a rosy-cheeked blond woman and a brown-skinned, bespectacled man sipping coffee together on the cover. "But Sheila Townsend has released three."

I remember that Sheila Townsend is Gal's favorite author. Stuart's always giving her a hard time for pushing Townsend's Coffee Cove novels on the neighborhood book club. "And that annoys you because . . . you have writer's block and she doesn't?" I guess. Maybe winning the lottery took the wind out of Stuart's creative sails. It's probably hard to be motivated to maintain your career when you don't technically need to earn money anymore.

"I don't have writer's block."

"Okay," I say, not seeing where this is going.

"I *am* Sheila Townsend." Stuart must be able to tell from my face that I don't know what he's getting at. "Sheila Townsend is my pen name." He picks up the other two books and holds them in front of his face like a fan. "I wrote all of these in less than two years."

"But you hate Sheila Townsend books."

"I hate talking about my own books in book club. I didn't want anyone to know." He rearranges the paperbacks into a pile and places them into my hands. "And if you read them, you'll understand why."

I look down at the books in my hand and then back up at Stuart. I'm still not sure what he's trying to tell me. Gal always said that Stuart was a literary snob. Is he embarrassed to be writing cutesy romances? He shouldn't be. Cutesy romances are the best.

"I started writing the initial book in this series after the first time Lynette and I got coffee together, just the two of us. She woke something up in me, I guess. Loving her made me soft."

My breath leaves my body like air seeping from a tire. "Loving her?"

"It's over now. Which is probably for the best. We let it go on for too long and neither of us want to break up a family. We've been selfish enough as it is."

"But you love her."

Stuart's eyes mist up behind his glasses. He swallows and his Adam's apple bobs. "I do."

"And does she . . ."

"Love me?"

I give him a sympathetic look. He heaves a breath.

"She said she did. But it's complicated. It has been from the start."

"Stuart, I'm so sorry."

"Don't be. This all had to end somehow. Might as well have been in a dramatic fashion. I reserve the right to write this into my next book by the way."

Stuart's kindness should be a salve, but it only makes me feel worse. "It's all yours."

"Good." He shoves his hands into his pockets. "Well, I should get going. I'm on a deadline and there's no better distraction than that."

He pats me on my shoulder as he passes by, leaving me alone on the porch with his stack of books. Another secret I've forced one of my neighbors to reveal.

As I watch Stuart go, it begins to rain.

I THROW MYSELF into reading Stuart/Sheila's first novel. It's lovely and vulnerable and heartwarming and gut-wrenching all at once. Just as every good romance novel should be. In Stuart's book, there is no other man, no clandestine rendezvous under the cover of night. Of course, there are complications, misunderstandings— even a few secrets—but in the end, all of the pieces fall into place. The main characters end up together. Happily ever after.

Stuart is not retelling his and Lynette's story, at least not in any obvious way. It's no wonder that Gal never caught on. But now that I know, the characters in his first book are so clearly based on him and Lynette. And the way Stuart writes about her is enough to make even someone as cold as Bob cry.

I read the first book in a day, only getting up from my spot on the couch to feed Potato or let her out for potty breaks, which ends up being quite an ordeal because apparently, Potato doesn't like the rain. I end up having to hold an umbrella over her little head every time she has to pee. She doesn't seem to care that I get soaked in the process.

I miss calls from Mom and Enzo. But I don't hear a thing from any of my neighbors.

Or Joel.

By the time evening rolls around, I'm consumed with guilt. I'm heartbroken for Stuart. And for Lynette. Not to mention Allan.

I dig a carton of frozen custard out from the freezer for dinner (I can't bring myself to cook) and follow Potato to the couch. I shovel one spoonful after another into my mouth, until I'm hit with a sudden bout of brain freeze. I squeeze my eyes shut and rub my temple with my free hand, waiting for it to pass. When it finally does, I hop up from the couch and pace the room. I'm not sure why, but I end up staring out my front window.

That's when I see Marge and Gal, standing on their front porch with Joel. He has two people with him that I've never seen before—a white guy with brownish hair and a Black woman in a chic coat—they seem to be a couple, about my parents' age. The man is resting his hand on Joel's shoulder and the woman is hugging Marge.

I drop my spoon when Joel turns his head to look back at my house. I can't quite make out his eyes, but I know he sees me. I give him a limp, pathetic wave. He smiles, but I doubt that it's genuine.

I STAY UP most of the night reading Stuart's second book, which is even better than the first. It's as though his talent grew in tandem with his feelings for Lynette.

In this book, the coffee date couple gets married. Naturally, chaos ensues. There are quirky, meddling neighbors who insert themselves (harmlessly) into the couple's big day. A tornado rips through the wedding venue a week before the wedding.

And there's a misunderstanding about an ex that nearly, briefly, threatens to derail the entire event.

I think the ex might be a stand-in for Allan. He and the female protagonist dated in college—just like Lynette and Allan. In the book, the ex is a self-absorbed, career-driven, emotionally unavailable jock who returns to town in a Hail Mary attempt at winning back his former flame.

Kind of like how Marco had. It's funny how much art can imitate life.

I fall asleep before I get to the end. I don't know how long I'm out, but when I wake up, well past my usual weekday alarm, there's a text from Joel on my phone.

> **Joel:** I'm sorry for going quiet. My parents came to town after everything happened with Marge. I wanted them to meet her.

> **Joel:** I want to talk, but I need a little time. I promise I'll text you soon.

I toss my phone onto the bed and then flop down beside it. I know exactly what "I need time" means. Marco and I had needed time. And look where we are now.

I roll over and go back to sleep. I don't wake up again until Potato licks my face, looking for breakfast.

I EMAIL JORDAN to let them know that I'll be taking the day off. I text Trish to tell her that I won't be coming in for coffee. I simply can't imagine working right now. I'm too consumed with guilt.

All I want to do is talk to Enzo, but we keep missing each

other. He's probably with his girlfriend. I have no doubt that she's much better company than I am right now.

I take the next day off, too. I tell Trish that I'm sick, which is partly true. She doesn't question it. She doesn't really have the time to anyway, because business has doubled since the festival. It's a small, glimmering shard of good news amid the gloom.

When Jordan emails me saying we need to talk, my fingertips go numb. Then my upper lip. And then my feet. That hasn't happened to me since I was a teenager. Right after Hannah.

I walk myself through breathing exercises. I stroke Potato's soft fur. I step outside for fresh air, making a point of noticing the electricity that permeates the atmosphere. I'd spent the morning watching fingers of lightning tap dancing across the lake. I can feel the worst of my symptoms ebbing, but a full-blown anxiety attack lingers in the wings. I try Enzo one more time, but his phone is off.

I have nowhere else to turn. I can't talk to Jordan in this state. My parents will be of no help. Plus, they'll be in the middle of the lunch rush at the bakery.

I CAN'T BRING myself to read Stuart's last book. I can't concentrate. All I can think about is how horrible I feel about everything that's happened. And for the first time in probably ever, my brain can't seem to formulate a way to fix it.

I don't know how to fix it.

I really am on my own now. I curse myself for not finding a new therapist when I moved. I would give anything to talk to Nora right now.

I tried calling Farah, but she didn't answer. Who can blame her? I can't call Carmen—she'd texted the group to let us know that Daisy is getting induced today. She has much bigger things to worry about.

I know Brittany would be useless. She's never been very sympathetic about my anxiety.

At least I have Potato. I owe her a long walk and some fresh air, but she's not holding it against me. Quite the opposite, actually. She's showered me with licks and snuggles and has refused to leave my side.

I don't deserve her.

I'm not sure when or how, exactly, but I start talking to Potato. I don't tell her about my conversation with Marco (she was there) or how I inadvertently exposed my neighbors' mega secret or dashed my chances with Joel (she was there for both of those, too) or how I might have grown apart from friends back home for good.

Instead, I tell her about what happened to Hannah.

Chapter Thirty-Nine

The week before the start of our junior year, Hannah and I went to Cammi Kong's house for her annual back-to-school sleepover. The plan was to give each other makeovers, play a few rounds of Twister, eat way too much pizza, and then watch both *Sisterhood of the Traveling Pants* movies back-to-back.

I'd been looking forward to it all summer.

The night was going better than I'd even hoped—Hannah had beaten everyone at Twister (she was inexplicably double-jointed) and Cammi's mom had come through with a massive Walgreens bag filled with wet n wild makeup for all of us girls to sample. Hannah promptly covered my eyelids in pink glitter. "Gorgeous," she'd proclaimed.

But then Hannah got a text that changed everything. I watched her face light up as her eyes danced across the screen, the subtlest of pits forming in my stomach.

"What is it?" I asked.

Hannah grinned, holding up the phone. "We're going to sneak out."

I snatched the Motorola from her hands. There was a text from Andy Rhodes, a senior boy with spiky hair and a cleft chin that Hannah'd been in love with since she first laid eyes on him in the cafeteria our freshman year. I'd even spotted her doodling "Mrs. Hannah Rhodes" in her notebook during algebra class on more than one occasion. Andy and his friends had secured a case of Smirnoff Ice and were headed to Ocean Beach.

"I don't know, Han," I said. "I'm having so much fun here."

"But it's *Andy*."

I looked back at the rest of the girls. They'd moved on from Cammi's makeup haul and were dancing to Jesse McCartney's "Beautiful Soul." The pizza would be here any minute. I didn't want to miss out.

"There will be other nights," I said futilely.

Hannah shook her head. "No, there won't. His parents are out of town this weekend. That's the only time he's able to stay out late."

I didn't know Andy or his friends and something about sneaking out of the party didn't sit right with me. "I think we should stay."

Hannah's green eyes were bright with mischief. She'd already made up her mind, I could tell. "I think we should go."

I sighed, resigned. "I'm not going to tell you what to do, but I'm not leaving."

"Suit yourself," she'd said with a shrug before firing off a text message and snapping her phone shut.

The last time I ever saw my best friend, she was creeping toward Cammi's front door, a sparkly purse dangling from her shoulder, a strand of wavy auburn hair tucked behind her ear. She gently slid the door open before turning back, flashing me a smile, wriggling her fingers in a wave, and mouthing "love you."

I never got the chance to say it back.

Andy's car was hit head-on by a drunk driver going sixty-eight miles an hour that night. He and Hannah died instantly. Two of his friends who were in the back seat survived, although neither could remember the moments leading up to the crash.

Memory loss aside, everyone agreed that Andy hadn't been drinking. His blood alcohol level was zero.

Not that it did Hannah any good.

Hannah's death shattered me. There were weeks where I couldn't get out of bed, couldn't keep any food down, could barely speak. I missed the start of the school year and I didn't care. I was broken, a shell of my former self.

For months, I replayed the events of that night, berating myself for not forcing Hannah to stay. I came to believe that it was my fault, that I alone could have stopped her.

Eventually, my parents got me into therapy and with time, I started to return to myself. Or at least a version of myself. The Eliza that reemerged post-Hannah was more serious, more cautious, more rigid.

My therapist was so adamant about my not being responsible for Hannah's death, that I started to let myself believe her. By the end of my junior year, I'd found some semblance of peace. I knew I'd never stop missing Hannah, but I also understood that I couldn't let her death define my life.

Because that was the thing I hadn't been able to see before. If Hannah had just made the right decision, if she'd stuck to the plan, she never would have been in that car.

And I was never going to make the same mistake.

That's when I started mapping out my life, carefully laying out a plan for every year, every milestone. It's why I'm so comforted by mysteries—because if I can find a way to explain why something terrible happened, it'll all make sense. And then I can avoid the same mistakes.

Potato stares up at me with her big brown eyes and whines gently. I don't know how long I've been talking, but I can tell I'm starting to stress her out.

I scratch behind her ears and soon she rolls over onto her back, asking for a belly rub. I oblige, thanking her for listening as I scratch her furry little tummy. I'm so grateful for this dog and in this moment, I decide that if nothing else comes of my time here in Juneberry Lake, she will be enough.

When my hand lands on the knotted lump where her missing front leg used to be, a realization hits me with such force, that I nearly tumble backward. I stare into Potato's eyes, her innocent, trusting eyes. I hate that she had to endure any suffering in her life and I almost never let myself think about what she must have gone through when she lay battered and bleeding on the side of the road.

But what I realize is this: none of what happened to Potato is her fault.

I don't know what led to that particular moment in her life, but I'm sure a million little things—most of them completely unconnected—had to go wrong for her to end up in the exact wrong place at precisely the wrong time.

For the past sixteen years, I've been living my life based on a lie. A lie that I told myself.

I'd believed with my whole heart that if I planned everything out just so, if I followed that plan to the letter, if I set out to accomplish everything I said I would do, that nothing bad would happen.

I'd believed that planning would protect me. I'd believed that I was in control.

But that had all been a facade. A mirage of my own making.

Hannah's death was not her fault. Maybe she was destined to die that night no matter what. Maybe she would have choked on a piece of pizza or bumped her head during Twister or had an aneurysm in her sleep. Or maybe she was just a silly teenager with horrible luck. I certainly have no idea how death or the universe works, but I suddenly know with every fiber of my being that Hannah did nothing wrong.

Tons of teenagers sneak out of their parents' houses on any given night and nothing bad happens. She was just being a kid. Sure, she made a dumb decision, but that's what kids do. Isn't that baked into growing up?

I'd promised myself I wouldn't let Hannah's death keep me from living. But, for the most part, that's exactly what I'd done. I'd wrapped myself in a protective layer of goals and achievements, rarely allowing myself to deviate from the script I'd written. And where had it gotten me?

It hadn't saved me from infertility or heartbreak or loneliness. It hadn't protected me from making the wrong choices over and over again only to end up alone.

I had to stop. I had to let this go. I had to give up on trying to wrench control of my life from the powers that be and start enjoying whatever might come.

I'm on the verge of an outright epiphany when I hear the doorbell ring. Once, twice, three times in rapid succession. For a moment, I consider letting it go unanswered—I'm in no condition to see any of my neighbors. But then it rings again, in three distinct beats, and my heart swells with hope. There's only one person I know who rings a doorbell that way. And he's the one person in the world who could make me feel better right now.

Chapter Forty

My brother doesn't enjoy hugs, but that doesn't stop me from falling into his arms and descending into wrenching sobs when I find him on my front step.

Enzo's body stiffens, but he doesn't recoil. He even pats me on the back. "I guess it's a good thing that I decided to come," he says.

It takes me a minute to pull myself together enough to invite Enzo inside. I introduce him to Potato (Enzo has always preferred animals to people, so they fall in love instantly), and give him a tour of the house. He makes a point of complimenting very specific things he likes about it—the couch is a nice shade of blue, not too gray, the windows don't end too much before the ceiling, the oven is well positioned for baking—but he barely notices the lake view. I've missed getting to see the world through Enzo's unique lens.

I pour us each a glass of ice water and we settle into the living room. Enzo and I take the armchairs because Potato has stretched out across the couch. It's amazing how much room she can take up given her diminutive size.

"Do you want to know why I decided to come?" Enzo asks.

"Of course."

He dips his head in a single nod, takes a sip of water and carefully places the glass on top of a coaster with an anchor on it. My heart constricts with love as I watch him. We both hate water rings.

"I swear I didn't tell Mom anything," he starts. "She probably overheard us talking."

"You mean she listened at the door outside your room."

"Exactly."

I smile knowingly and motion for him to continue.

"When I found out that she'd told Marco everything and that he flew out here to see you, I got really worried. I talked to Dad and then we both had a talk with Mom."

"Did you get through to her?"

"I don't think so. Mom is Mom."

Maybe this is a bit dysfunctional, but I agree, which is why I never got too angry with her. Mom has always been an overprotective meddler, but she means well. I guess I come by it honestly. But we should probably start setting more boundaries with her. We've let her get away with everything for years, mostly because she's our mom. I think the charming Italian accent helps, too—her less than perfect command of the English language is thoroughly disarming and I think she knows it. "It was worth a shot."

Enzo shrugs. "She wanted to come out here, but Dad and I agreed that it would be best if I came instead. I tried to call you, but we kept missing each other and I was worried that if I texted you, you'd tell me not to come, so I just decided to go for it."

Coming from Enzo, this was a Herculean act of love. My brother does not enjoy deviating from his schedule, being in large crowds, confined spaces, or traveling in general. I don't know if I've ever felt more loved than I do in this moment. "Thank you. You're the best brother in the world."

"Probably not in the world," Enzo says, before adding, "That's statistically improbable."

"Nah, you're the best. I don't care about math."

"Do you want to talk about everything?"

I do, more than I realized. I start talking and don't stop for quite some time. Enzo listens patiently, rotating between understanding nods, blank stares, and sips of water. He doesn't interrupt me once. When I get to my epiphany about Hannah's death, I finally take a long, steadying breath.

"Haven't I been telling you all of that for years?" Enzo asks, amused. "You never listen to me."

I toss a wadded-up tissue in his direction. He bats it away.

"How are you going to fix all of this?" Enzo asks, a wry smile dancing along his lips. "Another plan?"

I laugh for the first time in days. "I mean, it's me, so yes. I just have to think of something first."

Enzo dips his chin. "Just remember that no matter what happens, you'll always have me."

My heart threatens to break into a million little pieces. I press my hands to my chest in an effort to hold it together. "I love you so much, Enzo. I know you don't like hugs, but I really want to give you another one."

"I love you too," he says. "And you're hugging me with your words."

Chapter Forty-One

Enzo went back home on Wednesday morning, but he made me promise to call Farah before he left for the airport. I wish he could have stayed longer, but I know it's hard for him to be away from the bakery. And from Allison.

"I'm sorry to bother you," I blurt before Farah has a chance to say anything. "I know you're busy, but I really need to talk."

To Farah's credit, she drops whatever she was doing and steps into a quiet room.

I've come to realize that the very reasons that I had been drawn to Farah—she was safe, stable, predictable, and traditional—were now the things that were driving us apart. I'd started blaming her for the traits that made me choose her in the first place. I was the one who'd changed. Or more accurately, I was the one who buried my true self under a stack of achievements and goals and work.

Farah hadn't been perfect, but neither had I. She had been trying to support the version of me that she knew—the one who was on track to marry a stable guy, have 2.5 kids, and move to the suburbs, just like her. I never gave Farah a chance to respond to what I actually needed, which was permission to be myself, to fumble through this phase of life as I figured out my new reality. Because I never told her.

Worse, I stopped being there for her.

But before I can get any of that out, Farah says, "I'm glad you called. I've been thinking a lot and—I owe you an apology. This last year . . . I wasn't there for you in the way that you needed me to be and I'm really sorry."

That's not the response I was expecting. "There wasn't much anyone could do for me," I demure.

"Yes, there was," Farah says, her voice firm. "I should have supported your decision, even if I didn't totally understand." I hear her release a breath. "We'd just always been on the same path and then when you started talking about not having kids and broke things off with Marco . . . I don't know, I guess I just worried that I was going to lose you if you didn't want the same things as I did anymore." She lets out a small laugh. "God, that sounds so stupid when I say it out loud."

I know she can't see me, but I shake my head anyway. "It's not stupid. I felt that way, too."

She laughs. "Well at least we were being dumb together."

And I know we're going to be okay.

Now THAT THE stormy weather has passed, Gal insisted that I join her for a walk that afternoon. We trod along the lakeside path, Gal with a pack of five dogs on leash, plus Darla in her bedazzled pouch, and me with Potato. It's a welcome return to normalcy.

"How are things with you and Marge?" I ask.

Gal beams. "Never better. I'd been bugging her about letting me meet this kid for months and he's an absolute doll."

"So you knew about Joel?"

Gal looks at me like I've just asked whether she likes rhinestones. If *duh* were a facial expression, that would be Gal's face right now. "Does a loon fly over the lake? Of course I knew. Marge and I don't have any secrets between us. I've always known about the adoption and I knew that the baby—well, grown man now—had found her. I just didn't know who he was."

"Did that bother you?"

She purses her bright pink lips and shakes her head. "Nah. One of the keys to a good marriage is knowing when to push and when to back off. I knew Marge would introduce me when the time was right."

I'm dying to know if Joel has said anything about me, but I can't bring myself to swallow my pride enough to broach the subject. Instead, as we make our way back toward the cul-de-sac, I ask my other burning question. "So, is it fun to be superrich?"

Gal barks out a laugh, startling Darla from her nap. She turns toward me and lowers her sunglasses to the bridge of her nose, painted nails sparkling under the sunlight. "You know something? It's pretty damn great."

Gal invites Potato and me inside for a cup of coffee after our walk. I let Potato run freely in the backyard and my spirits lift as I watch her playing with the other dogs from the comfort of Marge and Gal's air-conditioned house. Gal tells me that it was Erica's love for animals with special needs, and specifically her one-eyed dog, Phil, that inspired them to start fostering. "And we can do it indefinitely since we're loaded." She says it with a wink before turning serious. "So long as we get that scumbag Gary off our backs."

It occurs to me that my neighbors' stroke of luck has long-reaching ripple effects. Their good fortune has allowed them to take in so many animals in need, including my little Potato. My stomach curdles at the thought of Van and Gary jeopardizing everything my friends have worked to create.

I have to find a way to fix this.

"Hey," Gal says when she sees me disappearing into my own

guilty thoughts. "We'll come up with something. It's our prob-lem, not yours. We just need to get creative."

"There must be something I can do. I've caused so much trouble."

"Eliza," Gal says firmly. "I want you to know that I speak for everyone when I tell you this: we love having you here and we don't want you to go anywhere. Whatever happens, you're one of us now."

"Are you speaking for Bob, too?"

Gal winces. "Maybe not Bob."

We're sipping coffee at the kitchen island when Marge gets home, presumably from one of her AA meetings. She gives Gal a kiss, hangs her keys on a hook next to all the leashes, and turns to consider me. After a moment, she wraps me in a hug. "How are you holding up?"

"I'm fine," I assure her. "Just a little wrung out."

She releases me from her grasp and pats me on the back. "We've had an eventful few days around here."

Gal nods her head in agreement as she passes Marge a cup of coffee and then grins at me. "I don't know if you heard, but I have a wonderful new stepson."

"Couldn't have raised him better myself," Marge cracks.

They're both beaming with pride. I'm so happy for them, but then my mind drifts back to how much I've missed Joel these past few days. My face must give me away, because Marge's ex-pression softens. "He just needs a little time," she says.

I know she's just being nice.

Chapter Forty-Two

October

The next morning, I find myself walking up the path to Bob's house. He swings the door open before I make it to his doorstep. "What do you want?" he barks. I might be imagining it, but his tone is even more gruff than usual.

I hold up my hands. "I come in peace," I say.

He doesn't budge.

I take a tentative step toward Bob. "And with a plan to get rid of Van Fischer."

The idea came to me as I was leaving Marge and Gal's yesterday—"We just need to get creative," Gal had said. She was right. But I wanted to get Bob's buy-in before I made my move. Given his background in law enforcement, he was, weirdly, the perfect person to help me with this scheme.

Bob's shoulders drop ever so slightly. He narrows his eyes, grumbles again, and then steps aside and gestures for me to come in.

I take a big gulp, literally swallowing my pride as I cross the threshold of my nemesis's home.

The inside of Bob's house is so tidy that I begin to wonder if they invented the phrase "neat as a pin" specifically to describe it. I don't think it's been updated in years—despite Bob's windfall—

and soon I understand why. "My wife, Tammy, picked everything out. I can't take any credit," he says.

I take in the delicate floral wallpaper in the dining room, the tasteful wainscoting in the living room, the classic outdoor furniture on the deck beyond. "She had great taste."

Bob grunts. Then he asks, "Can I get you anything? Maybe some tap water?"

This is the nicest Bob has ever been to me. I think we might be getting somewhere.

Or maybe it's a trap.

After handing me a glass of water with three identical ice cubes in it, Bob starts to talk. He tells me about his wife, Tammy ("We were married for forty-four wonderful years," he says. "She was the best person I ever knew"), their son, Robbie, who is stationed in South Korea with his husband and their two kids ("I wish I got to see them more often," Bob confesses), and how he spent fifty-three years in the FBI. "I started out in behavioral analysis and then moved into white-collar crime. Mostly financial fraud," he tells me, his posture not slipping even once.

The fact that Bob loved his wife and that he spent decades in law enforcement comes as no surprise. I'm most shocked that he has a good relationship with his son and seems to be perfectly fine with said son having a husband. I probably judged Bob too harshly.

He kind of deserved it, though.

"So do you like, profile people when you meet them?" I ask.

"Do you mean did I profile you?"

I nod.

"I could tell you were hiding something, so I didn't trust you."

"Likewise," I say, grinning. And then, I'm not sure why, but I decide to tell Bob about Marco.

When I'm done, he fixes me with a stare. His icicle eyes are intense, but warm. "For whatever it's worth, I've known lots of different people who've lived all sorts of lifestyles," he says. "There are a million and one ways to be miserable and a million and one more ways to be happy. You can't always control your circumstances, but you can control who you surround yourself with. That makes all the difference."

I know he's talking about his wife now. I wish I'd had a chance to know her, to see them together. I bet he was a big mooshy romantic around her.

Okay, maybe not mooshy, but I'd imagine he was sweet.

I think about this neighborhood, these people. On the surface, they're all quite different, but at their core, they're good people who would do just about anything for one another.

"And I'll tell you this—" Bob says, interrupting my thoughts. "You've already dumped that loser and gotten the hell out of California, so you're ahead of the game." I'd never noticed the way that the ice in Bob's eyes twinkles when he's making a joke.

Bob leans back in his chair, crossing his arms over his chest. "Now," he says, his tone suddenly businesslike. "Tell me about this plan of yours." The scary Bob stare is back. "It'd better be good because I think you might be the only person who can get this Van Fischer character to go away."

I take a sip of water, happy to leave him hanging for a moment. "Oh, it's good," I say.

BOB SPENDS THE better part of his afternoon preparing me for a meeting with Van Fischer.

"Are you sure you're comfortable lying to this guy?" he'd asked. Then he shook his head. "Who am I kidding? This street is full of liars and you fit right in. You'll be fine. Besides, he's not a federal agent so there's no law that says you can't feed him a bunch of bull crap and call it fact."

With Bob's guidance, I texted Van.

> **Me:** I think I know what happened to Erica.

> **Van:** How soon can you meet?

> **Me:** My house. Seven p.m.

It was almost too easy.

That night, I try to channel Bob's weird vote of confidence in my ability to lie when I see Van's car pull up. I attach Potato's leash and step out onto the front porch before he's even slammed the car door. I don't want to give him the impression that he's welcome inside my home. He isn't.

Plus, Bob's listening on the other side of the door.

Van drapes a leather jacket over his shoulder and ambles toward me. Potato's posture stiffens and I give her a reassuring pat on the head.

Van stops a few feet short of my steps and strikes what I believe he considers a power pose: all of his weight on one leg, hand on a hip, fingers poking through his belt loops. He doesn't bother to remove his sunglasses even though the sun has already begun to set. "Hey there, Van," I say. "Thanks for meeting me."

He gives me a curt nod. "So what did you want to tell me?"

I make a show of looking around the neighborhood, pretending to be worried that someone might be listening. Then, I bring him up to speed on my discovery about Bob and TRH Holdings and the deed to Erica's house.

"None of this is new information to me," Van says blandly.

I pause for effect. Bob had helped me perfect this very tall tale about Erica, and if I don't tell it convincingly, Van might never leave me or my neighbors alone. I drop my voice and lean forward. "But, it's so much more complicated than I first thought," I say. Then, I repeat the story that Bob made me rehearse upward of twenty times. "Bob's been trying to find Erica, too," I say, my tone is conspiratorial. "She stole money from him before she disappeared." My eyes widen. "Like a lot of money."

Van flips the dark lenses of his sunglasses up and narrows his eyes. "What are you talking about?"

I drop my voice. "I don't totally understand how it all worked, but as you know, Erica had gotten herself into a bunch of debt, but was acting like she was also about to come into some money, which is kind of weird, right?" I don't wait for him to respond. "Apparently, she conned Bob into giving her a short-term loan and agreed to put him on the deed of her house as collateral. He'd known her forever so he trusted her. Plus, she led him to believe that she was going to get a big lump sum from the divorce."

Van has dropped the power pose and is now leaning in ever so slightly. I think I might have him. "She's a total con artist."

His lips sputter with disgust. "That doesn't surprise me."

I nod gravely. "So Bob basically handed over his life savings and then helped Erica to sell her house. She took all the money and ran. He hasn't gotten even a penny back."

Van pretends not to be surprised, like he's suspected this all along. "I'll see if I can pull some financial records," Van says, mostly to himself.

"You won't find anything," I say a little too quickly. I hope Van doesn't notice. "Bob gave Erica the money in cash. He doesn't trust the banks." I make a face that says, *You know how those old guys can be.*

Van strokes his chin, lost in thought. Finally, he says, "Well has Bob found her?"

I shake my head. "She'll call him every once in a while to check in—he still thinks that she's going to get him his money back. She's spinning some elaborate story about it being tied up in offshore investments and he believes her."

"Didn't he work for the FBI?"

I make a sympathetic face and sigh. "Exactly. I think he can't accept that someone could pull one over on him. He's too far in."

"Would he be open to working with me?"

"Not a chance. He knows you're mixed up with Erica's ex. She's filled his head with all kinds of poison about Gary."

Van nods. "I guess I could follow him, wait around until the next time Erica calls."

"I was thinking that too, but she always calls from a different number and only stays on the phone for a minute or so. This woman is good."

Van crosses his arms over his chest. I think I've stumped him. I decide to go in for the kill.

"I'm going to level with you, Van. I know you're trying to do right by your client, and I know he's concerned about his ex-wife's well-being. But honestly? I think he dodged a bullet. The poor guy was married to a con woman for years. He's been through so much already. Plus, whatever money she has left is stolen, so even if he wanted to sue her or something, there wouldn't be anything to sue for."

Van frowns. "Yeah, she's a slippery one." I sense a grimy layer of misogyny in his reaction. I bet he's thinking all women are slippery. And that's why I don't feel bad misleading him.

Plus, I'm lying for a noble cause. I'm protecting my friends. I know I won't always be able to protect the people I love, but when I can, I will. Always.

"And if I were you, I'd leave old Bob alone." I lean up against the post of my porch. If I smoked cigarettes, now would be the time to light up. "He's getting pretty old and paranoid. And he has a gun. I don't think it'd be worth it."

I can see Van's wheels turning. I just hope they're going in the right direction. I can tell he's made up his mind when he stops rubbing his chin. He stands up straighter, shoulders squared. "Thank you for your help. It's been invaluable."

"Do you have a plan?" I venture. I can't help myself.

He leans toward me conspiratorially. "Erica's ex—my client—was under the impression that Erica had found herself a wealthy benefactor or won the lottery or something."

It takes everything in me not to react. "That's pretty out there," I say, shaking my head.

Van rubs the back of his neck. "I know. The guy's pretty outlandish to be honest with you."

"Sounds like it."

"Yeah," he says, rolling his eyes. "Anyway, when I tell him what's really going on here, I think he'll drop it. Case closed."

He bought it. I can't believe it. I wonder if Bob is on the other side of my front door doing a happy dance, but then I remember that it's Bob and he's definitely doing no such thing.

Van flips his lenses back down, and my shoulders loosen. I didn't like having to look into his oily eyes. "Thanks for your help, Eliza." He flashes me the smarmiest of smirks. "That wasn't so hard, was it?"

I suppress a shudder and somehow manage to force a smile. "Glad I could be of service."

Van nods and starts to turn back toward his car.

"Hey, Van?" I say, pushing off the post. "Just so we're clear, I'm ready to move on from all of this drama. It's not my fault that some old guy got scammed by the person who used to live here, you know?"

Van gives me a weird little salute. "Understood," he says. "I can lose your number . . ." He makes a show of looking me up and down. "Unless you might want to join me for dinner sometime?" His bushy eyebrows poke up from behind his sunglasses and I have to fight the urge to vomit.

"Lose the number," I say. Potato growls her agreement.

He laughs and it drips condescension. "Suit yourself," he says, before driving off.

If I never see that man again it'll be too soon.

Chapter Forty-Three

I decide to spend Friday morning working at Black Bear Brew because I can't stand to be alone with my thoughts. Now that things with Van and my neighbors are settled, I have to face the music with work and Joel. I've been putting off a call with Jordan for days and I'm convinced that they're going to fire me when we talk this afternoon, which has triggered an all-consuming anxiety.

For most of the summer, I was usually the lone laptop user in the café. But that's changed since Trish started her marketing push. More than half the tables are now occupied by well-caffeinated remote workers. Trish said business has increased by 30 percent since the festival.

At least I was able to do one thing right this summer.

Trish brings me an avocado toast without even asking. "You get me," I tell her. Potato, who'd been fast asleep in my lap perks up and starts sniffing my toast.

Trish makes a face like she's trying to solve a math problem. "I actually don't, really."

I shrug. "Join the club."

She pulls out a chair and settles in beside me. "Joel told me what happened," she says. For a second there, I think she means about Erica and panic rises in my throat. But then I realize she's probably talking about what happened between *us*. "You're not getting back together with your ex are you?"

I pull a face. "Not even close."

"But he spent the night."

"Where else was he supposed to go?"

Trish gives me the side-eye but doesn't say anything.

"So are you two going to talk this thing out? I know it feels big and bad right now, but in time, it'll just be a blip on the radar."

That's what I'd been hoping for, but now, almost a week later, I'm not so sure. I think whatever romance we had might be over, but maybe we can salvage a friendship. I keep replaying the stricken look on Joel's face when I pulled away from him. I know it looked like I was choosing Marco in that moment. I know I should have gone after Joel and left Marco there alone. I'd give anything to make Joel understand that it had nothing to do with my feelings for him. But, the fact that we haven't talked things out yet doesn't bode well. "I'm meeting him at his house after work tonight."

Joel had texted me yesterday to say that his parents were leaving in the morning and that he wanted to talk. But that was all he said. Honestly, I should get a medal for even dragging myself out of bed today knowing that I would probably be fired and dumped before the sun went down.

"Good." Trish pats my hand. "You two are adorable together."

Before I can respond, a group of college kids walks in and head straight for the pastry display. Trish told me she'd already run out of bear claws twice this week. "I better get to that," she says. She gives my shoulder a quick squeeze before disappearing behind the counter.

"Are you firing me?" I ask as soon as Jordan's face fills my screen. Then I brace my hands against my desk while I await their response.

It's not what I expected.

Jordan starts laughing. "Are you kidding? No way."

I grip the desk even tighter. "Really?"

"Yes, really. I mean, you've been pretty distracted lately, but you at fifty percent is better than everyone else at a hundred percent. I'll take what I can get."

My hands relax. "So what did you want to talk about then?"

"Well," Jordan says, sitting up straighter in their ergonomic chair. "I'm getting promoted."

That's not what I was expecting either. "Why didn't you just say that in the first place?" I ask. It would have saved me a lot of catastrophizing.

Jordan's mouth kicks up at the edges. "Because it's more fun to share good news in person."

They have a point. My mind quickly shifts from dread to bewilderment to elation. "Jordan, that's great! Congratulations."

"Thank you. The rumors are true. I'm amazing." Jordan pretends to dust dirt off their shoulder.

"Does this mean you won't be my boss anymore?" Selfishly, the thought dampens my excitement.

"Not exactly. We're growing, so I'll just be managing a bigger team . . ." They pause, eyeing me meaningfully through the monitor. "Which means, I need to replace myself. Would you be interested?"

Their question nearly sends me toppling out of my chair. I stammer out an incoherent "what" and Jordan repeats the question, amusement dancing across their face.

It takes me several moments to fully process what is happening. And what I realize is this: I've spent my entire career meticulously calculating every move, every step on the corporate ladder, working myself to the point of burnout year after year in pursuit of career advancement. But for the past three-ish months I've slacked off, been wildly distracted, and consistently turned in a work product that was acceptable—nothing more, nothing less. And now I'm being rewarded with a promotion years sooner than I ever expected.

It all feels so backward that it makes me dizzy, but I think I could get used to this whole not having a plan thing.

I smile at Jordan. "I might be open to that—with a few conditions."

Chapter Forty-Four

I've spent countless nights this summer sitting on my back porch and staring across the lake at Aspen Estates, so pedaling my bike through the ornate entrance feels more than a little surreal. The houses are much larger up close. I crane my neck in either direction as I cruise past stately homes with soaring windows, monogrammed front doors, and Corinthian columns.

It's wild to me that none of my neighbors decided to upgrade to this neighborhood after their windfall. But then again, it does feel pretty empty. Not really like a neighborhood at all.

Joel is sitting on the front steps of a comparatively modest blue saltbox house with white trim when Potato and I pull up. She lets out a little yip when she sees him. By the time I've gotten her out of her basket, my heart has crept all the way up into my throat.

"Hey there, Frisco." He's already picked Potato up, but her little tail hasn't stopped whirring with excitement.

"You promised you'd never call me that," I say, attempting a friendly tone that just ends up sounding sad.

He sinks back down into a seated position on the step and gestures for me to join him. As I do, I feel whatever steely resolve I'd attempted to build up over these past few days begin to weaken. Being in such close proximity to Joel makes me feel all melty. I think it's those warm brown eyes. Or maybe it's his dimples.

Or just him.

"So," he says.

"How did everything go with your parents?"

He brightens. "Actually surprisingly well," he says, scratching Potato under her chin while he talks. She squeezes her eyes shut. "They loved Marge and Gal—I mean who wouldn't? And I think Marge was relieved to see how great my parents are. It was kind of a full-circle moment."

I fight the urge to reach out and touch him. I worry that I lost that privilege when I batted his hand away for Marco's benefit. "I'm so happy for all of you."

Joel smiles. "Thanks. Me too." His face turns serious. "Don't get me wrong, it was weird for everyone at first. But yeah, I feel really good about it."

"That's so great, Joel." I mean it with everything in me, but my words sound hopelessly hollow. I brush a nonexistent fleck of dirt off my jeans.

"Thanks for giving me a little space. It was just a lot to process all at once and I felt like I needed to take care of my family stuff first, you know?"

When I turn to meet his eye, he looks like he's on the verge of tears. "I completely understand. If I were you, I would have done the exact same thing."

"I wasn't expecting to tell you about Marge that day and I certainly wasn't expecting your ex to show up at your house. And then when you pushed me away and Gal said he spent the night . . ." The way his face falls chips off a little piece of my heart. "I just knew I needed to sort out my thoughts first."

"It's over with Marco. It has been for months."

"I know."

"And you could have told me about Marge. I wouldn't have said anything to anyone."

"Well, to be fair, you were getting really close to Gal. Plus, we were digging into Marge's friend's past, so it felt . . . complicated."

He has a point.

I turn to face him. "I'm sorry for the way I reacted when Marco showed up. It was a shock."

"I think I get it. You were with him for a long time."

"Still, I should have gone after you. I'll always regret that I didn't."

Joel looks out toward the lake and I follow his line of vision. I can just make out the speck that is my house from his front porch. After what feels like an eternity, he says, "Well, you could always find a way to make it up to me."

I look over at Joel, who's now wearing a mischievous grin. "If you want to, that is."

I feel so relieved that it almost makes me nauseous, like the stress and tension I've been carrying around in the pit of my stomach has suddenly evaporated and created a vacuum. I take a moment to catch my breath. "How would I do that?"

"I have a few ideas," he says, scratching his chin. "You could let me win at *Mario Bros.* for once or maybe make me some more of that focaccia I tried at your disastrous lunch?"

"The focaccia can be arranged but I can't make any promises about Nintendo." I'm smiling like a big old fool, but I don't care.

"I can live with that." Joel nods solemnly, but the warmth quickly returns to his face. "But first, maybe you could come inside for a glass of Minnesota's finest rosé?"

"SHE WANTS TO meet you, you know," Lynette says. She's eyeing me over a cup of cider, her first of the season. The temperature dipped below seventy degrees today, which Lynette declared was the first official sign of fall.

I raise my eyebrows in confusion.

"Erica," Lynette clarifies. "We told her the whole story at book club last night. You're invited to the next one, by the way."

A few weeks ago, I would have been thrilled to finally score an invite to the mysterious neighborhood book club. But now I visibly cringe. "She wasn't mad?"

Lynette shakes her head. "Nah. She was flattered that you cared so much."

"That's a charitable way of looking at it."

"Well as you know, she's quite charitable," Lynette says with a laugh.

"How does Allan feel about you hanging out with Stuart?"

Lynette turns her attention to the lake. "Allan doesn't like it, but we agreed it'll only be at group events—which is totally fair. And things are a little awkward between Stuart and me, but we're figuring it out."

I wonder if Stuart has told the rest of the group about his alter ego yet. Maybe he never will.

I finally finished Stuart's third book. This one was different from his first two—it was about a heartbroken woman whose husband goes to jail for fraud. As time goes on, she starts to realize that she'd built her life on an illusion. She has to figure out who she is and what she wants for herself. Maybe I was reading into things too much, but to me, it felt like Stuart always knew he couldn't have anything real with Lynette. I think he'd been preparing for this eventuality from the start.

"I'm glad you're working things out," I say.

Lynette sighs. "Me too. Allan and I were long overdue for a heart-to-heart. We'd both been so determined not to let the money change us that we didn't let ourselves grow together." Lynette explained that Allan had a complicated relationship with their overnight fortune. *Easy come, easy go,* he'd said. He felt like he wanted to make his own way, to be the one to support the family. Meanwhile, Lynette just wanted him around. "It's going to be a long road, but I think it's going to be okay."

It's funny—my nice, Midwestern neighbors ended up being much more complicated than I'd ever imagined. They are sneaky, deeply flawed, liars—many of them hiding secrets from each other and, in some cases, from themselves. But they're also loyal and loving and kindhearted people who are mostly trying to do the right thing. Just like me.

Lynette tops off my cider and I take a long drink. It tastes like a cool, tart apple pie and leaves a hint of cinnamon lingering on my tongue. I look up at the trees that tower over Lynette's patio and my eyes land on a single leaf among the sea of green.

Its color is starting to change.

Epilogue

December

I answer my front door and am greeted by what has come to be a familiar sight—Lynette holding a hot dish. Her cheeks are rosy from the cold and she stomps the snow off her boots before stepping inside. I peer over her shoulder to see Ruby making her way up the ramp I had installed a few weeks ago. I wanted her to be able to stop by and knock on my door anytime, just like her mom. My shoulders do a little involuntary wriggle at the sight of her cruising up to my front porch with ease. Allan and Ned are close behind, hand in hand.

"Hi, Eliza," Ruby says. She's wearing a sparkly purple beanie with a massive pompom. Bubbles sits on her lap, peering out from beneath a plaid blanket. "Can I go look at your Christmas tree?" I tell her of course and she heads off toward the living room.

Ned gives me a high-five as he runs by. I'm shocked he can see straight through the ski goggles he started wearing when winter rolled around.

I pretend not to notice when Allan slides his hand around Lynette's waist and then down to her butt as they watch their kids greeting the other neighbors, both giddy with Christmas glee.

Allan's been home a lot more lately. Joel and I even bumped into him and Lynette at the Starling Lounge, acting like a couple of teenagers. I know Allan's schedule wasn't the only issue—Lynette told me that they've been working through a bunch of "old married people stuff" in therapy, too. But if the way they're looking at each other tonight is any indication, I think they're going to be just fine.

Marge and Gal are already here, helping my parents in the kitchen. Mom is making her famous ravioli and I can't wait for my neighbors to try it because Mom's ravioli is truly out of this world. The Christmas playlist I'd spent weeks perfecting—a tasteful combination of the classics, plus tons of Britney, Kelly, and Mariah—plays in the background.

Naturally, Marge and Gal showed up with a gaggle of dogs in tow, much to my parents' delight. Mom has already fallen in love with Macaroni, a deaf pit bull mix with a graying face and the wiggliest bottom I've ever seen. I overheard her telling my dad that they should rent a car and drive back to San Francisco so that they can bring "Mac" with them. The fact that she's already nicknamed the dog means it's a done deal. Dad won't be able to tell her no.

I finally told my parents the whole story behind my breakup with Marco. There were a lot of tears and even more questions, but in the end they were unequivocally supportive. I guess I could have trusted them with the truth from the start. Now I know.

Joel is playing video games downstairs with Enzo and his girlfriend, Allison, who, from what I can tell is basically a female version of Enzo. I already adore her.

I hang everyone's winter coats on the hooks by my front door before sneaking a glance into my living room where Bob sits in the overstuffed armchair by the fire with Potato on his lap. Potato diligently jumps down to greet each new arrival, but always goes back to Bob once she feels she's fulfilled her hosting duties. The two have become best buds ever since Bob started coming by to shovel the snow in my driveway every other day. When Potato hears that first scrape of the shovel, she goes tearing toward the front door and begs me to let her out. She likes to follow at his heels and tries to catch snow in her mouth as it flies off Bob's shovel.

Bob has already complained that my Christmas tree was too sparse ("I'll cut a real one down for you next year," he'd said) and he groaned when NSYNC's "Merry Christmas, Happy Holidays" started to play, but I know it's just an act. As Bob watches all the commotion from the corner of the room, he looks content in a way that I never thought he could. Like a proud grandfather.

Stuart will be here soon—with his new girlfriend. After things ended with Lynette, he decided he didn't want to hide at all anymore, so he dropped the pen name. There were a few detractors, but when Sheila Townsend's sizable fanbase discovered that "Sheila" was actually a single, handsome, forty-something-year-old man with a romantic streak, his love life improved dramatically. We're all very happy for him.

A new tattoo parlor opened up in town, in the empty office above the general store, which has also been able to avoid significantly reducing its hours this winter. I wish I could say that it was all thanks to me, but that couldn't be further from the truth. After I got Van Fischer off our backs, Bob agreed to not only drop his opposition to the Join Juneberry Lake program, but to invest in it—anonymously. "Change is hard for me," he'd explained. "Erica was part of my family and when she left, it felt like I'd lost a daughter. I didn't want to go through that again." It wasn't an outright apology, but I knew it was the best I was ever going to get from someone like Bob. Besides, with his support, the Committee for Growth could now subsidize local businesses to stay open through the off-season.

Trish is thrilled.

A lot of the businesses in town decided to invest a portion of their subsidies in marketing, which is where I come in. When Jordan offered me the promotion, I had a few requests. The first was more money (I'm a woman who knows her worth), the second was every other Friday off (because balance is important), and the third was that I wanted to be allowed to dedicate 25 percent of my team's resources to helping small businesses. I was shocked when Jordan agreed to all three. Swayy's small business segment is just a pilot program for now, but I've already heard from a few different managers who are interested in trying something similar with their teams.

Even better, I've started helping Trish out with the Join Juneberry Lake program in my spare time. We plan to welcome seventeen new residents to town in February and I'm hoping the lake stays frozen long enough for me to take the newbies ice-skating on it. If not, we'll just hang out at the Common Loon and watch the Super Bowl together. The Vikings still have a shot at making it. Marge is beside herself. She can't seem to stop yelling "Skol Vikings" every five minutes.

Joel hasn't told her that he's a Packers fan yet. One thing at a time.

The other day, as Joel and I were wrapping up some last-minute Christmas shopping downtown—which looks like one of my nonna's favorite holiday paintings come to life—I was struck by a sudden urge to visit the tattoo parlor. Thirty minutes later, I emerged with a new addition on the inside of my left wrist.

Hannah.

I was done trying to forget, trying to pretend that losing her hadn't profoundly changed me. I touch my wrist now and wonder what she would have been like as a grown woman. I like to think we still would have been best friends.

That had been the plan.

I can't say I'm done with planning entirely. That would require a hard factory reset and as far as I know those aren't available for humans. Even if they were, I wouldn't want it. I like the idea of integrating all of the different versions of myself into one as I continue to move through this unpredictable life.

"There's the hostess with the mostest," Joel says. He hands me a mug full of mulled wine garnished with a cinnamon stick. I beam up at him and will myself not to start crying. "What's that look?"

"I'm happy that I'm here."

He leans in and brushes his lips against mine and my heart feels merrier and brighter than a Christmas tree. "So am I."

Joel asked me to be his girlfriend after Hanukkah dinner at Marge and Gal's a couple of weeks ago. He'd had no idea his birth mom was Jewish and has enthusiastically embraced his newly discovered heritage. (I've been enjoying the fringe benefits of our interdenominational relationship and have been eating all the latkes I can get my hands on.)

I replied with an enthusiastic kiss which he rightly took as a yes.

Joel will spend tomorrow with his family, and I'll spend it with mine. We may regret this, but we've agreed to watch all of the neighborhood animals at Marge and Gal's the first week of January, when everyone heads down to—let's call it the Bahamas—to visit Erica and Phil the poodle.

Gal said they'd be happy to take Potato when Joel and I visit

San Francisco in a couple of months. He's always wanted to see the city, and I can't wait to introduce him to Farah and Carmen. Brittany and I haven't talked in months—once I stopped making an effort, she sort of just faded away. It doesn't sound like Carmen has been keeping in touch with her, either, which is probably for the best.

I know it's natural for friend groups to evolve over time. People's lives and needs and availability ebb and flow—it doesn't mean that anyone has done anything wrong or that we can't be close again in the future.

Maybe we all needed a change. Regardless of my reasons for pulling away, I do hope Brittany is happy with her new kitchen.

Farah—and Carmen, to a certain extent—have been better about staying in touch, and I've been better about going with the flow. We aren't as close as we used to be and my friends are on a different path than I am, but I'm happy for them (Carmen and Daisy's daughter, Bea, is cute as a button and Farah really is the best mom) but I can tell they want to be happy for me, too. I don't know how much more I could ask.

I look around my house and am overwhelmed with gratitude for the series of events that led me here. Maybe luck had something to do with it. Or maybe everything that happens in a person's life is completely random. Either way, I've warmed up to the unpredictability of it all. Because, if you embrace the unexpected, you might end up somewhere better than you could have ever imagined.

In a few hours, we'll all sit down for dinner around my dining table, my lifelong family and my chosen one coming together for a cozy, snowy Christmas Eve.

I couldn't have planned it better myself.

Acknowledgments

It's surreal to be doing this again! I think I feel even luckier than Eliza and her neighbors. Adequately expressing my gratitude feels impossible, but I'll give it a try.

First, thank you to Asanté Simons (honorable mention to her dachshund, Wellington) and my wonderful agent, Rachel Beck, for making my dream of writing a second book a reality.

Thank you to my fantastic editor, Laura Schrieber, for being so lovely to work with, for strengthening this story, and for coming up with the perfect title. And thank you to Alessandra Roche for all of the additional support.

To copyeditor Justine Gardner—thank you for patiently helping me to get this manuscript into proper shape.

Thank you to Laura Brady, Marie Rossi, and Brittani DiMare for your production work, Pam Barricklow and Hope Ellis for your editorial support, and Diahann Sturge-Campbell for the beautiful design.

Thank you to my family—the Raggios, Westlakes, McGees, Delucchis, and Gottheardts—and friends for your generous and enthusiastic support of my writing career. I'll never be able to capture everything you've done in full, but I'll try:

To my mom, for being my number-one hype-woman, salesperson, and cheerleader and to my dad for being pretty excited, too. Love you guys.

To my in-laws, Carol and Wally, for being beyond supportive and for sharing my book with so many of your lovely friends.

To Dana, for buying copies of my book from so many bookstores that she lost track, and to Aaron, Kendrick, and D'Voni for celebrating with me.

To Lauren, for being my stand-in publicist (you're amazing at it) and to Matt, Harper, and Logan for helping me to celebrate.

To Katie, for cheering me on (and for reading my story!) and Kayvon, Roya, and Layla for always being so much fun to party with.

To Bevin, for being so excited with me and to Mark, Camden, and Brice for making the celebration even more fun.

To Kaylan, for being so sweet and encouraging, to David for being a great friend, and to Lyle and Pancake for being too cute.

To my gurls, Megan, Christine, and Angie for making everything extra special and for always making me laugh. Your thoughtful gifts, tolerance for my anxiety spirals, and friendship mean more to me than you'll ever know. I'm so lucky to have had you as friends for forever and ever. Let's go see a psychic again soon.

To Sam for being a top seller and to Kevin for reminding me that I've already made it.

Thanks to Kate for being prepared to lie to me if the need arises and to Matt for being such a great bookseller. And to Sam ("shaka great wave!") and Adam (Busey)—hanging out with you two is always the most fun.

Thank you to Jenne Coler-Dark for being so wonderful and supportive, for inviting me to join your book club, and for throwing me the best book party ever, and to Blake for providing us with an endless stream of increasingly wild stories.

Thank you to the amazing women in my book club for your enthusiastic support. You're the best.

To Alyssa, Michael, and Tessa—thank you for being there to cheer me on!

Thanks to Nick, Erin, Alaina, Mark, and Greg for your support every step of the way and for coming out to celebrate! It means so much to me.

To my extra special cousins, Brigitt, for being the best friend and sounding board, and to Mandy for inviting me to your book club (and for being so much fun). Love you!

Thank you to my nieces and nephews—Mason, Maverick, Marley, Makena, Dominic, and Madelynn for being so very cute. And to their parents, Mark, Mel, Jess, and Randy, who are also pretty cute.

To Ellie, for being such a wonderful aunt to me, and to Kirk for being my brother.

To Chris Guarente, an incredible friend, aunt, mom, and Nana who we lost much too soon. Thank you for letting me be a part of your family. I'll always think of you when I order a martini or use my passport or shouldn't be laughing but can't not laugh. Kate, Matt, Brian, and I will remain Polite, Calm, and Classy in your honor (IKYK).

To Cathy Grosshauser, truly the best neighbor ever. I'm so lucky that I grew up down the street from you and your family (who feel like my family). Thank you for always welcoming me into your home, for feeding me so many dinners, and for teasing me for being ridiculous whenever I was being ridiculous. I miss you.

Thank you to the Women's Fiction Writers Association for connecting me with a wonderful group of writers. C.J. McGroarty, Margaret Rodenberg, and Leslie Ann Costello—your notes on my early draft were invaluable!

Thank you to Marla Daniels for once again helping me to improve my writing by leaps and bounds.

Thank you to Heather Lazare and the Northern California Writers' Retreat community for your continued support.

Thank you to Alyssa Jarrett for being such a fantastic debut friend and conversation partner. I can't wait to read what you write next.

To Carol Messina at Sweet Farm, Miyoko Schinner and Caroline Singleton at Rancho Compasión, and Amy Mack at Unconditional Rescue for taking care of the cutest animals there ever were, and for inspiring me every day.

Thank you to Dr. Erica O'Donnell and the team at VMSG Orange County for taking the best care of Indy. Brian and I are so grateful to all of you.

To Anna Meixelsperger for being such a supportive reader and an even better friend. I can't wait to go visit the cows with you.

To my fellow childless cat ladies and childfree dog moms— you're the best. Don't let anyone tell you otherwise.

Thank you to my sweet, supportive, ridiculously cute husband, Brian. You're my favorite person in the whole world and I'm so lucky to be married to you. Thanks for putting up with my zombie brain, for constantly making me laugh, for making the best iced coffee, and for always being down to pick up dinner. I love you the most.

And to our baby puppy Indy (also known as Indiana Jones, Jonesy, Dr. Jones, Frank, Bubby, Bubs, Dog, Je Bubbie). We love you even more than you love treats.

Last but certainly not least, thank *you* for reading my book! I hope you get your very own lucky break soon if you haven't already.

Jaclyn Westlake is the author of the novel *Dear Dotty* and an alumna of the Stanford Continuing Studies novel writing program. A recruiter turned career advice columnist, her work has appeared in *Forbes*, *Business Insider*, and *Inc.* She lives in California with her husband and their dachshund mix, Indiana Jones (but you can call him Indy).

Discover more from
JACLYN WESTLAKE

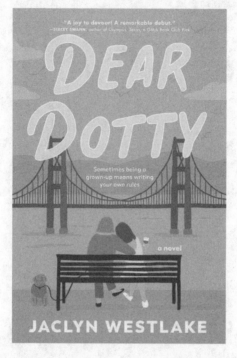

Rosie Benson does not have it all together. Like most twenty-somethings, she struggles to figure out life and soon finds herself following the advice of her late great-aunt through a series of revelatory emails about pursuing long-buried dreams rather than society's idea of perfect in this fun, highly relatable debut. Perfect for fans of Beth O'Leary, Lizzie Damilola Blackburn, and Sophie Kinsella.

"Compelling characters, a page-turning plot, and laugh-out-loud humorhumor. . . . A remarkable debut!"

—STACEY SWANN,
author of GMA Book Club Pick *Olympus, Texas*